HIMSELF

JESS KIDD

CANONGATE

First published in Great Britain in 2016 by
Canongate Books Ltd, 14 High Street, Edinburgh EH1 1TE

www.canongate.tv

2

British Library Cataloguing-in-Publication Data
A catalogue record for this book is available on
request from the British Library

ISBN 978 1 78211 845 9
Export ISBN 978 1 78211 846 6

Typeset in Bembo by Palimpsest Book Production Ltd, Falkirk, Stirlingshire

Printed and bound in Great Britain by Clays Ltd, St Ives plc.

MIX
Paper from
responsible sources
FSC
www.fsc.org   FSC® C018072

For my father

Prologue

May 1950

His first blow: the girl made no noise, her dark eyes widened. She reeled a little as she bent and put the baby down. The man stood waiting.

She straightened up into his second blow, which knocked her to the ground. She fell awkwardly, with one leg crumpled beneath her. He dropped down with his knees either side of her, so that she would hardly see the light greening the trees if she looked up, but she didn't look up. She turned her head to see her baby on the ground, with his face pale between the folds of the blanket. He'd kicked his tiny foot out, his toes all in a line like new peas in a pod. Because she couldn't hold her son in her arms she tried to hold him with her eyes as she willed him to be quiet, to be saved.

She did not see the man's hands as they moved but she felt each clear shock of pain in her dark little soul. She had once traced fortunes along the furrows of his palms with her dancing fingers. His hands could build walls, fell trees and turn a bull in its tracks. His hands could circle her waist, her arm, her ankle, to lightly plot her beauty. His fingers could play songs on her spine, or tuck a strand of hair behind her ear with a mother's tenderness. His fingers had spelt out complicated love messages on her belly as it had grown, salving the marks there with quiet reverence.

His next blow took her hearing, so that she knew her child was crying only by the shape of his mouth. She heard nothing but an endless rushing. Just like when she swam underwater in the wild Atlantic, a sea cold enough to stop your heart.

His last blow left her without sight. She lay at the edge of the world, finally willing it all to be over. She turned the mess of her face to her beautiful boy, thinking she could see him still, even through the darkness, a dim gleaming rose of the forest.

She couldn't have known it but it was then that her baby stopped crying. The void her son had fallen into without the cradle of her gaze was immeasurable. He lay as mute as a little mushroom.

The man held her. He watched with quiet devotion as each breath she took became a difficult triumph, flecking his chest with scarlet spume. He touched her hair, sometimes stroking it back from her forehead, sometimes turning the wet skeins about his fingers. And he rocked her, small in his arms, for the longest while. As she left the world she raised her hand like a dreaming child and with blind splayed fingers touched his chest. He kissed every one of her white fingers, noticing the curves of black earth under her nails.

When she was still, the man sheared her hair and took her clothes; he would bury them later, another day, another time. He couldn't give everything away, not now, not yet.

He looked down at her; naked and faceless she could be anyone and no one.

He wrapped her in sackcloth, rolling her body gently, tucking her limbs in carefully, swaddling her tightly.

A thick silence grew as the forest surveyed his dark work. The trees stopped whispering and the crows flew away, speechless with horror. But the child watched everything, as quiet as a stone, with his eyes big and unblinking.

Across the clearing, through the trees, the man saw the place that he would bury her: a low-tide island in the river you could wait years for and still never see. This wasn't a coincidence; it was a benediction.
He would dig her grave in the middle of the island. She was little bigger than a stillborn calf, but still he would be sure to weight her down, for the tide was coming in.

He bathed, washing himself clean of her for the last time as the light began to die. Then he remembered that he must also claim their child or his work would not be done. He must make one final deep hole, wrap his son in a blanket and put him into the ground. The earth would fill his mouth and eat his cries. He took up his spade again.

But whilst the man had bathed, the forest had hidden the infant.

Great ferns had unfurled all around the child, tree roots had surrounded him and ivy had sprung up to cloak him. Branches had bent low over his tiny head and had shaken a blessing of leaves down onto him. Moles had banked earth all around him with their strong claws, swimming blind and furious through the soil.

So that when the man looked about himself he could not find the child, however hard he searched.

Chapter 1

April 1976

Mahony shoulders his rucksack, steps off the bus and stands in the dead centre of the village of Mulderrig.

Today Mulderrig is just a benign little speck of a place, uncoiled and sprawling, stretched out in the sun. Pretending to be harmless.

If Mahony could remember the place, which he can't of course, he'd not notice many changes since he's been gone. Mulderrig doesn't change, fast or slowly. Twenty-six years makes no odds.

For Mulderrig is a place like no other. Here the colours are a little bit brighter and the sky is a little bit wider. Here the trees are as old as the mountains and a clear river runs into the sea. People are born to live and stay and die here. They don't want to go. Why would they when all the roads that lead to Mulderrig are downhill so that leaving is uphill all the way?

At this time of the day the few shops are shuttered and closed, and the signs swing with an after-hours lilt and pitch, and the sun-warmed shopfront letters bloom and fade. Up and down the high street, from Adair's Pharmacy to Farr's

Outfitters, from the offices of Gibbons & McGrath Solicitors to the Post Office and General Store, all is quiet.

A couple of old ones are sitting by the painted pump in the middle of the square. You'll get no talk from them today: they are struck dumb by the weather, for it hasn't rained for days and days and days. It's the hottest April in living and dead memory. So hot that the crows are flying with their tongues hanging out of their heads.

The driver nods to Mahony. 'It's as if a hundred summers have come at once to the town, when a mile along the coast the rain's hopping up off the ground and there's a wind that would freeze the tits off a hen. If you ask me,' says the driver, 'it all spells a dose of trouble.'

Mahony watches the bus turn out of the square in a broiling cloud of dirt. It rolls back, passenger-less, across the narrow stone bridge that spans a listless river. In this weather anything that moves will be netted in a fine caul of dust. Although not much is moving now, other than a straggle of kids pelting home late, leaving their clear cries ringing behind. The mammies are inside making the tea and the daddies are inside waiting to go out for a jar. And so Tadhg Kerrigan is the first living soul in the village to see Mahony back.

Tadhg is propping up the saloon door of Kerrigan's Bar having changed a difficult barrel and threatened a cellar rat with his deadly tongue. He is setting his red face up to catch a drop of sun whilst scratching his arse with serious intent. He has been thinking of the Widow Farelly, of her new-built bungalow, the prodigious whiteness of her net curtains and the pigeon plumpness of her chest.

Tadhg gives Mahony a good hard stare across the square as he walks over to the bar. With looks like that, thinks Tadhg, the fella is either a poet or a gobshite, with the long hair and the leather jacket and the walk on it, like his doesn't smell.

'All right so?'

'I'm grand,' says Mahony, putting his rucksack down and smiling up through his hair, an unwashed variety that's grown past his ears and then some.

Tadhg decides that this fella is most definitely a gobshite.

Whether the dead of Mulderrig agree or not it's difficult to tell, but they begin to look out cautiously from bedroom windows or drift faintly down the back lanes to stop short and stare.

For the dead are always close by in a life like Mahony's. The dead are drawn to the confused and the unwritten, the damaged and the fractured, to those with big cracks and gaps in their tales, which the dead just yearn to fill. For the dead have second-hand stories to share with you, if you'd only let them get a foot in the door.

But the dead can watch. And they can wait.

For Mahony doesn't see them now.

He stopped seeing them a long time ago.

Now the dead are confined to a brief scud across the room at lights-out, or a wobble now and then in his peripheral vision. Now Mahony can ignore them in much the same way as you'd ignore the ticks of an over-loud grandfather clock.

So Mahony pays no notice at all to the dead old woman pushing her face through the wall next to Tadhg's right elbow. And Tadhg pays no notice either, for, like the rest of us, he is blessed with a blissful lack of vision.

The dead old woman opens a pair of briny eyes as round as vinegar eggs and looks at Mahony, and Mahony looks away, smiling full into Tadhg's big face. 'So are there any digs about the town, pal?'

'There's no work here.' Tadhg crosses his arms high on his chest and sniffs woefully.

Mahony produces a half pack of cigarettes from his jacket pocket and Tadhg takes one. They stand smoking awhile, Tadhg with his eyes narrowed against the sun, Mahony with a shadow of a smile on his face. The dead old woman slips out a good few inches above the pavement and points enigmatically down towards the cellar, muttering darkly.

Mahony increases his smile to show his teeth in an expression of considerable natural charm altogether capable of beguiling the hardest bastard of humankind. 'Well, the last thing I need is work. I'm taking a break from the city.'

'It's the city, is it?'

The dead old woman draws close enough to whisper in Mahony's ear.

Mahony takes a drag and then exhales. 'It is. With the noise and the cars and the rats.'

'Rats, are there?' Tadhg narrows his eyes.

'As big as sheep.'

Tadhg is outwardly unmoved, although he sympathises deep in his soul. 'Rats are a very great problem in the world,' he says sagely.

'They are in Dublin.'

'So what brought you here?'

'I wanted a bit of peace and quiet. Do you know on the map there's nothing at all around you?'

'It's the arse end of beyond you're after then?'

Mahony looks thoughtful. 'Do you know? I think it is.'

'Well, you've found it. You're on the run in the Wild West?'

'Seems so.'

'A lady or the law?'

Mahony takes his fag out of his mouth and flicks it in

the direction of the dead old woman, who throws a profoundly disgusted look at him. She lifts her filmy skirts and flits back through the wall of the pub.

'She was no lady.'

Tadhg's face twitches as he curbs a smile. 'What are we calling you?'

'Mahony.'

Tadhg notes a good firm handshake. 'Mahony it is then.'

'So will I find a bed tonight or will I have to curl up with those antiques on the bench there?'

Tadhg withholds a fart, just while he's thinking. 'Shauna Burke rents out rooms to paying guests at Rathmore House up in the forest. That's about it.'

'That'd be grand.'

Tadhg takes a thorough glance at Mahony. He'll admit that he has a sort of bearing about him. He's not a bad height and he's strong looking, handy even. He's been into his twenties and he'll come out again the other side none the worse for it; he has the kind of face that will stay young. But he could do with a wash; he has the stubble of days on his chin. And his trousers are ridiculous: tight around the crotch and wide enough at the bottom to mop the main road.

Tadhg nods at them. 'They're all the rage now? Them trousers?'

'They are, yeah.'

'Do you not feel like a bit of an eejit wearing them?'

Mahony smiles. 'They all wear 'em in town. There's wider.'

Tadhg raises his eyebrows a fraction. 'Is there now? Well, you wouldn't want to be caught in a gust of wind.'

Tadhg can see that the girls would be falling over themselves if this fella ever had the notion to shave himself or pick up a bar of soap. And Mahony knows it too. It's there in the curve of his smile and the light in his dark eyes. It's in the way he moves, like he owns every inch of himself.

Tadhg stakes a smile. 'You'll need to watch the other guest who lives up there, Mrs Cauley. The woman's titanic.'

'After what I've been afflicted with I'm sure I can handle her.' And Mahony turns his laughing eyes up to Tadhg.

Now Tadhg is not a man given to remarkable insights but he is suddenly certain of two things.

One: that he's seen those eyes before.

Two: that he is almost certainly having a stroke.

For the blood inside Tadhg has begun to belt around his body for the first time in a very long time and he knows that it can't be good to stir up a system that has been sumping and rusting to a comfortable dodder. Tadhg puts his hands over his face and leans heavily against the saloon door. He can almost feel a big fecker of a blood clot hurtling towards his brain to knock him clean out of the living world.

'Are you all right, pal?'

Tadhg opens his eyes. The fella who is having a break from Dublin is frowning up at him. Tadhg reels off a silent prayer against the darkest of Mulderrig's dark dreams. He takes a handkerchief from his pocket and wipes his forehead. And as the hairs settle on the back of his neck he tells himself that this fella is really no more than a stranger.

Whatever he thought he saw in his face has gone.

In front of him is a Dublin hippy passing through the arse end of beyond.

'Are you all right?'

Tadhg nods. 'I am, of course.'

The stranger smiles. 'You open? I could do time for a pint.'

'Come inside now,' Tadhg says, and resolutely decides to lay off the sunshine.

Luckily the sun has a desperate struggle to get in through the windows of Kerrigan's Bar, but if it can seep through the smoky curtains it can alight on the sticky dark-wood tables. Or it can work up a dull shine on the horse brasses by the side of the fire, unlit and full of crisp packets. Or it can bathe the pint of stout in Sergeant Jack Brophy's hand to an even richer, warmer hue.

'Jack, this is Mahony.'

Mahony puts his rucksack by the door.

Jack turns to look at him. He nods. 'Get the man a pint, Tadhg. Here, Mahony, sit by me.'

Mahony sits down next to Jack, a strong square wall of a man, and, like all mortals, he begins to feel soothed. Mahony isn't to know that Jack has this effect on the mad, the bad, the imaginative, and skittish horses, whether off duty or on. Ask anyone and they will tell you it's what makes Jack a good guard. For here he is working his stretch of the coast, sorting out the wicked, the misjudged and the maligned without having to once raise his voice.

Tadhg puts a pint in front of Mahony.

'Now, tell me about it,' says Jack, barely moving his lips.

Mahony could tell him about it. Mahony could start by telling Jack what happened last Thursday.

★★★

Last Thursday, Father Gerard McNamara walked into the Bridge Tavern with a black leather folio in his hand and an envelope inside the folio. He was seeking one of St Anthony's most notorious alumni and had started by visiting the bars within a one-mile radius of the orphanage. For Father McNamara was heeding the advice of the local guards along with the principle that a rotten apple doesn't fall far from the tree; it usually lands and festers right next to it.

Mahony was emanating from the jacks with a cigarette in his mouth as Father McNamara came round the side of the bar.

'I'll have a word with you, Mahony.'

Mahony took out his fag and squinted at the priest. 'Sit yourself down, have a drink with me, Father.'

The priest threw Mahony a caustic look, put the folio on the bar and unzipped it.

Mahony pulled himself back up onto his stool and took hold of his pint with serious dedication. 'Ah, excuse me, I didn't shake your hand, did I, Father? You see I've just touched something far from godly but just as capable of inflicting great bliss.'

Jim behind the bar grinned.

Father McNamara extracted the envelope from his folio. 'Sister Veronica passed away. She asked for this to be given to you.'

Mahony looked at the letter on the bar.

'Have you got the right man, Father? Sister Veronica wasn't exactly head of me fan club now, was she? Why would she be leaving me anything? God rest her pure and caring soul.'

Father McNamara shrugged. He didn't give a shite; he just wanted to get out of the pub.

Mahony watched Father McNamara zip up his leather folio, put it under his arm and walk back out through the saloon door into the weak Dublin sunshine. Mahony finished his pint, ordered another and looked at the envelope. Then he found himself remembering.

He was no more than six.

Sister Veronica said that there wasn't a letter left with him. Wasn't he a little bastard that no one wanted and why would anyone be writing letters for him?

Sister Veronica said that his mammy was too busy working the docks to write.

Sister Veronica said that his mammy had only brought him to the nuns instead of drowning him because she couldn't find a bucket.

But Sister Mary Margaret had told Mahony a different story, while she had taught him to hold a pencil and form his letters, and recognise all the major saints and many of the minor ones.

Once upon a time Sister Mary Margaret had answered a loud knocking at the door of the orphanage. It was very early one morning, before the city was awake. All the pigeons had their heads tucked under their wings and all the rats were curled up tight behind the dustbins. All the cars and lorries were asleep in their garages and depots, and all the trains slumbered on their tracks at Connolly Station. All the boats bobbed gently in the harbour, dreaming of the high seas, and all the bicycles slept leaning along the fences. Even the angels were asleep at the foot of the O'Connell Monument, fluttering their wings as they dreamt, quite forgetting to hold still and pretend to be statues.

The whole wide city was asleep when Sister Mary Margaret opened the door of the orphanage.

And there, on the steps, was a baby.

Of all the things in the world!

A baby in a basket, with a quilt of leaves and a pillow of rose petals.

A baby in a basket, just like Moses!

The baby had looked up at Sister Mary Margaret with two bright eyes and smiled at her. And she had smiled right back.

Mahony clung on to the bar. He couldn't light a fag or pick up his pint, he couldn't move, the sweat was pouring off him. He closed his eyes and right there in his memory he found Sister Mary Margaret, as she was the last time he saw her.

He was not even seven. At first he had held back from climbing up, for fear that he would break her. But Sister Mary Margaret had smiled down at him, so he scaled the arctic landscape of the bed. Without that smile he wouldn't have known her.

Sister Mary Margaret had a cancer the size of a man's head in her stomach and was as good as dead under the ground. That's what they had told him but he'd come to see for himself.

He sat next to Sister Mary Margaret and let her wipe his nose with her handkerchief although he was too old for it. It took her hours because she kept falling asleep. He had wished to God that he wasn't trailing great lanes of snot. But Mahony always had a cold from the fact that the tops of his fingers were often blue and his socks were never quite dry.

She had looked at him with her shrunken face on one side and he'd looked back at the ridge of her eye bone.

'A letter was left with you,' she whispered. 'Sister Veronica took it.'

But then Sister Dymphna appeared and gave him a fierce slap and marched him out of the sanatorium.

Mahony wiped his eyes and glanced around the bar; the

drinkers were sculling through their own thoughts and the barman had gone to change a barrel. He was safe.

He looked at the envelope in his hand.

For when the child is grown.

A good solid schoolteacherly hand, slanted in all the right places.

On the back of the envelope was a seal of sorts. A tiny medal of wax stamped with the shape of some old coin or other. He liked that: Sister Veronica had kept it back from him but she hadn't opened it.

Mahony broke the seal.

Mahony will tell you to his dying day that the arse fell out of the barstool just after he opened that envelope. Then the barstool fell through the floor and the whole world turned itself about.

But then, when Mahony looked around himself, everything was exactly the same. The same smeared mirrors over the same dirty seats. The same sad bastards falling into their glasses and the same smell crawling out of the gents.

Inside the envelope was a photograph of a girl with a half-smile holding a blurred bundle, high and awkwardly, like found treasure. Mahony turned it over and the good solid schoolteacherly hand dealt him a left hook.

Your name is Francis Sweeney. Your mammy was Orla Sweeney. You are from Mulderrig, Co. Mayo. This is a picture of yourself and her. For your information she was the curse of the town, so they took her from you. They all lie, so watch yourself, and know that your mammy loved you.

His mammy had loved him. Past tense. Mammy was past tense.

They took her from him. Where did they take her?

Mahony turned over the photograph and studied her face. God, she looked young. He would have put her as his sister rather. She couldn't have been more than fourteen.

And his name was Francis. He'd keep that to himself.

Mahony lit a fag and turned to the drinker next to him. 'Paddy, have you been to Mayo?'

'I haven't,' Paddy said, without lifting his chin from his chest.

Mahony frowned. 'Jim, what's in Mayo?'

Jim put down the tea towel. 'I'm fucked if I know. Why?'

'I'm going to take a trip there, see how the land lies.'

'Grand so.'

Mahony stood unsteadily and picked up his lighter. 'I'm going. I am, Jim. Fuck it. What have I got to keep me here?' He included the bar with a wave of his fag. 'Nothin' – name one thing.'

'Parole,' said Paddy to his navel.

★★★

Mahony takes a taste of his pint and watches as Jack Brophy rolls a cigarette, deftly, with one hand. A hand as strong as a tree root, brown and calloused with big square cracked nails and deep gouged old scars. Mahony watches Jack and feels his brain slow a little. He breathes in tobacco, good soil, driving rain, calm sun and fresh air off the broad back of the quiet man.

Still. He'll tell Jack nothing of what happened last Thursday.

Mahony smiles. 'The truth is I've come here to get away from it all.'

A collie noses out from behind the bar.

When it turns its head Mahony sees that it only has one good eye, the other rests messily on the dog's cheek. Its ribs are caved in, leaving a dark sticky ditch. A dog that broken would have to be dead, and of course it is, fuck it.

Mahony sucks air in through his teeth and looks away.

The dead dog turns to lick Jack's hand, which trails down holding his cigarette, but its muzzle goes straight through and the dog, finding no response, folds itself up at the foot of his master's bar stool and rests the good side of its face on its faint paws.

Mahony studies his pint. 'All I really want,' he says, 'is a bit of peace and quiet.'

Sometimes a man is in no way honest.

'Aye,' says Jack. The word is little more than an exhalation of air. 'So that's it?'

Mahony feels no malice. He could tell them, ask them; he could start right here.

The two men look at him.

Mahony picks up his pint. 'That's my story. I have no other.'

Chapter 2

April 1976

By the third pint it's decided. Tadhg will bring Mahony up to Rathmore House to see Shauna Burke about the room, for he has a box of strawberries for the Widow Farelly that will go over if left until tomorrow. He hopes to be rewarded with a little kiss on the cheek or a squeeze of the hand. But he's by no means certain of that; so far the Widow Farelly has kept her gentler feelings well hidden. But then Tadhg knew that a decent woman would be slower to court: the higher the mind the trickier the knickers.

They walk out the back of the bar and jostle through a corridor lined with boxes of crisps, Mahony because of his rucksack and Tadhg because of his girth. At the back door Tadhg hands Mahony a half bottle of whiskey to break the ice with Mrs Cauley. For the dark-eyed fella is growing on him, despite the fact that he's almost certainly a gobshite.

Tadhg's car, a vehicle with its own notions of when to stop and start, is rusting out the back. Nothing grows here but empty bottles and broken crates. Tadhg tries the ignition, his top lip sweating with the effort of wedging himself in the driver's seat. The engine turns over consumptively then dies.

'Ah no.'

Mahony gets out of the car and aims his cigarette into the corner of the courtyard. He reaches into the back seat and pulls out his rucksack.

'Open the bonnet a minute, Tadhg.'

Tadhg puts his hand down to feel for the lever but can't reach it because his gut's in the way. He gets out of the car and leaning on the open door tries to squat, minding he doesn't shit himself or rip the arse out of his good cream trousers. By the time he's found the lever Mahony has the bonnet propped open and is walking round the car wiping his hands on an old bit of rag.

'Try it again now, Tadhg.'

Tadhg lowers himself back into the seat and starts the engine. Perfect. He gives it a rev to make sure.

'She didn't even sound like that when I bought her new. Wha' are you, some sort of magician?'

Mahony laughs and throws his rucksack in the car; there's a metallic clunk as it hits the backseat. He gets into the car, ignoring the expression on Tadhg's face.

'You've a bagful there.'

'Ah, I always bring a few tools with me.'

'Do you now?'

'You never know when you might need them.'

'I can see that – what did you say you do in Dublin?'

'I didn't.' Mahony grins. 'I buy old wrecks and sell them on. Cars, vans, you name it. Do them up. Respray even. That sort of thing.'

Tadhg looks almost convinced. 'I've a sky-blue 1956 Eldorado there in the garage, all done up to the nines like a mistress waiting on a night out. I've never been without a good car in my life, but she's one of the prettiest. Would you like to take a look at her some time?'

'I would.'

'I don't drive her much, for the roads around here would bollox her entirely, but we could go for a spin around the block and watch the skirt swoon over us.'

'Count me in.' Mahony taps the dashboard. 'We'll be off now, will we? While she's purring?'

Tadhg nods and coasts the car out towards the side road, relaxing a little as he turns the corner. 'Now, with the radio working we'd have a bit of the old rock and roll driving about the place.'

'I'll see what I can do.'

The dead are nowhere to be seen as Tadhg drives through the village, but the living have had their tea and are starting to show their faces. Tadhg drives slowly; he has the punnet of strawberries wedged between his great thighs and he doesn't want them bruised. He tells Mahony that he would do anything for the love of a good woman such as Annie Farelly.

Mahony sees some young ones standing on a corner gassing; they turn and watch as Tadhg drives by. When Mahony leans out the window to blow them a kiss they laugh and push each other.

It's just fun, he tells Tadhg. Mahony doesn't want a girl. He never has, not even close. He's happier alone – that's the way it's always been. He'll freewheel for ever. He'll never have a woman and a rake of kids hanging off him, holding him down.

They drive out past old stone-walled fields and white-washed houses. Sheets and shirts jackknife on lines in the yards, catching the breeze coming up stronger now from the sea below.

Tadhg squints ahead at the dry rutted road and tells Mahony that Mulderrig is a picture of heaven, framed by the most ancient of forests. Didn't St Patrick himself admire Mulderrig's trees whilst chasing troublesome snakes about the place? And didn't he bless this forest as he lashed through the undergrowth?

But then Mulderrig's trees have always been under some strange spirit of protection. A matchless treasure in a hoard of bogs and lakes and mountains.

Down all the long centuries of change this little forest has prevailed, unharmed by settlers and undeterred by soil, or weather, or situation.

And the trees still hold strong. Their canopies drinking every soft grey sky and their roots spreading down deep in the dark, nuzzling clutches of old bones and fingering lost coins. They throw their branches up in wild dances whenever a storm comes in off the bay. And the wind howls right through them, to where the forest ends and the open land begins and the mountains rise up. This is the place where, on better days, the sun and clouds play out their endless moving shadow shows.

From the bowels of the mountains comes the River Shand. Born twisting, it weaves through stone and land and forest down towards town, where it flows out to meet the estuary. In some places the river is banked and forded, in others wild and forgotten. In most places it's cold and tidal. In all places it's a law unto itself. For the Shand is a river of unpredictable bends and treacherous undertows, of unfathomable depths and unreasonable habits, of cursed bridges and vengeful willows. Of Denny's Ait: a sunken island, named for a drowned man, studded with gemstones, seen only at low tide, and then only rarely.

Now there's a fork in the road. To the left is the narrow

boreen that winds up to Rathmore House, just wide enough for a car. But Tadhg turns right onto a long gravel drive bordered by dour regiments of heathers.

'Would you look at that bungalow Annie Farelly had built for herself. Isn't it the bee's bollox, Mahony?'

'It's deadly, Tadhg.'

Rendered in grey and brutal in design, the widow's bungalow is entirely foreboding. At either side of the studded oak doorway, petulant stone horses sneer down flared nostrils. There's more than a suggestion of battlements around the dormer windows and a thickly planted hedge surrounds the entire building.

'It could pass as the gingerbread house. Magical, eh? And her net curtains – the fierce white of them. She's a wonderfully house-proud woman.'

Tadhg hooks the punnet over one fat finger and grins apologetically. 'I'd bring you in with me and introduce you—'

'Ah no, Tadhg, you go. I'll sit here and have a smoke for meself.'

'You wouldn't mind? I doubt if I'll get a squeeze anyways.'

'No, go on. Fill your boots. I'm grand here.'

'Right so, I'll just pop in for a minute.'

'Take your time,' Mahony smiles.

Tadhg hauls his big arse as politely as he can to the front door, where he stops, licks his hand and slicks down the front of his hair.

The door opens immediately and an astringent-looking woman comes out onto the doorstep. There's a brief exchange, with Tadhg shifting on his feet like a schoolboy as she peers over at the car. She shakes her head and trots out onto the drive. With each step her head hinges forwards from her upholstered body and her mouth chews silent curses.

She steams to a halt and stands, aiming eye-daggers in

through the car window. She takes in Mahony's long hair, the holes in his trousers and the dirt under his fingernails.

'This is a decent village. We don't want any filthy dirty hippies here.'

Mahony takes in the immaculate rows of nodding pin curls and the blue eyes as joyless as a Monday morning. He smiles. 'I scrub up all right.'

In a fight between them he would put his money on her. For the legs that emerge from the bottom of her plaid skirt are stout and muscled and there's a decent curve to her bicep. A nurse's fob watch is pinned to her strapping chest and at her hip she carries a set of keys on a loop like a jailer.

The Widow Farelly narrows her eyes. 'I doubt that. I know your sort. With your drugs and your loose behaviour – well, you can move on. We keep a close watch here. We deal with troublemakers in this town.'

'I bet you do. I bet you nip them right in the bud.'

Tadhg stands helpless on the path with his strawberries forgotten and his shoulders sloping. Dim faces have started to gather at the empty windows of the bungalow, quietly watching. Patient dead old faces that press apologetically through the windowpanes. Mahony resolutely ignores them.

'You live alone in there?'

'I do,' she frowns. 'What of it?'

Mahony shakes his head.

Annie Farelly leans in the window and points her finger at Mahony. 'Move on, bucko, or you'll regret it.'

She hurls him a look that could stop a strong heart and walks back to the house. Tadhg follows her in the door, his head bent and all hope of a quick feel destroyed.

Mahony sparks up a fag and puts it in the corner of his mouth while he unscrews the front of the radio. A little fair-haired girl skips zigzag down the drive and stops outside the car door.

'Hello, Mister.'

'Hello.'

'Will you play hide and seek?'

The child stands with her hands on her hips and takes turns pointing first one foot then another. Mahony is only just aware of the motion: point, change, point, change.

'Ah no, not now.'

Mahony takes the cigarette out of his mouth and puts it on the dash while he bites the plastic off a wire.

'Oh, pur-leeze. The forest is just over there.'

Something in her voice, at once disturbing and familiar, makes Mahony look up.

And there she is.

A little round face and a broad smile showing the gap where her front teeth used to be. She stabs her tongue tip through the gap.

'Close your eyes and count to ten,' she whispers, 'then come and find me.'

When she turns away Mahony sees that the back of her head just isn't there.

Mahony's hands are shaking as he puts the radio down on the passenger seat with all the wires and shit hanging out the back of it. He's not prepared for this. Not now. Five fucking minutes he's been here, keeping his shite together, keeping his fucking cool, and then this.

He hasn't seen them like this in years.

He rubs his forehead. When did he start looking out for them again? When he hitched a ride out of Dublin? Or when he rode a truck through Longford and slept rough in Castlerea? Or was it when he boarded the bus to Mulderrig?

Or the moment he got off and walked across the square?

He didn't see this coming.

He didn't see her coming.

A dead kid with a stoved-in head and a sweet little smile.

And it won't just be that one, oh no, she'll bring all her little dead friends.

She's there, up ahead by the trees, all fucking dead. She runs away a bit then stops to turn around, ballerina style, on the pale toe of one scuffed shoe.

'I had a yo-yo but I losted it.'

Mock pout, toe stab, she pirouettes back to Mahony and whispers dramatically. 'I think the forest stole it. It steals everything pretty.'

Her face is perfect; from the front it's fine, pale only. But it's not good from behind. No, it's not good. Her head is destroyed, oddly flattened on the left side with a mulberry seam running alongside. Inside the seam there's a dark glistening, a sickening sort of softness. Around this deep rift is a halo of fine pale hair, matted with dull blood.

Mahony had forgotten it could be like this. That sometimes the details come vivid and stay etched. The dim sheen on a twist of hair at the nape of a neck severed to the ligaments. Or the luminous curve of a bloodless cheek above lips bitter with poison, or a pale half-mooned nail on a drowned and bloated hand.

And when you look again, gone.

Glimpses, when you least expect it, when you're by no means ready. Sudden shocks of sharp detail then a glowing smear all the way to fade. Leaving images behind like the sun on your retinas.

Mahony looks away and listens; it's easier somehow. Her voice is high, metallic: a bad connection on a faraway exchange. He remembers that they sound like this.

The dead sound like this.

'Do you like my dress?'

He struggles. 'Aye. You look like a princess.'

'My mammy made it.'

'Ah, you're lucky then. What's your name?' Mahony forces himself to look at the dead girl, to smile at her. She stops walking and stands perfectly still, staring hard at her faint hands.

'How the feck should I know?' she says, and turns and skips through a tree trunk.

Tadhg got little out of the Widow other than the lash of her tongue, but even so he's in high spirits when he gets back into the car, for you can't keep a good man down. He sits propped forward with his nose on the windscreen as they drive up to Rathmore House. He is too vain to wear spectacles, for in his mind he's still the fine figure of a man who broke hearts at the village dance. Tadhg Kerrigan, with the car and the fine suits. Tadhg Kerrigan, with a good head of hair and a full set of teeth, with an engine full of fire and an eye for the girls. Hadn't he had his pick? He remembers them, back in his heyday. All lined up at the dances with their hands folded on their laps, smiling up at him in their bobby socks and ponytails. Although he's not knocking the miniskirts that have come in.

'Do the women have themselves on display in Dublin, Mahony?'

'There are a few sets of pins out and about.'

'Are there now? I'll have to come for a visit. Is there any free love about the place?'

'Not as much as you might expect.'

'No? With all that flower power? Is that good and wilted now?'

Mahony shrugs.

'Ah well, I'll come and visit anyways.'

'You'd be welcome.'

Tadhg squints at the road. 'I love a full woman. Did you see Annie? She'd just had a perm done, all those little curls, a head on her like a dandelion. Was she sharp in her greeting of you?'

'I'll cut my hair and she'll love me like a son.'

Tadhg laughs and drums on the steering wheel to Bill Haley. 'Well, you've worked a miracle here, Mahony. God, I love rock and roll. And I'd love to rock and roll Annie Farelly, Jaysus I would.'

'Then you're a brave man.'

Tadhg looks at him. 'You all right? You're a bit pale around the gills.'

'I'm grand.'

'Right so. Then we're here.'

Chapter 3

April 1976

Rathmore House is the highest inhabited place in Mulderrig. On a clear day you can lean out of a top-floor window and see for miles. Out past the trees to the patch-worked fields beyond, studded with tiny houses glowing white. On a clear day you can see the bay and the fishing boats coming in and out of it, and the lobster pots on the quayside, and the gulls rolling above them in the blue glassy sky.

Shauna Burke is in the big cave of a kitchen with her foot up on the draining board shaving her legs in the sink with her daddy's razor. She can't explain it but she'd felt, getting Mrs Cauley to bed, a definite change in the air. Mrs Cauley had felt it too and had been murderous. She'd taken hours to settle, demanding endless glasses of Pernod and asking Shauna to style out her good wig and wanting cream slathered on her leg sores.

Shauna is wearing little more than her drawers, so the sight of Tadhg's big face pressed up against the window gives her more than a subtle fright. She grabs a tablecloth to hold around her.

'Now then, Shauna, I've a guest for you,' roars Tadhg through the closed door.

'I'm not open.'

'Ah now, don't be like that. You've the room and the man's melted with tiredness.'

Shauna wants to stab Tadhg with the bread knife. She opens the door, clutching the tablecloth to her bosom, and looks blackly at Mahony.

'Is that my guest?'

'Aye, it is,' Tadhg nods enthusiastically.

'You can pay?'

'Aye, he can.' Tadhg pushes Mahony into the kitchen. 'Get the kettle on, Shauneen. He's destroyed by travelling. How's Mrs Cauley?'

'An old bitch.'

'Ah, the poor woman's afflicted.'

'Don't I know it?'

Shauna has the look of a rabbit about her, soft and compact, with light brown hair and pink-rimmed eyes She moves like one too, with quick dashes and small dazed pauses. Mahony finds her comforting to watch and his dark gaze trails her about the untidy kitchen. She's young, in her early twenties maybe, but she has the manner of someone much older. So that she fusses and mutters as she goes about her business, punctuating her tasks with sharp comments and sudden groans. She has changed out of the tablecloth into a dress and has pinned her hair half on top of her head. Her face has a clean, scrubbed appearance. A practical face: responsible, rushed and more than a little tired. She puts an ashtray down next to Tadhg's elbow with a pointed look. Tadhg ignores her as he sprawls at the end of the table with the whiskey bottle. Mahony sits at the other end with a cup in his hand. In the middle of the table, between empty jam jars and piles of dusty china, a ginger cat blithely licks its arse.

'I was having a spring clean, Tadhg.'

'You should see the cleanliness down at the Widow's, it's godly.'

'Don't talk to me about her, Tadhg. I've enough dealing with one bitter old wagon today.'

Tadhg smiles benevolently and tells Mahony that Mrs Cauley is both Shauna's finest patron and biggest curse. Mrs Cauley has the strong belief that she was once one of the greatest actresses to grace the stage of the Abbey Theatre. And of course wasn't she the muse of a multitude of highly talented writers and poets? She'd descended on Rathmore House twenty-odd years ago, when Shauna's mammy had run it as a premium hotel for English salmon fishers, and she'd stayed ever since. Mrs Cauley had paid very well for many years, keeping a roof on Rathmore House, a fire in the hearth and glass in some of the windows. Mrs Cauley had even stayed after the standards dropped when Shauna's mammy ran off to England with a guest, leaving Shauna's daddy hermited with grief in his workshop, reading about fairies and talking to himself in a Protestant accent.

'Don't tell lies now.' Shauna flicks Tadhg with the edge of a tea towel. 'Mammy is in Coventry helping Auntie with her angina. And there's nothing wrong with my standards.'

Tadhg winks and, clutching heavily at the side of the table, he bids them goodnight.

'Will he be all right driving back? He's three sheets to the wind.'

'He'll survive if he keeps on going past Annie Farelly's and doesn't chance his arm for a nightcap. God love him, that woman's steel and bolts.'

Mahony grins. 'All right, well, take me up to bed then, Shauna.'

Shauna warns Mahony to tread carefully in the hallway so as not to wake Mrs Cauley, who lies in state in the library. In its prime Rathmore would have been imposing; its bone structure still mutters about good breeding. The ceilings are high and the finishings are fine, but the house seeps with damp and is ravaged by dry rot. The woodworms sing in the skirting boards and the moths hang out of the curtains. The mice have the run of the guest rooms, shredding blankets, skating in the basins and nibbling the soaps.

They almost reach the foot of the staircase when a voice rolls out into the hallway and along the faded carpet. It's the sort of voice honed to turn corners, vault walls and open door handles.

'Is that someone with you there, Shauna?'

'No, Mrs Cauley.'

Shauna puts a hand on Mahony's arm to stop him walking forward but he's already held by the speaker's spell. It hardly matters what the voice says; Mahony would stop and listen to it anyway.

'Am I actually a fecking idiot?'

'No, Mrs Cauley.'

'Bring them in here then.'

'There's no one here.'

'If I have to get the leg out of this bed . . .'

'All right, I'll bring him in.' Shauna turns to Mahony. 'Come in and say hello to her or I'll have no peace.'

Mahony follows Shauna through a heavy door wedged open with an umbrella stand full of walking sticks. Inside is a corridor constructed from complicated strata of books, magazines, periodicals and papers. Some of the stacks are waist height but others reach up to well over ten feet high. Shauna stops to pick up a drift of pamphlets. She stuffs them into the cracks between piles.

'This was a beautiful room until she made it her lair.' Shauna points up at the thick cobwebs that trapeze the spaces between the books.

The smell is so strong that Mahony can taste it; a thick damp prowls into his nose and mouth, settles on the back of his tongue and starts to paw his throat closed. It is the smell of a million mould-blossomed pages, of a thousand decaying bindings, of a universe of dead words.

'She calls it her literary labyrinth,' says Shauna, kicking an avalanche of play scripts out of the way. 'I call it a bloody hazard.'

They emerge into a clearing. A bed, ringed by a low wall of books, is set before curtainless French doors. The night sky is captured in its topmost panes.

The bed is carved from dark wood and is horribly ornate. At the head of it stands a dead man holding his hat against his chest. The dead man looks up at Mahony with his eyes low-lidded and full. Mahony sees the famished hollow of his cheeks and the sad drape of his moustache. The dead man lifts his eyebrows imperceptibly then his gaze sinks down again to rest on the floor.

A reading lamp throws a web of light over the occupant of the bed: a very old bald woman who is reaching for a wig slung over the bedpost. Constellations of age spots pattern the waxy scalp.

'Wait until I am seemly, Visitor. I am preparing a respectable facade.'

She straightens the wig with some difficulty and a voice emanates from under it, mock sonorous. 'Come.'

Mahony draws closer and is staggered that such a body

can hold such a voice. Clad in a silk kimono, with her legs
half-covered by blankets, the formidable Mrs Cauley is no
bigger than a child. Her chest is startlingly concave in contrast
to her distended belly. This rounded abdomen, together with
her long, very thin arms, gives her the appearance of a benign
geriatric spider.

'Now there's a face,' Mrs Cauley whistles. 'Sit down here,
handsome.'

She gives Mahony an unsettling smile, revealing a set of
teeth like a row of bombed houses. 'You're a fine-looking
individual.'

Shauna pushes a pile of crumbling music scores from a
footstool and hands it to Mahony. 'He's only staying a few
days but.'

'He'll stay longer than that, sweetheart. Go and put on
a teacake, lightly tanned with a knob of butter.'

'You've not long had your tea.'

'And I the overpaying guest here? Get on, a bit of exer-
cise for those fat legs of yours.'

Shauna tuts and disappears into the maze.

Mrs Cauley edges upright in the bed. 'Good. Now we
can talk. You can't trust her, the slinkeen. That girl would
steal the eyes out of your head. I've had many personal effects
gone missing since I came here. Emerald-set jewellery and
bank notes and suchlike. There was a fox stole with glass
eyes, which was very fetching. That went.'

'Why don't you go elsewhere?'

Mrs Cauley scratches her scalp, moving her wig to a
new rakish angle. 'I like the forest around me, and all the
things that live in it, badgers and owls and fecking squirrels
running about. That one pushes me out onto the veranda
and I languish there all day listening to the trees sing. Hold
my hand; I want to feel some male warmth.'

Mahony takes her hand and holds it gently. He can feel her knotted bones through her fragile skin. 'What do your trees sing about?'

'All the lowlifes who inhabit the village.'

'So you know the villagers well?'

'Through the trees I do. I hear all the tales of illicit affairs and nasty actions. And what the trees don't know Bridget Doosey fills in with her slanderings. God, without her this place would be even more of a morgue. She's forensic, that one. Doosey could take this village apart and tell you what killed it in the time it takes you to break a girl's heart.'

Mahony frowns.

Mrs Cauley grins. 'Shauna hates having Doosey in the house; she says we're a bad influence on each other. That girl chews the ears off me with her relentless bloody nagging.' Mrs Cauley shoots him a mutinous glance. 'As soon as she patters off down to town I get Doosey in for a bit of hell-raising.' She leans forward and speaks low. 'We have a signal. I hoist my harvest festivals out of the window and Doosey stands on the quay with her binoculars.'

Mahony looks confused.

'I wave me knickers, boy. Harvest Festivals. *All is safely gathered in?*'

Mahony laughs. He puts Mrs Cauley's hand back on the bed and searches his pockets for his cigarettes.

'Of course I have to be careful Annie Farelly doesn't see or she'd report me to the priest for immoral behaviour.'

'I crossed paths with the Widow today; she's a charmer.'

'She's an article.'

Mahony watches as the dead man attempts to hang his hat on the bedpost. He gives up with a pained expression, puts it back on his head and drifts across the room, pulling his moustache morosely as he goes.

'That's a tall mouse you're watching there.' Mrs Cauley's voice is warm honey but the set of grey eyes she has clamped on him are splinter sharp. 'Have you always seen them? You do see them, don't you?'

Mahony takes out a cigarette and taps it on the packet. He refuses to meet her eyes. You'd need to know him well to realise that his hackles have risen, for his forehead is entirely smooth and there's a relaxed sort of smile on his face.

'You mind?' he says, holding up the fag and setting to light it.

'Not at all.'

They sit for a while in silence, two poker players waiting on the next move.

Shauna appears with a lap tray. 'Now, say good night to Mahony, Mrs Cauley.'

'I haven't finished with him.'

'You have of course; eat your teacake.'

Mrs Cauley puts her head on one side and sings back Shauna's own voice to her. 'I could take a little package of crisps, Shauneen, for something salty.'

'Good night, Mrs Cauley.'

'Good night, Shauna, good night, Mahony.' Mrs Cauley fishes up a teacake with her puckered fingers.

As they reach the foot of the stairs her voice careens out after them.

'Don't try it on with him, Shauna. He's way above you, both spiritually and in terms of his looks. And, Mahony, mind she doesn't get her hands on your gooter; she'd give you an awful dose. Just look at her: she's sex-mad.'

Shauna shows Mahony to a large room at the top of the stairs. It's powerfully musty despite the night air coursing in through the open windows. Mahony can hear the insistent chant of an owl, and some other noise, a panicky high-pitched bleat. Moths cast dancing patterns around the single ceiling light.

'You can leave the windows open for air, although it's noisy with the creatures in the forest murdering each other half the night.'

Shauna turns down the bed covers. Her movements are deft and assured when she doesn't know she's being watched.

'I'm sorry about Mrs Cauley,' she says.

'She's a handful, isn't she?'

Shauna nods. 'She's that. Don't listen too carefully to her, Mahony; she's a little touched.'

'I noticed.' Mahony folds his jacket onto the chair and puts his cowboy boots squarely underneath it. He walks to the window and leans out. The air is cooler now and filled with the elemental smell of earth and trees and sea and sky. Out past the cries of foxes and dying birds, if he listened, he would hear the black waves lapping against the quay and the owls hunting over the fields. Or the sound of the houses as they settle and sigh in their sleep, all the way down to the bay.

'I'm not really sex-mad,' Shauna says as she hangs a towel on the ring next to the hand basin.

Mahony laughs over his shoulder at her. 'You just haven't met the right fella,' he says.

Shauna gives the sink a quick wipe, blushing scarlet at the taps. 'Breakfast is at eight. Night-night, Mahony.'

'Night, Shauna, and thanks.'

'Sure, you're welcome.'

In the quiet room the night air steals in through the open window to whisper the soap dry in the dish. Mice bob around the boots corralled between the chair legs, stopping to nose at the worn heels and blunt toes, sniffing distant cities and a million steps from there to here. Inside the wardrobe a few crumpled shirts absorb the incense of mothballs and waxed wood. On top of the wardrobe a rucksack, heavier than it ought to be, is pushed back out of sight. Socks rest balled in a drawer, odd in their pairings.

Mahony is sleeping.

Come closer. Close enough to inhale tobacco and sweat, road dust and whiskey, sunlight and hair oil. Close enough to follow the swell of his shoulder all the way down to his inked and rounded bicep where a big-breasted mermaid swims. She blows you a kiss and fans her tail.

Come closer. Close enough to plot the lines on his forehead, the fine slope of his nose and the long-lashed crescents of his closed eyes. Now, hold your breath for this, slowly trace the teasing curve of his lips, open a little in sleep.

Look around you. The dead are watching too.

They rise through mouse-carved wall cavities and damp-blown stone. Through brittle flock paper and worn wooden floors. Through dust-dulled carpets and wide stone flags. They have been dead for a wing beat and for an age.

At the foot of the bed leans a pale blacksmith, his shirtsleeves rolled up and his dead mind still ringing with the chime of the hammer. His hands close around long-gone tools and he's pulling those easy shapes out of soft metal again.

A grey lady stands by the head of the bed. She walks Rathmore House in her dead dreams. Hers is the face in the painting in the hallway, where the last reach of stairs turns past the stained-glass window. In life she planted shrubberies and instructed servants. She poured tea from bright teapots and took up sugar tongs with an enquiring look.

As quiet in death as she was in life, she watches Mahony sleep.

Long-departed cooks arrive, wiping their foreheads and fretting over lost platters and tough pastry. Perished gardeners drift by, trying to remember the right way to espalier a fruit tree. Housemaids collect in dark corners, their dead knees remembering the hard kiss of polished wood.

Mahony is sleeping and the dead are gathering.

As the night passes, deceased farmers appear with their hats in their hands and spectral sailors wash up from the moon-sparkling bay below to pad wetly across the floor.

Towards dawn, thieves and saints, chieftains and beggars, clerics and tax collectors join the vigil.

Pale children run about in the early morning light in dim-glowing smocks and short trousers that will guarantee cold legs for all eternity. Babies stagger and fall like fat comedians, or else crawl bawling through their unformed for ever.

Be still. The dead are drawing in.

They wring their hands apologetically. They wait for his eyes to open so that they can be seen.

They only want to be seen.

Chapter 4

April 1976

It doesn't take her long to find him. When Mahony steps out into the morning with a hot cup of tea the dead girl is hopscotching along the veranda with her finger up her nose.

'Will you play with me, Mister?'

'I won't. I'm drinking me tea.'

She stands on one faint leg, dangling a little scuffed shoe, slap-slapping it up against her sole of her foot. 'I'll show you a secret.'

Mahony's hair is still wet from the water he's thrown on his face, his eyes are swollen but he feels all right. Shauna is making breakfast; he sees her through the window lighting the range with a long match, stepping back in a well-rehearsed dance when a big brutal flame kicks up. He likes hearing the noises she makes as she moves about. She sets a heavy pan on the flame and wipes her hands on the arse pockets of her corduroy skirt. A twist of light-brown hair hangs down her back.

The dead girl puts her pinched little face on one side and grins. 'Ah, go on, Mister.'

'All right, but not for long.'

She tries to hold Mahony's hand as they walk down the field towards the edge of the forest. She can't of course, her fingers slip through his, but she doesn't seem to mind.

At the bottom of the field Mahony leans against the gate while the dead girl pulls faces at the horses huddled nearby. They ignore her and stand with their flanks twitching in the early sun. It won't be long before the day's heat sets their backs steaming.

'Come into the trees, will ya? An' see the secret thing?'

Mahony searches his pockets for his cigarettes. 'Tell me about it.'

She thinks for a moment. 'I saw the dead girl's knuckles. I saw 'em in a maybush. The branches have grown all ways into them.' She threads her dim fingers together.

'What dead girl? You?'

She looks at Mahony with horror and holds her hands up. 'Not my knuckles, mine are here. I told you. *The dead girl's* knuckles.'

Mahony's heart turns crossways. 'Can you show me?'

Her voice is very small. 'I suppose so.' She walks through the wall and down to the trees miming a great load on her back.

The dead girl moves quickly through the forest. Mahony sees only glimpses of her. Sometimes the hem of a blue spectral cardigan, sometimes a faint little knee. Sometimes he just hears her: a laugh snapping back through the air like a sprung branch.

Mahony ignores a suicide to the right of him, hanging from an oak tree like a twisted chrysalis. As Mahony passes, the dead man swings round and gurgles through his crushed windpipe; if he had words he would curse the lure of a good rope and a sound branch. Mahony keeps his eyes low and looks only for the little scuffed shoes, pale against loam and leaf litter, running deeper into the forest.

Then, all at once, she slows down and starts to creep forwards, miming exaggerated tiptoes. Mahony follows her silently into a small clearing haunted by crows. Some are perched cawing on the carcass of a lightning-blasted tree. Some dance on the ground with their ragged skirts held behind them. As Mahony approaches, the birds wing it up into the sky and swear blackly down at him.

Beyond the clearing is a river; he can see it through the trees. The dead girl runs towards it.

Mahony walks along the bank, on a pathway of sorts, tripping over ridges of dried mud, hemmed in by undergrowth, searching for the dead girl. Around him is the rank smell of a world dominated by plants.

Then he sees her, crouching by the side of the river, winding a strand of pale hair around her finger.

'Maybe it's Ida,' she says.

'Your name?'

Ida smiles over her shoulder then looks back at the river.

It has dried up in the hot weather. Shrinking back from its banks so that the mud flats at its edges are as noxious as bedsores, infected and fetid, cracked and oozing. Mahony sees that in places, at slow bends, behind fallen branches, the water is pooled and clotted with algae. The air is laced with midges.

In the middle of the river there is a shadow of a dark bulk, a heaped mass under the surface. Mahony picks up a stone, feels its weight in his hand and throws it. The sound is unexpectedly loud, as surprising as a gunshot, the contact of rock on rock without water or silt to cushion it.

Ida glares at him. 'There's a secret island under there. Don't wake it.' She lowers her voice. 'If you wait until the river runs away you'll see it.'

Mahony finds another stone. 'A low-tide island?' He gets set to throw it, then thinks better of it.

'But you have to wait and wait. Mammy says you'll see it once in a lifetime if you're lucky and twice if you're blessed.'

'Have you seen it, Ida?'

'Maybe.' She peers up at him through pale eyelashes. 'You can walk on it. It's longer than a fishing boat and as wide as a bus. In the sunshine it sparkles, all the little stones like wet jewels.'

'You've walked on it, Ida?'

'Jesus, are you thick or something?' She sighs and looks up at the sky and continues in a flat bored voice. 'If you ever see Denny's Ait you're not to go near it. Even if you think you can jump it or wade it. Even if it's surrounded by less than a teaspoon of water. You're to remember the Protestant who went digging for old bones on it. You're to remember that when the tide changed, him and the island both drowned to death.' She bites her lip. 'Now *his* bones swim around and around it like long white fishes.'

Mahony looks out at the water. In the back of his brain something moves, shifts, a brief sickening feeling, like a wakening. He jumps up and walks back along the bank, needing to keep moving. He heads back to the clearing knowing she's right next to him, walking to heel like a puppy, still trying to hold his hand.

She is smiling. It's in no way a wholesome smile.

Say it, Mahony. Fucking say it.

'Where's the dead girl, Ida? The one you brought me to see?'

She stops smiling. 'What dead girl? I don't want to see no dead girl.'

'Then why did you bring me here?'

'To find my yo-yo. I lost it here and here and here.' She turns around and around with her hands stretched out.

Mahony rubs his eyes. 'Please, Ida.'

Ida puts her hands over her ears and drifts right out of sight.

Mahony makes his way over whorls of tree roots and through moats of leaf mould knowing that he's lost and knowing that he's watched. The dead of the forest are rustling in the undergrowth and winding up the tree trunks, twittering on branches and nosing through the loam.

Mahony feels them reach out to him as he passes.

He's almost relieved to catch sight of Ida sitting cross-legged on the ground up ahead, flickering very slightly.

'I'm not your friend no more. Just so's you know, *Gobshite*.' She picks her nose and wipes her finger on the sole of her shoe. 'I mean it. I'm not feckin' talking to you no more. Never. Not ever. All right?'

Ida is true to her word. By the time Mahony reaches the path to Rathmore House she hasn't cursed him once. She turns away with narrowed eyes, holding a finger over her fading lips.

Mrs Cauley is out in the garden when Mahony reaches the house, ensconced in a wheelchair with a lap tray on her legs. She is brandishing a sausage on the end of a fork in the direction of a greying priest who sits with a defeated sort of aspect on a garden chair at her feet.

'I'll hear no arguments. I do this for the church, Father.'

'Mrs Cauley, you are most generous but I'm certain my

superiors will want me to see the proposed script before you embark on another one of your productions.'

Mrs Cauley puts the fork down. 'Father Quinn, I cannot allow a collaboration. As an artist I must work alone.' She takes a long sup from her teacup. The priest watches on with thinly disguised impatience.

'But we must ensure that the production is suitable, Mrs Cauley, for it goes under the auspices of the church. Especially given the furore generated by your last production.'

'A resounding success.'

The priest throws her a sour look. 'I was unaware that the Holy Family featured at all in *West Side Story*.'

'It was but a meandering thought of mine.'

'But a contentious portrayal none the less, especially in terms of the costuming.'

'A loincloth is not to be sniffed at, Father.'

'I don't think you quite understand me, Mrs Cauley.'

Mrs Cauley hands Father Quinn her teacup with a patient smile. 'Father, the Son of God lived amongst us only briefly, but this much we know: as a man he had a fine physique and a splendid beard. That is well documented through holy statues and great works of art, is it not? And I think Tadhg made a valiant attempt once he got used to the safety pins. He may have been a big fat arse of a Jesus but you'd forgive him that for his superior singing voice.'

'We received many complaints.'

'And you sold a fair few tickets too. They came from far and wide,' says Mrs Cauley, smiling slyly now, 'especially after that article in the *Western People*.'

'All I ask is for the play to be suitable.'

'It is a travesty to require a play to be merely suitable.' Mrs Cauley takes up her fork coquettishly with her head to one side. 'If people choose to misinterpret my work what can I do?'

Father Quinn frowns. 'If I could only advise a more appropriate theme, Mrs Cauley, one that steers clear of—'

'Sadly, you can't. My creative juices only flow freely in the dark. My mind is like a mushroom: if you shine the light of the one true church on it, well then, inspiration may not spore at all.'

'Well, Mrs Cauley, at the very least you must consult me once you have the final draft ready. Otherwise the Bishop himself—'

'Ah now, look who it is, Father.' Mrs Cauley stretches her hand out to Mahony.

Mahony grins. 'Mrs Cauley, you are a picture.'

She has dispensed with her wig and is sporting a silk turban and a tweed coat. On her feet, over her bed socks, she wears a pair of strappy gold sandals. Mrs Cauley's dead admirer must have found somewhere to hang his hat, for he's skulking bareheaded in the rhododendrons. He ignores Mahony and continues to stare at the priest with an expression of concentrated contempt.

Mrs Cauley gestures gracefully at a vacant deckchair. 'Come and join us, Mahony. I'm afraid I've almost consumed your breakfast. Shauna held it as long as she could but one couldn't waste a lovely fry. I ate it alfresco to make full use of the weather.'

The priest raises his arse a little bit from the garden chair in welcome as Mahony sits down.

'Will you take a drop of tea with us? She's at least left me a pot.'

'I will.'

'Allow me, Mrs Cauley.' Father Quinn pours the tea with an air of spiteful servitude.

'Thank you, Father. Mahony is from Dublin, where he is a man of the world.'

'I can see that,' says Father Quinn, fixing Mahony with a hostile glare.

Of course Father Eugene Quinn has suffered the sort of misfortune that Mahony cannot possibly understand. Poor Eugene was brought up by respectable parents, in a respectable family, in a respectable town but, even so, the odds were stacked against him. He was unwelcome at birth, unpopular at school and disliked at the seminary. For Eugene had been afflicted with a face that inspired a strong and instinctive mistrust, or at the very least a nagging sort of doubt. Even his own mother had difficulty taking to him, so much so that she often neglected to bring him home. Little Eugene's forgotten pram was a familiar sight outside the butcher's, the baker's or the grocer's shop.

As he grew, the hapless Eugene retained about himself the appearance of a weasel or some such insidious creature, for his eyes could never be still and his top lip would always be damp, and his smile was never really genuine. For, after all, he had precious little to smile about.

His father thought long and hard about how he could propel Eugene into the world and as far away from home as possible. He decided that Eugene must join the priesthood, a position guaranteed to come with a good supply of unquestioning trust. For Eugene's father knew that Eugene's looks would work against him in any other business. Even the filthy wouldn't buy a cake of soap off his son.

So Father Quinn would readily swap places with Mahony, whoever the hell he is, just to have a face like that. A face that women can love on sight and men will smile upon. Mahony has the right tone in his voice and the right words to go with it. Mahony has a hand that people want to shake and a back they want to pat.

'How are you finding the village, Mahony?' Father Quinn smiles crocodilian through gritted teeth.

Mahony lights a cigarette and takes a deep drag. 'Ah, I haven't seen anything much yet.'

Mrs Cauley turns to the priest. 'But he'll be having a good poke around the village. Mahony is interested in even the smallest particles of village life; he has a very enquiring mind.'

The priest frowns. 'What is it you do, Mahony?'

Mrs Cauley interrupts. 'Why he's a tonic, just look at him! Do you know, Father, he's already raised my old heart right out of my chest and stoked up the embers? I'll not be the only girl in Mulderrig to fall for him now, will I? God help us in the face of Mahony's natural attributes.'

Mahony laughs and blows smoke out into the sky.

Father Quinn grips the handle of his teacup and appears to be fighting a fierce internal battle. Mrs Cauley turns to him. 'Father, will you ensure that the novenas are said for me?' She leans forward and pushes a small brown envelope into his hand.

'Certainly, Mrs Cauley.'

'Goodbye so, give my regards to Annie Farelly on your way down. You'll be calling?'

'Certainly, Mrs Cauley.'

Father Quinn pokes the envelope down inside his pocket with trembling fingers. Mahony makes out a firm clench on the priest's jaw.

Mrs Cauley calmly takes a sip of her tea. 'Well, send her up to me then, and inform her to bring a corner of her fruit loaf with her. For isn't the woman sainted for visiting the infirm? I may be having one of my naps, which, wouldn't you know it, is often the way when she visits. In which case you can tell her not to trouble a sick old lady but to leave the cake on the kitchen table.'

Mrs Cauley gives the priest a vacuous smile. 'God bless you and keep you, Father, for visiting me all the way up here. It always lifts me.'

Father Quinn nods to both of them and, being dismissed, is on his way with a seething heart. The dead man follows him down to the gate, gesturing at the priest's departing figure, before turning back across the lawn. Mahony notices that the dead man has no shoes on. Instead he carries them strung together over his shoulder, his dead feet milk-white and luminous against the grass.

Mrs Cauley shakes her head. 'When God was giving out charm that fecker was last in line.'

Mahony takes the tray from her lap unbidden and finishes the sausage.

'So, now we'll have the chat for ourselves, Mahony. And I'll start by asking you what you are doing here in Mulderrig.'

He takes a corner of cold toast and swirls up egg yolk. 'I'm on holiday.'

'And that's a crock of bollocks.'

Mahony shrugs and mops the plate.

Mrs Cauley smiles at him. 'I recognise your type, honeybee. You've had it tough, haven't you? You've been eating leftovers all your life?'

'I'm grand.'

'That you are. But when are you going to trust me? I trust you.'

Mahony glances up at her and, without expecting to, sees that she has the same kind of honesty that he does. The twisted kind: when something gets so wronged it gets righted.

She smiles. 'I can't vouch for anyone else in this town,

for they're mostly a shower of shites, but I can tell you that I'm upright where it matters. So now, Mahony, I'll ask again: what are you doing here?'

Fuck it, he thinks, he has to start somewhere.

Mahony licks his fingers, takes his wallet out of his back pocket and a folded envelope out of his wallet. He hands it to her. 'That was left alongside me twenty-six years ago at St Anthony's Orphanage in Dublin.'

Mrs Cauley searches for her glasses and holds up the envelope. She opens it and takes out the photograph and squints at it.

'Turn it over.'

She does, reads the back, and whistles through her remaining teeth. 'Damn it to hell, your mother was Orla Sweeney.'

'It looks like it.'

'Does anyone else know about this?'

'Not yet.'

Mrs Cauley nods. 'So you came undercover, thinking you'd case the joint first?'

'Seemed like the right thing to do, given what's written on the back of that photograph.'

'You're not just a pretty face, are you, Francis?'

'My name's Mahony.'

'And what do you want, Mahony?'

'To find out what happened to my mother just.'

'She's not here, honey.'

'I didn't think she was. Where is she?'

'That's something no one here pretends to know.'

'Did you know her?'

She looks at him. 'Our paths crossed briefly.'

'What was she like?'

Mrs Cauley remembers: a pale, dark-eyed ne'er-do-well.

They'd met during her first stage production. Back then Mrs Cauley was a newcomer, but then she always would be.

Orla had been hanging around outside the village hall, scowling, sneering, kicking the wall. The girl came with a warning, but after a few days of this Mrs Cauley had walked out, in clear sight of the village, to ask Orla if she'd be auditioning for the play. She held out the play script to her, and Orla, her full-lipped mouth sulky, had looked at it.

Then Orla had smiled.

My God, it was July after a tempest, the fury was gone and in its place there was bright fire. Orla took the script but she never came back.

But she had always looked for her. The girl would have burnt the stage down.

'She was like you,' Mrs Cauley says.

Mahony nods; that is enough for now. 'Have I any family here?'

'None at all. Your grandfather left when your mother was a child and your grandmother died ten years ago. They had no other children; Orla was a late blessing.'

'And my father?'

Mrs Cauley shakes her head. 'None as would admit to it. Your mammy was sixteen years old when you were born out of wedlock.'

Mahony finds that he isn't surprised and neither is Mrs Cauley's dead admirer, who shrugs and settles in a nearby flowerbed, listening closely.

'So you wound up at the orphanage. Rough, was it?'

'What do you think?'

'That an experience like yours could make a man partial to a drop of avenging.'

'I've told you, I'm here to find out what happened just.'

The dead man in the flowerbed shakes his head. He has been trying to blow down the faded petals of a clematis. But the flowers remain unmoved by his dead breath. He gives up and tries to knock their heads off with his cane in a disturbing expression of spectral violence.

Mahony picks up the photograph. 'Tell me what happened to her.'

'As I said—'

Mahony looks at her. 'If I don't hear it from you . . .?'

Mrs Cauley nods. 'Orla Sweeney was the wild bad girl of the village. She lived at the edge of the forest in a broken-down cottage with a drunken mammy and a long-gone daddy. By the time she was sixteen she was knocked up, unwed and Mulderrig's dirty little secret.'

The dead man gives up the fight and stands frowning amongst the flowers. He pulls at his moustache with his cane loose in his hand.

She speaks softly. 'Your mother refused to live by the rules, Mahony. She wouldn't be taken away with a blanket over her head and she wouldn't consent to being married off to some desperate old farmer. She wanted to have her baby and put it in a pram and bring it into town, and she was prepared to fight them for this.'

'Fair play to her.'

'But think about it, Mahony.' Mrs Cauley frowns. 'Can you imagine how the town responded, at that time?'

Mahony nods. 'I can.'

'The official story is that one fine day Orla upped and left Mulderrig, taking her fatherless bastard with her and leaving no forwarding address.'

Mahony shrugs. 'Everyone gets the hell out of these small towns sooner or later. She must have talked about it, planned it?'

Mrs Cauley thought about the question Orla had asked her that day. When the big-smoke actress had walked over to the little-village trollop with all the eyes of the town watching. It was a simple enough question. Spoken low, with a sense of wonder, disbelief even.

How could you leave?

Leave what – the city, the stage, the man? Mrs Cauley couldn't give Orla an answer.

Perhaps the question was enough? Perhaps Orla had glimpsed something, a world where a woman could leave anything and everything behind and strike out, alone. Afterwards, if she ever thought about the girl it was to picture her arriving at some new place, some new city. Stepping off a bus, a boat, a train, with her scowl and her smile and her brutal eyes. With her brand-new baby and her second-hand coat.

'She thought about leaving,' says Mrs Cauley. 'I'm sure of that.'

Mahony nods. 'So she left town, landed in the city, took a look around, got shot of her bastard.'

Mrs Cauley picks over her words carefully, soberly. 'I do not believe that Orla gave you up. Why would she, when she had fought so hard to keep you?'

'People change their minds; she was only a young one herself. Maybe it was tougher than she thought, alone with a kid. So she left me at the orphanage with a note to show she cared.'

'Except Orla didn't write that note, Mahony, that's a mature and educated hand. Your mother was on the mitch for years. She hardly saw the inside of a school.'

'Then she got someone else to write it.'

Mrs Cauley frowns. 'It's possible.'

'You're not convinced.' He studies her face. 'You don't think she made it.'

Their eyes meet; she holds his gaze. 'I'm sorry, kiddo. But then it's not what I think, is it?'

'I think the same.' His voice is quiet, steady.

Mrs Cauley looks relieved.

They sit in silence for a while.

'So you can stop asking yourself those same damn questions,' she says.

'What questions?'

Her voice is gentle. 'If she's living why did she leave me and if she's dead why can't I see her?'

Mahony regards the toe of his boot, his face impassive. On the lawn the dead man throws down his cane and sinks to his knees.

'I'm right, aren't I?'

Mahony pats down his pockets for his cigarettes, slips a fag from the pack and sets to light it.

'I'll tell you something that I know.' Mrs Cauley leans forward and touches his arm. 'Those we have lost return to us in their own time.' She smiles. 'You've been searching for her all your life, I know. But she'll come to you when she's good and ready.'

Mahony exhales sharply. 'You know a lot, old lady.'

Mrs Cauley looks away, out over the forest, into another cloudless day of bleached skies and pounding swelter. For a moment she yearns for the storm that she knows is coming. For when it does she'll be right here, watching the bright cords rip open the sky, with her old bones thrilling to the sound of hot air.

'Who's the dead eejit with the moustache?'

Mrs Cauley laughs. 'I believe that would be Johnnie.'

Johnnie takes a bow as he skips faintly along the veranda.

'And who's Johnnie?'

'Never you mind.'

Mahony forces a smile. 'So Mammy caused some trouble?'

'She defied the town and everyone in it.'

'I expect they didn't know what had hit them.'

Mrs Cauley nods. 'At the time people believed, maybe still believe, that your mother was unnatural, evil even. A few years earlier and they would have burnt her as a witch outside the Post Office.'

'Who's to say they didn't? According to that note there they dealt with her some way or other.'

They sit in silence. Johnnie settles on the lawn and muses too, cross-legged, stroking his moustache dolefully.

'You have to ask yourself why St Anthony's? Why take a baby so far?'

'It's a fair way to go to get rid of a baby,' says Mahony.

Mrs Cauley stares at him. 'They didn't take you there to get rid of you, Mahony; *they took you to there to save you.*'

Johnnie jumps up clapping his hands.

'Has it crossed your mind that if something happened to Orla you could have been in danger too?' Mrs Cauley continues, oblivious to Johnnie's applause. 'They needed to keep you safe, Mahony. Whoever left you there was giving you the chance to return, to put things right. That's why they left the note with you.'

Mahony nods. 'It's possible.'

Her face is grave. 'And it's also possible that they knew exactly what happened to Orla.'

Chapter 5

April 1976

Mahony hears the car before he sees it, and it sounds terminal. It pulls up alongside him, ploughing up the dust. Tadhg leans out, unshaven and wearing a woollen hat, despite the heat of the day.

'You're kicking your heels up there, Mahony. On the way into town, is it? Get in and I'll bring you down with me. Watch me jill.'

Mahony gets in, minding the ferret in the footwell. A length of string is looped in a harness around her long back and tied to the gear stick.

'We've been catching wabbits for the Widow.'

'Has she given in to you?'

Tadhg resumes his driving position, with his nose just short of the windscreen. 'She hasn't, but I'm wearing her down. Her resolve is weakening. Soon me slippers will be under her bed and me teeth will be in the glass next to hers. If only the church biddies would stop putting a bad word in. Mind you, Father Quinn is the top one there, advising her against me.' Tadhg throws Mahony a look of disgust. 'He's a teetotaller. Would you credit it? Not a natural vice in him.'

'I met him today – a sly cast on him like your ferret there.'

'Jaysus, don't insult the creature. Was Mrs Cauley dancing rings around him?'

'She was.'

Tadhg accepts a cigarette and Mahony leans in to light it for him. Tadhg's two hands grip the steering wheel and the fag bounces in his mouth. He murmurs through the smoke. 'Mrs Cauley has Quinn in her pocket, lulled by the clink of her gold.'

Mahony puts his hand down to the ferret; she shudders all down her back but she lets him touch her. Under her oily fur she is muscle, roped and hard. She turns her head to him and shows him one long fang.

'What are you doing in town now? Come by for a pint?'

'I will. I'll take a wander first, make myself known about the place.'

Tadhg looks at Mahony closely, as if he is burning to say something, then thinks better of it and switches on the radio.

The old ones are still where Mahony left them by the pump, but today there's a bit more life about the place. Vehicles roll up and down the main street; the doctor's black car passes twice alone. Villagers stand chatting outside shops and on corners. Babies sit on hips or in prams where they drool over pounds of sugar and babble at tins of cocoa. Some of the younger women nod and smile at Mahony, the older ones just nod.

Beside them stand their dead shadows, gossiping well into the afterlife. They squint at Mahony with mild interest before turning to call out to the frocked children who run hoop and stick through delivery vans and bicycles. A dead man in shirtsleeves passes by with his hat pulled down low over his eyes. He is singing, he tips his brim at Mahony and is gone, leaving the ghost of a song behind him. Mahony picks it up and whistles it as he walks.

A gaggle of girls sit on the edge of the pavement sucking aniseed balls and spitting the pips across the road. As Mahony walks by they get to their feet and scatter laughing, each with a wide red grin of stolen lipstick.

'Have you a girlfriend, Mister?' says the ringleader, a big girl wearing the last goodness out of an ugly dress.

Mahony shakes his head. 'Didn't I tell you I'm waiting for you? When you're grown we'll run away together.'

And he goes on his way, leaving her a queen in the eyes of her friends.

Today the shop doors are propped open, welcoming sea breeze and custom. Commanding the best view of the quay and spilling its wares freely onto the surrounding area, the Post Office and General Store sits back on its haunches and disregards the competition. For here Marie Gaughan will sell you anything: from rat traps to knicker elastic, from duck eggs to feather dusters.

Outside, reels of chicken wire jostle against sacks of potatoes with turned-down tops. There's spades and buckets hung up for the children to eye. Measuring the merits of colour and function, round turrets over square ones, pale blue over space-dust pink. Here Marie Gaughan will cut you a yellow ice from a thick block and sandwich it in wafers. Here rabbits are sold in cardboard boxes, along with water butts and garden hoes, banned books and jam made from hedgerows.

Mahony steps in off the street. Just inside the doorway a dead woman is standing on a pile of newspapers leaving neither print nor wrinkle. From her basket black beetles fall. They spiral through the air to melt, wriggling, into the floor.

'I wanted carbolic,' she whispers, near to tears, and disappears.

Mahony looks around him.

Marie Gaughan is behind the counter pretending to price dishcloths. Mrs Lavelle and her daughter Teasie are pretending to buy a tin of peas, and the lovely Róisín Munnelly is pretending to help them.

Here is a handsome stranger.

And here is more than one woman with the hairs rising on her neck nape and an unwanted memory shifting in the back of her mind. Past the place where old songs go to pass the time of day with forgotten hymns and nursery rhymes. Where long-ago cats are put out along with lost schooldays and expired coupons.

Later it will hit them. When they are waiting on the kettle or turning down the bed sheet.

His dark eyes are her eyes, the shape of his face, hers. The way he stands with his weight shifted back on his heels and his nose in the air, hers.

Then they will start up and call out, drink a hot cup of tea or something stronger and firmly tell themselves to cop themselves on.

But right now this memory is jumbled deep, tucked firmly behind the shopping lists and the ironing, the Friday fish and the Monday-morning gossip.

'Now,' says Marie Gaughan when Mahony gets to the counter. She spreads her arms out over the folded newspapers and squares her jaw.

Mahony asks for fags and a local rag. 'What's the news about the place?' he says in his hardest Dublin orphan voice.

You are.

Marie takes his money and gives him change. 'Ah, not much happens about the place. Sure, there's not much to keep a body here.'

'There seems to be a lot going on.'

'Not for those such as yourself, from out of town.'

Mrs Lavelle watches from behind the dry goods, where she's been having a scratch of her scalp, salting her shoulders with a fresh cascade. Marie has advised her to seek out a medicated shampoo and avoid black to lessen the effect, but Mrs Lavelle has been in mourning since the death of de Valera.

Mahony smiles at her and she draws nearer, followed by her daughter, Teasie, who clutches a can of peas to her narrow chest as if it would stop a bullet. Teasie's eyes flitter in the far-off depth beyond the surface smear of her spectacle lenses.

Mrs Lavelle tries out her voice. 'You're the fella from Dublin staying up at Rathmore House?'

'I am.'

'Is it comfortable there?' Mrs Lavelle breaks the long word into separate syllables, for she is speaking polite.

'It's grand.'

'And the breakfasts?'

Mrs Lavelle ignores Marie's little headshake. Mrs Lavelle had helped Shauna with the housekeeping for years only to be dismissed after a misunderstanding over a silver-plated cruet. She would like to know the place has gone to the dogs without her. Although she doesn't blame Shauna; it's the other one. Either way, it drew on an attack of her nerves, which put her in her bed for nigh on a month.

'Breakfast is grand too. Shauna does a good fry.' Mahony takes up his paper and pretends to read. 'I'll be staying on for a bit. I'm taking a holiday for meself.'

The women glance at each other.

Mahony looks up and smiles so brightly that most of them smile back. 'It's a breath of fresh air to be out of the city.'

He speaks low and kind about the lovely trees and the sea so that Marie's hands start to stroke the corners of the newspapers and Teasie Lavelle puts down her can of peas. Then he's asking if any of them have been to Dublin.

'No.'

'Not at all.'

'Marie, you have.'

Mahony gives Marie a soft kind of look. 'Then you'll know what I mean better than anyone else. It's not a patch on here, is it?'

Marie finds that she is leaning halfway across the counter gazing into the hot dark eyes of an unwashed stranger young enough to be her grandson.

'It was busy, the streets were dirty and you couldn't get a decent cup of tea,' she says, entranced.

'That's right.'

Mahony gives her an impossibly slow smile and Marie Gaughan is astonished to find the corners of her mouth responding of their own accord. She coughs herself red and begins to thumb through a copy of *Ireland's Own*.

Mahony folds his paper under his arm. 'Well, I'll be seeing you around the place no doubt, Marie.'

Marie nods, speechless. Behind the counter her toes are curling in her carpet slippers and the locked cash box of her heart is opening.

Words are capable of flying. They dart through windows, over fences, between bar stools and across courtyards. They travel rapidly from mouth to ear, from ear to mouth. And as they go, they pick up speed and weight and substance and gravity. Until they land with a scud, take seed and grow as fast as the unruliest of beanstalks.

By the time Mahony reaches Kerrigan's Bar everyone knows he's on holiday from Dublin, loves a fry and is capable of causing a smile on Marie Gaughan's face, a sight not seen in living memory.

The pub is heaving; even the plush seats are taken. Here are the farmers and the fishermen, the postman and the shopkeepers of Mulderrig. The dead have been pushed out by the living today. They sulk in the cellar and listen on the landing.

In the corner sits a bodhrán player. The music will start directly, once the rest of the band is here and the tall tales are toppled.

Tadhg nods to acknowledge Mahony as he steps in through the door but doesn't miss a beat; he's on fine form behind the bar.

'So there we were, me and this whale on the end of the hook, and the line reelin' out like judgment and this unholy bastard trying to pull me out of the boat and into me death.'

Mahony catches sight of Jack Brophy in the same place as before.

'So then this fella,' Tadhg points the nose of a bottle at a laughing man with hair like a wind-blasted bush at the far end of the bar. 'He says, "Ah, Tadhg, give it a flick of your wrist – isn't it all in the wrist action?"'

The pub howls.

'And Tadhg landed a monster of a two-pound mackerel!'

'It was a mermaid, wasn't it, Tadhg?'

'One with a new perm for herself?'

'Ah, watch it. Half the lies Tadhg says aren't true.'

Tadhg grins benevolently at his audience and spreads his hands wide. 'Ye can all ask me arse. Now, Mahony?'

There's a lull and Mahony feels the eyes of Mulderrig upon him.

Jack raises his finger half an inch from the bar towel. 'I'll stand him a pint. Take a pew, Mahony.'

Mahony takes the seat made free next to Jack, and the eyes of Mulderrig see the big man pat Mahony on the back. It's a benediction; Mahony knows it and is grateful. Jack smiles at Mahony, then turns back to listen to the man with the swollen face to the right of him talk with authority about the terrible malignity of horseflies.

A good pint has magical powers. It can solve the simplest of problems, heal surface wounds and cement minor friendships, all in one evening. As Mahony steps out into the soft Mulderrig night he feels as if he's finally found a place in the world, his own corner. His friends share the same face and he's unsure of their exact names, but they rate him and that's enough. He's been inspected in the smoky light of Kerrigan's Bar and, despite the Dublin accent, despite the leathers, despite the orphan scowl, they'd judged him to be a grand fella entirely.

And he'd disarmed them with his stories and the cast of Dublin characters he drew for them. From the boys who can hot-wire a car as fast as a fart, to the women with the broken voices selling black-market fireworks out of prams. Now they know all about the rooftops and the alleyways. They know about the good bars and the quiet doorways, and the grand houses and the wide parks. They have even seen the light on the Liffey as she turns like dishwater through the town.

As he falls out the door of Kerrigan's Bar and into the

gentle Mulderrig night, Mahony could almost forget what he came here for.

He walks through the sleeping town, sparking a fag with a tune in his mind. His boot heels spin echoes across the empty streets and he begins to sing low in his fine singing voice. The lyrics are pure, about love and sacrifice and good intent, but the tone in his voice makes the words dirty and hard. Curtains twitch and young girls in soft sprigged nighties with brush-gleaming hair look out dreamily. The dead drift down through floorboards and up through flagstones and through windows and walls and locked doors, listening, yearning.

Mahony walks alone in the blue-white moonlight, to the end of the village and up the steep road towards Rathmore House. The land exhales the heat of the day and the warm-bellied cows dot the fields in huddled shapes.

On a night like this it would be easy to forget, with all of Mulderrig soft and easy in its sleep.

He could forget, first of all, to ask what lit up her eyes, or if she ever laughed, if she liked apples or fucking pears.

He could forget his own name.

Francis Sweeney.

After all, it's a dead name: a name never taken, a life never lived.

This town took it from him. He won't forget that.

The night is clear from mountain to sea as Mahony climbs the dark ribbon of road. Ahead of him the starlit forest slumbers. Behind him the moonlight skims and breaks over the mild-skinned water of the bay, which is as still as milk tonight. For the wind is lying low, curled into the strong back of the deep-sleeping velvet mountain.

A man could almost forget what he came for, when the lovely Mulderrig night is for him alone.

Chapter 6

April 1976

There's a light on in the library and Mahony decides not to ignore Mrs Cauley's summons to join her for a nightcap. He finds her propped up in bed, wearing a poker visor and playing solitaire. She has listened all evening for his footfall in the hall, although she'd never admit to it.

Mahony turfs a pile of papers out of an armchair and pulls off his boots.

'Here.' Mrs Cauley fishes a bottle out from under her pillow. 'Pour us a drop of the hard stuff.'

Mahony pours her a tooth mug and takes a china cup for himself.

There's a nice silence just while they drink. The reading lamp beside the bed casts a mellow tent of light over the two of them. The dead and the mice draw in to watch, lulled and quiet. The damp settles in the corners of the room and stretches itself out along the wallpaper.

Mrs Cauley peers over at him. 'So how's tricks?' She collects up the cards, as quick as a croupier.

'Not bad. I had a good time at the pub with the boys.'

'The boys, is it?' She shuffles and squares the pack. 'Watch yourself. There's not a trustworthy soul in this town. Every one of them has at least two faces.'

Mahony puts his feet up on the bed and looks over at her. The visor shades her eyes but he's certain she's taking everything in. 'They seem sound enough.'

'Will they still drink with you when they know who you are? Do they know who you are, Mahony?'

Mahony gets up and pours himself another. He ignores the empty mug in her outstretched hand.

Mrs Cauley fixes him with her best poker face. 'So you didn't ask your new pals at Kerrigan's Bar what happened to your mammy?'

Mahony swirls the bad whiskey. It dances up the sides of the cup. 'I didn't.'

Mrs Cauley nods. 'That's a shame. They'd have spun you a story about Orla leaving town.'

'It would be no story.'

'So you believe she left town now?'

'If she were dead I'd know about it.'

'You're right of course. She'd be over there by the fire-place, knitting.'

Mahony knocks back his whiskey in one hit, before it can take the skin off the roof of his mouth. 'She could still be alive.'

'Because you can't see her?'

He shrugs.

'The dead are like cats, Mahony. You of all people should know that. They don't always come when they're called.'

Mahony shakes his head. 'They could be holding her somewhere.'

Mrs Cauley raises herself up on her pillows. 'For twenty-six years, Mahony?'

'It happens. I read about some kid found in a woodshed.'

'You think that's possible? A live wire like Orla in a woodshed?' Mrs Cauley speaks evenly. 'You think your mother was murdered and so do I. Now I thought we'd established that?'

Johnnie strolls through the French doors, throws his faint hat down on the end of the bed and disappears. In a moment Mahony sees a plume of spectral pipe smoke coming from behind a large stack of encyclopaedias in the far corner.

Mahony nods. 'So what's next?'

'We play to our strengths, isn't that how the best detectives work? With my mind and your unnatural talents we'll have this case cracked in no time.'

Mahony gets up, takes her cup and his and puts them on the bedside table. He pours another measure into each and wonders if he'll ever feel his feet again. 'All right, Miss Marple, but, first of all, how do you know so much about my unnatural talents?'

She grins. 'Husband number four was an eminent clairvoyant.'

'Four, is it? Jesus. So that would be the dead fella with the moustache?'

She shakes her head and smiles. 'No, Johnnie was my fiancé. We never married, although he was the most beloved.'

Mahony puts a drink into her hand. 'He was the one that got away?'

'Something like that,' says Mrs Cauley. She frowns. 'I want to try something, Mahony.' She takes off her visor and reaches for a headscarf hung over the bedpost. 'Is there a breeze tonight?'

Mahony looks at her. 'God knows. The night is still.'

'We'll give it a go anyways, although it's better with a drop of wind to get it started.'

Mrs Cauley sidles to the edge of the bed. 'Help me to get standing.'

'Where are we going?'

'Did you know, Mahony, that literature can be very illuminating?'

Mrs Cauley reaches for her walking frame and with Mahony's help moves her legs off the bed and puts on her slippers. With great effort she stands and Mahony sees how small she is, not quite five feet tall and the weight of dry hide and honeycombed bone alone.

She sways, curved and calcified by time, smiling up at him. 'Open the doors, Mahony.'

The French doors are stuck fast and blossoming with mould but eventually they give and the night air falls in around Mahony as if it's been waiting with its face pressed against the glass.

'That's it. Throw them wide.'

The night air stalks into the room and starts to tease the dust along the skirting boards.

Mrs Cauley takes a step forward, stumbling a little in her carpet slippers. 'Look around you,' she whispers. 'The room is changing. See? The lights are burning brighter? Can't you feel it? The books want to tell you something. They want to help.'

And then Mahony feels it.

The books, the papers and the magazines: all of them pulsing with a faint heartbeat. They're watching him, holding their breath. Mahony suddenly wants to shout against the pressure of all of these waiting words.

Mrs Cauley turns to Mahony and lowers her voice. 'I last did this when Shauna's mother left for England. I knew exactly what she was up to when *Lady Chatterley's Lover* started snapping at my ankles. To say nothing of the fact that

Ibsen flew across the room and nearly took the head off me.' She knots her headscarf grimly. 'It was *A Doll's House*, so I know she won't be back.'

Johnnie emerges from a dark corner. The ghost of a smile teases the ragged curtains of his dim moustache; with a nod to Mahony he lies down on the floor and glides under the bed.

The breeze whisks a flurry of play scripts up into the air where they drift in graceful arcs. As Mahony watches, their movements begin to change. They start to circle the room, slowly at first, then picking up speed until they whirr past with the dedication of Wall of Death bikers. Soon light pamphlets of philosophical thought start to join them, skidding across the floor and fluttering up into the whirling cloud of paper. Slim volumes of difficult poems come next, scuttling out from dark corners and flapping headlong into the swirling gyre. Even the most aloof classics join in, shedding their covers and flinging themselves, one after the other, into the vortex.

In the middle stands Mrs Cauley, clinging to her walking frame.

Then all at once the cyclone stops and the wind rushes out of the French doors.

And everything falls down to the ground.

Johnnie springs out from under the bed and, with a look of profound effort on his face, blows a sheet of paper through the air and into the outstretched hands of Mrs Cauley.

'Close the window, Mahony,' she says. 'We've got something.'

Johnnie collapses, flickering.

Mrs Cauley studies the sheet of paper. 'Now that's some class of a hint.'

Johnnie curls up at her feet like a dying beetle. Sometimes twitching out one long limb, sometimes moaning soundlessly.

'What is it?' Mahony wades through drifts of papers.

'It's a playbill, Mahony.'

He reads her name on it. 'You were in this play?'

'I'm right there.'

Mahony looks at the playbill. In the photograph a dark-haired girl stands smiling with her head tilted and her hands on her hips. Johnnie stops twitching and gets up off the floor. He straightens his waistcoat and tries to put his arm around her.

'That's you?'

'That was me.' She puts her hand up to her head and touches the few white hairs remaining on her naked little head.

Mahony spots her wig, caught on the leg of an upturned hat stand. He brushes it off and hands it to her.

She takes it and smiles, her eyes bright with checked tears. 'Pour us a drink, kiddo.'

Back in bed with a whiskey, Mrs Cauley watches the dust settle. She sucks at her teeth. 'Shauna will be hopping. She'll have to run the broom around the corners. She won't like that, the idle mare.'

The room is demolished; many of the larger stacks remain standing but the floor is littered with piles of papers and broken books.

Mahony hands the playbill back to her. '*The Playboy of the Western World*, by John Millington Synge.'

'A great play by a great man,' Mrs Cauley says, smoothing the edges of the paper gently.

Johnnie smiles at her from the end of the bed.

'But you're wondering,' she murmurs, 'what this play has to do with our investigation?'

Mahony looks outside. It's nearly dawn and he's buckled

on the worst kind of whiskey and in no fit state for guessing games. Somewhere in his flittered mind he marvels at Mrs Cauley's tolerance of cheap liquor, for, apart from the jaunty slant of her wig, she's as bright as a blackbird.

'And here it is.' She taps the playbill on her lap. 'The St Patrick's annual fundraising production presents a premium opportunity for the amateur detective.'

Mahony fights a wave of nausea. 'I don't get you.'

'Every man and his mother rolls into town for it – they all come, it's an event.'

Johnnie gets up and rambles through a knoll of pamphlets to the French doors to watch the sun rise behind the trees. His face is glowing. Mahony has never seen a dead man appear happier.

Mrs Cauley looks thoughtful. 'First off, we'll use the auditions to quiz the hell out of them. They'll be there in droves, lining up ready for a good interrogation.'

Johnnie nods primly and straightens his tie.

'Then we use the play to flaunt you, kiddo. To keep you right under their noses, in their line of sight,' says Mrs Cauley, jubilantly. 'We put you centre stage.'

Johnnie takes a bow.

Mahony stares at her. 'Ah now – Jaysus, I can't act.'

'Think about it, Mahony.' She leans forward in the bed. 'It won't be long before they work out who you are, if some of them haven't already. You're the spit of your mother: the same big wounded eyes and damaged little smile.'

Mahony squints at her; he hasn't the strength to argue.

'You can only remind them of Orla and, no offence, Orla is the last person this town wants reminding of.'

Mahony nods. 'Fair enough.'

'So you parading about on that stage as large as life will wind the bastards right up.' She pats her quilt gleefully and chuckles. 'Then we sit back and let them give themselves away. Get them rattled enough and someone's bound to point the finger.'

'So I act in the play?'

'You do. Have you another plan?'

Johnnie twitches his moustache in Mahony's direction in an attempt at a sympathetic smile.

Mrs Cauley narrows her eyes at Mahony. 'Are you the kind of cowboy to run from trouble?' There's a bad kind of delight in her voice.

Mahony laughs and shakes his head.

'So let's ride headlong into town with our guns blazing.' Mrs Cauley holds out her mug. 'Set 'em up.'

Mahony reaches forwards and pours out the last of the whiskey, wondering if the feeling will ever return to his fingers.

'A toast to you, my leading man. And to our investigation.' Mrs Cauley downs her drink in one, her eyes hardly watering. She grins, wickedly. 'And to the straight-up joy of getting Mulderrig's bollocks in a twist.'

Chapter 7

May 1948

Orla sat on a log squinting one dark eye against the smoke that rose from the cigarette in her mouth.

The man stood, tucking in his shirt, watching her. The man knew that she didn't care whether he was there or not. She wouldn't sit prettily like other girls. Look how she sat with her legs open. The slut. She was more like an animal than a little girl.

The man wanted blushes and shy kisses.

He wanted her to take his money with a bit of gratitude.

He walked over to her and took the cigarette out of her mouth. Her face was filthy and so were her clothes. Her body always smelt sour. Every time the man went home he was shaken with the fear that he couldn't wash her off him and that his wife would come to know what he had done, what he couldn't keep himself from doing.

The man finished the cigarette and threw it on the ground. He knew he wasn't the first. He knew he wasn't the only. He knew not to go empty-handed to the forest behind the cottage. He knew that for extra she'd fight back. But sometimes he had to beg. And he always had to pay.

When she was distracted, when her eyes were fixed on the light through the trees behind you, that was the time to look at her. Because when her hard black child's eyes were staring back at you, well, you just couldn't think.

When she was distracted she was a doll. Then she lay quiet under you with her chin tilted back and her mouth open. Then you could follow the faint trace of her veins, blue beneath the white of her skin. Then you saw all the details of her. The freckle just under her lip, her upturned nose and the way her baby finger sat crooked on her right hand.

Roll up! Roll up! Did you see bruises the size of saucers on her hips? You didn't ask in case she told you. In case she said, 'Ah, now that was where I was held and fucked by a seventeen-stone farmer for the price of a trip to Ennismore to sit in the dark at the pictures and have a good cry, even though the film was a comedy, ho-ho.'

She never came when he called her. He knew that. He would walk in the forest for long hours with his heart jumping out of him at every sound. He spent long hours sitting in the clearing, panting for her, in the middle of the trees. Sometimes he had the feeling she was watching him, toying with him. He could imagine that, with the mocking little half-smile she threw in his direction, for she never smiled properly at him, not a real smile.

And then she'd just appear. You'd look around and there she was, leant against a tree with her arms folded. Five foot barefoot, two inches taller in her long-gone daddy's boots lined with newspaper.

But there was a man that Orla let find her time and time again. And she came every time he called.

'How did you find me?' she'd ask.

'I asked my honeybees and they told me.'

He was a beekeeper, so he should know.

He told her about the hives, how he could make the bees dull and dopey with smoke so that he could pull out a frame of golden comb. He said that new honey glowed.

'But you are my queen bee,' he murmured, and he made a low buzz on her neck until she laughed.

Once Orla said that if she didn't want him to find her then he wouldn't.

He just looked at her and smiled and said he knew the forest better than anyone, better than her even.

He was the only one ever to have seen Tom Bogey. She had once gone to the camp to see if she could catch a glimpse of Tom. When he found out he had beaten her, calmly, regretfully, and told her to stay clear or the next time he'd kill her.

He said that his bees were always watching her.

And she believed him.

Orla looked up. The man was standing over her wanting her again. She almost felt sorry for him as she held out her hand. He handed her the money that was no longer destined for the neat leather coin purse of the missus, or for the rosy tin box on the top shelf of the dresser, or the bright till behind the cosy bar.

This was money that wouldn't be spent on potatoes and butter, flour and salt, tea and boot polish. It wouldn't be spent on new curtains, or schoolbooks, or a set of pans needed since last Lent. This was money that wouldn't be saved against Communion dresses and white leather shoes, Christmas bicycles or stair carpet.

This was the money Orla held fast in her filthy fist as the man took her on the floor of the forest in the thick of the trees. As he lost himself in her the man put one hand on the back of her neck so that she couldn't look back at him.

When the man was gone Orla counted the money he gave her and the money she took without his knowing.

When she had enough she would buy a new coat and go to America.

Until then she would hide her money in the Blind Room.

Mammy wouldn't go in there.

Mammy wouldn't cross the threshold for ten thousand bottles.

In the Blind Room Orla could sleep without dreaming. In the old days Daddy had stacked the peat to waist height there. The air was still haunted by a sweet dark smell. Orla would light the lamp and lie down on the bed. She had made drawers from wooden crates and in them she kept her patent shoes, her good navy dress and her lipstick. She would wear these the day she left. Sometimes she put them on to practise ordering train porters about or waving goodbye from the boat.

On a nail on the wall was the mirror she had stolen from Mother Doosey. Whenever she looked in it she would laugh in delight at the thought of Mother Doosey trying to comb her bit of hair without it. Then she would become distracted, trying her hair over one shoulder or the other. Breathing kisses on the glass and giving herself come-hithers.

For often, when the people were at Mass, Orla would slip down into town for a wander. She would climb through hedges and try back doors. She'd check in at the windows then slip inside. The houses were never locked, but if they were she knew the key would be on top of the doorframe.

The thrill of it! The rooms, waiting on their owners – even the air in these places belonged to someone else. She'd see the signs of recent occupation. The glove dropped under the table in the rush to leave, the cup left unwashed in the sink, the kettle still warm on the hob. The family had been here, only minutes ago, and they would be here again soon. That thought made her grin at her own terrible audacity.

Mostly she would just walk through their houses, trailing her fingers over mantelpieces and opening drawers, looking at family photographs or the dinner standing ready in the pans.

If the mood took her she'd help herself to a tin from the larder or a blanket from the press. She took small things mostly: a pearly handled fork or a handkerchief, a postcard or a new tin of tooth powder.

And she'd leave nothing behind but the faint musky scent of her hair, or a footprint on the clean linoleum, or a sticky kiss on the bathroom mirror.

Father Jim would go mad, if he knew. Maybe he did know. Maybe some little worm had already whispered in his ear. But she didn't care. She'd near enough had it with his stories and his charity, with Bridget's cats and barmy ways, with the cups of tea and the dinners round the table – *Will you pass the salt, Bridget? I will, Father.*

She went less and less to her job at Father Jim's. Sometimes she didn't turn up for weeks. Then she'd go home to find him sat with Mammy, not minding the smell. The filth. Talking to the old bitch as if she could even answer him.

When he saw her he'd stand up, his manner uncertain and a little defeated.

Or she'd see Bridget all over the town. She'd look up

and there would be Bridget, smiling mournfully at her, with her eyes watering as if in a fierce wind.

All in all, she was a shocking disappointment to them.

In the forest Orla peed on the ground and wiped herself with a handful of moss. 'I'd pull up my drawers now if I had any,' she said to the bees. 'Tell him that, why don't you? Tell him I'm a queen bee with a cold arse.'

She pulled on her runaway daddy's boots and was gone.

Chapter 8

April 1976

The auditions for Mrs Cauley's annual fundraising production are legendary. On this day villagers and onlookers flock to Mulderrig Village Hall, where animals are sold in the car park and marriages are brokered in the cloakroom, and the parts that haven't already been filled by Mulderrig's most reliable performers are ruthlessly fought over.

This is the time to bring new talent to the fore and if there isn't a musical number in the play Mrs Cauley will put one there. For many it's a rite of passage: two choruses of a song from *The Mikado* on a badly lit stage.

Mulderrig will applaud them.

For the town loves those who give it a shot, even if only to fall on their arses. A bad performance will only be half remembered, but a good one can have you riding high all year.

Mrs Cauley knows how to give the people what they want.

She's known it ever since she got off a train at Connolly Station with a suitcase in her hand. She'd looked at the buildings and the clouds and the parks and the people and she'd decided to stay. For the soft Irish skies suited her mood.

And so there she was, tripping to the Abbey Theatre with her brown curls bobbed under her hat and her little chin tilted up. Full-lipped and clear-eyed. Although her mind had always been old, her gloves and her accent were new. No more than an underfed foreigner with a pretty lisp and a stable of suitors.

There were so many men!

Men who gazed at her in the street, in the shops, in the bars, who held doors open for her, held out stoles for her, flagged down cabs for her, waited backstage for her with corsages and jewellery in velvet boxes. Men who sat in the stalls night after night (and sometimes twice on a matinee) and sighed as she held the wild dark breathing mass beyond the stage lights in the palm of her little immigrant hand.

You wouldn't know it to look at her now: the raddled old rook. But yet, as Mrs Cauley makes her entrance the crowds that gather in the village hall hush and part in reverence. Dressed in a beaded cocktail dress that's seen better days, with a tatty flapper-cut wig askew on her head, Mrs Cauley crosses the floor with a slow haphazard shuffle. Now and then she stops to return a nod or a smile, now and then she winks up at Mahony to disguise the pain.

Miss Fidelma Mulhearne (schoolteacher, spinster, deceased) watches closely from the back of the hall. She haunts the rooms she taught in when she wore a twinset and the building was a school. In death, as in life, Miss Mulhearne is a picture of respectable Irish womanhood. Her neat hair is waved and pinned, her low-heeled brogues shine dimly and her skirt hovers demurely above her ankles. She adjusts her spectacles and peers across the hall as Mrs Cauley and the fine-looking fella from Dublin take the stage.

He glances over at Miss Mulhearne and winks.

Miss Mulhearne flickers in surprise and flies into the kitchen to hide behind the tea urn with her dead heart beating fast. She wonders if she ought to be outraged as she undoes the top button of her cardigan.

Leaning heavily on Mahony's arm Mrs Cauley turns to face her audience.

The women of the Catholic Housewives Forum have turned out in force (with the exception of Annie Farelly, who has sent her apologies again this year). The quayside, the Post Office and General Store and Kerrigan's Bar are well represented, as are the outlying farms and houses and the coastguard.

Mrs Cauley shuffles to the centre of the stage and pauses; Mahony can almost feel her drawing the fibres of herself together. She lifts up her head and her voice comes, rich and rolling, big enough to fill the dusty corners. 'Good afternoon, ladies and gentlemen of Mulderrig, it is a profound pleasure to be amongst you and to see so many familiar faces.'

Mrs Cauley looks down the slope of her ancient nose. 'Today I will be auditioning for our twenty-seventh annual fundraising production.'

There's a round of applause.

She smiles. 'Of course we do not do this for artistic edification alone. Last year's production raised enough money for Father Quinn to indulge his flock with the purchase of an opulent set of new hymnbooks.' She takes a step forward with her walking stick and lowers her voice. 'And do you know, there was even enough money left over for Father Quinn to pay for some much-needed attention to his organ.'

Someone snickers at the back of the hall.

Father Quinn attempts a smile.

'As always, there's an open buffet provided by Kerrigan's

Bar.' Mrs Cauley sees Mrs Moran pick up her canvas shopper. 'So you'll get the run of your teeth if you're quick enough.'

She raises her voice. 'The roles we are casting are up on the board there. Take a copy of the play script from Shauna and be sure to study the marked parts as you wait in line to read for me.'

Shauna waves from her spot at the front of the hall; she holds up the scripts to show that she has them ready.

A note of steel slants into Mrs Cauley's voice. 'This year we will be performing an interpretation of *The Playboy of the Western World*.' Her eyes scour the room for any sign of mutiny but there's a cheerful outbreak of clapping and a few amiable whistles. Father Quinn is showing more teeth than is reasonable, given the circumstances.

'You need a playboy, do you, Mrs Cauley?' roars Tadhg. 'Then I'm your man.'

Mrs Cauley smiles. 'I'm delighted to inform you that Mahony here has agreed to grace our stage as our very own *Dublin* playboy.' She nudges Mahony in the ribs and he laughs and stands up a little straighter.

Father Quinn closes his eyes as a peal of wolf whistles sound. Mahony laughs and looks down at his boots. At the buffet table Tadhg shakes his head and wonders what Ireland is coming to when a playboy is shy of soap, scissors and razor and without a decent pair of trousers to his name.

The young ones flick back their hair and send Mahony smouldering glances. Mahony, not at all daunted by his lack of decent trousers, grins back at them.

Mrs Cauley bangs her stick on the ground for order. 'Not only was Synge one of Ireland's foremost dramatists he was a close personal friend of mine. I'm sure that many of you are familiar with the cultural heritage of this play.'

Mahony notices a resurgence of interest in the buffet table.

'Is there a bit of romance in this play?' roars Tadhg.

Everyone laughs and jeers.

Tadhg looks around himself in delight. 'Wha'? I'm only saying.'

Mrs Cauley rolls her eyes. 'Today we'll be casting the lead for the ladies. Our playboy's love interest: Pegeen Mike.'

Howls are sent up again, as the women of the village, young and old, bite their lips simultaneously and wonder how they can land the part so as to get their hands on Mahony.

'I also have jobs for those who'd prefer to work behind the scenes,' says Mrs Cauley with a confused smile, as if this is something she cannot conceive of. 'I need costume makers, set builders and musicians. Pat, will the band be free?'

'They will of course, Mrs Cauley.'

'Good man yourself.'

'I'll build the set, Merle,' says Jack Brophy, standing left of stage as tall and trustworthy as a locked parochial wine press.

'I was hoping you'd say that, Jack.'

'Is it a bar they're building? Isn't the play set in a bar?'

'It is, Tadhg.'

'Well then, I'll furnish it.'

Clapping and a few more whistles.

Mrs Cauley holds up her hand. 'Now, before we begin, I have something very regretful to tell you.'

The room falls silent.

'This will be my last production.'

Father Quinn amends his face and attempts to join in with the chorus of disappointment.

Mrs Cauley smiles sadly. 'I am of a great age and it's

time for me to dedicate myself to quieter pursuits. So let's make my last show one to remember.'

'Hear hear,' calls Tadhg, grabbing hold of a tray of cold tongue as Mrs Moran heads towards the buffet table with her elbows out.

Shauna has made the room to the back of the village hall as comfortable as she can, dragging in a high-backed chair for Mrs Cauley, who settles into it with the air of a slightly tarnished queen. 'Shauna, you stand outside the door and send them in one by one.'

'And Mahony?'

'We're a double act. He'll sit here beside me.'

Shauna looks at Mahony and shakes her head. 'I'll leave you both to it then.'

Mrs Cauley turns to Mahony. 'Isn't this just the opportunity to begin our investigations?'

Mahony sits down, laughing. 'This isn't an audition at all, is it?'

'No, I've already cast the play.' She ferrets in her opera purse and hands Mahony a list of names. 'Two lists: on the one side, cast, on the other, suspects.'

Mahony picks it up. On one side the page is blank. 'Not many suspects.'

Mrs Cauley takes back the list and shuts it in her purse. 'Isn't that why we need an interrogation? Now, will we start with the eejit-looking ones? They always know who the culprit is. They always know all along, it's just that no one bothers to ask them.' She adjusts the feather in her headdress. 'We should have this sewn up by teatime. The location of the body, the perpetrator, you name it.'

Mahony laughs. 'You're sure?'

'I'm Miss Marple remember? With balls.' Mrs Cauley

pushes a package of blank cards towards him. 'Write the name of the witness next to the key facts of the interview. Then we'll get a sample of their handwriting on the back to compare to your photograph, find out who brought you back. Get them to write that.'

She hands him a card with the line *The quick brown fox jumps over the lazy dog* scrawled on it.

Mahony takes the cards.

'Bridget Doosey,' announces Shauna.

'Is Bridget Doosey an eejit-looking one?'

'Not at all, Mahony. Bridget Doosey is the second sharpest old biddy in town. Show her in, Shauna.'

Bridget Doosey is a small woman with a shrewd look about her. She is wearing a pair of overalls and a fedora. Her one concession to femininity is her handbag, a relic of bygone glamour in tan crocodile with an ornate silver clasp. Like its owner it is full of sandwiches liberated from the buffet table.

'Will you help build the set again this year, Doosey?'

Bridget shakes her head. 'I won't. I'm after the part of leading lady.' She gives Mahony a comprehensive wink.

Mrs Cauley hides a smile. 'Aren't you a bit long in the tooth for the role of Pegeen Mike?'

Bridget ignores her and snaps open her handbag. There is a powerful smell of stale cologne and ham. She delicately extracts a pair of glasses and winds them over her ears.

'Have you the book for me to read?'

'I need an actor who can take direction,' says Mrs Cauley. 'I haven't forgotten your improvised rant, Doosey, halfway through act two of *The Man Who Came to Dinner*.'

'It fitted. It was politically pertinent.'

'It was in my hole. You're not going off-script again this year with all that communist nonsense. It bored the shite out of my audience; I could see it in their glazed fecking faces. They didn't pay their good money for that.'

Bridget narrows her eyes. She has the dishevelled appearance that comes from sharing her bed with cats and eating her meals out of a tin.

Father Quinn was cursed to inherit her as his housekeeper, as if he wasn't already significantly burdened. But Bridget came with the parochial house, just as her mother had before her. Bridget is the first to admit that she isn't a patch on her late mammy in the housekeeping department. Although she can rewire a house, drink Tadhg Kerrigan under the table and castrate a bull calf singlehandedly, none of these are prerequisites for a (successful) priest's housekeeper. In fact, stringent, swabbing old Mother Doosey would turn in her grave at her daughter's slatternly ways. Unlike her daughter, Mother Doosey took exemplary care of her priests. It was common knowledge that you could eat a meal from Mother Doosey's front doorstep without the slightest unease; nowadays Father Quinn rarely finishes his dinner without coughing up a hairball.

For Bridget holds no truck with the relentless drudgery of housework or the moral authority of Catholic priests. She sees both as unnecessary evils but stalwartly continues in her employment in order to support her roving pride of felines. And believing in honesty, Bridget will tell anyone who listens that she is daily destroyed with the effort of being polite to Father Quinn, who, after all, is nothing but a gobdaw in a black suit.

'As my esteemed friend and a woman of quality, I'd like to offer you an important role. Bridget Doosey, will you be my stage manager?'

Bridget snaps her handbag shut. 'You can whistle right up my arse, Merle Cauley. What would I want with that?'

'You'll do a fine job, take the headache out of it for me. Now. Where were you on the day Orla Sweeney left town?'

Bridget stares at her. 'Orla Sweeney? Ah Jesus, I knew you were up to something, you old bitch. What is it now you're involved in?'

'I would appreciate your honesty, Bridget,' says Mrs Cauley in a voice as unctuous as medicinal syrup. 'For Mahony's sake; he wants to find out about his mother.'

Bridget looks at Mahony intently, as if she is making some sort of uneasy calculation. Then she smiles. 'Could he be anyone else's?'

Mrs Cauley nods brightly. 'Exactly. So what happened to Orla Sweeney?'

Shauna's head appears round the door. 'They've asked Tadhg for a barrel. Will he bring it over?'

'He will,' says Mrs Cauley, with a dismissive wave. 'Carry on, Doosey.'

'I wish to God I knew.' She takes off her fedora and puts it on the table.

Mahony leans forward and offers her a cigarette. 'Just tell us what you do know.'

Bridget takes three, puts one behind each ear and leans forward to let Mahony light the third, puffing it alight.

'Tuesday, 2 May 1950.' She exhales. 'That was the last time I saw your mother.'

'Are you sure about the date?'

'Certain. She was coming out of the priest's house.'

'What time was it?'

'Early, around eight.'

'And she was coming out of Quinn's house?'

Bridget nods. 'I thought it odd at the time and I quizzed him about it after but I got nothing out of him. He said Orla had come for a blessing. Blessing, my arse.'

Mahony leans forward. 'Did you talk to her?'

'Hardly at all. She was agitated, in a rush. She said she would come up to the house later. But she never did.'

'Did she tell you what she was planning to do?' Mahony asks. 'Did she tell you that she was going to leave town?'

'As far as I knew, Orla wasn't planning on leaving. Things had been getting tougher for her, the town had long wanted her out, but she had resolved to dig her heels in.' She lowers her voice. 'She told me that morning that she'd decided to go to the Father for help.'

Mrs Cauley frowns. 'What, to Quinn?'

'That's what I thought she meant at the time. But why go to him when she must have known that he wouldn't lift a finger for her? He'd just arrived in town, you see, and was courting popularity. Still is, the weasel.'

Mahony blows smoke up to the ceiling. 'Orla wasn't talking about Father Quinn.'

Bridget points her fag at him and nods. 'You're the sharp one. It took me half a day to work that out.'

Mrs Cauley looks at her. 'How do you mean?'

'Tell her, Mahony.'

Mahony taps his ash into an empty teacup. 'She was going to the father, *my father*, for help.'

'Just so,' says Bridget.

Mrs Cauley whistles through her teeth. 'And did Orla tell you who Mahony's father was?'

Bridget purses her lips. 'She didn't. She wouldn't. And I don't have a clue. She always told me that she hadn't even told the man himself. But I believe on that day she took a chance and enlightened him. Then she asked for help.'

Mrs Cauley scowls. 'You never told me that, Doosey.'

'You never asked.' Bridget takes a long drag on her cigarette and exhales slowly, evenly.

Mahony nods. 'Did you tell anyone else who she was planning to meet that day?'

'I didn't. The next day I went up to her house and her mother told me that Orla had gone out the afternoon before with baby tucked under her arm and the clothes she was standing up in and she hadn't seen her since. I checked the house and not a stitch was missing. If Orla had left town she'd taken nothing with her, no coat, no nappies, no money, nothing.' Bridget purses her lips. 'I went straight down to the station to report you both missing to Jack Brophy.'

'And did the guards investigate?'

'If they did, Mahony, it was half-arsed. By then a few people had started saying that Orla had been seen leaving town, getting on the 3:15 to Ennismore with her baby and a suitcase.'

Mahony speaks softly. 'And do you think she got the bus out of town?'

'She couldn't have. The bus to Ennismore didn't run that Tuesday. The driver was having an abscess drained.'

Mrs Cauley raises her eyebrows. 'Are you sure?'

'I was the one doing the draining.' Bridget screws her fag out roughly. 'When I asked around, no one could recall precisely who had seen Orla leave.' Bridget looks at Mahony with a pained expression. 'In the days that followed I ran all over town searching for you and your mother. Some people agreed that it was strange for a young girl and a baby to disappear into thin air. But then, they said, look how wild she was, she probably upped and left with the tinkers.'

'Why didn't you tell me all this at the time?' murmurs Mrs Cauley. 'Why didn't you come to me?'

Bridget smiles at her. 'I hardly knew you. Besides, you

were already unpopular enough; you'd only been in town for five minutes before you had them hopping with your bloody plays.'

'Even so.'

'What could you have told me, old woman? You who had hardly even met the girl.'

Mrs Cauley shrugs and glances at Mahony. 'So you were the only one asking questions at the time?'

'Everyone was so relieved that Orla was gone that they didn't want to bother themselves with the how or the why of it. With Father Jim out of the picture it was as if the town no longer had a care or a conscience.' Bridget turns to Mahony. 'Father Jim Hennessy had been a friend to your mother. Now *he* would have raised hell to find out what happened to her.'

Mrs Cauley frowns. 'Father Jim died only weeks before Orla disappeared.'

'He did. God rest him.' Bridget nods. 'So the gloves were off. And then Father Quinn came slithering into town. He'd hardly unpacked his cassocks before Orla was God only knows where.'

'Now there's a set of coincidences,' murmurs Mrs Cauley.

Bridget stands up, hooking her monumental handbag over her arm. 'I've nothing more to say here. Come up to the house, lad, when you can. I'll be waiting for you.'

Mrs Cauley gestures to the card on the table. 'Will you copy down that sentence? We need a handwriting sample to help us with a piece of evidence.'

'Am I a suspect then?'

Mrs Cauley laughs. 'I was hoping you'd be on our side, give us a hand with the investigation.'

Bridget nods. 'If I can help I will of course. But I'll scribe for you some other time, Merle.'

At the door she turns to Mahony with a smile. 'Welcome back, son. You've been a long time coming home.'

Mahony pushes back in his chair and lights a fag. 'Is she a good sort?'

'She's a sort,' says Mrs Cauley. 'She's clever, but she's mad stubborn too. Doosey will help us all she can, but she'll do it in her own time and in her own way. I believe she was one of your mother's few friends.'

'There's something she's not telling us.'

'There's always something Bridget Doosey's not telling you. That one's deep enough to make a well look shallow.'

'Do you think it was her that brought me back? Could it be her handwriting on the photograph, I mean?'

Mrs Cauley shrugs. 'I don't know. It could be.'

Mahony looks at the blank card in front of him. 'Do you think she really tried to find us?'

'Doosey doesn't lie unless she's playing poker.'

'She didn't tell anyone that Orla had gone to meet my father. Why?'

'Maybe she feared for her own safety? Maybe she expected some kind of retribution?'

Mahony puts his head in his hands and Mrs Cauley watches him. If she had a heart it would break for him, just like a Communion wafer.

When he speaks his voice is low, clotted with fury. 'My own father.'

'You don't know that.'

'He did it to keep her quiet, to put an end to it. There it is. He was a man with something to lose. A job, married even.'

'It might not have been him, Mahony. You know yourself Orla wasn't short of enemies. Now, are you ready for the next one?'

'Bring them in,' says Mahony grimly.

In the main hall the villagers pull out chairs and sit and talk and eat while they wait their turn. Shauna gives out copies of the play. Some read them, most put them on their knees under their plates of sandwiches. The young ones touch up their lipstick and jealously eye each others' dresses, and the kids rage up and down the stage in magnificent unwatched productions of their own with a full cast of pirates, unicorns and ghosts in nightdresses.

Mrs Lavelle, in mourning black, sits in the corner with her eyes fixed on another realm and her tea growing cold in her hand.

Mahony nods encouragingly at the large woman in front of him. 'Thank you for the song, Mrs Moran.'

Mrs Moran folds her fleshy hands on her lap as delicately as a child at her First Holy Communion.

Mrs Cauley returns her hip flask to her opera purse. If she had nerves they would be as shattered as her eardrums. 'Despite that remarkable performance I'm afraid there are no singing parts this year, Mary.'

'That's all right, Mrs Cauley. I just wanted to do a turn for you and the young man. Will I be making the costumes again this year?'

Mrs Cauley grimaces. 'Under Róisín Munnelly's supervision.'

'Grand so, and there'll be a great call for wings?'

'There won't.'

'Are there not any quantities of fairies, Mrs Cauley? As there were in *A Midsummer Night's Dream*?'

Mrs Cauley's tone is final. 'There'll be no fairies this year, Mary.'

Mrs Moran looks disappointed. 'Is that so? Ah, I loved all the wire and the netting and such. What about birds? Will we have a few birds then?'

Mrs Cauley purses her lips. 'No birds.'

'What about a big terrifying robin red breast with a few spangles to catch the light? Or a macaw? That would be exotic, swooping down over the stage? I've a few bits of yellow felt that would do for the beak.'

Mrs Cauley throws her a stony glare and Mrs Moran obediently settles down and sits nicely.

'Is there anything else I can help you with, Mrs Cauley?' she finally asks.

'There is. Where were you on the day that Orla Sweeney disappeared?'

Mrs Moran looks at Mahony and smiles a round little smile, for like a Communion child she's been well prepared.

For by now the entire village knows Mahony's identity. From the babies threading their first sunny sentences together to the grandfathers propped up in the corner with more tea in their saucer than in their cup. Every worm and sparrow, crow and badger, tree leaf and grass blade has heard Mahony's story, such as it is. That he was abandoned on the steps of a Dublin orphanage and has come back to find his mother.

And the surprising thing is, no one is in the least surprised.

They were only surprised that they hadn't realised before. But then, as Tadhg pointed out, they were ignoring this slice of bad news as you would a fart in a confessional box.

And as for Orla?

Well, she's little more than a bad dream, a bad dream easily shaken off in the bustle of the village hall. The people look around themselves, at the familiar faces of their neighbours and friends. They can see that Orla isn't here and never will be again.

And as for Mahony?

Jesus, he's nothing like her at all! Save the eyes, and a certain wild spring in his step and that wicked curve of his smile.

Perhaps he's like his father?

All the women of a certain age breathe a sigh of relief. Mahony hasn't got Pat's titanic ears, or Eamon's walleye, or Declan's buckteeth, with which you could scrape the carrots. Mahony is entirely gorgeous; he's not a bit like their husbands.

The villagers look around themselves and see that everything is exactly as it was before. Nothing has really changed. Everything is just as it should be.

Then Mrs Lavelle rears up.

Mrs Lavelle's voice is distinctive. It's threadbare and nasal, with hysterical undertones, and is quite capable of carrying over the practising of lines, the ribbing and the rivalry, the cooing and the gossiping.

The first thing that everyone learns is that Mrs Lavelle won't be pacified by a cup of tea and a sponge finger. Teasie tries to move her mother away from the buffet table and into the cloakroom with a few gentle clucks and a supporting hand under her elbow.

The ensuing scene is terrible.

Teasie is knocked sideways by Mrs Lavelle's handbag and sent spinning into the ham sandwiches. Mrs Lavelle takes a few steps then is suddenly struck with the full weight of a premonition. She leans heavily against the corner of the trestle table with her sleeve in the coleslaw and her eyes wide.

Her mouth starts to move independently, recalibrating

itself in a number of violent twitches. Then, in a low tone of prophesied doom, Mrs Lavelle addresses a space just left of the ladies' powder room. Her words spew out over the teacups and potato salad, the cardigans and handbags, the polite nods and the time of day.

'She's woken,' announces Mrs Lavelle in a sabulous voice from beyond the grave. 'She's coming.'

The hairs stand up on the back of every arm. The babies begin to cry and the children wrap themselves up in the stage curtains or watch open-mouthed from under the table. Those of a nervous disposition bless themselves. A group of stalwart mammies crowd in and start to convey Mrs Lavelle out of the hall with the tenacity of a swarm of worker ants seeing off a trespassing wasp. Mrs Lavelle goes quietly until she reaches the threshold, where she clings to the doorframe moaning. There's an unladylike tussle as they unhook her arthritic fingers and lift her through the double doors. Teasie follows with her glasses fogged and a pocketful of stolen biscuits that she knows will be like dust to her now.

Afterwards, the tea is poured too brightly and received too gratefully. The villagers, as jittery as cats on elastic, remind themselves that Orla left town of her own accord. They tell themselves that she is most likely alive and well and causing havoc in another town, God help them.

And so they start to breathe again and even laugh a little.

For after all, who believes in ghosts?

Poor Mary Lavelle does.

The woman is away in the head. Entirely tapped. Utterly unravelled. Some think about her floor-bound gaze and the tremble in her hands. Some think about the drifting silences in her conversations. Some just think about the light on Teasie's glasses and the downward slope of her thin shoulders.

And the afternoon rolls on.

'So let's go back to the day that Orla disappeared, Mrs Moran,' says Mrs Cauley, purposefully.

'On that particular day, Mrs Cauley, I was suffering very badly with my legs.'

'So you remember it?'

'You couldn't forget pain like that.'

Mrs Cauley looks at Mahony with pointed despair.

Mahony speaks slowly and clearly. 'Mrs Moran, do you remember seeing Orla on the day she disappeared?'

'Disappeared, is it?' Mrs Moran opens her eyes wide. 'Well, I know nothing at all about that.' She looks coyly from one to the other of them. 'But I did see her slinking around the back of Kerrigan's Bar. There she was, sitting on a pile of crates, swinging the legs and smoking and talking to Tadhg. So I called out, "Now then, Tadhg, haven't you got a bit of gainful employment to be getting on with and not to be led astray from?" And Tadhg shouted out, "I'll be away back to the cellar in a minute, Mrs Moran. How're the legs?"'

Mrs Moran leans forward and lowers her voice conspiratorially. 'Tadhg was just back from England to take over the pub from his uncle, who was making a big point of dying at that time. Tadhg was one of the few young men in the town with money in his pocket and that lent a certain sheen to him.'

'What had Tadhg been doing in England?' asks Mahony.

Mrs Moran straightens up. 'He'd been boxing, and making a name for himself by all accounts. Then his uncle got involved with the whole dying thing and called him back.'

She smiles at Mahony. 'It's hard to believe it now, looking at the shape of him, but Tadhg was well put together in those days, a fine big strapping lad. And a temper on him like all the Kerrigans, great violent Irishmen the lot of them.'

Mrs Cauley looks at her with interest. 'You think so?'

'Tadhg was quick to hop in those days, Mrs Cauley. And when he hopped, like most brave young fellas with a temper, well, you heard all about it.'

Mrs Cauley nods. 'Go on.'

'As I said, there was I hobbling home the best I could down the lane and Tadhg asking after my legs and I said, "Oh, Tadhg, I'm in a terrible way." And he said he'd run me up home for he had the use of his uncle's car and in those days there wasn't many who could lay claim to that. Well, Orla didn't like this at all. She threw me this sour variety of look and said something under her breath to Tadhg. Maybe she thought I was an interfering old biddy. But then I didn't care about that.'

Mrs Moran shakes her head. 'I saw it all you see. There he was, a decent young man trying to make a go of it, and the last thing he needed was to be hooked by your one and her dirty ways.'

'You're talking about my mother there, Mrs Moran. You'd do well to remember it.' Mahony speaks low and soft, but it's his expression that startles. Cold-eyed and with a smile that says he could climb over the table and finish Mrs Moran off with his bare hands.

Her jowls wobble with indignant alarm. 'I meant no offence.'

'None taken.' Mrs Cauley nudges Mahony. 'Is there?'

Mahony nods imperceptibly but drops his terrible smile.

'There now,' says Mrs Cauley. 'Please continue in your own words, Mrs Moran.'

Mrs Moran narrows her eyes. 'I only say it how I saw it, Mrs Cauley.'

'And isn't that the best way, Mary?'

Mrs Moran takes a sly gander at Mahony. 'But if you'd prefer I dressed it up a bit? Tidied the corners?'

'Not at all, Mrs Moran. We are grateful for your honesty,' says Mrs Cauley with a rigid smile.

Mrs Moran, vindicated, allows her jowls to settle. 'Well, Orla kicked herself down off the crates and walked up to me in that brazen way she had about her and she said, "Jesus, will you get down off your cross and let Mrs Moran get up there?" And I said, "You should be ashamed of yourself talking about the good Lord in that manner." And she gave me such a smirk and turned on her heel and was off throlloping down the road. At the end of the road she turned and roared out like a fishwife, "I'll be seeing you, Tadhg. Don't you forget to meet me later."'

Mrs Cauley glances at Mahony. 'And that was the last you ever saw of her?'

'It was. But I'm not sorry about that. Nor did I ever think on her again.'

'Did you never wonder what happened to her?'

'Mrs Cauley, if you had a bad tooth you wouldn't send it a postcard when it was pulled out of your head, would you? I was just relieved she'd cleared off. What became of her, God himself only knows.'

'You've been very helpful, Mary. If you remember anything else will you let us know?'

Mrs Moran nods and gets up from the chair. At the door she turns and smiles treacherously at Mahony. 'It's a terrible shame that one was your mammy, for you seem like a decent individual.'

★

Mahony accepts a hip flask and Mrs Cauley accepts a lit cigarette.

'Tadhg, though?' says Mahony.

'Why not Tadhg?'

'I wouldn't have said he's the murdering type.'

'That's what everyone says about the murdering type.' Mrs Cauley inhales. 'Of course it's not bloody Tadhg; he'd have told the whole of Ireland he'd murdered her by now. But let's put him down on the list. Jesus, just for the sake of having a name.'

Mahony nods.

Mrs Cauley looks closely at him. 'How're you holding up?'

'Let's just get through it.'

'That's the spirit. Any dead ones coming through yet?'

'Haven't we enough with the living?'

Mrs Cauley watches as Mahony runs his fingers through his dark hair.

'I'm sorry you have to hear all this, kiddo. Will we stop for today?'

'We won't. We'll keep going, aren't we a fierce team?' He catches her look and smiles; there's a world of pain in his eyes. 'I'm grand. Tell Shauna to bring the next one of these horrors in.'

Mrs Cauley feels something she hasn't felt in a long time. She curses the smoke for bringing tears to her eyes.

Chapter 9

April 1976

Shauna sweeps the empty village hall and Mahony stacks the chairs and collects the plates and glasses. Mrs Cauley shifts the cards laid out on the table in front of her as if she is divining an indifferent fortune. She is annoyed that a fair few prominent citizens of Mulderrig have evaded interrogation. And she is annoyed at having missed Mary Lavelle's performance, for a cracked mind often gives a true picture.

Miss Mulhearne missed it too. She is just emanating from the broom cupboard as Mahony comes down the corridor looking for a mop. She flits back inside and toys with the idea of keeping the mice company as they gnaw the wasted beams in the roof space above. Mahony walks into the cupboard, shuts the door and props the mop under the door handle. He turns over a bucket and sits down for a smoke. Miss Mulhearne decides to stay.

At first Mahony feels her as a cool, soft presence behind him. As his eyes adjust to the dark, Mahony can make out her mild-eyed face by the light of the small window high above him. She stands very still, with her hands clasped together low, and she makes him feel calmer than he has felt all day.

Mahony smiles at her. 'Do you come here often?'

She nods.

'Do you like the people, the plays?'

'I like poetry,' she whispers.

'I don't know about poetry but I've got a couple of dirty limericks you're welcome to.'

Miss Mulhearne sighs, almost audibly. 'I can't remember any poetry really. I just know it was beautiful. I think I remember that Yeats wrote beautiful poetry, but all the words have gone.'

'Are you always here?'

'I teach here. But all the children have gone too.'

'Everything goes. That's how this whole thing works.'

Mahony draws bitterly on a cigarette. Miss Mulhearne moves imperceptibly nearer, as if to comfort him. A companionable silence fills the broom cupboard.

'The mice are still here,' she eventually says, very softly.

Mahony smiles in the dim light. 'I'll come back with some poetry then.'

Tadhg offers to run them back up to Rathmore House. He's bursting to tell the Widow about his role as Michael James, a publican playing a publican! There's goodness in that alone and she must approve of him helping to raise money for the church there.

On the way out of town Tadhg pulls the car up next to a roadside shrine.

It's a peaceful spot, with a grand view of the bay and the forest just across the road. It appears to suit the Mother of God, a strapping six-foot statue with a healthy colour. Her magenta face beams above robes that fall in folds of lancing cerulean blue. A stone grotto has been built around her to protect her from the elements.

Tadhg gets out of the car and takes a wrapped platter from the boot. With effort he bends down and pushes the plate onto the shelf beneath the plastic flowers that bloom perennially and the pot plants that come and go.

'I didn't know the Holy Mother liked a sandwich,' says Mahony.

Shauna smiles. 'It's for the fella who lives up in the forest.'

Then, on second thoughts, Tadhg goes back and throws down a couple of cigarettes.

'Tadhg isn't the only one at it.' Shauna looks out of the window. 'Daddy has me leaving all sorts there for him. Soap, pipe cleaners, you name it.'

Tadhg levers himself back into the driver's seat and starts up. 'Wha'? Who's this?'

'Tom Bogey,' says Shauna.

Mrs Cauley turns her head and peers over the passenger seat. 'He's a wood-kerne, a hermit, a speechless bard.'

Tadhg gives her a funny look. 'He's unravelled in the head only.'

'Apparently so,' says Mrs Cauley coyly. 'Only I've never had the pleasure and neither has anyone else. You see, Mahony, Tom sees no one and no one sees Tom.'

Mahony raises an eyebrow. 'Is that the case? How do you know that he exists?'

'Because Jack Brophy says he does. He's in cahoots with him.' Mrs Cauley widens her eyes. 'They go out skinning badgers and roasting squirrels together.'

Tadhg wipes his face with his handkerchief and starts the motor. 'That's some class of an imagination you've got there, Mrs Cauley. Don't listen to a word of it, Mahony. Jack looks out for the poor guy, that's all.'

Mrs Cauley shrugs. 'And would Jack know what Tom the bogeyman has squirrelled away in the forest? He may have more than a couple of pipe cleaners up there by now.'

Tadhg rolls his eyes. It's evident that he holds no truck with their investigations ever since his refusal to be interviewed by Mrs Cauley, claiming to be neither a murderer nor a slanderer.

'What's Tom's story, Tadhg?' Mahony leans forward with his hand on the back of the driver's seat.

Tadhg looks at Mahony in the rear-view mirror. 'The guy served with Jack's father in the war and was some class of hero. But he came out of it badly; what he'd seen shattered him. It ruined him for people, so he sought consolation in nature. That's the only story I know and that's from Jack himself.'

'So he's up there just roaming around? And Jack lets him?'

Mrs Cauley shoots Mahony a sly look. 'Why not? When the notion of Tom Bogey keeps the bad boys and girls out of the forest and away from all the no good they could be getting up to in there. For there Tom would be, hiding and spying amongst the trees, and reporting straight back to Jack Brophy.'

Tadhg frowns. 'Tom keeps himself to himself and the village lets him, and that's all there is to it, Mahony.'

'He's been around for a while then, Tadhg?'

'Been up there near thirty years.'

Shauna nods. 'Longer maybe.'

And Tadhg turns up Elvis singing 'In the Ghetto' on the radio and, because no one can argue with that, the conversation is at an end.

Chapter 10

April 1976

Mrs Cauley looks at the map spread over her knees in disgust. 'They saw us coming, the feckers.'

She's had five sherries.

Shauna sets out the hot water, a fresh towel and the medicated soap.

'I've plotted their evidence on this map here, Shauna, and it demonstrates that Orla Sweeney was in eight different places at the approximate time she disappeared. I know she slung it about a bit, but even so.'

Mrs Cauley pushes the map away. 'She was seen leaving town walking in five different directions whilst simultaneously boarding the bus to Ennismore, with and without a suitcase, a vanity case, a baby and a pram. All on a day when there was no bus to Ennismore because Bridget Doosey was lancing a boil on the bus driver's arse.'

Shauna tuts and folds up the map. She gathers the rest of the papers into a pile and dumps the lot on the footstool next to the bed.

Mrs Cauley shakes her head. 'How can I apply ratiocination to this dissembling shower of bastards?'

'Apply what?'

Mrs Cauley grits her remaining teeth. 'Logical thought, the process of elimination. Even Marple would be at a loss in this town. Jesus, they couldn't tell the thing straight if their lives hung on it.'

Shauna takes a clean nightdress from the press. 'Don't get yourself worked up now. What did Dr McNulty say to you about getting worked up?'

Mrs Cauley, grumbling, removes her wig. 'How can I bring reason to bear when Mulderrig doesn't conform to reason?'

Shauna shakes out the wig and smoothes it onto the stand. 'Why don't you take the statements from the most trustworthy witnesses and go from there?'

Mrs Cauley snorts.

Shauna takes a soft brush from the drawer to brush out Mrs Cauley's few bits of hair round the back of her head. 'There are still people you haven't interviewed, Mahony said.'

Mrs Cauley nods. 'Jimmy Nylon, for one; he was seen walking with Orla up towards the forest on the day she disappeared. There were three separate sightings of that.'

Shauna looks at her. 'Jimmy Nylon, really?'

'Oh, I know, Shauna. He's a malignant little fecker but I doubt he's capable of murder.'

'Not unless Orla was a pint.'

Shauna unbuttons Mrs Cauley's dress and lifts it over the old woman's head.

'Then there's Tadhg.' Mrs Cauley narrows her eyes. 'Mary Moran described him as a handy young fella with a fiery temperament. What's more, Orla had arranged to see him later that day.'

'Well, I don't think Tadhg is Mahony's daddy, or the murderer. You know he can't keep a thing to himself before he's off blathering it around town.' Shauna drops a flannel into the basin. 'Do you know he told Annie Farelly that you pretend to be asleep whenever she visits?'

'Did he now?' Mrs Cauley grins.

Shauna lifts Mrs Cauley's arm and begins to soap her armpit. 'Do you really think something bad happened to Orla?'

Mrs Cauley nods. 'I'd bet money on it. I told you what was in that note. She was a little troublemaker, so they finished her off.'

'It's awful. In a place like this?' Shauna rinses out the facecloth and gives Mrs Cauley a quick wipe down. 'Poor Orla, and poor Mahony, with him being an orphan and all that.'

'Don't you worry about Mahony. He's just the fella to apply a good swift kick right up this town's arse. You just watch him – he'll be taking a run up to it.'

Shauna drops the flannel in the bowl and reaches for a towel. 'I'd say it would be more of a swagger with Mahony.'

Mrs Cauley smiles grimly. 'Either way, that lad won't stop until he gets the truth.'

Chapter 11

April 1976

'Now that's just bloody horrible,' says Bridget Doosey.

On the back doorstep is the corpse of a recently deceased ginger cat with its head wedged in a wicker basket.

Bridget kicks open the lid of the basket and bends down to study the cat. 'Merle did right to call me.'

Its tongue hangs out of its mouth, swollen and black.

'Cream scones: poisoned. Something industrial.' Bridget takes a card from the basket and holds it up between her rubber-gloved fingers. 'And they weren't meant for this poor little bastard.'

Mahony's name is typed on it.

'I'd watch your back from now on, lad. It looks like your mother's fan club has reassembled.'

Mahony notices the cat, now dead, prancing in the flowerbed, snapping at a fly.

'Any ideas who?'

'Take your pick, Mahony. Your mammy wasn't a crowd-pleaser and now here you are poking your coulter where it's not wanted.'

'Even so.'

'You were dreaming of a different kind of welcome.'

'They seemed friendly enough.'

'Did they? Well, now you have the measure of them.' She looks at him closely. 'It could get rough. This town's as twisted as tits on a bull.'

Mahony frowns. 'Are you saying I should stop asking questions?'

'I'm saying that you might not like the answers.'

The cat stretches, shakes its dim tail through a series of exclamations and walks through the wall.

Chapter 12

April 1976

Mulderrig is asleep under the awning of the night sky. Above her, stars can be seen, now and again, through the inked smudges of ragged clouds.

By day Mulderrig appears respectable, a solid fat-ankled mammy dressed in patchworked fields. But at night, when Mulderrig lies down under the moon, she's gypsied to the nines, be-ringed and braceleted with fairy forts. And the moon looks down at her and smiles, tracing the dark waves of her forest and lighting the curved spine of her river all the way down to the bay.

Tonight Mulderrig is silent but for a moth beating against the window of a filthy cottage with a dolmen view. Where Bridget Doosey snores under a catskin quilt, busy spring hoeing and planting kittens in her garden. They wrinkle their little noses and mew as she sprinkles them with golden rainwater. She rubs her hands; soon she'll have tortoiseshell cabbages and tabby kale.

Mulderrig is silent but for the scuttle of rats in the basement of Kerrigan's Bar. In his bedroom above, Tadhg wallows heavyweight under a blanket of crisp packets on white pillows of stout foam. He's dreaming of screaming eels. He catches one with a fresh perm. She bites him, hard.

Mulderrig is silent but for the chime of a time-haunted clock in the fortified bungalow where Annie Farelly sleeps the fitful sleep of an old-lady-killer. She dreams only of dentures; they're coming for her. Snapping.

Mulderrig is silent but for the soft song of shale and the lulled ocean, heard in the bay-view bedroom where bachelorised Jack Brophy lies snug in housekeepered pyjamas. But does he dream? His slippers will tell you that when Jack lies down he enjoys the deep slumber of the upright. He only moves once, to turn the alarm clock off, at daybreak, just before it rings.

Mulderrig is silent but for the bats that sing in the key of darkest sonar as they spool in and out of the attic of Rathmore House. Where Mrs Cauley sleeps in her magical library, hairless and open mouthed, fat-bellied and spindle-armed. She's treading the boards again tonight, all night.

In her little turret room Shauna switches her legs like a cricket. She dreams only of Mahony. He's taking her under the washing line. She watches the hard-boiled dishcloths dance above her as he licks her ear rind, and she wonders what the neighbours will say.

And where is Mahony?

He's bollock naked in his bed with his boots by the door and his jacket over the chair until morning.

He's frowning.

He is back in the forest of his memory.

He's with Tom the bogeyman; they sit in a circle of bracken.

Tom has a bag. He opens it and beetles come running.

The beetles run lightly along Tom's crossed legs. They thread between his fingers.

Tom has gifts for Mahony. Found in the forest and kept only for him, until his return.

He lays them down one by one.

Look.

He has a sleek tibia, satin to the touch.

He has a pair of eyes like newly split conkers. A deep wet brown.

He has a clutch of molars; they glow in his hand like baby grubs.

He has fingernails, delicate veneers of pink shell.

He has a handful of smooth white knuckles, like the counters in a children's game.

He has a rope of black hair, as fluid as waterweed.

He has a skull that crumbles like a forest log, with chambers filled by the scurrying of a million insects. Listen.

He has the long-lost blackberry kernel of a heart.

But Tom says he will keep that.

Chapter 13

April 1976

In the first light of morning, with the air from the open window cold on his bare arms, Mahony leans over to his bedside table for his cigarettes. He has the picture of Orla propped up against the lamp so that he can study her face.

Does he look like her? He does.

He recognises the half-smile that plays on her lips and the shape of her nose and chin. She is dark like him; that much he can see. And she is young, too young; he can see that too, a kid really. She stands in a doorway offering up the bundle in her arms with an expression of shy pride; at least that's how Mahony reads it.

She strikes a pose in her too-big shoes, one foot turned out and pointed; her shoes are ridiculous, heavy lace-ups, which accentuate the frailty of her ankles. They could make him cry, those thin little ankles, if he let them.

He has always believed two things: that his mother was dead and that he had known her. In order to feel her loss he must have known her presence. And he does feel her loss, he always has.

Which is why he has been searching for her all his life: because he had loved her and because he had lost her.

He'd searched but she'd never answered.

Mahony takes a fag from the packet and lies back with it unlit between his lips, remembering right back to the start of it all, where his memories first began: St Anthony's.

By the age of four he knew the lie of every loose floorboard and squeaking hinge.

By the age of five he knew which corridors were patrolled and which handles were tried.

By the age of seven he was an expert on the enemy. So they moved him on.

Mahony lights his cigarette and inhales as a memory weighs in: himself standing on a chair with a blanket caped around his shoulders. At that time he'd fancied himself a Roman general taking leave of his legion.

'Hear this,' he'd whispered in parting to the younger ones. 'This could save your life.

'Nuns move fast and make no noise and they have eyes in the back of their habits: the eyes of the invisible saints that ride around on their backs.

'Nuns wear itchy knickers so they don't fall asleep at Mass, so when they look asleep they're not; they still have their eyes open looking at you.

'They have a lot of help on their side; there's a patron saint for everything – you name it, bicycles, owls and lost things (yeah, I *can* fecking name them: Madonna del Ghisallo, St Francis and St Anthony).

'The soft nuns wear socks inside their sandals. They won't beat the shite out of you but if you make them cry the hard nuns will beat the shite out of you for them.

'Don't look a nun in the eye for any more than two

seconds. They'll say you're being bold and you will get the shite beaten out of you.

'You can get onto the roof by climbing out of the dorm window and crawling along the ledge. Up there you can see the whole of the city.

'No nun has ever been known to check the roof but that doesn't make it safe from the patrol of the roof saint who reports back to the Mother Superior (yeah, I *can* fecking name him: St Florian, the patron saint of chimneys).

'A holy relic is a dry bit of old finger off a saint. This is what the nuns carry in their waist pouches. They rub their relics if they want to put a saint onto you. Then you're truly banjaxed.

'All the dinners come with cabbage.

'There are rubber sheets on the mattresses so the beds creak like ships in the night.

'The Church and the State are paying for the mistakes of your woeful mammies, who are feckless sluts.

'The Church and the State are paying for the mistakes of your useless daddies, who are feckless buckos.

'Avoid Sister Veronica as you would avoid death itself. The boys who have crossed her are hacked to pieces in a freezer in the basement. They're labelled up as pork joints.'

General Mahony twitched his cape. 'The rules for the priests you ask?

'They catch a beetle, yeah, a devil's coach horse, and they screw it into the head of their cane. This gives them speed and skill in their work. But if a priest breaks the cane over your arse then the beetle's soul will escape to take vengeance. This is the only way you have of killing a priest: make them break their stick by beating the shite out of you. If this happens it might take twenty years for the beetle to work on the priest, or he might fall dead there and then. There's no way of telling.

'Don't admit to anything in confession; they'll use it against you. Cross your fingers behind your back and then cross your hands. Then there's a chance that you might not go to hell, but only if it's not a mortaller. If you lie about a mortaller you're as good as burning in your shoes. But after all you can only be sent to hell once.

'And remember: although priests move slower than nuns they can see around corners.'

But there were no rules for the dead.

Mahony knew that from the first, when the recently deceased Sister Mary Margaret appeared to him on the first-floor landing.

There he was, sitting at the top of the stairs in a warm square of light from the hall window. He'd just been thinking on her. He'd been thinking on her lying under the soil.

Thinking about Sister Mary Margaret being dead was something that had taken up a lot of Mahony's time since she'd died. He'd wonder if they'd buried her with her teeth in or if they'd given them to another nun. If so, would they get her smile? He'd wonder if she could hear the weather inside the box. And was she cold down there in the soil? He didn't like to think of her being cold.

Mahony was thinking these thoughts, that day on the landing, when something rolled along the floor and stopped beside him. It was small and round and elderberry dark, as intricate as a walnut, with curved ridges and valleys. He was so fascinated that he forgot to be scared when he looked up to see Sister Mary Margaret drifting three foot above him. He could see the scuffs on the wall through her. He could see the light fittings through her. He could even see dust motes through her, still turning.

Sister Mary Margaret reached forward and picked up the dark fruit. She held it cupped and covered in her hands. Then she pitched it hard, like a fast bowler, through the closed window. Mahony jumped up, ran to the window and saw it turn through the air, up, up, up. Then it was gone and he was alone again, with his nose steaming a misty butterfly on the glass.

Mahony told Martin Doyle that he'd seen Sister Mary Margaret bowling her cancer out of the window and Martin Doyle went off, like a bollock, and told the nuns. Sister Veronica came down on Mahony like judgement and trailed him before the priest. Father McCluskey confirmed that there was a severe want in the boy that couldn't be rectified and gave him a sound hiding.

Mahony didn't mention the subject again, although the dead had become frequent visitors. Sometimes they just howled or sobbed by him. Sometimes they stayed a while, like old Mother Whorley, the cleaner with the lungs, who'd haunt the dormitory nightly, wheezing stories about dance halls and game girls. Or Mr Mullins, who fretted about the refectory for a lost key, knew all about birds' eggs and had died of pernicious gout.

But that's history, thinks Mahony, as he heaves his arse out of the bed, gives his balls a good scratch and lights his second cigarette of the day.

Mrs Cauley is breakfasting on the veranda with a coat over her nightdress and a silk scarf wrapped around her head. She looks a little tired today.

'Who did you say Johnnie was?' says Mahony.

'I didn't. Johnnie is Johnnie. That's all you need to know, kiddo.'

'Well, your man is down there lying on the path.'

'I know. I saw you step over him.'

Johnnie rolls over onto one elbow and blows Mahony a kiss, then lies back down to stare up at the clouds with his hands dipping through the paving stones. Mahony notices the dim caverns of his cheeks.

'What did he die of?'

'It wasn't good.'

Johnnie's foot twitches slightly in remembrance but otherwise he is still. A robin lands and hops through his left knee.

Mrs Cauley nods at the teapot and Mahony pours them both a cup.

'So, Sherlock, we've a missing girl, no body, a rake of motives and not one reliable witness.'

Mahony pulls up a chair. 'I was thinking on Tom Bogey.'

Mrs Cauley nods. 'A nice easy suspect, creeping about the forest, wearing necklaces of milk teeth and dreaming of sabre-toothed children traps.'

Mahony shrugs; it all sounds a bit obvious when she says it. 'Well, he's a suspect, isn't he?'

'Like every man between the ages of fourteen and dead on the day Orla left town.'

Johnnie stands up and saunters over to the flowerbed.

Mrs Cauley smiles foxily. 'Why don't you bring Shauna up to the forest with you? She can show you where to find Tom. It'll give me a bit of peace from all her prodding and poking and bloody cleaning. Get her out from under me feet.'

'You wouldn't be without her.'

'Don't tell her that.' She looks at him. 'Shauna is soft on you. But of course you already know that.'

Mahony grins. 'And?'

'Don't lead her astray. She's a sweet girl, Mahony.'

'And you trust me to take her into the forest?'

'I do.' Mrs Cauley stretches. 'While I stay here and have a quiet day with me squirrels.'

'And a game of cards with Bridget Doosey?'

'The thought hadn't crossed my mind,' she says slyly.

Mahony smiles and on impulse kisses Mrs Cauley on her cheek. 'You're a rare beauty, Mrs Cauley. Better looking than Dr Watson even.'

She is delighted. 'Ah, go on with you.'

Johnnie glowers at Mahony from the hydrangeas.

Shauna changes her clothes three times. She eventually puts on one of Mammy's good dresses, a navy shift dress that's too big for her, so she pulls it in at her waist with a cream plastic belt and puts on her good cream shoes with the heels. The rushing makes her feel hot and the clothes make her feel awkward. Shauna has a sense that she's unravelling as she walks out along the veranda.

Mahony jumps up out of his chair. 'Here she is.'

Shauna attempts a smile. 'Will I need a wrap?'

'For the forest?'

'Is that where we're going?'

Mrs Cauley looks up from the racing pages. 'Mahony needs a bit of help finding Tom Bogey; I told him you'd be delighted to show him the way.'

Shauna scowls across at her. 'Did you now? Is that what you meant when you said Mahony wanted to bring me out for a bit of a run?'

Mahony puts down his jacket. 'Ah, Shauna, if you can't spare the time — it's a bit of a long shot—'

'Ah no, that's fine, Mahony,' says Shauna, wishing she could go back in and change, but then she'd look an even bigger gobshite. What was she thinking? That Mahony wanted to bring her down into town on his arm and perch her up on a stool in Kerrigan's?

He smiles at her; his eyes are kind. 'Will you be all right in those shoes?'

'These are grand shoes. Just the thing for walking.'

'Like a cat on scissors,' says Mrs Cauley under her breath.

Shauna throws the old lady a withering look.

On the way to the forest Shauna tries to remember the stern talks she has had with herself. There is one theme: a romance with Mahony would only ever end badly. For having a man like Mahony would be like wearing slingbacks in a cowshed. Mahony is a luxury that she can't afford and doesn't need.

Mahony is not for her.

She will write it out a thousand times and chant it in her sleep.

The man she marries will paint window frames and round up chickens, grow turnips and poison rats, fix plumbing and plaster walls. When she thinks of Mahony stumbling around in overalls, broken by her nagging, hunched by duty, she could cry. He'd be a wild thing domesticated, his tomcattery shattered, his wicked grin the grimace of a yoked man.

Or else there he'd be at the doorway with his bag packed, turning up the collar on his leather jacket. There she'd be crying after him, tears falling on her big-again belly, the house falling around her ears, the dark-eyed twins in her arms bawling and Mrs Cauley roaring for a toasted teacake.

Mahony is not for her.

But still he's in her head when she's washing up the dinner plates, or filing Mrs Cauley's corns, or taking Daddy out his tea. Her senses search for him night and day, in the sound of closing doors and creaking floorboards, in the striking of a match and the pipes filling the cistern. She's put him out like a cat a million times but like a cat he has a habit of slinking back and curling up in the warm corners of her mind.

Now he's walking beside her; she glances across at him and there he is. With his dark eyes and his forearms brown against the white of his rolled-up sleeves. And a glimpse of hair through his half-open shirt and the way his shoulders fill the shirt.

He looks back at her with a smile on his lips. He's telling her stories about Dublin. She doesn't hear a word; she's listening to the sound beyond his words, to the thrilling low notes and the rough music in his voice. She can't help herself.

They find Tom's camp where Shauna thought it would be, in a thickly wooded area of the forest. At the centre is a caravan, bricks wedged behind its wheels. All around is the equipment for some sort of life: a chipped Formica table stacked with pots and dishes and covered with plastic sheeting, and a gas burner on a wooden workbench. The caravan door is propped open and a curtain hangs in the doorway.

'Come on.' Mahony takes Shauna's hand and they walk forward. There is no one inside; they know that even without looking, for the objects have the look of a beaten dog waiting for its owner.

'Stand here and keep watch.'

'Ah no, Mahony, don't go in. It wouldn't be fair on him.'

Mahony climbs through the curtain.

Inside the caravan there's a powerful smell of damp. When Mahony's eyes adjust he makes out piles of hoarded rubbish. Thick fans of flattened crisp packets, sour chains of milk-bottle tops, piles of crushed tin cans and empty bottles. A single mattress with no sheet or blanket lies in the corner.

Shauna calls in to him. 'Mahony, please, let's go, I don't have a good feeling about this.'

'Just a minute.'

Tom could be anywhere, she thinks, watching. She shudders.

Up on the roof of the caravan, as prone as a bathing lizard, Tom observes the light on Shauna's hair. He's almost close enough to see the pale hairs rise on her forearms and the curve of her turning cheek, her freckled clavicle.

Mahony sees that there's a kind of system in place: shelves have been built from floor to ceiling to hold the delicate bones of small mammals, lost buttons and carefully folded sweet wrappers. Hundreds of brass hooks stud the ceiling from which shredded orange nets and old tights hang. Mahony picks up a jar containing long rancid strands of grey hair.

'Mahony, please, I want to go.'

Mahony puts the jar back; he'll come alone next time.

As he turns to leave, something catches his eye.

A yellow yo-yo tucked on a high shelf just above the door, between a lead soldier and the handle of a skipping rope.

Mahony lights a fag and says nothing. Shauna knows she's annoyed him and she could kick herself, really bloody hard.

'Do you want to go back and wait for him?'

'No, we'll just go home.'

'I'm sorry, it just didn't seem right for us to be there.'

He keeps his hand in his pocket rolling something around and around. Shauna turns her mind apart for something to say and finds nothing. So she reaches out and touches his arm.

It's so easy. Here's his mouth on hers. One touch to

unlock him and now he's bending to kiss her. His spit tastes of cigarettes, stale and thrilling; his hand presses strongly into the small of her back. If her legs give way he's got her.

He pushes his tongue into her mouth until she pulls away just a little.

It's so easy. A groan and a word and he's walking her up against a tree. She wonders how many girls he's been with. She sees that it's a well-rehearsed dance for him. He expects her to step alongside; she doesn't need to know how – he'll lead. He pushes his hand up her dress with his eyes at close range, half-closed and unseeing.

He's moving against her. She's up against the tree, his lips are on her neck, he's opening buttons, calling her 'Baby, ah baby', with his Dublin accent hard and low. She hardly knows what to think, only that her face is scarlet. Mahony pulls away and Shauna opens her eyes to find him staring straight ahead.

Ida has wandered out through a tree and is standing with her arms folded and her face blank.

'For pity's sake,' Mahony says.

Ida sticks her pale fingers in her mouth and mock-gags as she skips past them.

And Shauna stands there with her mother's good dress all up around her waist and her knickers round her knees in the middle of the forest.

Chapter 14

April 1976

It is raining in Mulderrig. The heatwave has stretched, exhaled and picked itself up off the town all in one afternoon. And the rain has returned.

At first it fell lightly, uncertainly, as if it were testing itself, on the curious noses of cats and cows turned upwards to see if this news of rain was really true.

But the trees knew, and so did the bees, for they know all things.

Soon the rain grew confident, pattering on cobbles, bouncing along the tractor tracks carved in the hard-baked ground. Then, heavy and certain in its benediction, the rain began to fall steadily, blissfully, unlocking the smell of the ground.

The rain falls too on the roof of the village hall, dancing over the clogged gutters, ringing the ancient rusty school bell and running down between loose tiles to drip down the wall in the ladies cloakroom.

Inside the main hall Michael Hopper is sculling across the floor with the look of a creature of quarry about him. To his credit he's moving fast for a man whose knees are flittered with rheumatism. He almost clears the open ground before he is fastened to the floor by the steamrolling tones of Mrs Cauley.

'Michael Hopper, I'll have a word with you.'

And there she is, coming in through the double doors dressed in a high-necked coat of apricot lace, like a fortified wedding cake. She has her talons hooked over Mahony's arm, who is walking next to her with the air of a conquering hero, a fag upright in his mouth and his shirttails hanging.

The drip on Michael's florid nose stiffens to a sudden watchful stillness. 'Is it you, Mrs Cauley?'

'It is, Michael, and can you tell me where my cast members are?'

Michael Hopper looks rapidly from side to side as if connecting up the various parts of his mind.

Mrs Cauley fixes him with a dreadful glare. 'Correct me if I'm wrong, Michael, but there is no wedding, funeral or hurling match to account for a wholesale absence from the first rehearsal of my annual fundraising production.'

Michael Hopper curses his knees to hell. 'Will I go and have a look about the town, Mrs Cauley?'

'You do that. And mind you send Father Quinn in here to me, if you happen to turn him out from under a stone.'

'It's Father Quinn you want specifically?' Michael's nose reddens.

There's a dangerous light in her eyes. 'Isn't he the man in the know, Michael?'

Michael Hopper hotfoots it out of the door.

She looks about herself with disdain. 'Will you look at the filth of this place? He's not even set up the chairs. If there was work in the bed, Michael Hopper would sleep on the floor.' She sets her chin at a grim angle and squints up at Mahony. 'I smell a rat.'

'Do you now?'

'I smell a big cringing rat in a dog collar. Quinn is blocking us; he wants you out of town.'

'Maybe.' He pulls up a chair for her.

'We're upsetting the old order, Mahony.'

'But does he have that much influence? To call the lot of them out of the play?'

'Not at all, but sheep will cleave to a weasel if they're frightened by a wolf. Quinn is using Orla to get Mulderrig behind him.'

'Do you think?'

'With you here, and the play keeping you here, Orla will have retribution. Many of them were shook up by Mary Lavelle's premonition, that much is clear, and Quinn will jump right on the back of that. Fear, guilt and superstition, Mahony, it's a fine way to steer the herd. It always has been.'

'Well, time will tell. Is it tea you want?'

She nods. 'Go on then. We'll wait a while and see if anything turns up.'

Mahony tucks a blanket around her legs and goes into the kitchen. Miss Mulhearne is sitting on the draining board revealing a good inch of stockinged ankle. Mahony can see the piles of cups and saucers through her. She throws her arms girlishly around her knees and gives Mahony the kind of smile that makes her beautiful.

Mahony presses open a book. Amongst the empty cake tins and the rinsed milk bottles, behind the leggy wooden dryer and under the cobwebbed window, he reads poetry to a dead spinster. Miss Mulhearne stretches out the length of the serving hatch with her cardigan unbuttoned and her smile blissful.

As Mahony reads, rain sheers across the half-open

window and with the rain comes the smell of the wet earth rising. Outside the window the bushes beat time with their wet branches to the rise and fall of his voice, although the wind has abated now; she's holding her breath to listen.

Mahony reads, paying no mind to the wakening world.

Father Quinn pulls up a chair and waits, watching Mrs Cauley sleep. She has the same subterranean look as a bog corpse he once saw in a museum. She could easily have been spat out by some remote wetland, her body preserved by its dark juices. She's an archaeological find from another time, her skin as brittle as vellum and stained with age. She has a seedy string of pearls around her neck rather than a hangman's rope. And no doubt her stomach would give up a very good last meal, not a caked smear of gruel.

Father Quinn studies his enemy closely. He could crush her with the span of just one hand. But instead he arranges an expression of charitable concern on his face. 'Mrs Cauley?'

Mrs Cauley feigns bleary eyed surprise. 'Bless you, Father, for coming to me in my hour of need.'

'Michael told me that you sent for me.'

'I did, Father, tell me, where are all the people? Why are they not here? They've never let me down before.'

'Well, Mrs Cauley, and this is a delicate matter, but I have been made aware that the village has a few concerns regarding your production.'

'What concerns?'

Mrs Cauley is surprised by just how many teeth one man could have in his head as Father Quinn looks at her and smiles.

'I think you should consider changing your leading man, Mrs Cauley. Mulderrig is a little wary of strangers.'

Mrs Cauley smiles back at him radiantly. 'Mahony is not a stranger, Father. He was born here and he is fully entitled to return to the place of his birth. Not least to solve the mystery of his mother's disappearance.'

Father Quinn looks around himself, moistening his top lip to a wetter sheen with several erratic sweeps of his tongue. 'Orla Sweeney did not disappear, Mrs Cauley. She left Mulderrig of her own free will.'

Mrs Cauley leans nearer. Her voice is no more than a murmur. 'Neither of us believes that old chestnut now, do we? Look, Father, one of your flock must have confessed a little something or other. There's a reward posted, did you know that?'

Father Quinn raises his eyebrows.

'*Unofficially*, of course. Think of it more as a demonstration of gratitude from a rich old lady. All I'm asking for,' she says, with a roguish glint in her eyes, 'as a hitherto loyal friend to the church, is a few small nuggets of information.'

Father Quinn frowns.

Mrs Cauley unleashes a winning smile. 'And of course I keep my sources confidential, Father. As you know yourself, I'm very discreet.'

An expression of complicated disgust flickers over Eugene Quinn's face. He surges up from his chair. 'I'll not be—'

'Sit down, please, Father.'

The priest takes his seat, levelling a look of impotent fury at the old woman.

Undaunted, Mrs Cauley continues. 'Oh, I know all about the sacrament of penance and confessional seals and all that jazz. Just pop the name on a bit of paper and post it to me. Or type it. Or better still, cut the letters out of a newspaper like a blackmailer in an Agatha Christie.' She drops her voice to a whisper. 'You see it doesn't count if you don't say it out loud.'

Father Quinn shakes his head in disbelief.

'Then bang bang, you're on target for a new roof or a spanking new organ, a trip to Honolulu or whatever it is you want.' Mrs Cauley taps the side of her nose. 'And it's all between you and me, Father. All I need is a name.'

Father Quinn looks at her incredulously. 'Mahony has put you up to this.'

'He has not. I'm cutting a deal here. This is all me.'

'Mrs Cauley, I'm going to forget that we ever had this conversation.'

'And lose out on that cruise you've been dreaming of?'

'This just proves the disruptive influence Mahony has had on this village.'

'This village needs disrupting.'

Eugene Quinn slaps his legs with his long hands and makes his words those of swift business. 'No. I'll have no more of this, Mrs Cauley. Mahony has turned this town upside down. Mrs Lavelle in particular is distraught. She is greatly unsettled.'

'She's always been greatly unsettled.'

Father Quinn ignores her. 'This is my advice to you, Mrs Cauley: let Mahony return to the city. He doesn't belong here and the people don't want him here. He stirs up bad memories.'

'He only wants the truth.'

'He's a fantasist, Mrs Cauley. His mother abandoned him and that's the truth of it. He can't accept that truth, so he's come back spinning some dark tale, casting aspersions. You are not helping him by inventing these *crime fictions*.'

'Mahony will find out what happened to his mother.' Mrs Cauley smiles a smile of unsettling sweetness and folds her hands primly on her blanketed lap. 'In the meantime, he's going nowhere. For if there's no Mahony, there's no play. And if there's no play – now I'm no fortune teller but I predict a marked downturn in your parish income this year.'

The priest reddens.

'This is my last production and I will have it my own way: Mahony is my leading man. If Mary Lavelle wants to have a funny turn and the villagers want to light a few extra candles then let them.'

'Mrs Cauley, I only have your welfare and the welfare of this village in mind.'

Mrs Cauley lifts up her face, her eyes awash with honest fortitude. 'I'm dying, Father, I'm riddled. I've been sentenced by Dr McNulty.'

Father Quinn stifles an irreligious impulse and nods stiffly.

'I have many loose ends to tie up before I allow myself to expire. I must deal with all my worldly possessions, such as they are. My little crock of gold must find a home, I must place it wisely into safe hands, having neither kith nor kin to inherit.'

She smiles slowly, with a terrifying benignity. 'The grief of not having my own way may lead me to make irrational decisions at a time when a clear head is needed. Father, you of all people know that old women are feeble of mind. My mind could snap, just like a twig, with the very slightest of pressure, then who knows what would happen to my nest egg? It could roll off anywhere, in any number of directions.'

Father Quinn is bitterly aware that he must strike a deal of Mrs Cauley's own making. 'Mrs Cauley, I will, temporarily, advocate tolerance with regard to Mahony but this inquiry into the fictional death of his mother must desist. I want no more talk of murder. You must stop your amateur detective games. Do I have your word?'

Mrs Cauley shrugs imperceptibly.

'And I shall be keeping a close eye on Mahony and I will apply the full weight of the church and of the law should he put a foot wrong.'

Mrs Cauley nods, clearly unimpressed.

'And you must give me your word that Mahony will leave this village and go back to where he came from immediately after the play is over.'

Mrs Cauley smiles slightly.

The priest rises haughtily from his chair. 'Furthermore, I shall also expect Mahony's presence at Mass on Sunday and his public acquiescence to all codes of acceptable behaviour.'

Mrs Cauley stifles a laugh and looks up at him with an unconvincing expression of ardent respect. 'May God bless and preserve you, Father Quinn.'

Mahony finds Mrs Cauley where he left her, fanning herself with a play script.

'Take me to the pub, Mahony. I'm dying.'

The wheelchair only gets stuck twice on the way to Kerrigan's Bar. Mrs Cauley sings filthy songs all the way, refusing the umbrella Mahony tries to put over her and turning her face up to the lashing rain.

By the time they crash through the doors of the saloon bar Mrs Cauley has lost her spectacles, her left shoe and every last ache in her joints.

'How are the men?' she roars. 'Tadhg, I want to buy Mulderrig a drink.'

The early drinkers raise their eyebrows and their glasses to her.

'Perch me there in that corner and make mine a double-double.'

Tadhg gives Mahony some bar towels for Mrs Cauley to knot about her head while her wig dries off. And there she sits at the table, flushed and beaming, decadent and regal, hopelessly frail and blazing with life.

As the day wears on, the village starts to come in through the door to be lured to Mrs Cauley's corner of the bar, where she holds court, downing shorts and telling her ancient theatre stories with the slippery skill of a card cheat. Mahony watches their faces as they turn to her, enthralled, even a little grateful, like she's the morning sun after a cold night.

Tadhg pours a couple of pints and motions Mahony over to a table in the corner. 'Mrs Cauley in full flow is a beautiful thing. I haven't seen her like this in a long time. You do her good, Mahony.'

Mahony smiles and sits down. A long-dead drinker settles himself in the empty chair beside him and gazes at Mahony's pint on the table. The dead man nods to Mahony and attempts to pick up the glass.

'Well now, Mahony, it seems you've set the cat amongst the pigeons with a carving knife.'

Mahony takes a cigarette from Tadhg and lights it. 'Why's that then?'

'Mary Lavelle says that you have woken the dead. She says they reared up out of their graves the very moment you set foot in town.'

Mahony laughs.

'It's no joke, pal.' Tadhg frowns. 'You're getting their imaginations riled; it's affecting them.'

The dead drinker draws closer and tries to lick Mahony's glass.

'They just get caught up in it; it can happen to the best

of us, the old superstition.' Tadhg leans forward. 'I remember a tinker scaring the life out of me once. She'd said she'd seen my grandfather riding around town on my mother's back. The man had been dead six months and in that time my mother had suffered terrible pain. Now my grandfather was a bad bastard, God rest his soul, so you really wouldn't want to be carrying him about your person.' Tadhg raises his pint to his mouth. 'But then Mammy went to the doctor's and found out that it was sciatica she'd had all along.'

The dead drinker stares forlornly at Mahony's pint.

'It's all this talk of your mother, her disappearance, murder even. You need to let it go. We both know Orla is out there somewhere, alive and kicking.'

'I don't know that, Tadhg.'

Tadhg reddens. 'Where's your evidence then? If Orla is dead then where's her body?' Tadhg shakes his head. 'Where's the crime here, Mahony? I don't see one.'

The dead drinker nuzzles up to Tadhg's shoulder, crying in quiet despair.

Tadhg screws his fag out in the ashtray. 'Call off the search, Mahony. Enjoy the play, have your break and you'll leave on better terms for it.'

'That's your advice?'

'That's my warning. You keep winding them up and every last one will take against you.'

Mahony shrugs. 'And prove that they're hiding something.'

Tadhg looks at him in disbelief. 'Have you heard nothing? Drop it and move on. That girl was a curse.'

'That girl was my mother,' says Mahony, hard-eyed.

Tadhg looks away. He pulls out a handkerchief and gives his face the once-over. 'Now there's Jack up at the bar for me.' He gets up. 'Think it over, Mahony. Before it's too late.'

The dead drinker follows Tadhg to the bar, hopping up

onto the stool next to Jack Brophy to sit looking in boundless despair at a pint with a virgin head on it just like a drift of thick cream. Mahony finishes his drink and waves his glass at the bar boy for another.

Mahony looks at the outstretched hand in front of him.

'You were asking after me, Squire?' says the man.

Mahony gets up and shakes the man's hand. 'Aye, I was. Take a seat. Jimmy Nylon, is it?'

The man grins in delight. 'It is. How did you know?'

'I took a wild stab.'

Jimmy Nylon sits down and crosses his legs, ankle to knee, stretching his slacks to the limit. He has the look of someone whose soul got up and walked away in disgust a long time ago. He holds up his hands as if he's parting a biblical sea of troubles. 'Now, first off, whatever you heard about me isn't true. I'm a lad with a bit of a reputation.'

'You know what I want to talk to you about?'

'I have an idea,' says Jimmy, shooting Tadhg a furtive glance as he stands watching them from behind the bar with his arms folded.

'Then what do you know about the disappearance of Orla Sweeney?'

As Jimmy begins to finger the flayed edges of his magnificent golden hairpiece, Mahony can only look on in fascination.

And rightly so, for Jimmy is a local legend, that much is clear. Ask anyone and they'll tell you that what you have, right there, is a man of unwavering purpose. A man who spent decades as bald as a rock until one day he left town in search of the right hairpiece, at the right price.

His travels took him all over Ireland.

Some said he'd killed a man for his wallet in Athlone

and some said he'd bought it with the money left him by a maiden aunt in Ballycroy.

Either way Jimmy had struck gold. Literally.

He returned to town with a flaxen toupee of prodigious style and quality. Here, finally, was the perfect marriage of easy-care manmade fibres and a dazzling blond hue.

Jimmy leans forward in his chair and points at Mahony. 'On the day Orla left town I saw her propping up the wall outside the General Store.'

'Was she alone?'

'She was alone an' looked a bit downcast for herself.'

'In what way?'

Jimmy sucks air in through his teeth. 'Now don't get me wrong, I never had anything against your mother. But it didn't do to be seen to be *involved* with her. It wasn't good for the old reputation.'

Jimmy's hand travels down his leg to tap on his crossed calf then his knee and back again. Tap, tap. His fingers go up to rim around the cuff of his wig, then back down to his knee again.

Mahony smiles. 'She wasn't popular. I get that. The town wanted her out.'

Jimmy narrows his eyes, sensing a trick. He leaves go of his knee and hooks his hand up behind his back. 'Ah now, I wouldn't know about that. The truth is I felt a bit sorry for her. She was different, you see, running around the forest day and night. There was a notion that she wasn't quite right, that she was a bit touched.' Jimmy taps a pattern on the side of his head.

'But you spoke to her that day?'

'I did, because it looked as if she'd been crying. She had this pinched-up look about her.'

'Did she say why?'

'She didn't. I told her a few jokes to bring a smile to her face then I said, "Mind how you go now, Orla" and she nodded. I never saw her again but I often thought of her and hoped she was all right.'

'So you didn't take a walk up to the forest with her?'

'Jesus, no, why would I? I was working; I had the post to deliver.'

Jimmy grabs a beer mat off the table and spins it. 'I told you, I saw her outside the General Store, spoke to her for half a minute, tops, then I went on my merry way.' Jimmy holds out his arms and turns in his chair. 'I've a rake of witnesses to that.'

'There were several sightings of you walking with Orla up towards the forest on the day she disappeared.'

Jimmy sneers and leans in close. 'Speaking as a man of the world to another man of the world, I have my enemies.' He whispers. 'Envy is a terrible thing; there's some that don't like to see people get on in life.' Jimmy gently pats his hairpiece, crosses his arms and levels an unconvincing smile at Mahony. The interview is as good as over.

'He's keeping something under his hairpiece, Mahony. Now you wouldn't trust Jimmy Nylon as far as you could throw him, would you?' Mrs Cauley takes a sip of her stout.

'He's a little shifty.'

'He's a little bastard, and a dirty one at that. Bridget Doosey once accused him of stealing knickers off her line. She would catch him eyeing her nether garments when he was up there on his rounds.'

'Was there any evidence?'

'Only that by the time he left the Post Office Bridget was down one brassiere and two drawers. She often had to go regimental.'

'Jesus. I didn't need that.'

Mrs Cauley grins into her pint. 'You're a great man for the moral decency, Mahony. I can't imagine you stripping washing lines.'

He laughs.

Mrs Cauley looks him dead in the eye. 'You're a bang-straight gentleman, Mahony, under that profligate exterior. I know that, I know your heart is made of pure-gold honest-to-goodness bullion.'

Mahony catches her look. 'What are you getting at?'

'Shauna. I take it upon myself to look out for the girl. Since her mother ran away with a paying guest and her father ran away with the fairies. I consider her family.'

'And?'

'I give a shite, about the girl and about you. I don't want either of you maimed by what some people call love and I call disaster.'

'You're telling me this because . . .'

'Something happened up in the forest.'

'She told you?'

'She didn't need to.' Mrs Cauley looks at him. 'You may have turned her head but it's still screwed on.'

'Meaning?'

'Shauna wants a steady life, Mahony, she always has. You know, the husband and the children. She has these dreams of restoring the house; she has it all planned out.'

'Fair balls to her, for knowing what she wants.'

'You're a good man, Mahony, but you have to ask yourself are you the right man for Shauna?'

'Are we getting married? After all of five minutes?'

Mrs Cauley smiles. 'Shauna's the type to fall very deeply. She's been stung before and badly. Young fellas, you see, will make all manner of promises for a quick rattle.'

'What are you saying to me now?'

She pats his arm. 'Just help the girl do what's best for her, lad. That's all.'

Mahony frowns.

She nods. 'Grand so, will we have another pint?'

It's still hammering down when they leave Kerrigan's but once they get the wheelchair loaded in the back of the squad car it's straightforward sliding Mrs Cauley into the back seat. She's out like a light, breathing heavily through her open mouth. Mahony puts his jacket over her and checks that she's still holding on to her damp wig.

'She was on fine form tonight, God love her,' says Jack Brophy, getting into the driving seat.

'Thanks for the lift, Jack.'

'Not at all.'

They drive in silence for a while.

Jack turns the wheel to avoid a bundle of sheep at the edge of the road. Mahony sees them, greasy clouds picked out by the headlamps. Then nothing but a darkening sky above the darker outline of the stone wall below.

'Jack, how well do you know Jimmy Nylon?'

'What's he trying to sell you?'

'Nothing.'

'Then he's a grand fella.'

They drive in silence, bumping through potholes. Jack turns the windscreen wipers up faster.

'You know Tom, don't you? Who lives up in the forest?'

It takes a while for Jack to answer. 'I do.'

'What's he like?'

'He's had his troubles but he's a peaceful soul.'

'So he's harmless?' Mahony thinks about Ida's toy, tucked away on a shelf in Tom's filthy caravan.

Jack curses a pothole to hell. 'You're still playing detective, Mahony?'

'Did the guards get involved? Did they look for Orla?'

'I can't discuss that with you, Mahony.'

Mahony finds his fags and offers one to Jack. He takes it. Mahony leans forward to light it and in the brief flame sees Jack's face, frowning.

He drives on in silence for a while. 'They followed up on some of the concerns expressed by one of the villagers.'

In the back seat Mrs Cauley gives a deep snore.

'What did they find?'

'Nothing. There was nothing to find.' Jack's voice is kind but there's a hardness to it that says he'll stand no shit. 'Your mother left this town in one piece, Mahony. She got a bus or a lift to Ennismore and then took a train. There was not a shred of evidence to suggest otherwise.'

'A note was left with me. It says that Orla was the curse of the town so they took her from me.'

Jack takes a drag on his cigarette; the lit end of it burns and flares. 'What's to say she didn't write it herself?'

'The handwriting: it wasn't that of an unschooled kid.'

'Then she got someone else to write it for her.'

Mahony says nothing.

'Look, no one took her from you, son; she left you, and that's the truth of the matter, isn't it?'

'The truth of the matter is that she fought this town to keep me, only to give me away in Dublin? It doesn't add up, Jack.'

'The girl could hardly look after herself, let alone a baby.' His voice softens. 'Maybe she wanted a better life for you.'

Mrs Cauley mutters to herself in the back seat.

'You have to ask yourself, Mahony, does this seem like the kind of place where someone could murder a young girl and then kick over all traces? A village where no one as much as farts without someone rushing to tell you about it?'

Mahony looks out of the window; he can't see a thing. Up ahead, in the headlamps, there is only rain.

Chapter 15

May 1976

They meet in the hallway; she's carrying Mrs Cauley's break-fast tray, he's coming down the stairs with wet hair and bare feet. She hasn't time to scuttle into the library before he sees her. She curses, softly.

'There you are then,' he says.

There she is, standing gawking with a tray in her hands.

It's desperate and she knows it is. She fights the urge to edge back into the kitchen or put her head down and run the length of the corridor.

Her nerves are flittered from avoiding him.

She has to say her piece. She'll make herself say it. Here in the hallway, with Mrs Cauley's porridge getting cold and the poached eggs slithering under her nose, there's no better time.

'I want to speak to you.' She reddens. 'About the other day, in the forest.'

He nods. His eyes are kind. There are none kinder. He smiles at her.

She can feel the heat coming off her as she roasts with mortification. She imagines herself as he sees her, with a big red face on her and her eyes blinking with confusion.

She tightens her grip on the tray. 'Will we forget about it?'

She feels sick inside.

'If that's what you want.' He's still smiling at her, God love him.

'No hard feelings?' She's nearly crying with the effort of saying it.

'Go on with you. Give me that.' He crosses the hall and takes hold of the breakfast tray. 'I'll bring this in to her Highness.'

'Thank you, Mahony.'

'Sure, it's nothing at all, Shauna.'

Shauna stands over the sink for the longest time. Eventually she'll notice that the tap needs a new washer, when she hears the drip that's been keeping time with her. Then she'll wipe her face, fill the kettle and put it on the hob.

Chapter 16

May 1976

It's standing room only at St Patrick's this morning. For throughout Mulderrig the beaks have been busy and the birds have shared a fine seed of news: that Father Quinn and Mrs Cauley are going head to head over Mahony and that Mrs Cauley will be worshipping this morning.

Mrs Cauley is as rare a sight at the church as the devil himself.

Wearing dark glasses and an emerald silk turban she takes the front pew with such an awful sort of majesty about her that more than a few members of the congregation start to regret their decision not to show up for rehearsals. Mahony sits beside her in his leather jacket with his dark hair brushed back.

The young ones nudge each other. Don't the pair of them look glamorous? As if they have just stepped off a film set? But if Mahony notices the village girls making eyes at him he doesn't let on, he just keeps talking low to Shauna, who sits the other side of him blushing a shade to rival her fuchsia cardigan.

'It looks like the whole flock have turned out today

then. Have you seen the sour face on Annie Farelly?' says Mrs Cauley in a voice designed to carry.

The Widow is almost level with them across the aisle. She stares stiffly ahead with a rigid halo of curled hair and her gloved hands folded on her broad lap.

Mrs Cauley frowns. 'Sanctimonious old bitch, there's always been something fishy about that one. She's in cahoots with Quinn. I'm certain they both know something.'

Shauna throws the old woman a stern look.

Mrs Cauley leans in close to Mahony and whispers loudly. 'Of course, getting anything out of them would be like getting shit from a stone.'

Mahony watches as a line of dead priests in faint vestments take up their positions behind the altar.

Mrs Cauley grins and nudges Mahony. 'And there's Tadhg next to her, trying not to scratch the crack of his arse. And Jack Brophy, bless him, sitting with Bridget Doosey. God love her, she's wearing that old collar made of dead cats.'

Mahony looks over at Bridget, who is fanning herself with a hymnbook.

'She'll start to smell gamey soon – just wait until the church starts heating up with all the action.'

Mahony laughs, Shauna glares, and the dead priests begin to shuffle and look off in different directions as Father Quinn steals in from the wings to bring the church to a hush.

And all the mammies start writing shopping lists in their heads and all the daddies start thinking about the comfort of the bar stools at Kerrigan's. The old ones concentrate on staying awake and the young ones on trying to kick the arses of those in the pews in front without getting caught.

Father Quinn unfolds an oily smile. 'This morning I invite you to reflect upon the subject of superstition. I am talking about the bad old country ways.' He glances around the church with an incredulous look on his face. 'I've started *seeing things*.' He drops his voice. 'Incredible things: owls nailed to barn doors, salt scattered in patterns, stones ranged about doorways.'

Father Quinn spreads his hands, opening his fingers. 'We are not pagans, are we? We do not need charms and magic in this day and age. This is the year of Our Lord nineteen seventy-six. Should we fear vampires, ghouls and spectral attack?' He looks around himself with an excited kind of expression, like he's just won a big prize but he has to keep it secret.

Something flickers in the cave of Mrs Lavelle's mind. A thought is sewn together in the shadows there. She moistens her lips. Teasie holds on tighter, her knuckles white on her mother's arm.

'Or should we rather fear the corrupting wind that blows in from our cities?' Father Quinn looks at Mahony. 'The wind of progress, of modernity, they say. I say it is the wind of vice, of wanton fornication and absent morality.'

In the front row Mrs Cauley farts audibly.

'It's all this talk of wind,' she says under her breath.

A few children snigger.

Colour rises under Father Quinn's collar. 'I ask you all to join me in prayer.'

He bows his head and the congregation avert their eyes from his bald spot, which has a private nakedness about it as it nestles in his thatch of coarse greying hair.

'Almighty and merciful Father, unite us against the trouble that has stalked uninvited into the heart of our village and bind us together in our fight against sin and darkness. Let us not invite heathen evils, old or new, into our community, our hearths and our hearts.'

The priest looks up, his gaze sweeping over the congregation to alight on Mrs Cauley. 'Heavenly Father, forgive those who seek to resurrect old stories and promote bad histories, thereby corrupting the feeble-minded, the gullible and the ignorant.'

Mrs Cauley winks at him, sending the muscles in the priest's jaw hopping.

'We ask you to forgive the weak among us who have erroneously turned to dark traditions. Banish from us all spells, witchcraft, maledictions, evil eyes, diabolic infestations, possessions and ghostly curses.'

Father Quinn takes a step back and the row of dead priests open their eyes in alarm. One tries to flap him away with the sleeve of his alb.

Mrs Cauley nudges Mahony. 'He's getting to the point now; he looks like he's about to pass a difficult shit.'

Father Quinn adopts the spiritually authoritative face he has perfected in the bathroom mirror. 'Bring clarity and wisdom, Lord, to those who question the priest's homily and who fail to take his direction, which is only ever given for their own good.'

In the front row Mrs Cauley snorts loudly.

Above Mahony's head are the Stations of the Cross. He counts fourteen painted wooden plaques, each the size of a platter of Tadhg's sandwiches. The pictures are numbered, so that you can follow Christ's journey as he hauls his cross through town.

In the picture just above Mahony, Jesus is centre stage, his legs are buckling under the weight of his cross, his eyes are narrowed and his muscles are roped. There are women in long robes stretching out their hands towards him in a way that would really piss you off if you had something heavy to carry. Jesus scowls back at them with the lean countenance of a bare-knuckle fighter.

Mahony knows how it will end.

On a wide stone pillar just right of the altar is a six-foot cross with a marble Jesus nailed to it. Jesus's eyes look up to heaven and his beard curls down.

Mahony lets the familiar tide of sound and counter-sound lap at the edges of his mind. And lulled, Mahony gets down on his knees or up onto his feet with the best of them as he is rocked in the cradle of old words and swaddled by the murmured refrains.

The bright chalice is raised and the bell rings, clear and pure through the calm air. The altar boys move lightly and the people make the sign of the cross with intimate and simple grace.

They offer each other the sign of peace, taking each other's hands without reservation.

'Peace be with you.'

'The Mass is ended, go in peace.'

Mahony is the first out of the door, disappearing round the side of the church and out into the graveyard for a smoke. The graves are dotted with bell jars full of Virgin Marys and wreaths of plastic roses. To the right the graveyard wall slopes down towards the bay and to the left there's a clear view of the mountains.

In the far corner of the graveyard is a quiet spot, where the graves are natural and unvisited and the Celtic crosses are softened by the weather of years. Here the uncut grass is scattered with pink-tipped daisies and the dark darts of crow feathers.

Mahony throws himself down between Patrick James Carty 1901–1925 and Joseph Raftery 1880–1913. Paddy and

Joe have vacated their eternal resting places and are sitting up on the church roof nudging each other and whistling at the young ones walking home. They melt laughing into the lead.

Mahony lights a cigarette and lies back, turning his face up to feel the sun before it hits another bank of clouds. With his eyes closed he hears the gulls wheeling overhead and the voices below him as they swim up through the soil.

Tell Maggie her hair still shines as red as cherries and I kiss it when she's sleeping.
Tell Johnny Gavaghan he's a terrible bastard and when he dies of the drink next spring, by God, I'll be waiting for him.
Tell Paddy I did it.
Tell Agnes I never did.
Never, ever, ever.

Mahony opens his eyes to see pale faces sprouting, like pockets of mushrooms, from every crevice. The dead blossom amongst the gravestones and monuments and push up between the stone flags. They shake themselves off and weave towards him with a famished look about them, as if, given half a chance, they'd lick the salt wind off the headstones.

Bridget Doosey, who has come wandering into the graveyard to visit her mammy, jumps a full foot off the ground when Mahony sits up and smiles at her.

'Mother of God and all the Blessed Saints, are you actually trying to kill me?'

Mahony laughs. 'I'm having a quiet smoke for meself. Will you join me?'

She puts down her handbag and takes three cigarettes from his offered pack, tucking two up the sleeve of her cardigan. She accepts a light and strays over to a headstone across the way.

'There's herself. She wanted a quiet corner away from the bustle of the main drag. Mammy was a thin woman, so they could shoehorn her in just here.'

'It's a grand spot.'

Bridget nods. 'We had to shave a foot off her memorial. It's lucky she had a short name.' She rests her backside against the edge of her mammy's headstone. 'Do you know, I've loved this woman since the day she died. We have great debates now.'

Mahony watches as the late Mother Doosey climbs up out of her grave and tries to nudge her daughter away with a faint pair of fire tongs. He takes off his jacket and spreads it on the ground next to him. 'Come and take the weight off.'

'Why not?' She settles herself next to him, stretching out her short legs. She's changed out of her overalls into a shapeless dress but has left her boots on. Mahony suspects that they might have steel toecaps.

'So how did you manage to drag your woman into the church?' she says.

Mahony reclines on his elbow and looks up at her, paying no attention to his peripheral vision. 'She dragged me in. She said she had a deal with the devil.'

'Another deal, is it?'

Ignored, the dead begin to gather and complain. Mahony makes out a hazy clump of them squawking in a nearby yew. Several stand around in the shadow of the church wringing their hands and shaking their heads.

'Father Quinn tried to warn her off me. We're appearing to play ball.'

'Ah, take no notice of him, the gobshite. I'm destroyed

with the effort of being nice to him and not spitting in his fecking cocoa.'

Mahony laughs and Bridget looks sideways at him. 'He's an ignorant man and an intolerant man. Father Jim approached things a different way. You'd be happy to make the effort for him now. Father Jim's passing was a blow to all of us. Did you see Mary Lavelle in church today?'

Mahony nods.

'I don't think she's ever really got over the death of Father Jim, or de Valera for that matter. But then she's always been very morbid in her outlook.'

'It sounds like she's been causing a stir.'

Bridget shrugs. 'It's Teasie I feel sorry for. Yesterday Mary made her fill a hip bath from the old horse trough outside the village. Then Mary got in it and wouldn't get out again. She said it was the safest place in the house, what with the ghosts circling the ceiling. After five hours of this, and with Teasie worried that her mother's pharyngitis would flare, Dr McNulty visited and administered an injection.'

'Poor Teasie.'

Bridget smiles. 'Of course Father Quinn heard about this behaviour and went round to warn her off it.'

Old Mother Doosey rambles slowly past. She fixes Bridget with a disapproving glare and tries to polish her headstone with the corner of her apron.

Bridget screws her cigarette out on the ground. 'Quinn is an interfering bastard; why he can't leave people to their own notions I don't know. Mary told him straight up that water from the old horse trough was nearly as good as that from a holy well formed by the tears of St Brigid herself.'

'What did Quinn say?'

'He told her to pray to the Good Lord for wisdom in

the face of ignorance and superstition. Then he threw her water over the buddleia and said let that be an end to it.'

'And was it?'

'Not at all. Mary told him the story of the Protestant sheep washers. You know it?'

Mahony shakes his head.

'In 1876 there was a holy well up the coast, along Belmullet way. Now one day the Protestants visiting the big house got wind of it and had a laugh about it and they had a flock of sheep brought to it. Then they washed the filthiest animal they could find in the holy well. A sheep with shit up to its oxters.

'Sure enough this angered the well and of course wells can be spiteful as well as bountiful.'

'So what happened?'

'The well upped and moved along the coast to Portacloy, where they were very pleased to have it. And every last one of the individuals involved with the sheep was struck down the very next day.'

'What happened to them?' asks Mahony.

'They were out riding their horses across the fields, having a splendid time, when a blinding bolt of lightning came out of the blue and melted the lot of them on the spot.' Bridget purses her lips. 'For years the outline of the riders was seared right there on the ground. You could even see the horses, hooves raised mid-gallop. To this day no crops will grow in that field and no animal will feed in it. Even the rain won't fall there; I swear to God it slants away before it hits the ground.'

Mahony smiles. 'So Father Quinn should look over his shoulder now?'

'He should. I'm away back to the house to put some nails in his pockets. He's a marked man as soon as there's a hint of a storm. Now, talking of looking over your shoulder, Mahony.'

'No further attempts.'

'Well, keep your wits about you, son.'

'Have you any ideas?'

'I'll keep you posted.' Bridget squints up at the clouds. 'I have my suspicions.'

Mahony watches Bridget Doosey thread her way back through the graveyard with old dead Mother Doosey following behind her, waving a dim set of fire tongs.

Mahony must have slept, because it's cold when he wakes and the church is empty. Even the dead have gone. He wipes saliva from the side of his mouth and gets up off the ground.

As Mahony heads round the side of the church he sees her standing with her back to him. She's wearing a dress so faded that for a moment he's not sure if she's dead or alive. But when she turns to face him Mahony knows that she's alive, for the pain is real and raw on her face and Mahony has to fight himself from reaching out to hold her.

Róisín Munnelly gives him an apologetic smile and searches blindly in her bag for a handkerchief. Her face is delicate, honed by grief, so that her fine cheekbones show below the grave brown eyes that look into his.

'No, I'm sorry. I'm sorry,' she says.

Without a thought Mahony smoothes a loose strand of hair behind her ear as gently as a mother would and whispers, 'It's all right, it's all right.'

They sit on the ground, one each side of the grave, and Róisín tells Mahony about her daughter. While she talks, she absently plays with the little white chippings spread inside the marble kerb. Róisín tells him that at first she found it very hard to leave her daughter up here in the graveyard. That she still feels an urge to tuck her in when she leaves, for the ground is cold all year round. But on a nice day it's not too bad, if the sun is out and the birds. And recently she's had a growing feeling that her little girl is no longer down there.

When they told Róisín, it took her feet right from under her. She has a scar above her eyebrow where she hit the dresser on her way down.

Her daughter had been missing for two days when the guards found her on the Carrigfine road. Her injuries were compatible with a hit-and-run. They never found out whose car it was. The ground was too dry and the tracks had all blown away.

Her husband tells her that she shouldn't keep coming up here, because it can't bring her back. He says that she has the boys to think of now.

When Mahony bolts the gate behind him he can still make out a little speck of colour. It's a yo-yo, balanced carefully on the top of a small, white, heart-shaped gravestone that reads *Margaret Ida Munnelly, 20 November 1961 – 12 May 1968*.

Chapter 17

May 1968

Mammy told her to keep to the fields nearby only and she could take her toy. It was round and yellow and perfect. Uncle Eamon brought it out from his pocket with a smile. He showed her how to flip it and trick it and walk the dog with it and Lord knows what. Mammy laughed and put her hands on her hips and Ida looked at her face and knew that Mammy had forgotten all about the pots on the stove and the Sunday dinner and the smell of cabbage lifting the lids and the steaming potatoes splitting their skins in the bowl ready for the butter to go on. Maybe they were laughing too. Laughing potatoes. Daddy was in his armchair behind his paper.

'That's grand, Margaret,' he'd said. 'That's grand.'

No, she thought, I'm not Margaret. I don't want that name. That's not what I call meself.

She had seen a great deal already that day.

She had seen all the hairs on Mrs Lavelle's top lip as she bent forward to shake hands with Mammy at Mass.

'Peace be with you.'

She had seen Ruth Quigley's new sailor coat from

· 152 ·

England, navy blue with little anchors on the brass buttons. Mrs Quigley said Mr Quigley had sent it over; he was there working ever so hard and ever so successfully.

'I have a yo-yo,' Ida told Mrs Quigley. But Mrs Quigley didn't hear on account of her getting stuck into telling Mammy all about Mr Quigley's important work.

Ida tried to touch the white piping on Ruth Quigley's hem. It was made to look like real rope twined all about but Ruth Quigley said to leave off with her filthy dirty fingers. On the way home Mammy told Uncle Eamon that Mrs Quigley was always blowing her own coals. Ida imagined Mrs Quigley with her head in the fire and her big arse sticking up behind and her mouth full of air. Puff. Puff.

The priest had shaken Ida's hand and smiled at her with all his teeth.

'Peace be with you.'

'Peace be with you, Golden Margaret,' said Uncle Eamon.

'That's not my name,' she'd whispered. 'That's not what I call meself.'

There were five girls in her school with yellow hair, but she had the finest. Mammy didn't know where she got it from, for hers was brown and Daddy's was ginger.

'Look it. Like spun gold. Goldilocks.'

Golden Ida. Hop, skip, point, down the lane on a good-weather day in her best dress with a cardigan for the nip in the air. Mammy had wanted her to get changed into her day clothes. Then Uncle Eamon started talking to Mammy and winked at Ida so that she could slip out.

Slip out, like her tongue through the gap in her teeth. She hissed over to the cows and climbed up on the gate. She made her hand go like a snake. Snap. Then she felt sorry for the cows and she showed them her toy, taking it from her pocket, shyly uncovering it.

'It is a yo-yo.'

She rolled the sound in her mouth and made big shapes with her lips as she said it. She opened and shut her jaw with the saying of it. Yo-yo.

The cows looked impressed, as well they should, up to their hocks in shit with no entertainment.

Hop, skip, point, to the Gallagher's.

Eileen and Phyllis had a biblical case of head lice. They'd be in there with their hair heaving and their mammy having a good rake around with the nit comb. Their hair was dead straight, so you'd think the nits would just slide off. Ida wondered if their mammy had cut all their hair off like she'd threatened she would. She said she'd see them scalped. Ida thought about them with their eyes all red and their hair all tufted and shorn, like baldy baby birds. She laughed and climbed up on the gate and showed her toy to the outside of their house.

The empty windows blinked back at her.

'It's a yo-yo, don't you know?'

The shut front door listened but didn't comment.

Ida danced off up the road.

She had seen a great deal already that day.

She had seen the tidemark in the breakfast jug where the milk had gone sour in a little ridge. She had pushed it with her nail then wiped her nail on the tablecloth.

She had seen a web as big as a piano. Although she felt it more than she saw it when she ran through it. It brushed her face and got in at her mouth. Ida spat on the ground for ages. For she knew that if you swallowed a mammy spider the babies would grow all inside you and would crawl into your ears and make you as deaf as a hedge. All you'd hear was the rustling of spider feet as they ran about your skull.

When Ida got to the forest she got her toy out of her cardigan pocket and showed it to the trees.

'This,' she announced, 'is a yo-yo. Don't you know?'

She showed them how to flip it, trick it and walk the dog with it, and although the trees were impressed, Ida knew better. She'd seen it done for real. She wound the string up and the yellow moon fell straight down again. She wished for it to bounce and run back up the string again. She glared at it.

It took ages and ages and ages to wind the string up. That was the boring part. You had to get it right. She poked her tongue through her tooth gap as she concentrated, breathing through her nose.

There.

It was shiny and round and perfect and yellow. She licked it but it didn't taste of yellow, although she didn't know what yellow should taste like.

Her yo-yo had come with her to make boats and sail them on the water. She'd use anything: a leaf or an acorn cup, a raft of moss and a weave of twigs. Passengers sailed too, on awful cursed kinds of crossings. Across wild uncharted seas to savage shores. The captain was a woodlouse and the passengers were ants, but all were condemned – God bless their souls! She would wave bravely and sob into her hankie as they sunk all the way down to the silty bottom of the Shand.

Hop, skip, point.

In the dirt with her best shoes on – Mammy would roast her!

She wasn't allowed near the river. Sometimes the edges were thick with slime. You had to break it to launch the boats; you had to poke them through, leaning right over. Maybe even step in a bit, even if you were wearing your school shoes, or else you were a baby.

But you always had to be careful that the river didn't grab you.

Ida had already seen a great deal that day: Uncle Eamon's gleeful green eyes as he promised to marry her, the potatoes laughing their skins apart and steaming up the rim of Mammy's good blue bowl. She had seen the dog nosing in the garden heap, a line of wet around his snout, and her school shoes filled with paper by the fire, drying.

Ida skipped through the trees with her toy in her hand and there he was.

A man with a sack and a shovel, kneeling on an island in the middle of the river.

Ida stared and stared. The island was longer than a fishing boat and as wide as a bus. The wet silt sparkled. It was all true – it had been down there all along, just hiding under the water watching the old bones swim round it!

And now it had a man on it.

The man wasn't a stranger, she knew him all right, although he wasn't wearing his cap or his smart coat. He looked up at her, unsmiling, then he glanced down at the sack by his feet.

The sack moved, she was sure of it – a sack full of kittens, Ida just knew.

With ears too big for their little pointed faces and tails so small they'd wrap only once around her finger.

She would take them all, really she would, on her life she would. They'd never bother him again, the kittens. She would feed them milky tea with a spoon and kill mice for them. They would ride to school on her shoulders and sit in her desk all day. At night they would sleep around her head like a furry halo. They would be brindled and tabby, grey and white, ginger and black. They would be tiger-striped and leopard-spotted. With combed-out whiskers and pink paw pads. She imagined herself smiling down at them. All the nearly drowned kittens in the world looked up at her and purred gratefully.

But when she opened her mouth to tell him, the words got stuck.

The man pretended a smile.

Ida had seen a great deal that day: the light on the water and on the green branches, drowsy bees in the wood sorrel and glossy beetles in the moss. And a low-tide island you'll see once if you're lucky and twice if you're blessed.

But Ida wasn't lucky and the man wasn't blessed. He had waited for eighteen years. He had studied the weather and the tides. And now he would shore up his troubled lover's grave and return the things he had taken from her. He would hold her in his arms again if he could, there in the middle of the river, with the water shrinking from him and the stones shifting under him.

For nightly, still, she came to him: she rose up out of the Shand, shrugging off her cape of silt. A river goddess, worn as smooth as an ancient carving, wearing waterweeds and dropping diamonds with every step. Her footprints dented rocks.

On the riverbank the little girl stared and stared.

He picked up his shovel.

'Come here to me, Margaret,' he said.

As Ida turned to run she dropped her toy, but it was only as she hit the ground that she realised her hands were empty.

Chapter 18

May 1976

'Now, I'd say this one was more of a warning,' says Bridget Doosey. 'Gelignite, you see. A drop more and we'd have seen some real damage.'

Mahony surveys the letterbox. The wire has blasted out and the plastic coating has melted onto the doormat. There's a plume of smoke damage along the wall and the coat stand is charcoal. Skeletal umbrellas lean in a blackened umbrella stand.

'Poisoned cats and letter bombs are a strange field of expertise.' Mahony offers her a cigarette.

She takes one and he leans forward to light it. 'The field of attempted murder is more commonplace than you think.' She exhales. 'Call it a hobby of mine.'

'So Mrs Cauley did right to call you?'

'Of course, I know my onions.'

Bridget picks up a charred piece of paper from the blackened tiles. 'Guess who.'

It has his name typed on it.

Chapter 19

May 1976

Mahony has walked for hours, keeping out of the forest and circling back up to Rathmore House by way of the open fields, for he needs time to think. The clouds are blowing in from the Atlantic, so that when Mahony sees Rathmore House, behind an ancient horse chestnut and just over a stile, the light makes the stone as colourless as rain

He almost doesn't see her, on the road up ahead of him, crouched on her hunkers. Her face is in profile and with her upturned nose and heavy-lidded eyes she is as sweet and pale as a graveyard angel.

'Pooky Snail, put out your horns,' Ida lisps as she stabs a pale finger through a snail. She tuts, stands up and puts her hands on her hips. 'Pooky Snail, would you ever put your feckin' horns out?'

'Ah, he's asleep, look it,' says Mahony, and picks up the snail to show her.

'He's not asleep. He's dead.'

'You're right of course.' Mahony pitches the empty shell over the wall.

They walk together, Mahony in his leather jacket and Ida in her scuffed shoes he can see the road through. She reaches her arms up to him and Mahony's heart turns over. 'You know I can't carry you, chick.'

Ida folds her arms and flutters down at the side of the road with the impeccable grace of a prima ballerina. She takes something out of her cardigan pocket and holds it up. She licks her finger and rubs an imaginary smudge from it. Mahony swears that for a moment the yo-yo glows brighter in her hand.

'You got it back then?'

Ida nods and Mahony notices that she looks just like her mother. She has the same stiff, serious little smile as Róisín. She starts to wind up the string.

Mahony sits down next to her. 'Do you remember how you lost it?'

She grimaces. 'Mammy said I wasn't allowed to go into the forest on me own, but I did. She said I wasn't to go near the river, but I did that too. I went up to play acorn boats, but he was already there, drowning kittens at the river. Where I showed you.' Her eyes widen as she remembers. 'The island, I saw it! The water had all run away.'

'You saw Denny's Ait, near the clearing?'

Ida nods. 'And the man was on it. He had this sack and this shovel.'

'How did you know there were kittens in there?'

Ida frowns at him. 'What else would you put in a sack to go into the river?'

Mahony shrugs.

'Eejit,' murmurs Ida, soft and low. She purses her lips. 'And I shouted, "Don't kill them, Mister", and he looked up at me and did a pretend smile, and said, "Come here to me, Margaret", and I knew I was in trouble because he sounded cross. Then I ran and then there was a flash behind my eyes and then I dropped my yo-yo.'

'You saw his face?'

She looks down at her shoes. 'Maybe.'

'And you knew him, didn't you?'

'How do I bloody know?' Ida jumps up. 'Jesus fecking Christ.' She slips her yo-yo back into the pocket of her cardigan and is gone.

Shauna is coming out of the back door with a tea tray. The late sun catches her hair and gives it a reddish cast as she moves into the light. She leans the tray on her hip as she closes the door behind her, with movements quick and unthinking, her lit face familiar and lovely. She negotiates the steps, frowning as a wayward hen scrabbles across her path. Watching her sets up a calm bright feeling in Mahony: here life continues, against the landslide, against the darkness. If he could he'd kiss her for it. Shauna looks up at him and smiles.

'I'm taking Daddy down his tea.'

Mahony takes the tray off her. 'Jesus, do you ever stop running with these trays? Can the man not get his own tea?'

Shauna laughs with him. 'The man would die of thirst rather.'

Shauna leads the way past a series of outbuildings in different states of disrepair, where hens peck distractedly around an overgrown courtyard and a dead ginger cat prowls amongst the weeds.

'I've been thinking, Shauna.'

'Steady on.'

'It's best if I leave.'

She glances back at him. 'Best for who?'

Mahony watches his step on the cobbles. 'For you and for Merle.'

'Where would you even go? I can't imagine anyone else in town opening their doors to you.'

'That's not the point. That's the second attempt—'

'And they've said their piece. It would devastate that old woman if you left now; she loves the bones of you.'

'What if one of you gets hurt?'

'Don't be thick, Mahony. It's you they're after, not us.' Shauna shrugs. 'Anyway, those were only warnings. If they'd have wanted to kill you—'

'I'd be dead by now? Cheers.'

He follows her down a narrow path by the side of a greenhouse; the remaining panes are fogged with moss and the floor is littered with old feed bags. He picks his way carefully, keeping everything upright on the tray. Shauna smiles over her shoulder.

'Stay here with us, Mahony. It's where your friends are.'

Mahony is bowled over. He smiles down at a tea cosy.

Shauna stops outside what used to be a stable; some of the doors have been glazed and it's been given a recent coat of dark-green paint. She opens a door at the end. She goes to take the tray off him.

'I'll take it in,' says Mahony.

'Ah no. Daddy won't have strangers in his workshop.'

Mahony laughs. 'I live in his house, I'm hardly a stranger, am I now?'

'Well, just put it down on the table there and come straight out so you don't disturb him.'

'I won't; I'll stay for a while with him.'

'Ah no, Mahony.'

'The man doesn't see a soul from one end of the day to another.'

'That's the way he likes it. Now don't make him touchy for me, for then he's the devil to deal with.'

'Go on up to the house. I'll be up later. The talk is probably bursting out of the poor fella.'

Desmond Burke is of an unfavourable disposition, until he takes himself down to the old stable. The horses are long gone, although cobwebbed bridles and tattered paddock rugs still hang tangled on hooks in dim corners.

Desmond has it all set up. The stalls are knocked through to make one long room lined with bookcases, and electricity is routed from the house in order to run the lights. He has a wood burner he can use on cool days and an old easy chair he can sleep in.

At the far end is Desmond's desk, with a lamp arranged, just so, to throw light on a clean wide blotter. Every morning, at seven, Desmond walks down the garden, opens the door and takes his place at his desk. He smiles at the leather-bound books on the bookshelves and takes a paisley cravat from the drawer. He puts on his cravat and opens a book from the neat pile next to him. Then he picks up his pen and starts to make notes, in a good solid schoolteacherly hand, slanted in all the right places.

Lost in his scholarly reveries, Desmond wouldn't notice if the goat itself brought him his tea, as long as it didn't bleat.

Mahony sets the tray down on a table just under one of the windows. 'Evening, Squire, I've brought your tea down to you there.'

Desmond studies Mahony for a moment then screws the top on his pen. 'Can I help you at all?'

He speaks with quiet deliberation but Mahony sees impatience in his pale blue eyes. He has the same mildly startled look about him as his daughter.

'I've brought your tray down to you there.'

'So I see.' Desmond looks at Mahony without interest and Mahony looks back at him with a winning smile.

This is the guest from Dublin then.

Desmond sees the long hair and the leather jacket, the stubble and the dirty trousers. He wonders if Mahony smokes drugs up there in his house. He expects they have a load of drugs in the city, on every street corner, in every bar, in every pocket and pipe. All the people are bewildered out of their minds on it.

Mahony sees that Desmond – once a fine figure of a man no doubt – has been ruined by the books. For too long he's leant over them, like an old toad nursing a fly. And now, like an old toad, he's bowed of back and thin of leg.

Mahony holds out his hand. 'I'm Mahony.'

Desmond looks at Mahony's hand. 'If you'll excuse me.'

Mahony, unperturbed, steps over to the bookcase. 'You have your books in better order than Mrs Cauley; the woman has to summon a windstorm to find what she wants.'

Desmond snorts.

Mahony traces his finger down the spine of a collector's edition of the work of Thomas Crofton Croker. But when he leans forward to manhandle an antique Lady Gregory from her place on the shelf Desmond almost swallows his teeth.

'Don't touch my books.'

Mahony looks up in surprise. Desmond has his arse half out of his chair and his hand clutching the edge of the desk.

Mahony speaks gently. 'I'm sorry, pal. Look, I won't touch them.'

Desmond settles warily in his seat.

Mahony smiles. 'It's just that I've loved books ever since I was a wee boy in the orphanage.'

Desmond stares at him. 'The orphanage?'

'Aye, the orphanage.' Mahony turns back to the bookcase. 'Where dear old Father McCluskey read to me every Saturday afternoon; I was his favourite you know? He would bring down a book from the cabinet, sit me on his knee and we'd look at that book together for hours and hours.'

Desmond Burke appears to be riveted. Mahony, heartened by such an attentive audience, could even start to believe his own story and forget the fact that the only time he ever went to Father McCluskey's office was to have nine kinds of shite belted out of him.

Mahony pulls up a stool and sits down at the side of the desk. 'Then one day, Father McCluskey said wasn't I the lucky little fella, because he was going to show me the best book of them all.'

Mahony pauses and looks off into the far distant corner of the stable. 'It was beautiful, bound with leather and on the cover were these gold deep-cut letters that you wouldn't believe. Real gold surely?'

Desmond shrugs helplessly.

'And when I opened the pages the paper inside was as thin and crisp as a slice of fresh cloud. And there were all these pictures of temples and Romans and each picture covered by a tissue wisp to keep it nice.'

This was true. There really had been a book of such beauty in Father McCluskey's office, in a locked glass cabinet. Mahony remembered it well.

On that particular day, just as the priest was getting into the swing of Mahony's chastisement, he was called away to give Extreme Unction to Mother Maria Consuelo, who'd been dying for twenty-odd blashted years. Father McCluskey had left Mahony behind in the room with the instructions to pull his trousers up and get the hell out. Mahony nodded with hardly a tear in his eye, for after years of walloping, his arse was as tough as footskin.

Mahony had searched in all the unlocked drawers until he found a half pack of cigarettes. He had pocketed them, taken a book from the bookcase and sat down at Father McCluskey's desk for a smoke.

'It was a truly beautiful book and I treated it with the respect I would give to Father McCluskey himself.' Mahony smiles as he remembers how he'd watched a gentle arc of his golden piss fall on the leather-bound cloud-thin pages. 'So you see, Desmond, I'd only treat your possessions with the greatest of respect. I wouldn't even breathe on them.'

Desmond Burke sits speechless. He has taken up his fountain pen again and keeps screwing the lid on and off, unaware that he is in real danger of breaking the thread.

Mahony lights a fag. 'What are you reading about?'

He holds out the pack to Desmond, who shakes his head. 'History. Folklore. That sort of thing.'

'Grand so. Is there anything about the dead in all that?'

Desmond looks confused. 'The dead? In what context?'

'In the context of them coming back, having a look about the place and then telling the living who did them in?'

Desmond takes off his glasses and hopes that Mahony can't see his hands shake. 'I don't know.'

'By the way, that necktie looks well on you, Desmond. Very distinguished. The professors at Trinity College wear those when they're walking about talking to themselves.' Mahony smiles at him and against his better judgement Desmond Burke smiles back.

★

'So let me get this straight, Desmondo, in the story with the bold boy chasing this bewitched hare up the side of the mountain—'

Desmond downs the last of the dry sherry and nods. 'Yes, "The Fate of Frank M'Kenna."'

'That so, his friends all come down the mountain when the weather turns but M'Kenna stays out hunting because he's a gobshite?'

'Because he's a headstrong young man, yes.'

'Aye, he's a gobshite, so he dies running about after the hare in a snow storm.'

'Well, William Carleton is telling us that no one quite knows what happens to the boy after we lose sight of him.'

'And the father is beside himself, having cursed the boy to death for breaking his plough on a magic stone.'

'No, that was the other tale we read. In this story the father remonstrates with Frank M'Kenna for putting his love of hunting over attending Sunday Mass. He warns his son of the dire effects of habitual and unchecked pleasure on his mortal soul.'

'And then, because the son disobeys him, the father curses the son's soul to hell that he might come back a corpse from the mountain for his defiance.'

'He does.'

'And they find the poor bastard when the snow thaws and bring his body back to the village strapped to the door of his own house.'

'They do.'

'And when the ghost of Eejit M'Kenna returns, he returns for one reason and one reason only.'

'He does, Mahony.'

'And that's to tell his friends who should get his good trousers.'

· 167 ·

'That's right.'

'Nothing else?'

'No.'

'Not how he died, or if the hare was a witch after all, or about how she got him?'

'No.'

'Stop the lights! That's just like the fuckin' dead.'

'So then, Desmond, the purpose of folklore is that it has no fuckin' purpose at all?'

Desmond takes a cigarette from Mahony; he won't remember that he doesn't smoke until tomorrow. He adjusts his glasses with a very serious kind of deliberation.

'Now concentrate, Mahony. Folklore is the record of a dying civilization, romantic Ireland, the ancient untarnished imagination of the pure and noble peasant making sense of the harshness and beauty of their life and the landscape.'

Mahony hits the table, narrowly missing Lady Gregory, who sprawls open next to an empty bottle of whiskey.

'Imagination, me hole. Who says this stuff doesn't happen? There's a lot of truth in folklore.'

Desmond frowns.

'Can you not see the dead roaming about the place? What about that old fella sitting on that armchair over there?'

Desmond squints across the room. 'That's a commode.'

'A commode?'

'We got it for Mrs Cauley but she refused to use it.'

Mahony laughs. 'I'm not surprised – there's a priest already hatching on it.'

'What does he look like?'

Mahony peers across the room. The dead priest sits with his head sunk to his chest, rolling his thumbs one over the other, round and round. A haggard bulk of a man, he's the most impressive-looking priest, dead or alive, that Mahony has seen.

'He looks like you wouldn't mess with him.'

Desmond leans forward and whispers in Mahony's ear. 'It's fitting, it came from the parochial house.'

The dead priest hunches over his dim hands, oblivious, grinding his big square jaw.

'A priest haunting a commode.' Mahony sways gently on the stool with an unlit fag in his smile. 'It's the place to be if you've a bit of time on your hands.'

Desmond smiles back at him. 'You have your mother's eyes.'

'I do? Now, did I tell yeh who I was?'

'You didn't need to. I'd have known you anywhere.'

'An' what about me daddy? Do I look like me daddy?'

'I've no answer for you there, Mahony.'

'My daddy was anyone and no one, was he?'

Desmond looks down at his hands. 'You were a bye-child; there wasn't anyone that could have made her decent.'

Mahony lights his cigarette. 'What was she like?'

'I don't know. She never said more than four words to me.'

It's a soft lie, badly delivered. Mahony wonders if Desmond would have had the nerve to try it on him if they were both sober.

'Jus' tell me something about her.'

Desmond studies his knuckles. 'Orla was from another world. As I said, I didn't really know her.'

Chapter 20

May 1976

In the comfortable library of the parochial house Father Quinn wakes to a gentle parade of droplets on his nose and face. He had fallen asleep after a passable chop in front of the fire, and now, opening his eyes, he sees a playful spring bubbling up in the approximate centre of his hearthrug. Father Quinn watches it in a rapt sort of amazement, becoming aware of a strong smell of leaf mould all around him. Soon the air is thickly glazed with mist and the water is rising with a purposeful gush. When a jet of it spurts directly into his chest, knocking the breath out of his lungs, Father Quinn is galvanised into action. He leaps up from his chair and sinks to his ankles in the boggy substance of a wool-mix shagpile.

Bridget Doosey and Michael Hopper have been passing the evening peaceably in the kitchen. Michael has been flirting with the idea of applying putty to a windowpane he replaced last Thursday. It's a pressing job. But having considered the failing light and the location of the putty in relation to himself (in the shed at the bottom of the parochial garden) he has almost decided against it. What's more, he is enjoying the comfort of the kitchen and his current view of Bridget Doosey's womanly proportions as she half-heartedly scours the burnt cooking pots.

The terrified wailing that begins to emanate from the library brings them both running, Michael with his heart in his mouth and Bridget clutching the soapy handle of a frying pan.

Opening the door to the library they find Father Quinn sunk to his knees in the carpet and clinging on to an occasional table. Afterwards, Bridget will remark that it's lucky the priest is a tall man, given the considerable delay they had in laying hand on a coil of rope to haul him out, for otherwise Father Quinn would almost certainly have drowned in his own home.

By the time the weeping priest has been led into the kitchen and given a brandy, the water is tumbling out along the hall and down the garden path. Where it stops, just short of the gate, laps back on itself and becomes as still as glass.

Bridget Doosey smiles. She'll widely proclaim the miracle of Mulderrig's very own holy well, just as soon as she has led Father Quinn upstairs by the hand and tucked him firmly into bed.

Chapter 21

April 1944

The confessional in St Patrick's church had always lapped up tales of suffering and spite. It fed on shame and remorse with quiet, ligneous devotion. Its deep shine was not just wood polish and spinster's spittle; it was the gilding of guilt, rubbed over the years to a saintly lustre.

Inside, on one side of the brass lattice, sat Father Jim Hennessy, full of hard-won wisdom and indigestion. On the other side of the brass lattice sat Orla Sweeney, eyes wide in the dark.

She pressed her fingers into the grill until the tips of them disappeared. She could hear the priest breathing on the other side.

'I talk to the dead, Father,' she said. 'They've been giving me messages since last Tuesday.'

Father Jim was trying to release gas quietly. For he was a big-framed strong man more suited to the rigours of farming than the sedentary life of a man of the cloth; his spiritual calling had all but destroyed his digestion. He carefully raised one cheek but it reverberated on the wooden bench. He apologised to the Lord and straightened his stole.

'Child, this is a terrible fantasy to put into your head and it is false. You must look to the Lord God to find truth and peace in your life.'

'I know it's wrong to talk to them, Father, but they're so lonely. At first there was only a few but now they keep coming up out of the ground and through the walls with all these things they want telling to people and I don't know what to do.'

Father Jim learnt two things that day. First, that quantities of radishes did not agree with him and second:

'Dorothy says it wasn't your fault, Father.'

Father Jim's breath halted inside him.

'She says she would have died anyway, even if you hadn't tried to baptise her in the cowshed. It wasn't the chill that took her away; it was her heart.'

Father Jim went as white as a sheet in the dark. He was where? In the confessional, trying to keep breathing.

Breathing what? The familiar incense smell, beeswax and lilies, the damp wool coats of the congregation, their balsam and hair ointment, their stale smoke and cough sweets, the vinegar of last night's alcohol.

But he was half in the past again. A child of little more than six, already with a vocation, practising the priesthood and knowing it was wrong, but wanting to. Oh wanting to, wanting to do his great loving terrible God's work always, always.

There was his new baby sister with her face still wrinkled with brine, and there was the cup dipped again and again into the bucket in the cowshed. The low winter sun filled his eyes to the brim, spilling all around, catching cup and bucket. He remembered still the bright metal glint and the light burnishing the straw to gold and the cobbled mud to bronze.

He had baptised her Dorothy, although her name was Margaret. He drew a cross on her tiny forehead and blessed her blissfully, whispering the words like a spell.

Mammy couldn't understand why Babby was wet in the cradle. All her things soaked. She wasn't to know it was holy water, for the cows were in the milking shed now and the bucket was no longer a font lit by God in heaven.

And Dorothy? A livid spot on each cheek, otherwise a china doll.

A coffin small enough for Mammy to hold on her knees.

God bless, Dorothy.

The real priest was solid black; Jimmy watched from under the table with his little soul frozen with a terror that had never quite thawed.

Until he was absolved by a ten-year-old girl.

Father Jim stumbled from the confessional and shut himself in the sacristy. He looked around the familiar room. At the press with his vestments inside and the baptismal candles that lay waxy in a row. At the bottles of Communion wine and the linen, reverently folded, a mystery of worn fabric and belief. The whiskey in his hand didn't warm. The shelves of books didn't reassure.

This was the first time that Orla made Father Jim Hennessy cry.

Orla sat all alone in the confessional with her hands on her lap. A dim white face pressed its way through the wooden wall. Rising up from her unmarked grave just south of the altar, an ancient abbess had travelled through cold soil and colder church stone to whisper wisdom in Orla's ear:

'You're on your own, treasure. Don't expect any help.'

She shut the mild curves of her eyes and dissipated. Later

she would stalk the organist, who was never warm when he sat down to his work, despite the thick socks on him.

Orla sat very still and thrilled to a brand-new idea.

She was a magician with a big white rabbit. She could reach into her black hat and pull out a man's worst fear or his greatest reassurance. The dead saw everything. She saw everything. Feck.

The first to come through last Tuesday had been Mrs McHale's husband. In life he had ordered, with great pride, a threshing machine from Westport, which had his right arm off on the second day he'd used it. Mr McHale had bled to death in the far field. His arm was recovered and bandaged back on again so that his hands could be joined together for his final prayer. As if in protest, his hands refused to meet. So a framed picture of St Isidore, the patron saint of farm equipment, was placed between his punctured fingers. Mr McHale was not a popular man. The cause of Mr McHale's demise was sent back to Westport, where it was re-oiled, resold and gave twenty-five years of uneventful service to a farmer just outside Castlebar.

A little after nine that morning Orla had been scraping the porridge pan for the chickens when she saw Mr McHale walking towards her with one arm significantly longer than the other.

'Here, Dolly,' called out the dead farmer. 'Tell my missus I don't want my good shoes going to the bloody charity box; she should keep them for the boys.'

Mr McHale flickered slightly in the early morning sun. He didn't look bad considering he'd been dead for over a year.

'And tell her to get off her fat arse and sort out the rats in the barn,' he said. 'They're getting big enough to ride around the town, so they are.'

'Right so, Mr McHale,' said Orla, and she watched the dead man turn and walk through the hen house.

After Mr McHale they came thick and fast.

When Orla walked in the forest she saw faint nooses filled with twisting lumps of men. When she walked in the village she saw the faint forms of skipping children in white dresses. Some of the dead wore quaint costumes and glided. These tended to hold their fingers up to their lips and vanish. But some were as real as Orla's own hands and would stand before her scratching their arses and swearing.

At the graveyard they sat about in groups, lolling against the stones or swinging their legs on the wall, just like she did. When she approached, some melted into the ground and some walked forwards holding their arms open.

Soon Orla began to feel wanted. She began to feel important. She would lie between the gravestones of Patrick James Carty 1901–1925 and Joseph Raftery 1880–1913 and listen to the dead. Paddy and Joe would politely vacate their eternal resting place and flitter up to the top of St Patrick's church, where they would stretch their dead backs out against the roof and smoke invisible cigarettes.

Down below, the spirits would gather and jostle.

'Silence, please, ladies and gentlemen. Wait your turn.'

Orla listened to them in rapture.

What she heard, she knew, could set the town hopping. The only problem was how to deliver their messages.

She wasn't allowed in the shops because of the thieving, and she wasn't made welcome at the school any more, for being wayward. If she turned up at Mass they'd ignore her and if she went up to their doors, well, it would be the mop bucket. Orla listened, then she regretfully explained to the dead that they'd chosen the wrong girl. But the dead just folded their arms and shook their heads.

Two days later Orla had a remarkable idea.

The next morning she arrived at the graveyard with stolen paper, pen and ink. She only knew the four letters of her name but that didn't stop her, because on that day, note after note was written, each in an entirely different hand. Some were executed in fluid copperplate and others were in hard-pressed capitals. Some were no more than smudged spider scrawls and some were sprinkled with excitable loops and florid crosses. As the sun died, Orla stretched out her aching hand and the dead smiled and drifted away arm in arm through the church tower, looking as relaxed as she'd ever seen them.

By the next morning the messages from the dead had reached the living. They were found in letterboxes and pinned to doorways, propped behind clocks and folded on kitchen tables. Adulteries were exposed and grievances were aired. Real fathers were named and bastards discovered. Old sins were brought to life and played out for the rest of the village to watch.

But the letters could not be refuted.

The stories they told were incontrovertible and the handwriting, in every case, was a perfect and demonstrable match to that of the deceased. These were the words of the all-seeing dead and the living knew this.

The town looked around itself in horror.

Spinsters were accused of witchcraft and black cats were strung up. Windows were smashed and bureaus were forced open. Insults were smeared from door to door as the villagers sought the source of this terrible, evil outpouring of truth. Orla smiled and returned to the graveyard with a rake of paper and a fresh pot of ink, and who knows what would have happened to the village if Benny Ganley hadn't caught her in the act.

Benny, a helper at St Patrick's with a drinker's nose and a hand that shook under the collection plate, was walking through the graveyard when he saw a little pair of feet sticking out past a headstone. As he rounded the grave he saw the child propped up against the marble slab with her face bent to her work. She was biting her lip with concentration and Benny watched in amazement as her tiny hand travelled over the paper, neatly and cleanly, without snag or hitch. Occasionally she stopped and cocked her head and nodded, as if listening intently.

Benny, riveted, moved closer, but in doing so disturbed her. She jumped to her feet with her hands held behind her back and the kind of bold expression that invited violence.

Benny gamely lunged forwards to grab hold of her and give her a bit of a shake. But as soon as he laid hands on her she came alive and twisting under him, all teeth and hair. Then the little bitch laid a fierce bite on his hand. It was a bite that could have come from a rat or a dog. (Indeed, Benny would still have the stamp of Orla's teeth on him seven years later when he died roaring of a tumefied liver.) The child fled from the graveyard, dropping a handful of papers in her haste. Benny picked them up and was astounded. By the time Benny took the evidence to Father Jim, he had already told ten people.

Orla was in deep shit.

Chapter 22

May 1976

Mahony is a natural.

As soon as he gets up onto the stage a peculiar kind of magic starts to happen. Some spit on his name, but they feel it. Some wish him to hell, or back to Dublin, but they feel it. Every last judgemental do-gooder, backstabbing old biddy and jealous boyfriend feels it.

Mrs Cauley looks on in delight. It is what she expected and better than she expected. The town is needled, its bollocks are truly twisted, for try as they might they can't resist Mahony.

She had known this from the start.

And so Mulderrig is caught between love and fear, spite and affection, with Mahony always on their minds. It's everything Mrs Cauley could have hoped for: confusion, bewilderment and a good shake of their parochial notions.

She grins. The play is a Trojan bloody horse, landing Mahony right inside their defences, where he can disarm them with nothing more than a lively stride across the stage in an open shirt and a tight pair of breeches.

Such is the power of theatre.

Such is the power of a handsome, dark-eyed, daring man.

Father Quinn stands in the wings, watching.

Only he sees the peril of this ambush, this infiltration, which must lead to dropped guards and careless talk.

But still, he has to admire the cunning of his enemy. For he has no doubt it was Mrs Cauley's plan from the first to take Mahony's brazen charms and amplify them with the pagan spell of her theatre.

Father Quinn sees it all: a town run by an actress and a libertine, where illegitimacy is honourable and morality a crime. Where Orla Sweeney is a saint not a sinner, and those who fought her diligently, with unimpeachable resolve, for the sake of the village, are vilified.

This is no more than a second wave of corruption, bringing with it all the evil of the first. Orla is back, riding the village into submission; only her tactics have changed.

Father Quinn tirelessly monitors village opinion, sending out legions of poisonous whispers and whole armies of noxious slanders to counteract Mahony's growing popularity. The villagers nod and agree but they forget to despise Mahony the moment they lay eyes on him.

It appears that nothing can destroy Mahony in the eyes of Mulderrig. Not scandal, not truth, not history. Mahony will take the good character freely hung on him as his past falls away like the arse-end of a burning comet.

Father Quinn watches and waits in the wings. He starts to follow Mahony everywhere, looming like mortality in dark corners, as shifty as a fox with a hen in every pocket. He starts to mutter and scrawl in notebooks. Sometimes he forgets to shave and change his underpants.

But he sees it all.

Soon most of the village are showing up at rehearsals and soon all of them could understudy, the way they mouth each word silently in chorus. Mammies start bringing down scones and sandwiches to keep the audience going and Tadhg has the bar boy running over and back with a tray from Kerrigan's Bar until his legs threaten to fall off him.

Jack Brophy comes in off-duty. He watches Mahony out of the corner of his eye and smiles as he raises the set out of wood and canvas. Soon there is a cut-away cottage with half a thatched roof. Bridget Doosey paints the views beyond the open door using bruised colours in big strokes and the audience begin to see a far-off bay and mist-shrouded mountains.

The house on the stage becomes the exact place remembered from childhood or visited in dreams. The walls are whitewashed and the troughs are planted. Furniture arrives, solid and old-looking. The shelves of the bar are stacked with stone jugs and bottles. A bucket and mop are propped in the corner. Someone thinks to bring a mousetrap, or a jam jar full of flowers, or a pair of gingham curtains.

Róisín Munnelly brings her sewing down so that she can sit in the corner and listen as she finishes the costumes. And soon it is Róisín that Mahony's looking at when he says his lines most gently, and she scuppers more than a few easy seams in confusion because of it.

Father Quinn sees it all.

And he bites his hands in the dark and waits for his moment to come, for he knows how this will end.

Mulderrig will bring down a plague on itself and it won't be the first time.

Chapter 23

May 1976

It is a truth universally unacknowledged that when the dead are trying to remember something, the living are trying harder to forget it.

Mrs Cauley has been interrogating her commode for the past half hour. In the absence of reliable testimony from the living she has decided to turn to the dead. Recognising the dead priest's description from Mahony's anecdotes of his drunken evening with Desmond, she has had the haunted commode moved to her bedside in order to extract a statement from the late Father Jim Hennessy.

Mahony is lying on the floor reading poetry and smoking.

Upstaged by the newest dead man in her life, Johnnie is nowhere to be seen. But Mahony suspects, from the tapping of a cane on the ceiling above them, that he's most likely pacing the master bedroom.

'A priest haunting a commode,' chuckles Mrs Cauley. 'It's sublime, isn't it? Is he there now?'

Mahony glances up at Father Jim, who is in the corner leaning on a bookcase. 'After a fashion.'

'Then he needs to get his dead finger out and tell us

who did him in.' She studies the empty commode. 'There's no doubt in my mind that he was done in. How did he die? He succumbed to a short and violent illness. Someone had a hand in it.'

Father Jim scowls. 'Pneumonia, he had a hand in it, along with his good pal heart failure.'

'Think about it,' Mrs Cauley whispers. 'The town was desperate to rid themselves of Orla. She was wild, unpredictable, a real troublemaker.'

'Does this wagon ever stop?' mumbles Father Jim.

Mrs Cauley purses her lips. 'Having someone like Hennessy fighting Orla's corner would have presented a major obstacle to getting rid of her. He wouldn't have taken any of their crap.'

Father Jim nods and searches in his pocket for his pipe. 'She's right there. Tell her, lad.'

Mahony looks up from his page. 'You're right. He wouldn't have taken any crap.'

'They had to do away with Hennessy before they could get to your mother. Which is why Doosey kept her own counsel; she realised it was a dangerous game to be on Orla's side.'

'What with all the letter bombs and poisoned scones and the like?'

Mrs Cauley looks at him. 'Don't be flippant.' She picks up the doorstop and sets it again on the middle of the tea tray. 'Hennessy may just hold the key to this case.'

'It's not always that easy.'

'You underestimate these dead you know. They hang around the place, don't they, watching, haunting? That makes them prime witnesses in my book. You just need to know the right way to talk to them.' Mrs Cauley pushes herself up in the bed and fixes the commode with an exacting glare.

She speaks very slowly and very loudly. 'Now then, Hennessy, tell us what you know about the disappearance of Orla Sweeney.'

'I'm dead, I'm not fecking stupid,' mutters Father Jim. He sits down at the end of her bed, chewing the stem of his pipe. Even in death he has a fine high colour to his cheeks.

'Come in, Hennessy. I'm not receiving you.' Mrs Cauley taps the tea tray pettishly. 'Now, Father, will you stir yourself and move this doorstopper? Isn't it light enough even for a dead old badger like yourself?'

Father Jim shakes his head. 'How do you put up with this, lad?'

Mrs Cauley listens carefully for a moment then she glances across at Mahony. 'He must have heard something in confession. They're all in there day and night bleating about their sins and holding out their gruel bowls for holy redemption.'

Father Jim grimaces. 'Oh, they came to confession all right. It was all "Forgive me, Father, for amn't I after getting a baby from using the wash flannel off me husband?" Or, "Forgive me, Father, for I looked at me cow the wrong way."'

'Ask him, Mahony.'

'Tell her she's an eejit.'

Mahony puts down his book. 'He said he heard nothing useful.'

Mrs Cauley grunts. 'Does he know that the seal of confession doesn't apply if you are a priest who is mortally dead?'

'Sweet Lord Jesus Christ, give me strength,' moans Father Jim.

'He's aware of that.'

'Let's try this then.' Mrs Cauley's hands scuttle across the tea tray. 'Listen carefully, Hennessy. What happened on the day Orla Sweeney disappeared? Did this happen?'

Mrs Cauley slides the doorstopper towards the words 'fowl play', the nearest she could find to 'murder' in Bridget Doosey's back copies of *Ireland's Own*.

Father Jim passes a hand across his forehead. 'Make her stop.'

'Father Jim's off for a bit of a lie-down.'

Mrs Cauley frowns. 'He's been dead for twenty-six years, hasn't he had enough of a lie-down?'

Father Jim wanders back to the commode and sits down. He lights his pipe with the faint flame of the afterlife, which always burns cold. Occasionally he glowers over at the figure on the bed.

'You can't expect too much from them,' says Mahony.

Mrs Cauley puts her head on one side, her eyes narrowed under her poker visor. 'I think you're reluctant to get properly involved. You're holding back, Mahony.'

'How do you mean?'

'Well, if you were to listen to them . . .'

Mahony looks up at her. 'Then no doubt they'd have me running all over the town. Pouring libations onto Biddy Gavaghan's grave, delivering a kick up Frank Kiernan's hole, that sort of thing.'

'Exactly. You don't want to be put out.'

'It's not that. It's just that they don't always have great memories. They're a little lost.'

Mrs Cauley purses her lips. 'So Father Jim, sitting scratching his holy bollocks on the commode there, is of no use to us?'

Mahony shrugs. How can he explain? How can he explain to Mrs Cauley that Father Jim is just a vague copy of his former living self? That just like any other dead person, his mind, if you can call it a mind, has ceased to exist. For the dead don't change or grow. They're just echoes of the stories of their own lives sung back in the wrong order: arsewards. They're the pattern on closed eyelids after you turn away from a bright object. They're twice-exposed film. They're not really here, so cause and effect means nothing to them.

Mahony knows that only very rarely, and through no fault of their own, will the dead tell you something useful, like the whereabouts of an unread will, or a box of furled banknotes, or the name of a killer.

Mrs Cauley shakes her head. 'Well, it's a shocking waste of a good weapon. You should be wielding your shining sword of clairvoyancy against your adversaries; I know I would be.'

Father Jim raises his eyebrows. Mahony picks up his book of poetry.

'Squandering. That's what it is.' Mrs Cauley pushes away her Ouija board with disgust and takes up her map to plot likely sites for an illicit burial in and around Mulderrig.

Peace settles nicely on the room; now and then there is the quick sharp scuttle of a mouse along the skirting boards, now and then the shifting sound of a book settling into a deeper sleep.

Mahony is just closing his eyes when the dead priest jumps up from the commode with a terrifying roar.

'*He started to drive her home,*' he screams, and lurches towards Mahony. 'That was when all the trouble started. It was *him*, don't you see? It must have been him: he had a car.'

'Jesus. What?' Mahony is up off the floor, moving out of his way.

Father Jim frowns. '*The daddy* – for the life of me I can't remember his name.' Father Jim grins triumphantly. 'But I know this, you little gobshite: she stopped letting me walk her home because he would give her a lift.'

He turns and walks off through a bookcase, punching the air without as much as displacing a dust mote.

Mahony stares at the space where the dead Father Hennessy used to be. 'Who owned a car around the time that Orla fell pregnant?'

Mrs Cauley looks up from a promising patch of alluvial wasteland. 'Ask Bridget Doosey, she'll know.'

'Ask Daddy, he'll know,' says Shauna, coming in the door with the tea and the biscuits. She looks at Mahony. 'You could take him down his cup of tea and ask him.'

'I could.'

'And maybe you could get him to change his socks and go out for a walk?'

'Daddy doesn't like going out; leave the man alone,' says Mrs Cauley, pushing biscuits off her plate.

Shauna looks at the old woman in despair. 'If you don't want the biscuits just leave them on the side.'

Mrs Cauley claws up a plain one. 'I told you, not the creamy ones.' She scowls. 'You know I'm trimming to get into that lamé number for the play and you're trying to sabotage me. Thundering little witch.'

Shauna rolls her eyes. 'If you do head into town you might want to go and see Father Quinn. He's left another message for you.'

'He's been trailing you for days,' says Mrs Cauley. 'You should go and see what he wants, the shitehawk.'

Mahony pulls on his jacket. 'All right, I'll take your old fella down for a stretch of the legs to town.'

'You won't get Daddy further than Roadside Mary but you can leave him there for a bit. He says he won't mix with the village philistines.'

Shauna wraps the biscuits in a napkin. 'Take these down for Tom Bogey; if she won't eat them he will.'

'And watch your back with that priest one,' says Mrs Cauley. 'An interview with Quinn is like fighting a yellow snake in a sandpit.'

Desmond Burke won't change his socks but he'll come for a walk down to the shrine and back again. He's got an article on woodturning that might interest Tom. He thinks he might like to look at the pictures.

'Have you never met the man?' asks Mahony as they cut across the field to join the village road.

'No.'

'Not even a glimpse?'

'No.'

'Seriously, and no one else has?'

'No, Jack Brophy only; he helped him move there.'

'So Jack could be making him up to keep the kids from running mad in the forest.'

'Tom is real. We leave food, a few necessities and he leaves woodcarvings.'

'And no one's tried to find him? To get a look at him?'

'We respect his solitude.'

'Or there's Jack Brophy to answer to?'

Desmond glances up at Mahony with the trace of a smile. 'There's that too I suppose.'

'Why do you think Jack protects him?' Mahony asks.

'He's a guard; he has a sense of duty.'

Mahony tries not to snort.

Desmond refuses go any further than Roadside Mary, not even for a pint.

'When was the last time you had a pint?' asks Mahony.

'Do you know, I can't even remember,' smiles Desmond.

They sit down by the side of the road under the ruddy gaze of the Holy Mother.

'Tom left something,' says Desmond. He passes it to Mahony. 'It's hawthorn, I think. He uses this kind of wood often.'

Mahony takes it and turns it over in his hands. It's a small round bee, its wings folded along its back and stripes scored over its abdomen. It is cleverly made and no bigger than a conker. Mahony goes to hand it back.

'Take it.'

'Ah no, I've nothing to give him.'

'Take it anyway. It doesn't matter.'

From here Mahony can see the rooftops of the village houses as Mulderrig unravels below them. He can make out the road curving round towards the quay.

'This is a place of remarkable beauty, Mahony.'

'It's that all right.'

'Will you stay?' asks Desmond, quickly, awkwardly.

'I hadn't thought—'

'No. Right so.'

They look out over the village. Birds alight on television aerials and chimney pots. Dogs bark at washing lines or at nothing. Someone somewhere is singing along to a radio. Above the bay the seagulls turn in the air.

Mahony hauls himself up. 'Now you're sure you won't come down for a pint with me?'

'No, son, I'm best off left quiet.'

Mahony nods and leaves Desmond Burke sitting by the side of the road, gazing down upon the town.

Michael Hopper opens the door to the parochial house and lets Mahony into the hallway, which smells like an open peat bog. Mahony watches as a gaggle of frogs flop down the stairs and wriggle under the library door one by one. Michael Hopper seems not to notice; he is more intent on trying to get Mahony's jacket off his back. Mahony wonders if the old man is trying to frisk him.

'Go into the kitchen there and I'll go an' tell the Father you're here. Róisín is cleaning out the oven on account of it being as black as the devil's eyebrows.'

'Where's Bridget?'

'Father Quinn had to let her go.' Michael Hopper leans forward so that his nose is an inch away from Mahony's face. 'He caught her selling water from the holy spring in the library by the bucket.'

'The holy spring?'

'Didn't the priest insult Mrs Lavelle's horse trough by disbelieving in it? Well, now its big brother is here.' The corners of Michael's mouth twitch into a contemptuous smile. 'He's had a rake of plumbers in, from as far as Westport even. They've searched high and low for leaking pipes and left scratching their heads and their arses.'

Róisín has her sleeves rolled up to her armpits and her hair is wet with effort. Mahony feels like pulling her out of the oven by her ankles and planting kisses on every last bit of her. He tugs at the back of her apron until she laughs.

'Behave yourself, Mahony. Father Quinn has asked me to get this place up to scratch before the new housekeeper starts.'

'Who is the new housekeeper?'

Róisín puts down the scourer and pushes her hair out of her eyes. 'Well, that's the problem. With the holy spring and everything he's having difficulty filling the position. I said I'd stand in till he finds one.'

'The place is taking on a cursed aspect,' mutters Michael Hopper, heading to the door. 'It was never so in Father Hennessy's day, God rest him. I'll go and see if himself is ready.'

Mahony lets go of Róisín's apron and helps her to her feet, grinning to see her blush as he pulls her towards him.

'Mahony—'

Michael Hopper comes back into the room wiping his hands delicately on the seat of his trousers. 'He'll see you now. Only don't let on you notice the spring or he'll get as mad as a wet hen.'

Michael glances at Róisín, who is scrubbing the hob with serious dedication. 'Father said would you be so kind as to do out the scullery before making his meal. He'll have the fish and the lightly steamed vegetables.'

Róisín nods and continues her work with her smile bright and her eyes brilliant.

Father Eugene Quinn has positioned himself behind the desk in front of the bay window. Hearing the knock on the library door he takes up his fountain pen to lend himself an air of authority.

'Enter.'

Mahony keeps to the edge of the room as he heads to the desk but, even so, the water goes halfway up his boots. The room is pleasantly warm, with the feeling of a tropical glasshouse about it. Water gushes happily up from the root of the spring just near the fireplace and a thick layer of frogs seethe in heathen ecstasy where the hearthrug used to be. Father Quinn looks rigidly unperturbed; he is wearing rubber boots and his chair is covered in waterproof sheeting.

'I like what you've done with the place, Father. It's like the outdoors indoors.'

'Sit down, Mahony.'

'I'd rather stand.' Mahony leans against a bookcase where sodden books sink in their spines.

The priest looks at him with a profound dislike. 'I won't beat about the bush. I've called you here because I have a proposal for you.'

'Yeah?' Mahony lights a fag and holds out the packet to the priest, who shakes his head.

'An anonymous member of the community wishes to become your benefactor.'

'Those frogs are having a great time of it on your rug there, Father.'

Father Quinn peels apart some papers on his desk. 'This generous individual, who wishes to remain nameless, is offering you a truly wonderful opportunity. The sort of opportunity that a man like you ought to be extremely grateful for.'

'If those are all St Brigid's tears she had an awful lot of crying to do, God bless her.'

As if in answer a wave laps gently at the toe of Mahony's boot.

Father Quinn's colour begins to rise, starting at the peripheries of his temples and the strip of his neck just above his collar. 'The benefactor in question would like to fund your passage to America.'

'The land of opportunities, Father?'

'Indeed. They are also prepared to furnish you with a modest sum to help you start a new life. Perhaps you will even find some use there for your – various talents.'

Mahony turns and wades towards the spring with his cigarette in his mouth. He holds out his hand and the water twists and gushes affectionately towards him, like a cat rubbing its chin over his fingers.

'Once you have accepted I'm to furnish you with a ticket and personally escort you to the airport.'

Father Quinn unlocks his desk drawer and extracts a banded pile of banknotes. 'And just before I see you onto a plane and wave you goodbye I'm to give you this.' He lays them on the desktop. 'It is all here for the taking, Mahony. Everything you need to begin your new life without delay.'

Mahony smiles and sculls to the edge of the desk and sits down on it, smoking thoughtfully.

'That's a big pile of money there, Father.'

Father Quinn nods. 'It is.'

'And this generous benefactor wants me to go to America?'

'They do.'

'To make my fortune and then come home a rich man?'

The priest's smile is unwavering. 'There would be no coming home, if by home you mean Mulderrig. That's the only stipulation your benefactor makes.'

Mahony laughs. 'And why the hell would I come back to Mulderrig if I was living the high life in the U-S-of-A?'

'Precisely,' says Father Quinn.

Mahony stubs out his cigarette in Father Quinn's antique inkpot, leans forward and picks up the money. It's a lot of money. Closely bound, with perfect edges, neat, clean, new. Someone made a special visit to the bank for this. Mahony smiles at Father Quinn and the priest shows him every single one of his long teeth in return.

'Father Quinn, I would like to thank this kind benefactor from the bottom of my heart for their generosity. But I can't leave Mulderrig. Call it unfinished business.'

Father Quinn's smile drops right off his face. 'If you're holding out for more, Mahony—'

'Not at all.' Mahony puts the money down on the desk

and smiles at the priest. 'You should know, money isn't everything, Father.'

Father Quinn's eyes bulge out of his head. 'You won't get another offer, Mahony. I'd advise you to take the money.'

'And no doubt that would be sound advice. But if it's all the same I'll leave it.' He holds up his empty hands. 'Well, it's been grand gassin' with you, Father. I'm sure I'll be seeing you around.'

Mahony walks towards the door and Father Quinn sees, with an unholy variety of rage, that at each step the water ripples back to leave only dry carpet beneath Mahony's feet.

Chapter 24

May 1976

'Now I'd say that this was deliberate, wouldn't you?' says Bridget, holding up the severed end of the metal flex. The stage is littered with fallen scaffold.

'Who's in charge of the lighting, Mahony?'

'Eddie Callaghan's nephew.'

'And has he got it in for you?'

Mahony kicks the shattered casing of a spotlight. 'Not that I know of.'

Bridget stands up. 'If you hadn't jumped out of the way in time—'

'I did though.'

Bridget looks closely at him. 'You had your back to it, Mahony. How in God's name did you see that coming?'

Mahony smiles. Over by the curtain, Johnnie takes a bow.

Chapter 25

May 1944

She told Father Jim she had nothing inside the house to
give him and pulled the door to behind her so that he
wouldn't catch sight of the state of Mammy in the chair.
Father Jim said not to worry, that it was her he'd come to
see. He asked if she'd like to walk with him.

They went down to the cliffs and the priest took off his
coat and they sat side by side on it. It had been a fine
morning but now full-bellied rainclouds bruised the sky for
miles. Over the horizon the sun was breaking through a
bank of cloud; it skimmed the sea with mackerel streaks of
light.

Father Jim turned to her and asked her if she was still
conversing with the dead. Orla refused to meet his gaze.

'And the notes, Orla? Any more of those?'

She let her fingers run through the grass.

'The town's in uproar.' Father Jim looked out at the
sea. 'When they settle down again they'll find they mostly
don't believe Benny Ganley. I've done what I can to smooth
things over but you have to promise me that there'll be
no more.'

'Did you believe Benny Ganley?'

Father Jim smiled. 'I know my own mother's handwriting. But I also know that she's been gone eighteen years.'

Orla studied her palms and spoke quietly. 'They're liars and cheats the lot of them. I was only after giving them the truth.'

Father Jim nodded, then he said, 'I've a job for you, keep you out of trouble.'

Orla scowled down at her knees.

'I could use some help down at the house. Bridget has taken over from Mother Doosey in the housekeeping department.' He lowers his voice. 'She's entirely clueless, so you'd be doing me a great favour.'

Orla glanced up at him. His face was brown and spare and his jaw looked like it could stand a few punches. He wasn't flabby around the gizzard like some old fellas.

He didn't look like a priest at all. He looked like a cowboy.

No, he looked like a sheriff. A sheriff who could ride a mad crazy horse and shoot a gun straight. Who'd seen a lot of action and was maybe on the wrong side of the law himself once.

'I'll think about it,' she said.

As the priest walked her home he talked about the state of Bridget's cooking and had her grinning into her hair. Once or twice she laughed out loud but she disguised it as a cough.

After he left her home she climbed up on the gate and watched him out of sight, willing him not to turn round to wave like an eejit. He didn't. He just kept on walking with the gait of a man who had temporarily mislaid his horse. She cocked an imaginary pistol at him, taking aim along the steady edge of her finger. But not being the kind of girl to shoot a cowboy in the back, she holstered it again, sent a spit over the wall and ran back into the house.

The job wasn't so bad. Every Wednesday and Friday Orla was to help Bridget dust the library, clean the fireplaces, wash the windows and scrape the dirt off the vegetables for the dinner. Then they would cook the meal, and if there wasn't a visitor, which there never was, Father Jim would join them at the kitchen table and they'd all eat together.

Orla was quiet at first. She'd sit and eat and listen to the two of them talking. It was then that she realised Bridget was cleverer than she looked. That she'd had a dream of going to university but that she'd had to stay and look after her mammy until it was too late for her. Sometimes Bridget took Orla to see the litter of kittens she had hidden in the turf shed. Orla thought that Bridget was a bit old for kittens but she didn't say anything because of the way Bridget smiled at her. Soon Orla was smiling back, even though she felt a little goofy with all of it. Bridget told Orla she could take a kitten and Orla picked a black one with green eyes. Bridget laughed and told her she'd chosen a witch's cat.

After dinner Father Jim would bring Orla home. He said it was so he could walk off Bridget's puddings but Orla knew it was because of the kids that lay in wait for her on the edge of town with their pockets full of stones.

Bridget always gave Father Jim a few bits in a basket to carry up to the house: a bar of soap, a loaf of bread, or a twist of tea. As they walked, Father Jim would tell Orla stories about Jesus. They were so boring she could hardly listen. Instead she would study her shoes and nod as if she was concentrating hard.

One evening, as he walked her home, Father Jim told her a story that wasn't boring. They were a little later than usual, for it was Bridget's birthday and they'd had cake after the dinner. The sun was setting through the forest and it would be dark soon, but for a while there was the orange of the dying sun and the black of the trees against it, like a warning.

Whether it was these colours that made Father Jim think of the story, Orla never knew, but this was the first story he had ever told her that made her forget to look as if she was concentrating.

And it wasn't about Jesus.

Once upon a time, he said, in a quiet village, there lived a woman. She was a good woman who kept busy about her tidy cottage. She had a few hens that laid eggs. She sold the eggs and saved the money from them against a donkey so that she wouldn't have to walk the long miles to market. The hens lived in an outhouse that she had made strong against the foxes that would sniff about outside all night long, slavering for the plumpness and the freshness of the hens.

One day the woman was collecting the eggs in her little basket when she came across an egg the likes of which she'd never seen before. She put down her basket and carried the egg out of the henhouse and into the light. It was nearly five times the size of a normal egg, and the shell felt thicker and silkier. It was pure white but with a shifting cast of gold and when she held it up to her ear she heard a smooth ticking sound.

The woman looked at the egg for a long while, then she picked up one of her quietest hens and she brought both hen and egg into her cottage. She set up a box by the range and filled it with clean straw then set the hen over the egg. At first the hen clucked angrily and moved away, but the woman was patient and she picked up the hen time

· 199 ·

and again and put her back on the egg. She fed the hen with strips of bread soaked in warm milk until the hen was content and closed its eyes and curved its beak down into its soft, feathered neck.

The woman fed the hen day after day until the hen grew fat and its eyes grew glazed, and still it sat on the egg. The woman began to despair that the egg would ever hatch, so one day she lifted up the hen to see if there were any cracks yet in the wondrous egg.

And she saw, with great confusion, that the egg was gone and the hen was dead.

She felt the hen all over. Its belly was bloated hard and it was heavy in her hands. She put the bird back into the box and stared at it. All of a sudden, the hen's neck flopped backward, showing the gullet.

The woman watched, riveted in horror, as something began to move inside the dead bird's throat. Now drawing it taut, now laying it loose.

A bloody beak began to tear through the neck of the dead hen. The woman hardly had the wits to scream. The beak was followed by a head, which poked obscenely out of the dead bird's carcass smeared in gore and blinking its eyes. And so the woman realised that the poor hen had hatched a chick so monstrous that it had eaten her from the inside out.

The woman fought against the repulsion rising in her as she carried the box outside with shaking hands. The chick, halfway out of the dead hen, was as soft and naked as an earthworm. It squinted up at her with its swollen eyelids half-closed against the sun. The woman tried not to look at the terrible chick as she banked dry wood around the body of the hen. The chick opened its beak and sang quietly. The woman tried not to hear its small song as she added newspaper to make the fire burn quicker. The chick tried the stumps of its wings, flapping about in the box as the woman added turf to make the fire burn deeper.

The woman lit the fire she had set and watched it burn with her heart sickened over the poor dead hen and the monstrous chick. Then, no longer able to stand it, she returned to her cottage and shut the door and sat by the range looking at the empty space on the ground where the box had been.

The next day the woman went to the scorched smear in the courtyard and began to sweep up the ashes.

As she did so, something moved beneath her brush.

Before her eyes a blackened ball was collecting itself, rolling over the ground and drawing itself upward. The graphite dust whirled tighter and tighter to become more and more densely packed and sparkling. It grew bigger, blacker, sharper, until it formed an undeniable shape, not unlike a swan, only bigger. It opened its wings and rushed up into the air.

The ashes fell away, so that the bird was revealed as it circled above the woman. Its body was the colour of copper lit from the inside. Its tail feathers were a fierce orange that flashed and burnt as the bird flew around the roof of the cottage. It landed on a chimneystack from where it looked down the length of its beak at the woman with long almond eyes the colour of hot iron.

And the woman finally saw that what is terrible can also be beautiful and she lifted up her arms to the bird as it flew away into the west.

The woman cried for a long time, then she wiped her face on her apron and got up from her knees. As she walked back to the hen house to shut her hens away from the hungry foxes, something caught her eye.

It was a gift from the firebird.

A feather lay smouldering in the mud. It was the rich red of a velvet-lined trinket box, a deep, secret red. It was longer than her forearm and curved from root to tip, like a foxglove. The woman picked it up and found that it was warm to the touch and soft against her lips. She took it into her house and heated a candle. Then she carefully pushed the quill of the firebird's feather into the softened wax. For the rest of her life the feather glowed. She set it at the window, in case the bird ever flew her way again.

Chapter 26

May 1976

In the parochial library Father Eugene Quinn and the Widow Annie Farelly are sitting pious and silent, clad in rubber boots and a rain bonnet respectively, and stalwartly ignoring the holy spring that spurts and babbles at their feet with pagan enthusiasm. Their conversation has been temporarily halted whilst Róisín sets down the tea things.

'Will I take some of the frogs out with me, Father?'

Róisín nods towards the bucket at the door, which she fills to the brim with writhing amphibians at least six times a day. But however far away she takes them the creatures always seem to find their way home again.

Yesterday she packed a crowd of them in a picnic hamper and took them on the bus all the way to Ennismore. Yet she swore the exact same frogs were waiting for her in the hallway by the time she got back again.

Róisín doesn't have the heart to kill them. As long as they keep out of the kitchen she doesn't mind them. They're even a bit of company about the place. So when Father Quinn enquires as to whether she's destroying them as he asked her to, she bursts into song, or pretends not to hear, so that Father Quinn begins to think that Mrs Munnelly is a little touched.

'No, that will be all, thank you, Róisín.'

Now Róisín will tell you that she's not at all the type of individual usually given to listening at doors. But there's something in the way that the priest looks at her as she leaves the room. Or maybe it's the cat-cream way in which Annie Farelly raises her teacup to her mouth. Or perhaps it's a certain bitter smugness on both their faces.

So that when Róisín closes the library door, God forgive her, she kneels down on the hall runner and puts her ear to the gap under the door to listen.

'As I said, I support you, Father, one hundred and ten per cent. For if the late Father Hennessy (God rest his soul and reward him in heaven) had helped us to control the mother before she even had her issue we would not be experiencing the infestation of Mahony himself now. As you well know, Father Hennessy advocated tolerance and forgiveness, of all things, when there she was running wild and sticking her fingers up at the lot of us. I can say that it angered a great many people. They simply did not understand why Father Hennessy wouldn't act to remove Orla Sweeney from the village.'

'Tolerance and forgiveness have their place but not when the moral fabric of a town is threatened.'

'Quite so. There was a blessing in Father Hennessy's passing that brought you to Mulderrig, Father Quinn.'

'You nursed Father Hennessy?'

'I was with him when he died.'

'Did he ever regret his stance on this matter?'

'I believe he did in the end, Father.'

'But yet the town loved him?'

'Ah, the town will be in your pocket soon enough,

Father. It's just a case of them getting used to you. How long have you been with us now?'

'Twenty-six years.'

Róisín smiles behind the door.

'Ah well, they are slow, Father. In most things they are very slow. And so Mahony refused the money?'

'He did. He's adamant he's staying.'

'And he couldn't be encouraged to leave by a greater sum of money, Father? Perhaps his anonymous benefactor could increase their donation? I'm sure that would be feasible, given the circumstances.'

'I don't think so. Mahony believes he is here on a mission. He says that he has unfinished business.'

There is the bright sound of silver on china.

'Thank you, Father, just one lump.'

Róisín removes a toad intent on burrowing into her hair.

'You see Mahony believes that his mother met with a bad end, and of course Mrs Cauley with her *imagination* is egging him on.'

'She is a truly awful individual. I've heard that they were interrogating people up at the village hall during the auditions.'

'They did, Mrs Farelly; they treated them like crime suspects.'

'How dare they? And then of course the play, which is no more than a chance for her to spread her wanton influence. With him cavorting on the stage, half-dressed and spewing profanities. But the people are enraptured by him, are they not, Father?'

'His growing popularity is of mild concern to me.'

'Mrs Cauley planned it that way, of course. Mahony has his feet under the table now, so to speak. Can't you stop that play?'

'I only wish I could, Mrs Farelly.'

There's a pause and a faint murmur, and Father Quinn's voice again, softly. 'I hope you understand, I had to ask.'

'I don't know any more than you do, Father.'

'Could the girl really have left town, baby and all?'

'It's possible, but . . .'

Silence.

'Would it be fair to surmise that someone took the matter into their own hands?'

'I think it would, Father.'

'Some poor soul finally driven to act, through desperation?'

'Yes, Father.'

'Then God forgive them.' A sly tone comes into Father Quinn's voice. 'Sometimes there's no agency in digging up the past, is there, Mrs Farelly?'

'None whatsoever.'

'Whatever grounds Mahony is here on, whether justified or not, he is clearly a corrupting influence on our village.'

'He is, Father.'

The priest sounds louder and brisker, as if he's got up and is pacing the room.

'I can assure you, Mrs Farelly, that I shall preserve the good in this town and protect the villagers by removing this second threat quickly and cleanly.'

'The village will thank you for it, Father.'

Róisín frowns and extracts a small frog from her cleavage.

'I spoke to Jack Brophy to see if the guards could assist us with this matter. I told him that I have reason to believe that Mahony poses a serious threat to Mulderrig. I said that in my considered opinion the man is mentally unstable.'

'What did Jack say, Father?'

'He said he's had a few jars with Mahony and he seems like a grand lad.'

Róisín smiles.

'Brophy told me that unless Mahony stepped out of line there was nothing he could do.'

A momentary silence falls in the library.

'Just how difficult can it be to encourage the illegitimate son of an underage whore to step out of line?' says Father Quinn, his voice oiled and crawling.

'Exactly, Father, exactly, but if he doesn't?'

'He will.'

'But he's a cute one; he has the village on his side.'

There's a long pause.

'Couldn't we find out a bit more about him, Father, something that would put people off him? He's come wearing his best face. He may have left another one behind in Dublin.'

'Bravo, Mrs Farelly. I'll start digging today.'

'There's sure to be a rake of dirt on a man like him. You could start at the orphanage perhaps?'

'St Anthony's? I have it in my notebook here.'

There is a low murmur that Róisín doesn't quite catch, and then they both laugh.

Róisín shakes her head in dismay. For the widow and the priest have become even more unwholesome than the snub-nosed toad sat in front of her licking its own eyeball.

Róisín shuts herself in the kitchen. She takes her apron off and puts it on again. She picks up a potato and starts peeling it in an agony of indecision.

She has to go and warn him. Róisín looks down at the potato. But if she runs out now the priest might guess that she's been eavesdropping. She drops the potato into the bowl in the sink. She'll find Mahony later and tell him exactly what she's heard.

She'll tell him to watch out for himself.

As Róisín rinses the cut potatoes and sets them on the hob she thinks about Mahony. As Róisín rolls the priest's liver in flour she thinks about Mahony. As she cuts onions into the pan, ready for the meat, she thinks about Mahony.

She blots her eyes with the hem of her apron, realising that they are watering more than they ought to be. As she slides the liver from the pan into a warming dish Róisín finally admits to herself that she's in love with him. She's in love with him wildly, against each and every sensible thought. Róisín sobs into her apron and the frogs watch her sympathetically from just outside the kitchen door, like a row of polite cinemagoers.

By coincidence, it just so happens that right now Mahony is thinking on Róisín Munnelly as he sits in an empty kitchen at Rathmore House with no more company than a dead tomcat and a dozen dusty jam jars. The dead cat stares back at him with an expression of complicated disdain. For Mahony has just informed the cat that he has a powerful liking for the lovely Mrs Munnelly.

The dead cat looks pointedly around the room. At Shauna's slippers by the backdoor, her cardigan over the back of the chair, and the pot she's not long set to boil.

Then the cat turns the dim lamps of its dead eyes back to Mahony and fixes him with a provoking glare, as if waiting for an answer.

Mahony shakes his head. Shauna doesn't come into this. She's already spoken for by her future. She has the whole thing planned out.

The cat looks doubtful.

Mahony lights a cigarette and pictures Shauna's Future drawing nearer.

Mahony can see him now, Shauna's Future, driving into town. Red-faced, palms wet, with his hair brushed flat and a ring in his back pocket.

First off, he'll be a wholesome, hard-working lad, a fine upstanding young fella. You couldn't wish for better. With a good job, a good name, a pure heart and his mammy and daddy's blessing.

Even so, he's hardly worthy of her, he knows that – Jesus, who would be? But he's solemnly vowed to God and every last saint in heaven that he'll make Shauna happy, or he'll die at her feet trying.

He'll be walking up the path soon, Shauna's Future, wiping his hands on the backside of his trousers, ready to say his bit. Maybe he'll surprise her when she's pegging out the washing, go down on the knee, do it properly. Blushing to the tops of his ears. Maybe he'll even cry a little bit when she accepts him.

He'll shake hands with her father and Desmond will give him a pen, or a cravat even. Mrs Cauley will pretend not to like him at first, but who could take against a young fella so obviously in love?

Mahony glances out the door, expecting to see him hovering on the doorstep, hand raised, eyes shy.

The dead cat softens its glare and lowers itself on its haunches, wrapping its tail around itself. It blinks. And so?

Róisín is a grown woman; she has ten years on him, Jesus, she knows what she wants and it isn't a husband. She has one; she doesn't need another.

The dead cat looks unconvinced.

There'd be no risk. They wouldn't get caught; he'd make

sure of it. For how could she hold her head up around town if anyone found out?

He imagines a thousand opportunities. In the forest, tangled together in the tree roots. Or rolling on a down-coast beach as the gulls scud overhead and the sea rings the shingle. There will be a million looks darting between them: in the street, in the town, at the Post Office and General Store. There'll be the sudden sparks of a hundred accidental touches as Mahony helps her on with her coat, or carries her bag for her, or hands her up onto the bus. And when he looks at this trim housewife in her respectable dress, with her hair neat and gleaming, he'll know that he's loved every last inch of her and that his kisses burn her skin still.

The dead cat yawns and stretches and jumps down through the table.

Mahony lights another fag. He'll wait for the rain to calm down a bit then he'll take a walk into town and find her.

Mahony flicks his cigarette into the ashtray on the table.

It's a great ashtray, *A Souvenir from Mulderrig*, with all the local sights picked out in bright paint: the quay, the pub and the River Shand.

He stares at it.

Mahony twists out his fag and gets up to find his boots.

Mahony looks out at the river. Shaded by the overhead branches it looks wide and dark. A tide of scum laps at the edges but otherwise it's still. Too still.

He takes off his underpants and drapes them over a bush next to his jacket and his trousers. Now he's only wearing his socks; when he takes them off he'll have to go in.

The questions he's been asking himself all the way from Rathmore House are still clattering around his brain.

If the sack wasn't full of kittens, what then?

Something the killer had kept?

Something he needed to lose?

And why here, all those years later?

And Ida, surely that was no accident?

Mahony takes off one sock, then the other, and balls them together. He slaps his arse and his legs a couple of times to get the blood up.

As he looks around, he feels a bit on display here. Surely it's only the birds watching up in the trees, or the odd badger or squirrel having a good laugh at his antics?

They should wait and see his breaststroke.

Mahony climbs down the bank and lowers himself into the dense silt that smells like sump-water, and dear fuck it's cold.

But at least it behaves like water should, for Mahony had half expected a quicksand to grip him and suck him straight down. But the river lets him move into it with no more retaliation than to draw green-flecked tidelines on his thighs and stomach as he wades in deeper.

He strikes out and swims towards Denny's Ait.

And the river changes.

It's as if the river is fighting against him. An undercurrent rips below the surface and he cannot swim through it, however hard he tries.

Mahony steps out of the water, sleek and shaking, pale and cursing. He pulls his clothes over wet skin and picks up his boots.

As he walks back through the forest he hardly notices the ferns wave and flatten behind him. Once or twice he glances over his shoulder, perhaps sensing something. But seeing nothing, he carries on his way.

Chapter 27

May 1976

Just out of town, up on the brow of a hill, lies a cottage nearly as ancient as the dolmen it has sight of just across the field. Mahony draws nearer to it, carrying a bag that has trailed an unholy stench all the way from Rathmore House. At the gate he puts the bag down to untie the rash of difficult knots, for Bridget Doosey doesn't encourage visitors and it is testimony to her clean-living lifestyle that she can still throw her leg over her garden gate whenever she herself wants to come and go.

Hidden eyes watch Mahony's meandering progress from gate to turnip patch, from turnip patch to runner-bean wigwam. For there is more life in Bridget Doosey's garden than you can imagine. Maybe it's due to the nearness of the dolmen, or maybe it's due to the real love she pours into the good black soil, but a lot more than rhubarb grows here.

Mahony spots her, headfirst in a flowerbed. 'Your garden's a picture, Bridget.'

Bridget squints up at him. There are stripes of soil across each cheek as if she's been trying out camouflage.

'Fish heads.' Mahony flaps the bag at his side.

'You'd better come in then,' says Bridget, with a feral look in her eyes.

The house is dark with a foxy musk smell, a smell that rolls out along the hallway in place of a carpet. Luxuriant patches of many-coloured cat fur adorn every surface. Constellations of saucers moulder about the place, showing dried milk rings or licked smears of tripe. Some of the feline residents greet Mahony and his irresistible cargo. Others just watch benignly from a felted card table or a cobwebbed window ledge. Bridget pushes forwards, kicking furry pelts aside as she goes.

'Come through to the kitchen.'

As she opens the kitchen door Mahony considers burying his nose in the bag in order to save his life. For the smell that issues from Bridget Doosey's kitchen is antique and complicated, rich and vile. It's a thousand boiled fish spines and a hundred fossilised cat craps. It's decades of damp washing, rancid fat and stale dishwater.

Bridget beckons Mahony past a cracked Formica table, thick with cats, to a cooker painted with grease. She points to a lidded pot flecked with fish scales. Mahony knows this to be the epicentre of the smell.

'Tip 'em in there. I cook 'em up for the creatures to aid the digest. All those lovely salty-eyed fish snouts. Now, I suppose you'll be wanting the cup of tea and the bit of softness, won't you? I have a half loaf of fruit bread that'll still be decent if I give it a bit of a scrape.'

'Ah no, I won't need a thing. I just came with them from Shauna. I'll be off now.'

'You won't. You'll sit down there and drink a cup of tea with me.'

She leans forward and pats his arm. 'I have the list you wanted.' She searches amongst the cats on the table and liberates a crumpled piece of paper from under a sleeping tortoiseshell.

Mahony casts his eye over it. The title reads: *Men from Mulderrig (between the ages of 15 and 80) and its Environs with the Use of a Vehicle During the Summer of 1949*.

Mahony nods and, keeping his breathing shallow, folds the list and puts it in his back pocket.

Mahony has an ashtray at his elbow, a mug of whiskey in his hand and a young white cat with pink-rimmed eyes nuzzling against his ear. It reminds him of Shauna, so he gives it a little stroke, for he's enjoying his visit now, as Shauna said he would, despite the fish heads.

Bridget is getting used to him too, for although she continues to break wind extravagantly she has stopped looking around herself in surprise.

'You have the garden lovely.' Mahony lets the slim white cat slip onto his lap, where she settles, spiralling down to the size of a pair of boot socks.

Bridget nods, with a terrible glint in her eye. 'I do, but there's no getting away from the fairy host issuing forth every night across my rhubarb.' She lowers her voice. 'That dolmen is a gateway to the underworld you know.'

The dead old woman by the back door glances up to the heavens and takes hold of a faint broom. Mahony recognises Mother Doosey from the graveyard; she twitches the corner of her mouth in greeting. Cats scatter as she cuts a path through the kitchen.

'So you leave out a saucer of milk out for the good people, Bridget?'

'Now that would attract the dead. Mary Lavelle knocks the head off Teasie whenever the poor girl forgets to put the milk away. She says that even a dribble of it will have her coming home to find a load of thirsty ghosts drawing up to her kitchen table, rubbing their cold little hands.'

Mother Doosey sweeps past looking skeptical.

'She has Teasie building a ring of rocks round the house now,' says Bridget. 'It's not so successful with the dead but it's great against the devil. Interferes with his hearing apparently.'

Mahony smiles. 'Do you believe in what she sees?'

'Each to their own, that's what I believe. If Mary Lavelle wants to see ghosts and bloody spectres hanging from her curtains, that's up to her.'

'She says that the dead were resurrected when I walked back into town.'

'As if you haven't enough demons to deal with?' Bridget fixes him with shrewd eyes. 'As you know yourself, Mahony, you've more to fear from the living.'

By the back door Mother Doosey nods gravely and drifts out into the garden to stand with her hands pressed into the downcurve of her back, gazing up at the passing clouds.

Bridget smiles at him. 'I'll tell you what though, I'll worry about the dead the day they work out how to poison a scone.'

Mahony laughs.

Bridget picks up a fork and scratches her head with it meditatively. 'I've got something for you, in exchange for your visit.' She points the fork at him. 'It takes great strength of character to walk five miles with a bag of fish heads, don't think I don't know that.'

'So you were testing me?' Mahony laughs.

'I know your mettle.' Bridget narrows her eyes. 'You're your mother's boy.'

Chapter 28

May 1976

Mahony concentrates hard on the flies circuiting the light bulb. The bulb itself is ordinary, naked for a shade; it hangs down on a fifteen-foot cord, to the left of the middle of the ceiling. It has dictated the position of the furniture in the room; it is directly above Mrs Cauley's bed. The bulb is a hot spot around the clock. Later on, when the flies lay off, the moths will take over.

Mrs Cauley is propped up in bed wearing an auburn wig, powder-blue crêpe de Chine and a frown. She's not watching the flies. She's watching Mahony. Only sometimes her eyes turn to the suitcase on the low table between them. Mahony screws out his cigarette and gets up off his chair. He goes over to the French doors and leans against the frame. Johnnie and Father Jim are drifting up and down the veranda, driven outside by the tension. Father Jim is holding forth, deeply engaged in a sermon of sorts, Johnnie meanders alongside him, looking down at his feet with his hands clamped over his ears.

Mahony will go out to them. He'll have a walk and clear his head. He'll hear what Father Jim has got to say.

Then maybe he'll go down to the bay. Then maybe out to sea, and to America even, keeping Mulderrig, Rathmore House and the suitcase firmly at his back at all times.

'Christ on a crutch, Mahony, will you open the case and be done with it?'

Mahony pushes out against the doorframe and turns. 'I will, yeah.'

Mrs Cauley feels for him, she really does, so she speaks gently. 'Let's start by running through what Bridget told you.'

He sits back down on the chair.

'Inside that case are the worldly possessions of your mother.'

There is a frayed pink ribbon tied around the handle.

Mrs Cauley continues. 'When your grandmother died, Bridget went up to the house and she found these things and saved them. Maybe to prove to herself that Orla and her baby had existed, maybe to keep them in case Orla ever returned.'

The lock has rusted.

'Open the case, Mahony. You need to know what's inside.'

One of the hinges will break as he opens it. It has held on for such a long time.

Some things are too much.

Inside there are baby clothes. Little vests, a knitted cardigan with ducks on the buttons and a pile of folded nappies, yellow with age. There's a pair of shoes, black patent and worn at the heels. Mahony cradles one in his hand and looks inside. The shape of her toes is still pressed into them. There's a dress made of shiny fabric, with the ghost of a stain under each armpit, a few blouses in differing sizes and a coat with a badly ripped lining. At the bottom of the case they find a purse with money in it, a play script and a silver-backed hairbrush, deeply tarnished. Caught in it are several long inky hairs.

Mahony doesn't feel Mrs Cauley's hand on his arm. He doesn't hear her say his name.

He kicks over the table and walks out of the room.

There's beauty today in the changing landscape. The sky is a freshly washed blue and the wildflowers along the road bend their bright heads, dipping through the long grass. Birds spin through the glass air to land on washing lines and survey lawns sprinkled with breakfast crusts.

It's the time of the day when mammies shake out the dead with the doormats and set about making the dinner. They catch sight of Mahony from a casement window, or an angled mirror, or a propped-open back door. Then the housewives of Mulderrig patter out to stand on their door-steps with a dustpan in hand, or a bowl of peelings, or a clutch of eggshells. Mahony strides past without a nod or a smile, with his hair whipped back off his face and his gypsy eyes burning.

They've never seen anyone like this: a Mayo Heathcliff. All curses and windstorm, black passion and fury. The women watch him until he is out of sight, for he's as compelling as the weather.

If they saw what followed him, well, they wouldn't wonder at the speed of his feet. For the dead are drawn to those with shattered hearts. They flit down from barns and outhouses, and dart out from attic rooms and cowsheds to join in the march.

'Róisín, always a pleasure.'

'What's happened here, Mrs Cauley?'

The contents of the suitcase are strewn across the floor.

From the bed Mrs Cauley is endeavouring to hook a nappy rag with a back scratcher. She sinks back into her pillows.

'An autopsy; would you be so kind as to put all that back, Róisín?'

'Of course.'

Róisín kneels on the edge of the rug and starts to fold. 'Is Mahony here?'

'He's not. He went out for a walk.'

'Do you know where he was heading?'

'I don't.'

Róisín nods. She hesitates to reach out for a little white knitted cardigan.

'Where did all this come from?'

'It belonged to his mother.'

Róisín recoils slightly. 'You ought not to keep this in the house.'

'Why not?' says Mrs Cauley reasonably.

Róisín continues folding the piles into the case. 'It can't do Mahony any good. He needs to move on.'

Mrs Cauley's smile drops a notch. 'Mahony needs to find out what happened to his mother – that's why he came here.'

Róisín shakes her head. 'No disrespect, Mrs Cauley, but this is someone's life you're meddling with, someone's feelings.'

Mrs Cauley licks her lips slowly. 'Meddling?'

Róisín gets up off the floor and brushes her knees. 'I know you mean well, Mrs Cauley, but you're upsetting people, stirring up all these bad memories. Can't you let the past alone? Can't you let Mahony lay this to rest and get on with his life? This is certain to cause trouble for him.'

Mrs Cauley's eyes are arctic. 'What did you want with Mahony?'

'I've heard something he needs to know. That's all.'

'What is it?'

Róisín doesn't like the look on the old lady's face. 'I'd rather tell him directly.'

'We have no secrets between us, Mahony and I.'

'Well then, he can tell you after if he wants to.'

Mrs Cauley's smile doesn't falter. 'As I'm sure he will. Isn't he lucky to have a friend like you taking care of his interests?'

'Oh, I wouldn't say—'

'But still, you ought to remember your place, Róisín. You're a married woman and people gossip.'

Róisín laughs a little too loudly. 'I don't think of him like that.'

Mrs Cauley smiles up from the bed; dressed in the softest blue she's as harmless as a soapsud. 'Of course you don't, dear. You wouldn't compare a man like Mahony to your Noel, would you? Isn't Noel the only man for you?'

Róisín colours.

'You can live with Noel's psoriasis and his drinking and his old mammy in the guest room if you've the kind of love you two share. Can't you, dear?'

Róisín flares into tears and flees, dropping the kind of look on Mrs Cauley that could almost make a body feel guilty.

Alone in her library, Mrs Cauley takes out the play script and opens it. Her name is marked inside the cover: *Property of Merle Cauley.*

She was still Merle in those days.

Green-grey branches bleed from her name. They spread out across the page. Mrs Cauley touches them, traces their path. She imagines Orla, pencil in hand, dreaming. Lying on her stomach, kicking up her heels. Or sitting curled up in some quiet corner, biting her lip, absorbed, her hand moving across the paper.

Mrs Cauley turns over the page, following the branches as they weave through the words of the text, becoming darker, denser, more convoluted. They twist and writhe, weave and twine. Soon the words are hidden, obliterated, by the growing branches.

They reach downwards to form trunks and roots; they reach upwards to break apart into showers of leaves and stars. Here, a fat orange sun rises above autumn leaves. There, a winter storm cloud is caught between a tree's twiggy fingers.

Mrs Cauley turns the page and animals begin to appear in Orla's forest. A thin red fox noses delicately from one corner and a murder of flapping crows fly by, patterned deep blue and charcoal. Mrs Cauley turns the page and a hare with protruding eyes hops shyly through the undergrowth where giant black beetles swarm with great antlers.

Owls appear, moon-faced and sinister amongst the branches, in a forest shaded with heavy lines so that Mrs Cauley understands that it is night. The owls gaze down upon a crop of strange heads that sprout from tree trunks, or hang from branches, mild-eyed and pale, with blunt noses and unformed mouths and tiny starry hands.

Mrs Cauley turns the page, going deeper into the forest. A satyr-like creature grins up at her from behind a tree, with hairy haunches and a pointed chin. A swarm of bullet-headed bees pass by, with sleek plush bodies and fine gauze wings. One stares out at her with blue human eyes. Mrs Cauley turns over quickly.

On the final page there is a clearing in the forest, and a stage.

An audience has gathered. All the inhabitants of Orla's

forest are here: the fox and the satyr, the hare and the moon-faced owls. The bees are seated, with their wings folded neatly along their backs, and the mild-eyed heads bob gently in the orchestra pit. The trees at the edges of the clearing lean in a little, as if they are listening politely. Their branches are crowded with attentive crows.

The stage has red curtains and is swagged by a garland of flowers and fruit, the likes of which Mrs Cauley has never seen in nature. She holds up the script and looks closely. Each fruit is an eye: green, brown, blue. They nestle amongst the foliage, some frilled with lashes, some narrowed, some closed.

At the side of the stage lies a baby, swaddled in rose petals on a bed of ivy. At the centre of the stage stands a girl with open arms, a red curve of a smile and a halo of black hair.

Mrs Cauley wipes her face on the bed sheet. What could she have given this girl, after all? Stage lights and sequins, props and costumes, gloss and sparkle. She thinks back to the woman she was then, when Orla met her. Her sparkle a little faded, her gloss a little tarnished.

Running west, away from Dublin, the sea had stopped her. She had wavered for a while, then drifted along up the coast until she had somehow got stuck.

At first she had missed what she had left behind with a grief that threatened to unwind her. Some days she'd put on her brightest lipstick, pack her case and drag it back into the hall. She would sit there for hours, dry-eyed and rigid, between her past and her future. She felt them both, one on either side of her, whispering in her ear. Some days she even found out timetables, settled her bills, said heartfelt goodbyes.

But it was all an act; she could never go back.

She would never leave Mulderrig. But Orla . . .

She closes her eyes and sees Orla still, stepping off a bus, a boat, a train, into some new city, with her brutal eyes and her startling smile, with her brand-new baby and her second-hand coat. It is springtime, morning, and the weather is kind. And Orla has time to set the world on fire.

Chapter 29

May 1976

Out on the coast road Róisín sees Mahony ahead of her.
She hasn't the breath to call out to him. But then he's
turning, looking behind him, waiting for her. He's heard her
chain click or her wheels on the road. Before she knows it,
to spite Mrs Cauley, and despite herself, Róisín is off the
bike and up against him.

They leave her bike against a hedge and walk on together,
hardly realising they're holding hands or that a fine soft rain
has begun to fall.

By the time they reach Orla's cottage the clouds have
begun to turn inland and the sky is growing clear again.
The sun picks out the gable, lighting each wet stone.

The cottage is small and low set. Bordered on one side
by open fields and on all others by the hem of the forest,
which skirts around the back of the house and looks to be
sidling nearer yearly. The roof has long caved in and a young
ash tree grows up through the middle of the house. The
front door stands ajar, held open to the weather by a lush
clump of weeds.

The sunlight follows them inside and Mahony sees how

it illuminates the rich patterns of mould and damp, moss and lichen that cover the walls. The burnt leg of a chair is propped in the fireplace, the mantelpiece is swagged with ivy and the hearth is littered with matted feathers.

Mahony could walk from one end of his mother's house, his house, to the other in ten steps.

To the left of him there's a windowless room that smells like a cave. The roof is still intact and a sturdy lock is rusted on the door. At the other end of the cottage there is a smaller room with a hole in the wall, where the breeze from an empty window stirs the leaves around the floor.

They sit together in the middle room on Mahony's jacket. Róisín draws up her knees for something to hold. Their hips are touching and sometimes their arms and shoulders touch too.

They don't speak about loss, although it is there with them in the broken room. There's no mention of pain, but that's present too. Róisín wears the frown she shares with her daughter. Mahony regards her with his mother's eyes. They see the dead written on each other's faces. They don't mean to, but they do. Even now, drawn together in the stillness, they are not quite alone.

Mahony looks at her hand in his; she's waiting for an answer.

'So they want to get rid of me out of the town?' he says.

Róisín nods.

'Do you think they'll manage?'

She studies him closely and shakes her head.

Mahony kisses her.

★

The sun slants through the roof and onto their faces. They lie together with the smell of wet stone and earth all around them and the sea birds calling out and the wind playing over the blasted cottage.

Róisín has her hand curled on his chest. He puts his fingers in the well she makes with hers and they stay like that until she sits up and pulls her dress round her.

With this action she lets the world back in. The grief they had put out of their minds returns and insinuates itself between them. Pity will follow, and regret: here they are, pawing at the door.

Mahony drives them away; he concentrates on plotting the curve of Róisín's spine, the shape of each stacked vertebra and the freckle just under her shoulder blade. But then he sees how frail she is, how naked, her skin pale, her shoulders narrow. She is shivering in the breeze up off the sea. He wills her to get dressed, but she just sits there with her arms around her knees. Perhaps she is listening. If you listen you can hear the waves crash and fall in Mahony's cottage.

Mahony stands at the doorway. She'll go alone, she says; she has her bike. He looks around him like a man waking up. The dead have amassed; they circle the cottage at a polite distance. They stand silently, eyes lowered, their caps in their hands, as if they are paying their respects.

Róisín opens the gate and for a moment Mahony sees her framed against the coast road, captured by the setting sun, her hair coming down around her shoulders. He waits for her to turn and wave but she doesn't.

Mahony walks alone in the garden, finding things in the long grass. There are jam jars and hinges, bent spoons and pram wheels, a rusted bath of brown rainwater and a spent pitchfork. His inheritance.

He fills the jam jars with water and kicks through the brambles to the early roses that climb up the side of the cottage. They bow and dip in the breeze off the sea, confused by the clement weather, some budding, some already blown. He takes out his knife and cuts the thorny stems. Mahony puts roses in each room before he leaves. So that if his mother returns there will be light in the darkest corners of their shattered home. The dead nod and watch. Several smile, but not unkindly.

Chapter 30

May 1976

Shauna stands surrounded by towering mounds of laundry, reading the list she has found in the pocket of Mahony's trousers.

She reads: *Men from Mulderrig (between the ages of 15 and 80) and its Environs with the Use of a Vehicle During the Summer of 1949.*

> *Jack Brophy*
> *Eddie Callaghan*
> *Pat Conway*
> *Cathal Doyle (deceased)*
> *Desmond Burke*
> *Gerry Heeher*
> *Pat Keenan (deceased)*
> *Tadhg Kerrigan*
> *Dr Maurice McNulty*
> *Jimmy Nylon*

She bites her lip and reads it over again, *Desmond Burke*, and her heart beats in time with the twin tub on a spin cycle.

Chapter 31

May 1976

'Father Quinn is here to visit you, Mrs Cauley.'

Mrs Cauley purses her lips. 'And he's about as welcome as the clap.'

Father Quinn emerges into the clearing, stepping over piles of books. 'If another time would be more convenient, Mrs Cauley?'

Mrs Cauley waves him towards a footstool.

'I'll leave you to it, Father,' says Shauna, fixing Mrs Cauley with a look.

The priest sits down. The stool is uncomfortably low for a tall man. With his long legs folded awkwardly the priest has the air of a malevolent cricket.

'Thank you for seeing me, Mrs Cauley.'

'As much as I revel in your visits let's make this snappy, I've a Dubonnet and a bed bath on the agenda this afternoon.'

'It won't take long, Mrs Cauley, I can assure you.'

Mrs Cauley feels a predictive itch starting up under her wig, a sure sign that this interview is unlikely to go her way. This notion is confirmed by one glance at the priest, for he is radiating smugness.

Father Quinn rests his long hands on his elevated knees. 'It's about Mahony.'

The itch goes mad. Mrs Cauley reaches for a cocktail stirrer. 'What about him?'

'I have made some enquiries.'

'Good for you.'

'I've traced him to a variety of institutions. I have it on authority from one Father McNamara that the records from St Anthony's Orphanage alone show a history of criminal tendencies and profound instability.'

Mrs Cauley puts down the stirrer. 'Mahony had a difficult childhood. One must expect fluctuations in the development of a person of character.'

'Mahony then went on to commit a succession of offences and serve a number of custodial sentences.'

She waves her hand. 'Who cares?'

'A *succession* of offences, Mrs Cauley: disorderly conduct in a public place, affray—'

'Boyish high spirits, Father.'

'Then there's accessory to automobile theft, resisting arrest and offending public decency.'

Father Quinn watches as Mrs Cauley's lips draw a questionable curve. 'Father, haven't all God's children sinned? I know I have. I've sinned long and hard and in a multitude of different ways. Like me, Mahony is reformed.'

The priest looks at Mrs Cauley through his knees. 'You don't quite understand, Mrs Cauley. By being here Mahony is breaking his current bail terms for aggravated assault.'

'Aggravated assault?'

'With a portable electric fire,' says the priest triumphantly.

The itch goes mad.

The priest folds his hands together piously. 'You see, Mahony is a wanted man.'

'And I suppose you've told Jack Brophy all of this?'

'Not yet.'

'What do you want, Quinn?'

Father Quinn smiles. It's his biggest yet.

Mahony looks out across the veranda. Across the lawn Johnnie is stalking one of the dead housemaids. Even in death she is ruffled, her hair coming down from under her cap and a chamber pot in each hand. Mahony taps on the windowpane and shakes his head. Johnnie stops, peers back at him and hastily fastens his trousers. He flitters up to the roof of the woodshed and sits pulling at the side of his moustache with a mutinous expression.

'Low-down dirty fucker,' says Mahony.

'It's a quality I always look for in my priests,' murmurs Mrs Cauley and drains her glass. She's finished with the Dubonnet and started on the gin and grapefruit. It suits her sour mood. 'Maybe I've underestimated Quinn.'

'Well, he has all the dirt on me now.' He smiles grimly. 'I was arrested for fighting over this one at a wedding.'

'Angry boyfriend?'

'Angry bridegroom, best man and two uncles on the bride's side. It was self-defence, but the guards made sure it didn't come out that way.'

'I'm sorry, kiddo.'

'How much time will Quinn give us?'

'Three days, then he'll call in the guards.'

Mahony exhales. 'Then we don't stand a chance of finding her, do we?'

Mrs Cauley speaks softly. 'You don't know that. We could be on the verge of a breakthrough. Have you spoken to Mary Lavelle? Teasie's been coming up to the house every day asking for you. There may be something in that.'

'And what about the play?'

Mrs Cauley shrugs. 'We'll survive. Half the village know your lines.'

'And I'm not to return?'

'And you're not to return.'

Mahony nods. 'Well, we'd better get on with it then.'

Chapter 32

May 1976

Róisín waits in the forest. She looks tired, her hair unpinned, her beauty a little blurred. He's over an hour late but he just grins and bends down to kiss her.

He throws his jacket on the ground and has her lie down on it. He kneels in front of her and unbuttons his shirt. His body is very white and his hair is very dark. It runs in a line from his stomach to his chest. Here he smells of sweat, there he smells of smoke, or peat, or the sea. She looks at the light through the leaves as he moves above her.

He lights a cigarette for her and she smokes it. He says she is quite the professional now and she thinks about blowing a smoke ring as he pulls on his trousers.

She will tell him now.

That she'll come away with him. That she'll give up everything for him: husband, house, even her children. She'll leave the dishes in the sink and the school shirts soaking and the burnt pan on the hob. She'll abandon the rugs that need beating and the beds that need making.

She will follow him anywhere. Dublin. London.

They'll rent a room and stay inside it for weeks. Wearing the skin off each other. Kissing each other raw.

After a while she'll get a job in a café and smoke drugs and throw away her bras and go out dancing. They'll fight and make up again and she'll sleep in his arms every night and wake to him every morning.

He stands up and lights a fag for himself and with it in his mouth he walks over to a tree and starts to piss.

'I'm going to leave Noel for you,' she says.

Mahony almost dies. She can see it on his face. He even stops pissing.

Before he can speak she's pushing things into her bag, finding her shoes.

'Róisín . . .'

He's on the ground next to her. He knows better than to try to hold her. He lays a hand on her arm, cautiously, as if petting a stranger's dog, as if she might bare her teeth. He speaks low, calm; he tells her that it wouldn't be right, that it wouldn't be fair.

She waves her hand at his jacket on the ground. 'And this is right, this is fair?'

'It's not that I don't want you . . .'

She needs the whole sentence, so she finishes it for him. 'But there's someone else.'

Three, four heartbeats and the words she has put before him, unpicked, hang heavy. His face is stricken, his eyes bitterly kind, he takes his hand away from her arm.

Five, six heartbeats and she's on her feet, she's running through the forest knowing he won't follow her.

Chapter 33

May 1976

Teasie has had the tray set ready for a long time. There's dust on the teaspoons and an ossified moth in the sugar bowl. She shows her guest into the parlour and turns to the complicated task of handing round the tea with her nerves entirely shredded. She hopes to God he doesn't want sugar, for her hands are shaking too much to work the little tongs.

Mrs Lavelle sits silent in the corner. The room is as dirty and joyless as Mrs Lavelle herself, wearing her customary black, speckled with alluvial drifts of dandruff.

Teasie holds out a heap of soft biscuits to Mahony. Mahony smiles up at her and she almost drops the plate.

He has eyes like black sloe berries and eyelashes like a girl. His jacket smells of leather and smoke, sweat and hair oil; she knows this because she held it to her face when she hung it up in the hallway. Mahony balances his cup on his knee and asks Mrs Lavelle how she's keeping. He keeps his voice loud and bright.

Mrs Lavelle doesn't quite catch the question. A muscle twitches in her face and her hands grip the armrests. She is watching the sideboard. Her tea is getting cold on the table next to her.

Mahony turns to Teasie. 'Have you any honey to sweeten the tea?'

'I have of course, in the pantry,' she says. She leaves the door ajar behind her.

Mahony leans forward and pats Mrs Lavelle's hand. 'You have something to tell me, don't you?'

All at once, as if automated, her eyes revolve in her head. She glares at him, as unblinking as a tomcat.

'Take it with you,' she hisses. 'It belongs to you. Take it with you.'

Mrs Lavelle looks away as Teasie comes back into the room.

'I've no honey. Will treacle do?'

'I'd prefer the honey, if it's all the same.'

Teasie peers through her smudged glasses with an expression of great uncertainty. 'I could pop along to Mrs Moran and borrow a spoonful.'

'That's the plan right there! You could so, Teasie. I'll sit with your mammy. She'll be fine with me, won't you, Mrs Lavelle?'

There is no response from Mrs Lavelle; her eyes are riveted to the pot plant in the corner.

Teasie hovers.

'You'll be no sooner gone than back again.'

'Right so, I'll be a minute just.'

'Take your time,' Mahony smiles.

Teasie goes out into the hallway and takes down her overcoat from the hook, pausing only to inhale Mahony's jacket once more.

★

There's a shadow in Mrs Lavelle's front parlour, she says. It's stretched out there along the sideboard, *watching them*. It fidgets the hem of the tablecloth and fingers the china plate. It shakes the curtains and pinches the cat. Its breath flutters in the empty grate and fogs up Teasie's glasses. The shadow let itself in the day Mahony came to town and now it's taken up residence.

Mrs Lavelle tentatively brings her hand up to wipe the corners of her mouth with the handkerchief knotted in her fist.

The shadow kept to the corners at first, she says. It hid behind the dresser, under the bed, in the hatbox on top of the wardrobe.

It waited and it watched.

Soon she began to hear footsteps on the stairs, a naked little patter, sticky wet. Watery footprints began to appear, on the lino and on the carpets, up the walls and along the windowsills. The place developed an underwater smell.

They found silt on the doormat and gravel on the hearthrug.

Mrs Lavelle took to wearing a nail tied around her neck, for such shadows can't abide iron. But each morning the shoelace lay empty at her throat and the nail was gone. Soon the footsteps were iron-shod; they rang out on the kitchen flags and fell heavy up the stairs.

Soon her prayer cards were missing, and her crucifix, and her blue glass rosary beads. All gone. The shadow had eaten them.

The shadow grew braver and began to lick up the holy water she put around the place. It banged doors and left handprints in the butter dish. It threw saucers and howled down the hallway.

Mahony looks around the room. A framed portrait of

the pope, with one hand raised in blessing, hangs over the fireplace. A few parched pot plants hang on grimly in the corners, and a pair of ugly ceramic dogs grace the mantelpiece. Anything that can be covered with an antimacassar is wearing one. A good layer of dust shrouds everything else.

There is not one dead person in sight.

Mahony speaks to her very gently. 'You mustn't upset yourself, Mrs Lavelle. Sure, there's nothing here but us two. The only dead thing in this house is that moth in your sugar bowl.'

Mrs Lavelle clenches her handkerchief to her mouth and cries, 'That's because it frightened all the others away.'

Mahony's heart jumps. 'Who is it, Mrs Lavelle? Tell me.'

She shakes her head. 'Where are my pills?'

'I'll get you your pills now, Mrs Lavelle. Just tell me who you see.'

She starts to rock herself with her hands balled to fists at her sides. 'The dead pay back. You shouldn't cross them. You mustn't cross them.'

'Who did you cross, Mrs Lavelle?'

Teasie hears the screaming as she lets herself in at the gate. She runs into the parlour to see Mahony on the floor in front of her mother's chair. He has hold of her mother's knees and her mother is looking down at him in stricken horror. When Mahony sees Teasie he lets go of the old woman and immediately the screaming stops. Mrs Lavelle slumps back in the chair with her eyes closed, twitching. Teasie hears herself asking him to leave in a voice that isn't her own. In the hallway Mahony turns to her.

'I need to talk to your mother again, when she's feeling better. It's important, Teasie.'

Teasie shakes her head. 'Get out. Get out. Get out!' She

is still holding the pot of honey in her hand as she locks the door behind him.

In the parlour Mary Lavelle stares, her knuckles white on the arms of her chair. Her nightmare is crawling towards her, all along the skirting boards.

Chapter 34

March 1950

The fire was nearly out when Orla heard the sound. It wasn't one of the night sounds she knew: an owl hunting over the fields, or the mournful cry of a vixen; these sounds were familiar to her.

This sound was different. It was muffled and heavy with threat.

In a moment they were inside. Men with their caps pulled down low, stark patterns from their lanterns, shouting, knocking over chairs.

She ran to take up her baby.

A man grabbed hold of her and tried to put her arms to the sides but she was too quick. She twisted herself free and took up a bottle and broke it against the wall. She turned and pushed it into him. She saw him stagger backwards.

She looked around for her boy.

A woman stood holding him across a sea of people, moving shapes in the light. How could she swim through them?

★

She was outside. There was blood in her mouth. They'd split her lip for her. She was running into the trees. When she reached the heart of the forest she slowed and stopped and started to feel by degrees.

She would curse them all to hell for this.

She came out of the forest just before dawn and circled the town, silent and iron-eyed. By the time the sun alighted on the rooftops Orla was standing in a dew-wet garden. The back door of the house was open. In the heavy silence of the morning she heard a baby cry and went to claim her son.

Chapter 35

May 1976

'I just wanted to say fair play to you.'

Mahony, sitting outside the village hall, running through his lines and smoking, glances up.

Noel Munnelly is standing over him, tall and apologetic looking, with his right hand outstretched. His forehead is angry with blisters and his hair is badly receding. Behind him two curly-haired boys wearing matching sweaters are jumping on and off the kerb.

Mahony puts his fag in his mouth and stands up.

'For the production an' all,' says Noel.

Mahony shakes Noel's hand and manages a smile.

'Róisín hasn't been the same, since, you know. But since you've come an' all this.' Noel gestures at the empty car park. 'It's given her a new lease of life.'

The boys spin off whooping into a far corner where they slap each other and run back again.

Noel shrugs. 'That's all I wanted to say.' He nods and turns and walks away. The younger boy runs to put his hand in his father's, and Noel smiles down at him. The older boy lags behind, looking back at Mahony without curiosity.

Mahony lights another cigarette. He'll go back inside in a minute just. He runs his fingers through his hair.

Around him the dead are crowding into the car park, drifting through the low wall to line up by the dustbins. They stand watching him with pale faces.

Mahony can make out Miss Mulhearne trailing through a parked car. She hovers near the group to the right of him, steadfastly studying her own shoes.

A hushed silence falls.

Mahony recognises a courtroom when he sees one.

A dim figure pushes through the crowd and staggers towards the steps, his right sleeve blood-soaked and flapping.

'Here, Gobshite.'

Mahony looks at him.

The dead farmer glances around him and licks his lips. 'Didn't I tell you to get your own?'

In the empty car park the dead clap and jeer.

The dead farmer shuffles a little and grins. 'Time to mend your ways.' Mr McHale fondles the sodden end of his vacant shirtsleeve thoughtfully. 'And that's coming from a rotten one-armed bastard like me.'

The gathered dead agree. Their murmured assent echoes around the car park, metallic and distant, like a recording played backwards.

'Settle down,' urges Mr McHale. 'One good woman and all that.' He narrows his eyes and leans forward, so close that Mahony feels the dead man's breath on his face, as stale as the crypt. 'You're gone on her anyway, son.'

Mahony closes his eyes. When he opens them again the car park is empty apart from a crisp packet skittering across the tarmac, filled momentarily by the breeze up off the bay.

Chapter 36

May 1976

Mrs Cauley and Bridget Doosey are amusing themselves in the kitchen with a game of cards and the last nippings from a bottle of Irish. Mrs Cauley is clad in brushed velvet and is wearing an alarming cascade of dark curls. Shauna is washing up at the sink. Now and again she scowls over at Bridget, who has her boots up on the table and is smoking a cigar.

'I have a hand like a foot,' says Bridget.

Johnnie, peering over her shoulder and pulling at his faint moustache, nods in agreement.

Mahony sits down at the kitchen table and declines Bridget's offer of a Dominican.

Mrs Cauley glances up at him. 'Where've you been? We have developments.' She puts down her cards and pushes a folded piece of paper towards him.

Mahony picks it up and the two women grin at him. 'What's this?'

'The name of your generous benefactor,' says Mrs Cauley. 'The kind old soul who put up the money for your bribe.'

Mahony unfold the paper and looks at it. 'You're serious? I thought it was the priest's money.'

'That tight bastard?' Mrs Cauley shakes her head. 'He'd pull the socks off a dead man.'

Bridget blows smoke up to the ceiling. 'You have to ask yourself, Mahony, what kind of an innocent bystander would put up that kind of money to buy a body out of town?'

Mrs Cauley pushes forward two coins and a matchstick. 'And she had a motive.'

Mahony frowns. 'Which was?'

Bridget deals another card. 'Who would Orla really annoy?'

'The sanctimonious, the bigoted and the pious.' Mrs Cauley folds, pushing her cards across the table pettishly. 'The Widow Farelly has always been head of that department.'

Bridget points with her cigar. 'Full marks to old King Charles there.'

Mrs Cauley tosses her black curls and narrows her eyes.

'But do you really think that the Widow could commit murder?' asks Shauna. 'I know she's a bit sour and all that.'

'Well, I don't think it was hands-on. It think the Widow was most likely the brains behind the operation,' says Bridget.

At the sink, Shauna raises her eyebrows.

Mahony smiles grimly. 'Either way, I think it's time I paid my generous benefactor a visit.'

Chapter 37

May 1976

Mahony stands on Annie Farelly's doorstep with his finger on the doorbell.

A dead old man zimmers out through the wall and into the flowerbed; he leans on his walking frame and fixes Mahony with a charming toothless grin.

Mahony nods his head. 'She's in there hiding, is she?'

The dead old man laughs soundlessly.

Mahony bends down to roar through the letterbox.

'Annie, will you open the door? I know you're in there.'

Silence.

'Do you want me to say my piece in front of the whole town? At the church maybe? I've the kind of voice that carries. Or at the General Store? I could even shout it across the square to you, Annie.'

Mahony hears the scraping of bolts and the door opens. The Widow Farelly stands before him with a face that would curdle the milk inside a cow. She has put on a clean apron and has a syringe, with enough sedative to drop a carthorse, cocked and loaded in the dresser drawer.

You can forgive a lone woman for taking precautions.

Otherwise Mahony is quite safe. For Nurse Farelly has hung up her uniform in the empty wardrobe in the never-visited guest room.

For over forty years she was dedicated to efficiently dispatching her duties at Kilterhill Nursing Home. A place where she cared for those who repulsed her more than anything else in the entire world: the old and infirm.

Even as a child, poor Annie was monstrously horrified by old age. It was her job to wash, change and feed Grandma, a fine upstanding woman, who, at the tail end of her life, wound up mewling by the milk pail and flashing her bits at the postman.

When Grandma finally died from the head injuries she sustained from beating herself repeatedly with a copper bedpan, Annie was sent to nursing school to develop her vocation of care. Annie returned to Mulderrig with a second-hand fob watch and a solid reference. Within a week of her return, her daddy, a practical man, had won her a position at Kilterhill Nursing Home. With Annie as the family's new breadwinner, her daddy could dedicate himself to the full-time occupation of sitting on his arse.

All Annie's hopes and dreams ended the day she walked in through the front door. It was a daily horror of ripe bedpans and clotted dentures, rivers of incontinence and weeping bedsores. Every evening poor little Annie would go home and cry herself to sleep, for the smell of the old people was still on her. It was in her nose, her mouth and her lungs, in the pores of her skin and the fabric of her hair. She breathed in age and swallowed decay.

But Annie was very good at her job. She saw things the other girls wouldn't: the unlocked medicine cart and the soiled sheets under the bed, the smears on the teacups and the stains on the nightdresses. Within a month Annie had received a pay rise and the offer of more shifts than her daddy could dream of.

And then came the first death.

On an ordinary Kilterhill morning Annie found that Mrs Kiernan was uncharacteristically unresponsive to her morning cup of tea. Annie felt Mrs Kiernan's grizzled neck for her pulse. Then she patted her hand and smiled at the woman for the first time.

Later, as Annie stripped the bed and opened the window to let in the fine grey rainy day, she felt a profound sense of completeness. It was just how she felt when she had finished all her tasks neatly and well, but it was stronger, clearer. As if she were entirely secure in the knowledge that things were exactly as they should be.

The manager was glad that the next five residents all died on Annie's shift, for she dealt with things so marvellously. She was indeed a grand girl. Little Annie always had the facts and figures ready for the duty doctor so he hardly needed to throw his eye over the corpse. Annie would even have their coffin clothes picked out, pressed and ready for them.

How Annie lived for those days. She would wake up in the morning with a calm sort of feeling, a happy anticipation. She would eat a hearty breakfast and cycle joyfully to work. She would smooth down her immaculate hair and pin her white cap in place. She would tie her apron and check her fob watch. Then she would go up into their rooms and close their doors gently behind her.

Annie dealt first with the Problem Patients, those who scampered naked down corridors or moaned half the night and sang half the day. Then she tackled the ones who complained that their beds were too hard and their eggs were too soft. Then she fixed the ones who talked to her, or touched her arm, or tried to make her return their smiles. But even as she sent them out the back door in a casket there were always more crawling in through the front door to replace them.

And Annie's patients still plague her, even in her retirement. Her house is filled to the rafters with them; they haunt her every corner. Poor Annie isn't to know it but they are the cold breath on her porridge and the tapping in her loft, the whistling in her chimney and the static on her rug. They crack her china cups and fog her crystal vases. And they take turns staring at her as she sleeps badly every night.

Mahony follows Annie into the parlour through the crowd of dead pensioners orbiting the hallway. As Annie draws near they flinch and scuttle through the walls into well-vacuumed corners.

He flings himself on her settee, puts his feet up on her table and takes a good look at his sparring partner.

The Widow appears benign enough in her pastel cardigan and pleated skirt with the gold cross over her spotless blouse. But then there is the grim line of her shoulders and the iron tilt of her chin and the spite in her eyes. Mahony sees that she is locked down and bolted. If she were a castle she would have wound up the drawbridge and woken the archers by now.

Mahony smiles. 'Well now, Annie, this is nice.'

Annie speaks softly. 'I told you to leave town, didn't I? You're filth, just like your mother was.'

'Away with you! That's just who I want to talk to you about. So you knew her well? Me mammy?'

'Your mother was a whore.'

Mahony lights a cigarette and inhales fast and deep. 'That's no news to me, Annie. I came for something fresh. Let's start with what happened to her?'

'Your mother left town, that's all there was to it.'

Mahony's face sets hard. 'Come off it, Annie.'

'Even if I knew I wouldn't tell you.'

'But you put up a lot of money to bribe my arse out of town. That tells me you must have a very guilty conscience.'

Annie narrows her eyes. 'I'm saying nothing.'

A dead old lady meanders into the room and settles on the settee next to Mahony. She draws out her knitting with a friendly nod.

Mahony speaks slowly, like a courtroom hero with the odds stacked against him but who'll be winning anyway. 'Now, Annie. Just tell me what happened to my mother and I'll leave right now and never bother you again.'

'Or what?'

Mahony shrugs, his eyes cold.

Annie looks straight at him. 'She got what she deserved.'

The dead old lady shakes her head and tuts.

Mahony smiles. 'What did she deserve? Don't be shy now.'

Annie holds out her hands. 'How could I possibly say?'

'Did you kill my mother, Annie?'

'I didn't.'

'Because you're no murderer, are you, Nurse Farelly?'

Annie stares at him. 'Get out or I'll call the guards.'

'And tell them what?' Mahony takes a drag on his cigarette. 'Maybe we could entertain them with some of the highlights of your nursing career.'

The dead old lady nods and points at Annie, then she draws her knitting needle over her faint throat. Mahony admires the gesture; it shows spirit.

Annie sits down in an armchair opposite, smoothing her skirt around her knees with careful deliberation. Mahony watches her closely; she doesn't look in the least bit rattled. After all, he has nothing on her, just a hunch. So a few old people died at the nursing home? Well, that's hardly news. He sees that she'll bluff without flinching and give nothing away, unless she wants to. If they were playing poker he'd be leaving without his wallet.

'So you want to know the truth about your mother? I'll tell you about your mother,' she says, her face impassive.

'I've an ear for the truth now, Annie.'

'She lived with her drunken mother on the edge of town. She had grown up fatherless, running wild. One day she marched into town with her head held high and her stomach grown big and said that she was going to have a bastard and that she wanted to be treated like everyone else. Of course all of the decent people would cross the road rather than talk to her and she had already been banned from every one of the shops.' Annie pauses, a smile plays on her lips. 'She said if she didn't get the respect she deserved she'd tell the town who had fathered her bastard.'

'And did she?'

'She didn't. She had the baby and she wound her neck in and waited, like a snake about to strike. So the good people of the town decided to act first.'

'What did they do?'

'They petitioned the priest but he would not help them. Instead he urged forgiveness and acceptance, charity and understanding, and if that wasn't possible, he said he'd come after anyone who so much as looked sideways at her.'

'And what did the town say to that?'

'They said that she'd bewitched the old fool.' Annie absently touches the gold cross at her neck. 'So the town decided to take matters into their own hands. They would round up the bastard and give it to a decent Catholic family. And they would bring the girl to a place where she could do no more harm.'

'What place?'

'An asylum.'

Mahony looks out. In the garden a starling is dragging a worm out of a trim lawn. It tugs and then hops away, jerking its wings ready to attack again.

'They went up to the cottage late one night, planning to come upon her in surprise.' Annie leans over and bangs on the window. The bird flies away.

'Who went?'

'I wouldn't know. As they entered she rushed at them like fury and escaped into the forest leaving her bastard behind, filthy dirty, underfed and too weak to cry.'

Annie's eyes are milled metal, hard-set. But Mahony can take her stare; it glances right off him.

'They found an old woman rocking herself in the corner of the room, drunk out of her mind. It took them a while to recognise her for the respectable woman she once was. "Has she done this to you?" they asked her. "Yes," she said and pointed to the door. "But that one is not my daughter; my own baby has gone. The devil climbed in at the window and took her and left his own behind in the crib."'

Annie stands up and walks over to the sideboard and smiles down at the ornaments arranged there, a row of dancing ladies in crinoline dresses. Along with the potted palm, they are the only decoration in an otherwise drab room, for the walls are without pictures and the colours are uniform and cheerless.

Annie pushes one of the dancing ladies back into line. 'The girl was a changeling, the old woman said. The moment she appeared, accidents and illness befell the family, animals died and visitors sickened as soon as they crossed the threshold.'

She picks up the last dancing lady, frozen mid-waltz with

her furled parasol aligned with her leading right foot. She tips her backwards, cradling her in the cup of her hand. 'Soon the birds stopped flying over the cottage and the white roses bloomed red. Even the mice ran away.'

Annie puts the dancing lady back down. 'And all the time the girl watched the woman with eyes that went right through her. So that the woman began to shut the child away in a windowless room where they kept the turf. The woman had her husband fit a strong lock on the door but the child just kept on staring at her; she could feel her eyes right through the door.' Annie fixes him with a look of terrible triumph. 'It was in this room that the child led her own father to commit a terrible sin.'

Mahony stays very still.

'Now, the woman went often to church, morning and evening, and since she was unable to take the girl with her (for the child would fall into a fit within sight of it, screaming herself insensible) she would leave her behind, locked in the room.

'One evening, finding herself suddenly unwell on the coast road, the woman turned back. As she entered the cottage she saw that the door was no longer locked. The woman went forward and pushed open the door.'

Mahony notices the dead old lady on the settee beside him put down her knitting and cover her ears.

'As the light fell across the threshold the woman saw them together.'

Mahony doesn't move. He's underwater by a mile.

'Her husband ran from the house and she never laid eyes on him again. That night she took a lamp and went to look. The child was peaceful and flushed with sleep. But the woman saw that the girl was monstrous. As full as a tick on an animal's hide. Full and bloated with the soul of a once good man.'

'And what did the people of the village make of the woman's story?' asks Mahony, keeping his voice even, his face composed. 'After all, were they not the judge and the jury?'

Annie folds her hands primly on her lap. 'Several of the men didn't wait to hear more. They ran straight out to find the girl, but of course she was long gone. So they took the baby down into the village and waited. And of course that lured her out of the forest.'

'Orla came down to claim her baby.'

'She came down to fight.' Annie sneers. 'The villagers would have shipped the both of them off and heard no more of it. But somehow the priest got to hear about their plans. He demanded that the bastard was returned to her and they were let alone to live in their hovel.'

'And then the priest died?'

'And then the priest died.'

Mahony sits forward with his elbows on his knees. 'A coincidence?'

Annie smiles. 'Coincidences happen. Of course, the new priest gave hope to the people of the town. He was on their side.'

'You mean he turned a blind eye?'

'I mean that Orla was strongly encouraged to leave and never return, and finding herself without a friend in the world, she left.'

'Now that's where you're lying, Annie. Didn't I tell you I've a great ear for the truth?'

'That's all you'll get from me.'

Mahony shakes his head. 'But you still haven't given me the name of my mother's killer. She was killed, wasn't she, Annie?'

Annie says nothing; she gets up off her chair and walks to the door and opens it. 'Get out.'

Mahony stands. 'You won't give me a name? Then I'll give you one, shall I? *Mary Waldron.*'

The dead old lady looks up from her knitting. Annie stares at him.

'I'll give you another?' Mahony says. '*Cathal Doyle.*'

Annie grabs hold of the doorframe.

'*Maggie Hoban.*'

Annie cries out; she can't help herself.

Mahony walks towards her. '*Kathleen Irwin, Michael Joyce.*'

'Please.'

'*Bridget Lawless.*' He grabs her by the wrist. 'Look at me.' He pulls her close to him. She can feel his spit on her cheek. She closes her eyes.

His voice is flat, oddly metallic. '*Maura Cusack, Theresa Walsh.*'

Annie slumps down with her hands over her head.

Mahony clenches his fist.

Then he sees them: a shield of dead pensioners, their arms linked, their faces patient and apologetic. They shake their heads in dismay. They stand between him and the woman until he stops shouting, until he unclenches his fist, until he sees with the surprise of a sleepwalker waking the woman sobbing on the floor, until he leaves.

Chapter 38

March 1950

They told Orla to be quiet, that her baby was safe. They told her that they would find a good home for him. That he would go to live with a good Catholic family who would raise him to be decent. Orla spat and howled and tried to get out of the bed until Dr McNulty came.

When she woke again they put Francis into her arms. She took him unseeing, blinded by tears.

They told her she was lucky. That she had a friend. They told her to get out of the town and never come back. *Last chance,* they said.

Chapter 39

May 1976

The portents came just before dawn, starting with a steady trickle of soot falling down every chimney into every unlit hearth at Rathmore House.

This was not the only sign of the coming storm.

At first light the swallows began to dip lower and lower over the field beyond the house.

For the bees it was old news. They'd told each other about the storm days ago with a dance of their plush behinds. And of course the trees knew too, but they just plumbed their taproots deeper and held their own counsel.

By now even the dead are jittery. Most of them have taken refuge in the basement, with the exception of Father Jim, who is smoking a pipe in the roll-top bath on the third floor, and Johnnie, who is sitting cross-legged on top of the cistern watching him.

Of course Mahony knows none of this as he stands barefoot in the kitchen waiting for the kettle to boil. He's given up trying to sleep. So too has Desmond Burke, who appears soundlessly in the doorway.

'Mahony, there's something you should know. Something I should have told you.'

Mahony glances up at him. 'Jesus, Desmond, you look like shit.'

Desmond takes a notebook from his pocket and throws it onto the kitchen table.

'Look at it, Mahony. That's my writing.'

They sit together in the garden, on chairs wet with dew, with the forest silhouetted by the brightening sky. Mahony watches as Father Jim, searching his pocket for his pipe, wanders out onto the veranda; the priest nods in his direction and drifts up onto the roof of the henhouse. Johnnie follows him, in a hat, a waistcoat and a pair of sagging drawers, his arms outstretched to welcome the new day.

Mahony doesn't need to look at Desmond to know that the man is crying.

'It was late, Mahony, really late. I was up reading. I answered the door and it was him.'

'Who?'

Desmond puts his head in his hands and cries hard.

Father Jim lights his pipe, a spectral flame flickers for a moment then goes out. Johnnie drops his underwear and hopscotches down the garden path, his bare arse winking in the early morning light. The priest averts his eyes.

Desmond wipes his face with his sleeve and sits up in his chair. 'He wouldn't come in, he stood outside in the dark, he sounded terrified. He said that Orla was dead.'

'Who was it?'

Desmond looks at him. 'Tom. From the forest.'

'Tom? Tom killed her?'

'No.' Desmond pushes the heels of his hands into his eyes. 'She was already dead when he found her.' He squints up at the sky. 'He had you with him, up under his coat.'

'Who killed her?'

Desmond shook his head. 'He didn't know.'

'You asked him?'

'He said he didn't know, Mahony.' Desmond frowns. 'She was in a lot of trouble, with the town. All Tom wanted to do was get you out of here.'

'And he came to you?'

'He knew I had a car.' Desmond glances at Mahony. 'And he wanted to leave something with you. A note to tell you who you were and what had happened. I would write it in my best hand.' Desmond pauses. 'He would tell me how it would read.'

Johnnie lies down on the grass with his legs open and looks up at the sky. A bird flies low and he quickly puts his hat over his mickey.

Mahony takes the photograph out of his wallet and hands it to him.

Desmond takes it. 'I took this, of you and her.'

'So you did know her.'

'She asked me to take it. When she heard I had a camera.' He studies the picture. 'Leaving it with you seemed like the right thing to do at the time.'

'And now it doesn't?' Mahony watches Desmond's face. 'You didn't think I'd come back, did you?'

Desmond gives him a broken smile. 'I hoped you wouldn't.'

Mahony shakes his head. 'You took your fucking time telling me all this.'

'I was worried about how you'd take it.'

Mahony looks at Desmond. The man is lucky he still

has a head on him. Desmond must know it; he's shaking like a shitting dog.

Mahony thinks for a while. Something isn't adding up. 'How did Tom know he could trust you? How did he know that you would help him?'

Desmond shrugs. 'I don't—'

'You already knew him, didn't you?'

Desmond looks down at his shoes. 'Not when I opened the door, not straight away.'

'Who was it, standing at the door, Desmond?'

'Orla's father, Thomas Sweeney.'

They sit in silence, Desmond with his head in his hands, Mahony smoking a cigarette. A mist is rising off the fields now and the birds are staking their claim on the morning. Mahony listens to their song echo in the early empty landscape.

'Who else knew that it was Thomas Sweeney living up there in the forest?'

'No one.'

'What about Jack Brophy? He must have known Tom's real identity?'

Desmond nods, hesitantly. 'He would have, yes.'

Johnnie gets to his feet and saunters to the nearby flowerbed scratching his flute. He begins to dress, lifting one thin limb, then another, into spectral linen and tweed.

Mahony forces himself to say it. 'And her body?'

Desmond shakes his head. 'When we came back there was no sign of it. Thomas looked.'

One question leads to another. 'Where did it happen?'

'In the forest.'

Mahony's heart pitches. He wants to cover his ears. Or shout. Or punch the stricken man sitting next to him into the ground. He does none of these things.

'Whereabouts in the forest?' Mahony says, his voice cold, calm.

'I don't know.'

Mahony speaks slowly, trying to make sense of it. 'And you never told anyone what had happened that night? What Thomas saw?'

Desmond starts to cry again. 'I couldn't. I'd made a promise to him.'

Then Mahony remembers: the child found in the arms of her father, the husband running out of the door, never to be seen again.

'What if Thomas had killed her? Did you ever think about that?'

'He couldn't have.' Desmond's face is bewildered. 'She was already gone when he found her.'

'And you believed that?'

'Thomas was a good man. He took me fishing as a boy.'

'Jesus, Desmond, he took you fucking fishing?'

Desmond looks at Mahony. How can he describe Thomas as he'd known him, with his slow smile and his hat pulled down? The hand-tied flies Thomas would make for him and the patient catechism that took place on peaceful banks, on the wild brown trout and the salmon, on the weather and the water.

'Thomas would never have hurt his own daughter,' Desmond says.

Mahony can't trust himself to talk.

They sit in silence. Mahony lights another fag and smokes it through to the end, bitterly. Desmond sits next to him, demolished.

'But not to tell a soul?' says Mahony. 'A young girl murdered and you tell fucking no one. You're going to have to help me out with this one, pal.'

'I wanted to, but Thomas said that they mightn't believe us, that they might say we did it.'

'Why would they say that, Desmond? Give me a fucking reason.'

Desmond can't look him in the eye. 'I'd been involved with her.'

Mahony stares at the man in horror, as the thought of Shauna in the forest with her dress up to her elbows rolls through his mind. 'Oh Jesus Christ, you're my father.'

'No.' Desmond shakes his head. 'I'm not. I was with her before that.'

Mahony breathes out. He searches in his pocket for another fag with his heart jumping. This man will kill him.

'Orla had been asking me for money. I'd just got married, Mahony. She threatened to tell my wife. What I'd done with her was illegal.'

Mahony regards him with amazement. 'For fuck's sake, Desmond.'

Desmond starts crying again.

Johnnie yawns and takes out his pocket watch.

'Get your boots on,' says Mahony. 'You're coming with me.'

'Where to?'

'To find Thomas Sweeney.'

Johnnie starts to roll up his sleeves.

In the library Mrs Cauley is woken by a loud rumbling sound. She opens her eyes in time to see a billowing avalanche of soot spew from the fireplace and roll towards her.

She watches with wonder as the cloud of soot comes to a halt at the foot of her bed. It hangs there for a while, arranging itself into a denser patch of a darker pitch. The morning light catches the particles as they move, giving the cloud a showy kind of shimmer. Mrs Cauley leans forward and pokes it with her walking stick. It quivers for a moment then re-forms.

An excitable person, thinks Mrs Cauley, with a cracked sort of nature, would remark on the fact that the soot is taking on a definite kind of shape there. Mrs Cauley scratches her scalp as a wolfhound-shaped cloud of soot cocks its head to one side and looks back at her.

Something catches Mahony's eye: a waist-high blur moving parallel to him in the field beyond. When Mahony stops, the blur stops too.

'Let me take a piss, Desmond.' Mahony walks over and the blur draws nearer to waver behind a stone wall.

He stares at it. 'Ida?'

Her face is unfocused, blurred. All Mahony can really make out is the blue of her cardigan and a blotch of bright hair. Her voice comes to him low and hissy. 'Get away. Go home. You will get hurted. He will hurt you.'

Mahony glances over his shoulder. Desmond is holding the map at arm's length and squinting through a lopsided pair of glasses. 'Wha' him?'

The blur dances, its voice an angry sob. 'You'll get hurted. To death even.'

Mahony realises that Ida is stamping with frustration.

'We're going into the forest to look for Thomas Sweeney.'

'No.'

The blur suddenly fades.

'Ida?'

He can't see her but he knows that she's still there and that she's frightened. He can feel it. He can feel the careful step of her foot on broken twigs and the folding of her dimpled knees as she crawls further inside a sprawling hawthorn. He knows that she is hunkering down and covering her ears. He can almost hear her hum her happy tune.

He walks back to Desmond, who looks up, pushing his glasses up the bridge of his nose with his forefinger.

'If we cut across the next field there's a path that should take us to the river. Thomas has his main residence due north from there, and then there are a couple of probable boltholes I know of. We should cover them all in a few hours.'

'Right so,' says Mahony, and puts his hand in his back pocket to check for the haft of his knife.

In the fields around Rathmore House the swallows have started flying into the ground. They lie with their wings snapped, dying in the furrows, with their feet curling and their eyes turning filmy.

Inside the house every fireplace, from the shell-shaped affairs in the bedrooms to the grand marble job in the library, is expectorating extravagantly.

From soft terminal gasps to the heartiest of coughs, every fireplace joins in and together they raise great marauding packs of soot clouds.

Mrs Cauley roars muffled commands from her wheelchair, where she sits with her head wrapped in a bed sheet like a geriatric Lawrence of Arabia. Shauna makes do with a pair of knickers; she has the leg holes hooked over each ear. With streaming eyes she raises her broom and curses each outpouring that rushes through her legs.

Neither of them is surprised that in a moment of crisis a man is nowhere to be found.

Soon the soot is everywhere.

It bounds over beds and under doors and licks at the windows. It rolls down the stairs fighting and tangles itself up in the curtains. It wags itself apart over occasional tables and lies doggo beneath sideboards or under rocking chairs.

'Go and find Bridget Doosey,' Mrs Cauley says to Shauna, her voice made distant by the bed sheet. 'There's something fishy about all of this.'

They speak little. Desmond frets with the map from time to time, wondering which field to cross, or if they are too far down to catch the right path. Mahony drops behind to watch him. Surely the man's harmless?

But he could be a giant if he pulled back his shoulders and sometimes there's a desperate kind of look in the eyes that squint out from behind the glasses.

Mahony searches in his pocket for a fag and sets to light one, hardly hearing the car draw up alongside.

'You all right there, fella?' Jack Brophy leans an elbow out of his squad car.

Mahony realises that he's walking alone. Where Desmond has vanished to is a mystery but Mahony doesn't miss a beat. 'I'm grand, Jack, yourself?'

'Grand. Enjoying this bit of weather?'

Mahony nods and looks up at the sky, a rain-washed blue without a hint of cloud.

Jack smiles. 'Where are you heading?'

'Nowhere. A bit of a stroll just.'

'A stroll, is it?' Jack slaps the side of the door with the flat of his hand and nudges the car into gear. 'Well, give my regards to Desmond behind the wall there.'

The squad car bounces over the tracks up towards Annie Farelly's.

Desmond stands up behind the wall.

'What the hell's the matter with you?' says Mahony.

Desmond gives Mahony a cock-eyed look.

'Jesus wept, will you give me that map, Desmond? Come on.'

All over town the strangest things are happening.

In Mulderrig Post Office and General Stores spiders are swarming. From big square russetty house spiders to dot-bodied spindle shanks spiders, from flying spiders to money spiders, it is clear to Marie Gaughan that every last arachnid in Mulderrig has arrived at her shop.

Now Marie is not a woman of a nervous disposition, but the sight of great regiments of spiders marching over the tinned peas and the packets of semolina is enough to send anyone on the turn. She throws down her mop and locks herself in the back room, pressing newspapers into the crack under the door and chain-smoking menthol cigarettes with a shaking hand.

An army of rats is marching across the basement of Kerrigan's Bar. Tadhg has never seen the like of it before. He puts on an oven glove and reaches down to pick one up. Its legs keep moving like a wind-up toy. The rat snarls like a bad Elvis impersonator; Tadhg shudders and puts it down.

In the parochial house Róisín Munnelly hides under the table as a colony of bats swirl around the kitchen. They land on the floor and drag themselves towards her on leathery knuckles; she swipes at them with a dishcloth.

A clan of badgers knock Michael Hopper down on the Carrigfine road.

Mrs Moran is nearly drowned by a labour of moles. They surge across the lawn in velvet waves as she stands weeping on a garden chair.

Mulderrig proclaims that nature has turned insane.

★

Mrs Cauley, unaware of these aberrations of nature, has been singing lullabies to the fireplaces. The fireplaces, becalmed by her golden voice, have stopped expectorating and started listening. So that by the time Shauna appears in the hallway with Bridget Doosey, the outpouring of soot is no more than the odd dyspeptic burp and the occasional smutty cackle.

Bridget Doosey sucks air through her teeth. Shauna begins to cry.

Mrs Cauley rolls her eyes. 'It's only a bit of soot. Dry your arse and wheel me into the kitchen. You might as well cut us a few sandwiches while you're standing about wailing. Doosey, you get the medicinal brandy out and pour us all a large one.'

Shauna sits down at the kitchen table and takes a deep breath. She fans her hands over the oilcloth, lowering each finger in turn. She is surprised at how dirty it is; she makes handprints in the fine dusting of black.

There is a hot draft on her ankles and she lifts up the edge of the tablecloth. Underneath the table a dog-shaped cloud of soot turns belly up for a scratch.

'Oh God, there's all soot under here.'

Mrs Cauley nods. 'Yes, but that's an Irish wolfhound.'

Shauna knocks back her drink in one.

Bridget looks under the table. 'I'd say that was more of a terrier.' She pours another brandy. 'Of course, this isn't normal soot. It's a sign.'

'What sort of sign?' Shauna wails.

'A sign that a terrible storm is coming,' says Bridget.

Shauna points to the window. 'But there's a clear blue sky.'

Bridget nods, 'And doesn't it seem harmless? Don't be fooled, Shauna. There's a tempest on its way that will level this town.'

Mrs Cauley wipes her face with a corner of her sooty kaftan. 'Well, we'd better get another one down our gullets then, for fortification.'

By the time Jack Brophy arrives Mrs Cauley is in the drawing room conducting the Glenn Miller Orchestra on the record player and Bridget Doosey is flapping the soot back up the chimney with an ornamental parasol. Upstairs, Shauna is dancing and coughing along the corridors with a wicker rug beater, her pink-rimmed eyes streaming.

All of them are twisted on brandy.

Jack returns to his car and comes back up the drive holding a gas mask confiscated from an armed robber in Castlebar. Shauna puts it on with a whoop of delight and waltzes off again.

Bridget raises a vase full of brandy. 'Chin, chin,' she roars.

Jack laughs. 'I won't ask. May I?'

Mrs Cauley nods and Jack turns off the record player. From the hallway they can hear the muffled strains of a song of Shauna's own design.

Mrs Cauley smiles up at him, her face filthy and her eyes bright. 'To what do we owe this pleasure, Jack?'

Jack takes off his cap. 'I'm afraid I'm not here on pleasure, Merle.' He glances at Bridget Doosey.

Mrs Cauley waves her hand. 'Say your piece, Jack, don't mind that old crow, she knows all my business soon enough anyway.'

Jack puts his cap down on the table and runs his fingers through his hair. 'Someone matching Mahony's description was involved in a robbery this morning.'

Mrs Cauley stops smiling. 'What do you mean?'

'Gavaghan's Wholesale was turned over.'

Bridget anchors her broom in the middle of the Persian carpet. 'On the Carrigfine road?'

Jack nods. 'There's a witness. The assistant caught the thief red-handed and took a hiding for it. He's up in the hospital now.'

'What has this to do with us, Jack?'

'The witness gave Mahony's description, Merle.' Jack says quietly.

Mrs Cauley shakes her head. 'No way; it wasn't Mahony.'

Bridget sweeps herself forward. 'He must be mistaken.'

'Let's hope so,' says Jack. 'But it's my duty to check it out. You understand that, don't you, Merle?'

Mrs Cauley nods slightly.

Jack puts his cap back on. 'Is he here? I'd like a word with him.'

Mrs Cauley purses her lips. 'He's not in at the moment.'

'Have you seen him this morning?'

'Of course I have.'

'At what time?'

'Time? Oh come on.' Mrs Cauley gestures around the room. 'I've had my hands full, Jack, as you can see.'

'I see. Is it OK if I go up to his room? Take a look around?'

Mrs Cauley looks doubtful.

'I could come back later with a warrant?'

'I'll call Shauna.'

'There's no need to bother her. I'll go on up myself. I know the way. The guest room to the front of the house?'

Mrs Cauley draws herself up in her wheelchair. 'What did you say the name of the witness was?'

Jack goes out of the door. 'I didn't.'

★

As Jack gets into the squad car he holds his hand up to Bridget at the window.

Bridget drops the net curtain. 'I don't know why he's smiling, when there's a biblical variety of storm coming.'

Mrs Cauley frowns.

Bridget pulls on her cardigan. 'Now don't fret. Mahony wouldn't get involved in that kind of thing. You know that. There are a thousand Irishmen fitting his description: tallish, dark and handsome.'

'Of course it's not bloody Mahony. Someone's trying to frame him.'

'It's possible.'

Mrs Cauley looks up. 'Something doesn't feel right. With *him*.'

'*Him?*'

'That one, Brophy.'

'What?'

'Oh, I don't know.'

'Well then, neither do I.' Bridget ties a scarf about her head, tucking her sooty hair under it. 'You worry about that lad too much. Mahony is cast iron, you know that.'

Mrs Cauley nods. Thoughtful.

'I'm off home to shut the felines in. I'd advise you to batten down your hatches, old lady.'

Mrs Cauley, already a million miles away, waves her hand. 'Leave that bottle where I can reach it, Doosey.'

Chapter 40

May 1976

The portents are right, as portents usually are, whether anyone heeds them or not: later on that day a biblical storm hits Mulderrig.

Down by the quay the fishermen are stunned. For in the space of a rapid fart the waves in the bay have gone from flat to grown. Above them the lightning is hopping and the thunder comes in sudden deafening peals. The wind slams past them, forcing their eyes shut and ripping the nets from their hands and the caps from their heads. It's all they can do to stagger back up the quay, and when they fall in through the door of Kerrigan's it takes three of them to close it behind them.

Bridget Doosey listens to the storm roar with her windows closed and her back door bolted. She has cats under the quilt, an illustrated guide to forensic toxicology and a freshly wicked lamp for the night ahead.

She shakes her head and thinks about the poor women with their wash out and their knickers all blown away in the blink of an eye. She considers the farmers in the fields, holding on for dear life to a cow, or a sheep, or a goat, or a gate. She hums a Patsy Cline song to the kittens huddled at her armpit. And what of the young ones who've crept into the forest for a bit of loving? You wouldn't want to be out in this with your trousers round your ankles. You'd take it as divine punishment and you'd never get your flute out again. Or, just think it, the mammies with the babies squalling terrified in their prams. Oh Lord, imagine them, dropping shopping and grabbing little Martin and Michael. Running up the hill with the storm at their heels. Ah Jesus, run, save yourselves, save your children.

She wonders why she didn't see it coming, having fireplaces of her own and being used to keeping an eye out for such things.

A thought suddenly strikes Bridget.

She eases herself out from under her cats, wanders over to the fireplace and runs her finger along the hearthstone. There's dust, dead moths and cat hair.

But not a speck of soot.

So there's more to this storm than meets the eye, and Bridget Doosey is betting it has most to do with one particular occupant of Rathmore House. And so, cursing her meddling tendencies, Bridget puts on her good gripping boots and winds herself into a sheet of tarpaulin the size of a topgallant. Then, taking hold of a stout walking stick and thanking the Good Lord for the ballast in her behind, Bridget Doosey sets sail for Rathmore House.

It was no surprise to Shauna that the men of Rathmore House were nowhere to be found the moment she needed a bit of help. She'd to get every one of the animals in herself. Blown all ways across the courtyard with a chicken under every arm and the roof tiles skittering along the ground after her.

Shauna sits at the kitchen table with a cup of tea in her hand.

Apart from the rioting storm, all is quiet at Rathmore House.

Mrs Cauley has fashioned herself a pair of earplugs from the obituary page of the *Western People* and settled down with her suspect list to embark on a bit of ratiocination. Apart from her usual demands for leg rubs and advocaat cocktails Shauna knows she'll get no further conversation from the old woman.

Shauna closes her eyes and listens as the house sings the backing vocals to the song of the storm outside. Floorboards groan and windowpanes shudder. Somewhere a door slams in time while the keyholes whistle the high notes. And then a loud banging starts: fast, near, persistent. Shauna opens her eyes and lets out a cry of horror.

A beast is hurling itself against the back door.

It's clawing at the door handle and fogging up the glass. It screams out to her with two twisted mouths and kicks the doorframe with its many tangled limbs.

Desmond and Bridget sit in the chairs Shauna has drawn up for them at the foot of Mrs Cauley's bed. They each hold a full glass. The pair met on the road to Rathmore House and helped each other through the storm. Bridget is blithely smoking a cigarette with her feet up on a footstool. Desmond is still insensible.

Mrs Cauley watches Desmond closely; she knows that expression. 'Desmond, look at me.'

He shudders. 'It's my fault he's out there.'

Mrs Cauley nods. 'It is of course.'

'A man is out there alone in the forest because of me. Lost and in danger. I must go and search for him.' Desmond makes a half-arsed attempt to shake off the blanket tucked around his knees.

'You'll do no such thing, Daddy. You'll sit there and dry off.' Shauna flicks at him with her tea towel as she bends to put an ashtray next to Bridget's elbow. 'Listen to Mrs Cauley, she's already told you there's nothing you can do.'

Bridget exhales and waves her cigarette at him. 'What you have to understand, Desmond, is that this is Mahony we're talking about. He's a Dublin orphan, which means that he could survive on an iceberg in just his socks. You, on the other hand, are as helpless as a fruit fly out there.'

Desmond lets out a soft whine. 'How can you know that?'

Bridget sneers and downs her whiskey. 'Aside from that is the obvious fact that this is no ordinary storm; it has a design to it: a *supernatural* design. This storm is here to help Mahony, not finish him off.'

Desmond looks at her in bewilderment. 'I don't even know what you are talking about.'

Mrs Cauley sits herself up in the bed and frowns at him. 'That's enough, Desmond. Be quiet now.'

Bridget holds up her empty glass to Shauna for another. 'A supernatural variety of storm will always be heralded by rolling clouds of soot from every fireplace and a rake of diving swallows. Exactly like today, eh?'

Shauna nods. 'There was soot all right, and swallows.'

'Well, there would be. This storm is a symptom of the huge quantities of paranormal energy that have been converging on this village. Jesus, the weather hasn't been normal in weeks, has it?'

Desmond goes to open his mouth; Mrs Cauley stops him with a look. She turns to Bridget. 'What do you expect from this storm, Doosey?'

'What does this investigation need most of all?'

Mrs Cauley narrows her eyes. 'A body.'

'Exactly.' Bridget nods. 'This storm will unearth Orla Sweeney. It will lead us to her body.'

Shauna shivers. 'Oh God. Can't anything just be normal around here? Can't a storm just be a bloody storm?'

Mrs Cauley holds up her hand. 'No it can't. Go on, Doosey.'

'Tomorrow we go out and we find Orla's body, because tonight the forces of nature will unearth her. That's what I risked my arse to come up here and tell you.' Bridget sits back in her chair triumphantly.

'So she'll just be there on the lawn in front of me? I'll be falling over her bones when I put the washing out?' asks Shauna.

Bridget is undeterred. 'Maybe not, but there'll be clues. Lightning-struck trees, boulders rearranged in a circle, that sort of thing. They will lead us to her grave.'

'Shauna, go and find a shovel,' says Mrs Cauley, with a terrible gleam in her eyes. 'We move out at first light.'

Bridget toasts Mrs Cauley with a loaded glass. 'And some rubber gloves. We will no doubt be handling evidence.'

Chapter 41

March 1950

The priest walked the floor outside the door all night, praying hard and fast. Annie heard his voice grow louder on every exhale, his breath propelling an urgent murmur of words.

She was only here at his asking.

She would be the first to see what came out of this devil.

As the morning broke, the mottled grey moon of a baby's head appeared.

The girl looked at it. It was no more than a scrap of skin, smeared and alien in her arms. Annie dressed the umbilical with gauze and wrapped the afterbirth in newspaper and hauled it into a bucket. By the time she had turned back, the girl was asleep.

Annie took the baby and laid it on the table.

Mucus whitened each wrinkled fold. A halo of black down surrounded a soft walnut skull. Its limbs twitched, and then floated, in turn.

Annie stared down at its face.

It didn't look like him, if he was even the father. It didn't look like anyone.

Its grey eyes, membraned and cloudy, stopped slaloming and gazed right back at her. It flexed its tiny hands, the fingers, with their too-long nails, furling and unfurling in some sort of pagan prayer. It opened the pink wound of its mouth to speak. It was casting a druid's spell, putting a curse on her. Annie felt it heating up the base of her spine.

She should have dashed it against the wall but she could hardly bear to touch it. So she swaddled it quickly, holding her breath, hastily tucking in the limbs. She dropped it in the wooden box at the foot of the mattress and pushed the box with her foot to the corner of the room.

Then Annie turned to its mother.

The girl had her head at an awkward angle, tucked in a little to her chest. Her hair was wet and her mouth was open. Annie slid the rubber sheet away, folded a thick pad between the girl's legs and pulled her nightdress down over her thighs. She put her arms down by her side and tucked a sheet firmly in and around her body.

Then Annie took up a pillow.

With the blood rushing in her ears she didn't hear Bridget Doosey come into the room but she felt her firm touch on her forearm.

'I'll take it from here, Annie. You can go now,' she said.

Bridget rocked the baby in her arms by the hearth and he sucked her finger, which gave her a deep thrill of delight. His eyes flickered over her, sometimes hesitating, sometimes sweeping on. He's reading me, she thought, and she smiled warm at him.

Father Jim got up from the table. 'I should take him now, before she wakes.'

'She'd never forgive you, Father.'

'It would be the right thing to do.'

'He belongs to her.'

The baby closed his eyes but his grip on Bridget's finger didn't diminish. She blessed him in his sleep. 'She wants to bring him up herself.'

The priest ran his hands through his hair. 'They'll never accept it.'

'They'll have to.'

The priest looked down at her. 'It's only a matter of time before they take matters into their own hands. You know that as well as I do.'

'It's all talk, Father.'

Father Jim seemed to have aged a thousand years. He shook his head. 'Is it? She is collecting enemies, and this little fella isn't going to help. I can't protect them for ever.'

'I won't let you take him, Father.'

'She's a child, Bridget.'

'No, she's a mother.'

The priest lightly touched the wrapped bundle in Bridget's arms before he left.

The light was out on the front porch so that Father Jim could only make out a dark shape moving against the wet leaves of the ivy.

'I'm sorry to call so late, Father.'

'Oh, it's you, is it?'

'It is, a quick word, it won't take long.'

Father Jim opened the door. 'All right, come inside now.'

'That would be grand, Father. Here, look, I've brought something to wet the baby's head.'

The priest stepped in over the threshold and held the door open. 'Now, I don't think—'

'Will we go into the library, Father? I've some information that may be of interest to you.'

Chapter 42

May 1976

The world is arsewards – sky, rain, branch, leaf, earth and stone, whipped and merging.

Mahony stumbles ahead by degrees with his hands held out in front of him. He hears only the rush and howl of the wind in his ears. But his guts hear the bass roll of thunder and his nerves catch every shotgun crackle of lightning as it forks and courses over the trees.

He keeps moving forward, caught by brambles, lashed by branches backlit for split seconds but otherwise just blacker fissures in the darkness.

Where Desmond is, the prick, God only knows.

When the lightning is overhead Mahony tramples a hole in the undergrowth and squats down on his hunkers with his feet together and his arms wrapped around his shins. He tucks his head between his knees.

So he doesn't see a thing coming.

Chapter 43

May 1976

The wind is still and the storm has passed and Father Quinn is up with the surviving larks before the town is even awake enough to find its bollocks, let alone scratch them.

He's a happy little figure this morning, for he has a great piece of information, spoon-sized, and he plans to have a really good stir with it.

He combs the thick wedge of his greying hair and buffs his crocodile teeth.

'I go,' he announces to himself in the bathroom mirror. 'I go, look, how I go, swifter than arrow from the Tartar's bow.'

Róisín, coming up the stairs with a pile of clean face-cloths, knocks on the door. 'Are you all right in there, Father?'

What could be more natural than a priest out at daybreak, striding about a storm-tossed village, doing all he can to help his community? Although today, like any other day, Father Quinn is as welcome as knob rot.

He's just one more affliction in an already blighted land-scape. The Shand has burst her banks and dead fish swim in hedgerows. Ancient trees have dominoed down in the forest and the birds nest a foot off the ground. Roofs and crops and flocks have been lost. Water still surges down through the town, filthy with ruined livelihoods and drowned dreams.

Father Quinn makes short shrift of the village central and the outlying farms, and, finding himself able to turn to the real business of the day, he starts to make his way up to Annie Farelly's.

Having all the luck of the malignant, the widow's bungalow is largely untouched by the ravages of the storm. Father Quinn finds her in the garden.

'You have survived the storm, Mrs Farelly.'

Annie sheaths her secateurs. 'I have, Father. Thank you for your concern.'

'Not at all. Actually, there's a matter I need to discuss with you. It's a little delicate.' The priest offers her a smile that would make a lesser woman recoil.

Annie nods and pulls off her spotless gardening gloves. 'Come inside, Father.'

Mahony wakes with the mother of all headaches.

He's lying on a wet mattress in a broken-down caravan.

He touches the side of his head. Something is stuck to it with duct tape. The tape goes across his cheek and extends into his hairline. Mahony sits up, fighting the urge to hurl. The arse and legs of his jeans are caked with mud, as if he's been dragged along the ground. He has no shirt or socks. His boots wait by the door, in a muddy puddle that has formed in the dipped and pitted linoleum.

Annie puts down her teacup and turns to Father Quinn with the disgust barely concealed on her face.

'How dare she?' she whispers.

'I'm afraid Mrs Cauley has long believed that she is a law unto herself. You could say that she has grown too big for her boots.'

'And you say she actually bribed the clerk?'

Father Quinn nods sadly. 'The girl is distraught. Not only did she take a bribe but she also divulged confidential information concerning the bank's valued clientele. Needless to say she has lost her position.'

'Well, at least it explains Mahony's visit.'

'Mahony visited you?'

'Yes, Father, and it wasn't a pleasant experience at all.'

It's a while before Mahony can stand. When he can lift his arms he gets the dressing off his head and finds it's made from a balled-up piece of his shirt. The gash on his forehead bleeds a little. He dabs at it with the cleanest corner he can find.

He finds his jacket folded on the table and his empty cigarette carton and matches next to it.

Mahony sits down on the doorstep and looks out. The clearing is strewn with Thomas Sweeney's possessions, half-submerged in mud, flung into bushes.

His grandfather is nowhere to be seen.

Mahony sees a blur of blue and hears the faint babble of song interspersed by emphatic swearing. Ida hopscotches into the clearing through upturned buckets and broken chairs. She stops in the middle of an upended bathtub and executes a perfect curtsy.

Mahony puts on his boots. Soon he'll feel the early sun on his chest; until then he'll shake with the cold. He pulls his jacket around his bare shoulders and gets up to follow Ida home.

★

This morning Shauna doesn't care about anything.

She doesn't care about Mrs Cauley's bed bath or Daddy's eggs. She's not worried about the laundry or the beds. The rugs can go unbeaten and the mice can go untrapped, the roof can go on leaking and the curtains can stay drawn forever and ever.

She just wants Mahony back.

So whilst Daddy and Bridget Doosey might be out searching for the supernaturally unearthed remains of Orla Sweeney, she herself is looking for a real living man.

Her man.

She walks out into the forest with a flask of tea and a blanket. She has a shovel with which to dig Mahony out from under fallen trees and a sling for his arm if it should be broken. She has a dry pair of socks, a ham sandwich and a bottle of brandy for the shock, hers or his.

Mrs Cauley may not fear for him, but she does.

He's the whole of her world right there.

Annie Farelly crosses the garden and lets herself in at the back door of Rathmore House. Shauna is out; her slippers are waiting for her, pigeon-toed on the doormat.

Annie makes her way through the kitchen. There's a burnt milk pan in the sink, the floor is unwashed and a breakfast tray is half set. She steps into the hall, past the mahogany coil of the staircase and opens the door to the library.

She follows the path through Mrs Cauley's labyrinth. It's been a while since Annie has walked through it and she wonders at the height of the piles that stretch up towards the ceiling. Now and then she hears faint scuttling sounds and detects some movement out of the corner of her eye. She has a feeling that she is being watched, no doubt by the legions of mice that are nesting and gnawing in the heaps of decaying books.

Until, right there in front of her, is Mrs Cauley.

A ray of sunshine in a nightdress of yellow flannel, stranded in a sea of dead words, fast asleep in her bed.

Annie draws nearer with a sense of relief. How small Mrs Cauley is when she's quiet. How much frailer she is with her mouth shut.

The old bitch could be dead already. She's hardly breathing; Annie has to look closely to see her chest rise and fall. Her liver-spotted hands are clasped beneath her swollen belly. Under her fingers there's a map of the town, covered, from the coast to the mountains, with little black crosses and question marks.

Without her wig Mrs Cauley is barely human, she's more like an ancient turtle with her round speckled head. Her jaw lolls slack and open. She's in a very deep sleep. She mustn't have slept at all with the storm last night. Heaven knows, Annie hardly did, but then she hasn't slept a great deal since Mahony's visit.

Annie takes a folded square of muslin from her bag, spreads it on the edge of the bed and sits down. What sort of a person would want to live like this? Like a dirty old spider webbed up in her dusty books. She'd burn the lot if she were Shauna. She'd haul all these books and papers out of the door and onto the veranda and build a bonfire. She'd set Mrs Cauley at the top and put a match to it. She'd go up with a big whoosh, with her old papery skin and dry bones.

Annie leans forward and wipes her finger along the headboard, sending a drift of dust into the air. As if in answer, Mrs Cauley's nostrils twitch very slightly. Annie looks at the bedside table; there's a ring-marked pad with an empty glass on it. She picks up the glass and sniffs it: some sort of cheap spirit. Then two words, scrawled on the pad in capital letters, catch her eye.

BROPHY. MOTIVE.

Annie picks up the pad. The writing is very bad. She puts on her glasses and holds the paper towards the light from the French doors, turning back through the pages. She closes the pad and looks at the sleeping woman for a long time. Then she reaches into her shopper and pulls out a pillow.

Shauna wants to cry. Mahony's face is dirty but his smile is warm. Warmer than it's ever been.

'You're a sight,' he says.

'And you're a picture,' she says.

Mahony, shirtless and covered in filth, with a nasty cut on the side of his forehead and his hair plastered to his neck.

He grins. 'What are you doing with the shovel, Missus? Burying me?'

Shauna shakes her head and laughs so that he laughs too. Mahony touches her arm. 'You came looking for me?'

Shauna colours. 'Bridget is convinced that the storm will have unearthed Orla's body.'

Mahony takes the shovel off her. 'That sounds like one of Bridget's finest. Tell me about it over breakfast?'

Shauna nods. 'What happened to your head?'

'I've no idea.'

'Does it hurt?'

He touches it. 'No, it's grand.'

Shauna takes a step forward and kisses him.

It's so easy: one kiss and she's pressed close to him, her hands passing over his back, his shoulders, learning the shape of him with his hair wet against her face and his mouth hot on hers. He holds her fast in his arms; if her legs give way she knows that he has got her.

By the time they reach the road to Rathmore House Shauna has her hand in his and Mahony has her cardigan on. He's knotted it high over his stomach and keeps looking through his eyelashes at her in a way that makes her laugh.

Everything is entirely brilliant.

Shauna starts to realise that this is the natural way of things: Mahony walking beside her, smiling and listening to her wittering on about the storm, about Mrs Cauley's earplugs and Bridget Doosey's theories. They move easily around fallen trees and craters of water. Shauna marvels at the ravines cut on either side of the road by rivers of rainwater, dammed here and there with dead rats, their eyes as bright as jet buttons. In the field a flyblown sheep is lullabied by gentle breezes, her rinsed wool lifting. She's an earthbound cloud! Her open mouth sings of eternal love and her bloated tongue talks only of marriage. The crows picking over the flooded fields are dancing the fandango and the farmers that applaud them are their biggest fans.

As they walk back to Rathmore House they have all the time in the world and soon Mahony has his arm around her with not even an inch of air between them.

'It's just another kind of sleep,' says Annie Farelly to the slumbering old woman. 'You shouldn't fear it at all, Mrs Cauley.'

As soon as she feels the unfamiliar kiss of a properly laundered pillowcase Mrs Cauley's eyes flicker open. There's no fear, only mild amusement, so that for a moment Annie falters, confused.

And then it hits her.

An illustrated copy of *Wuthering Heights* howls by, glancing her left temple.

Annie releases her grip on the pillow and looks around. There's no one there. So Annie picks up the pillow again and applies a bit of heft.

Then all hell breaks loose.

A large-type edition of *War and Peace* starts the counter-attack proper. It launches down from the top of a ceiling-high pile onto Annie's cranium, knocking her to the floor. Saved only by the coiled density of her perm, Annie is more than a little dazed as she drags herself up the side of the bed only to be set upon by *The Complete Works of Jane Austen*, which rain down variously on her head, arms and décolleté. Annie regains her feet just as *The Magic of Ernest Hemingway* begins a vicious offence on her ankles, snapping like an unschooled terrier.

Clutching her shopper against her chest, Annie makes a dash around the bed only to stop dead in her tracks. Up ahead, a huge darkly bound book appears to be mustering force. *Masterpieces of Russian Literature* rears up before a flock of flapping periodicals. For a moment it hangs ponderously in the air then it shudders open and begins to ripple its thick yellow pages. Annie screams and hurls herself at the French doors, stumbling out onto the veranda with a game copy of *On the Origin of Species* launching itself repeatedly at her rear to give her a good, thorough kick up her hole.

Mrs Cauley chuckles through her broken nose before the stage lights go out.

Shauna is setting the kettle on the hob when she hears Mahony roar.

He's standing at the open doorway of the library.

Before him is a sacked city, a ruin.

Here and there a book still scuttles or flaps. Occasionally there's a scraping groan as great plates of periodicals meet, jostle and finally settle. Every high-stacked tower has been toppled, so that Mahony can see right across the room.

A sharp wedge of light shines through the dusty air, illuminating an unsettling tableau. Mrs Cauley lies on the bed, wigless and blanket-less, with blood on her face and her closed eyes already bruising.

Two faded angels stand over her.

As Mahony steps into the room the taller of the figures shakes his head. The other brushes away the dim tears that have joined the downpour of his limp moustache.

Floating above the bed is a woven arc of books, a miniature vaulted ceiling. Spired with twists of paperbacks and lined with yellowed music scores.

Mahony slides forward over the litter of books and papers, hardly knowing he's shouting.

Mahony holds the old woman in his arms. She has stepped off the stage at the Abbey Theatre to find Johnnie waiting in the wings. She trips up to him, shaking back her brown curls, her eyes on his. He smiles, straightens his tie and holds out his hand.

The next voice she hears is Mahony's, gunfighter raw in her ear.

It tells her to get up. The bullet missed, see? The undertaker is pocketing his measuring tape and putting his hat back on; the bartender is sweeping up the broken glass.

She lets go of Johnnie's hand and opens her eyes.

Dr Maurice McNulty dresses Mrs Cauley's nose and wrist, and gives her a shot for the pain. He tells her that her injuries should be taken as a stark warning against the dangers of excessive reading. Mrs Cauley smiles through her butterfly of gauze and tells him that, on the contrary, *books save lives*. Dr McNulty looks unconvinced. He tells her that if an avalanche of books doesn't claim her then the dust surely will. Bookcases are the way to go, he informs her, coupled with thorough and regular housekeeping. He looks pointedly at Shauna, and Mrs Cauley laughs like a drain behind her bandages.

Mahony surveys the blackening shadows of the trees as the daylight dies.

'How long have you suspected him?'

Mrs Cauley shrugs. 'It was a hunch only. But a phone call to Gavaghan's confirmed that there was no burglary yesterday.'

'And he knew I wasn't here at the house. He'd met me on the way up here. The sly bastard.'

Mrs Cauley raises herself on one elbow. 'Well, he found nothing. You have the photograph with you in your wallet.'

'I left my wallet behind, up in the room.'

'Jack took it?'

'It's not there now.'

'I'm sorry, kiddo. Our one real piece of evidence.' She looks closely at him. 'Our enemies are breaking cover. We must be getting warmer.'

Mahony walks over to the bed and sits down by her side. 'I don't want you involved in this any more. What if I'd lost you today?'

'To the Black Widow? Come on, Mahony.' She smiles and taps his arms. 'I'll have a cigarette.'

'You shouldn't smoke.'

'I think I deserve one.'

Mahony lights a cigarette and threads it between her fingers. On impulse he bends down and kisses her forehead.

'Soft boy.'

Johnnie smiles up at Mahony from the end of the bed; Father Jim is sitting next to him, smoking his pipe with a shaking hand. The dead men look even more ashen than usual.

Mrs Cauley draws herself up in the bed. 'Don't even think of cutting me out of this investigation, Mahony. You need me.'

'I don't know. This is getting nasty.'

'Then we'll call in the guards.'

Mahony snorts.

She purses her lips. 'Don't bloody start. We'll go over Brophy's head. Inspector Kelly in Westport is credited with having a brain. Only we'll need something concrete first, given that Jack's one of them.'

'I'll think about it.'

'Grand. We'll get Bridget to bring Kelly in as soon as we've got evidence. She hasn't got form.'

Mahony glances up at her.

Mrs Cauley smiles lopsidedly through her bandages. 'Drunk and disorderly.'

Mahony laughs.

'In the meantime,' she says, 'it's business as usual. We've a play to stage tomorrow, Christy.'

'You want me to take the part?'

'Of course.'

'And have Quinn call time on me? That was no idle threat.'

'It wasn't.' Mrs Cauley drains her glass. 'And of course you being arrested right now would complicate things, if we didn't have a plan.'

'Now what are you up to, you devious old biddy?'

'It's not me, it's Doosey; she has it all under control.'

'How?'

'Let's just say she has been busy cultivating a few un-
desirable contacts,' says Mrs Cauley coyly.

'Oh Jesus, what are you going to do to the priest?'

'Never you mind, you've enough to worry about.'

Mahony gets up off the bed. 'Then the less I know the
better. I'll go and find a blanket; I'm sleeping here tonight.'

'Don't be thick.'

'I'm not leaving you.'

Johnnie nudges Father Jim, who gets up, clamps his pipe
in his mouth and shuffles off towards the door of the library,
where he will spend the night leaning against the doorframe,
puffing distractedly. Johnnie puts his cane under his arm and
fades with a sober salute. Later, Mahony will glimpse him
passing and re-passing the French doors as he patrols the
veranda.

Mahony clears a space on the floor next to the bed. Mrs
Cauley watches him, tapping her cigarette into a teacup.
'They won't be back you know. Not straight away. They'll
know we'll be on the lookout.'

'You can't know that. I don't want you left alone. Get
Bridget Doosey up here to stay until this is over.'

'Shauna's here.'

'All the more reason,' says Mahony. 'I want you both
safe.'

Mrs Cauley smiles. 'She found you then, Shauna, when
you were out wandering through the wilderness? Tempest
tossed.'

'She did.'

'She said she would. She said that she would haul your
arse home with her whatever your condition. I bet you
haven't heard that before from a woman?'

Mahony laughs.

They sit in silence, Mrs Cauley smoking her cigarette and Mahony watching night fall over the forest.

'She loves you, Mahony.'

Mahony nods. He looks up at her with a half-smile playing on his lips and his eyes full of black fire.

Mrs Cauley's ancient heart leaps. She grins widely. 'Bridget Doosey it is then. She'll guard your chicks in their nest. She's got a gun, so if Bonnie and Clyde try any more funny business we can just shoot the fuckers.'

'Jesus Christ.'

'This is war, Mahony.'

'Get some sleep.'

'You make a handsome couple, very well suited.'

'Go to sleep.'

Mahony watches the sky until the stars come out. Then he gets up out of his blanket and shuts the windows.

'I wasn't scared you know,' says a well-loved voice from the bed, rich and ribald, honeyed and vicious, with a new nasal quality from her injury

'Were you not?' he says. 'I would have been.'

'I can't die like that, Mahony.'

Mahony lies down again, so near that he can hold the old paw that comes knocking at the side of the bed, searching for his hand.

'You can't die? What are you, invincible?'

'I mean, I won't die on my back. I'm going out like Cúchulainn. I want a noble variety of death.'

Mahony looks up at the ceiling with her fragile hand in his.

'Picture it,' she speaks softly. 'There he was, Cúchulainn, mortally wounded, tying himself to a standing stone with his own entrails. Do you know, it was only when a raven landed on his shoulder and wiped its beak on his beard that his enemies realised he was dead?'

Her hand squeezes his. 'I plan to die like a warrior: fiercely and upright.'

Tears run unannounced onto Mahony's pillow, for love is just as heartbreaking as pity.

Chapter 44

May 1950

The man laid his fingers on the dog's snout so that she would understand and stay and be quiet. He took up his sack and his shovel and made to go.

But the dog was wise and she knew that the man had darkness in his mind, more darkness than she'd ever seen before, despite their long years together. So when he walked into the forest she followed him, for she couldn't leave him, even if he bid her to.

She walked close at heel, waiting for the soft scattered language from above, the clicks and whistles, the half-looks and hand motions.

But the man took hold of her neck and said, 'Stay. Stay. Stay.'

But she felt the darkness behind the man's eyes and she could not stay.

She had never defied him and he had never punished her.

She knew nothing but sun and rain, rabbit holes and falling leaves, sea-spray and sheep. And the miles and miles and miles they went together over beaches, bog, field and hill. Her long bright face curving back, always curving back, curving back to him, as he walked behind with his hands in his pockets, throwing his whistle through the air as straight as a stone.

His fingers said stay. Stay. Stay. They lifted her off the ground and pushed her away. Stay.

She knew nothing but coarse rugs and rich bones, warm ranges and gravy-soaked crusts. She slipped under the fence and joined him at heel.

The man put down his rope and his spade and he took off his belt and put it around her neck, looping one end to a fence post.

'Stay. Damn you.'

But she was canny and fast and she slipped the loop to rejoin him at the edge of the forest. This time she sang out to him. She sang to him with her strong bark; she told him she wouldn't leave him. She sang out against the darkness.

He broke her hind leg, shearing down her shin with the back of his boot heel to a point halfway. Her bone gave way with an empty sound.

'Stay. Damn you.'

Now she knew pain – the white pain of the leg she pulled after her – but still she sang out loud against the darkness in his mind.

She tried to sing him back to the world of sky and trees, half-dug holes, warm floorboards and full bowls. She howled with love, not pain.

She made him stop and turn and walk back to her.

'Be quiet. Damn you.'

She licked the wrist of the strong hand that held her down, as in the work of a moment he splayed her ribs with the backblade of the spade held low hilted.

'Damn you to hell.'

He dug a blow that tore her face away then he walked on, certain she could neither sing nor follow.

But she tried. Digging forwards with her long front paws, her useless hind legs twisting behind her.

But she tried. Her snout pushing forwards in the dirt and her black and white fur rinsed with the waves of red that smeared a wake on the ground as she moved.

She died at the gatepost, calling soundlessly to him as her eye dimmed in her raw-open head.

Chapter 45

May 1976

The old and the young wives of Mulderrig are rising uneasy this morning, for last night a visitor came uninvited. It blew open their latches and skipped over their thresholds. It patted their cats and climbed their stairs. It whispered in their ears and eased the rings off their fingers. It stretched out on their beds and grinned at their sleeping husbands. The old and the young wives watched behind closed eyes, helpless in their dreams.

They remember now. As they stand waiting for the kettle, or feeding the baby, they look down at their fingers where their wedding bands used to be. They search in soap dishes and along window ledges, in drawers and on dressers. They run outside to ransack the potato peelings. But all the time they know that they never took their rings off – they never would! And their husbands will say, 'Ah, it's bound to turn up, along with my shaving mirror and my belt buckle.'

So the village shrugs and goes about its business.

For isn't it the day of the play?

Who has the time to notice a few missing things?

Who has the time to mark the space left by an old

copper kettle or a dusty horse brass? Or a dented christening cup or a tarnished candlestick?

And if anyone does notice, well, they are soon caught up in another drama, which is far more distracting. For the villagers are now discovering that there is not a drop of milk to be had in the whole of Mulderrig. From unopened pints in refrigerators to netted jugs in cool pantries, every drop of milk in Mulderrig is found to be bitter and curdled and clabbered enough to stand a fork upright. What's more the butter is rancid, the cream has turned and the cheese is entirely rotten.

Mulderrig has gone sour.

Of course, ask Bridget Doosey and she would tell you that milk products are particularly vulnerable to malevolent supernatural forces. Keep the dead away from the dairy, she'd advise. But Bridget Doosey is happily unaware of the plight of the rest of the village, for right now she's enjoying her fifth cup of tea of the day up at Rathmore House, which has its full complement of shiny objects and the milk pours fine and fresh from the jug on the kitchen table.

Bridget, in her new role as dresser to Mrs Cauley, has curled the wig, pressed the brocade and de-flead the silver fox, Shauna having resigned the position due to hostilities over a scorch mark on Mrs Cauley's bird of paradise kimono.

Shauna refills the sugar bowl and sets it next to Bridget. 'How's she coming on?'

Bridget empties a handful of sugar into her cup. 'She's primped and painted. She wanted a moment to herself, so I left her outside swearing at the squirrels.'

'She's in that kind of mood?'

Bridget stirs her tea, licks the back of the spoon and puts it back in the sugar bowl. 'She is.'

'How does she look?'

'Terrifying. Like the Virgin Queen herself.'

'Well, she wanted the Bette Davis style.'

'She did.'

Shauna, at the sink, looks over her shoulder. 'I'm glad you could help her.'

'She wanted you really.'

Shauna rolls her eyes.

'She's a twisted old bitch, granted, but she cares about you, Shauna. She'd be lost—'

'Ah, don't.'

Bridget lifts the teapot. 'Isn't there anything else to pour the tea out of? I could piss straighter than this.' She fills a cup and pushes it across the table. 'Cross my palm?'

Shauna sits down, rooting around in the pocket of her apron. 'I've nothing – a sweet wrapper?'

'I'll accept that.'

Shauna drinks the tea then hands the cup back. She loves this. It's a joke, sure, but there's always something in it that makes her think. She sits in silence and watches as the tea leaves move around the cup under Bridget's narrowed eyes, swilled anticlockwise. Bridget tips out the excess liquid, sets the cup right and peers inside.

Shauna leans forward expectantly. 'What do you see?'

Bridget sucks air slowly through her teeth. If she holds the cup at an angle and squints a bit she can make out a battleaxe, Italy without its boot heel, and a fly swat. Or it could be a butterfly, a pair of one-legged trousers and a frying pan.

'There's travel abroad to a hot climate.'

'Is there marriage? A future between us?'

'Well, you're half-suited.'

'Is that it?'

'And if you don't go over water you'll pass it.'

'No babies?'

'And watch yourself about the kitchen, Shauna. Hot fat doesn't bode well for you.'

Bridget hands the cup back to Shauna. 'Let him take you out a bit first. Let him court you. Just think it. Down to Ennismore for a view of that premium John Wayne film.'

Shauna joins in. 'Dinner afterwards at the Atlantic Hotel, with the prawn cocktail.'

Bridget taps her arm. 'That's it! And if you're meant to be with him you'll be with him. Although it'll be like strapping yourself to a bloody rocket.'

Shauna grins.

Bridget laughs. 'A rocket ride, is that what you want? Well then, the best of luck to you, girl.'

Bridget finishes her tea and turns her cup, upends it, rights it and studies it for a long time.

'What does it say, Bridget?'

Bridget looks up, her face suddenly tired. 'It says nothing. Nothing at all.'

Today will surely be the last fair day. After today, everyone says, Irish weather will resume and it will be downhill all the way to Christmas. After today, the rain will be a constant visitor, drawing up its chair and putting on its sitting britches. But the rain seems far away right now as the sun roars down from the cloud-bald sky.

By midday the sun is belting down on the coachloads arriving in the square from out of town. It sends the daddies gasping into Kerrigan's Bar and the mammies sweating and muttering as they unpack babies and granddads, flasks and sandwiches.

The same sun alights on the astounding figure of Mrs Cauley as she sits smoking a cigarette in her wheelchair.

Over her head, slung from one end of the village hall to the other, is a sign, *The Playboy of the Western World by John Millington Synge*, in big gold letters. There are flowering shrubs on either side of the doorway tied with green and gold ribbons. Inside the door Teasie Lavelle and Mrs Moran are at their stations selling tickets. The people form a queue and wait their turn as Teasie counts out the change and hands them a programme. They begin to take their seats in the hall, the mammies and the daddies dug out of the pub, the old and the young, familiar faces and some less so.

Teasie smiles across at Mrs Moran, feeling her nerves uncoil. She has wrapped Mammy up well and left her at home with a flask and a plate of sandwiches. She has locked all the doors and checked them twice. She is looking forward to a full day with no one roaring any predictions at her, or gabbering in tongues, or staring around them glassy-eyed and moaning.

Mahony, costumed to the hilt, steps outside to a chorus of wolf whistles.

'Here he is now.'

'Here's himself.'

'You're a fine figure of a man, Mahony.'

They roar.

Mahony salutes them and walks over to Mrs Cauley. In his white shirt and tight britches he looks younger; he's shaved and maybe even washed his hair. Mrs Cauley could kiss him.

He lights a fag and scowls up at the sun. 'Am I Christy enough for you?'

'You are,' she says. 'Don't we make a fine-looking pair? Jesus, we're blessed.'

Mrs Cauley is majestic in fur, gold brocade and a foot-high ginger pompadour. Her make-up has been applied with an unsparing hand, even over the bandage across her nose. Her blackened eyes beneath lend a kind of damaged drama. The rest of the bruises she hides with a mandarin collar and a man's silk cravat.

Mahony watches as Johnnie runs out through the wall, stripped to the waist. He stands out in the road dancing suggestively and waving his shirt.

'It's a great day for Johnnie. He's on top form,' says Mahony.

Mrs Cauley smiles. 'He's with me now, isn't he? I can feel him.'

Mahony looks up. Above them Miss Mulhearne is attempting to hide behind the old rusted school bell. She's sobbing or laughing, Mahony can't tell which, only that her dim shoulders are shaking. Johnnie points up at her, throws down his shirt and starts to unbuckle his trousers. Miss Mulhearne covers her eyes.

Mahony smiles at Mrs Cauley. 'So you can. He never leaves your side.'

Mrs Lavelle opens her eyes wide. Awake and lucid she throws the blanket off her knees, stretches her legs and stands up. She walks around the room, trailing her hand over furniture, picking up ornaments. She licks her finger and draws in the dust on the mantelpiece. Four letters. She reads the name back to herself and finds that she's hardly surprised at all. She finds a hairpin and without knowing how she picks the lock on the parlour door and slips out into the hallway.

She stands in front of the mirror and takes a good look.

Mrs Lavelle is not herself any more.

She takes a scarf and ties it around her head.

She breathes kisses on the glass and gives herself come-hithers.

She tries the front door: it's locked, as is the back door. With remarkable dexterity for an elderly woman with rheumatoid arthritis, she levers the kitchen window open with a bread knife, hitches up her skirt and climbs out of it.

Outside, Mary Lavelle kicks off her carpet slippers and dances barefoot through the garden.

Inside, it's quieter than it has been for weeks. Now the only dead thing in Mary Lavelle's house is the moth in her sugar bowl.

Chapter 46

May 1976

Jack's squad car is parked on his drive when Annie Farelly arrives at his house. When she rings the doorbell he comes round the side of the house in his uniform, wiping his hands on a cloth.

'Annie, I'm just in the garage, getting a few tools together before I go down to keep an eye on the set.' He smiles. 'Tadhg trips over the threshold every time he crosses it.'

Annie tries to smile. 'He's throwing himself into the role.'

Jack laughs. Then he stops, noticing the bruises on her temple, on her jaw, under a dredging of face powder.

'What happened to you?' He reaches over, as if to touch her.

Annie colours. 'I fell in the bath.'

He puts his hand down and looks at her closely. 'Come to the play with me, Annie. I can bring you down to the village in the car.'

'Ah no, it's not for me. But thank you all the same, Jack.'

Jack, like a gentleman, won't press her. 'So what do I owe this pleasure to?' he smiles, his eyes kind.

'It doesn't appear that you have time to talk. I'll come back another time.'

'Of course I've time, there's always time. Will we go inside the house?'

'Ah no, I won't keep you.'

'Well then, come round to the garage. You can talk to me while I pack a bag.'

She nods.

He opens a deckchair and sets it by the workbench and spreads a clean rag on the seat for her. She sits down and, bolstered by the expression of patient concern on his face, she begins.

She tells him everything she's left unsaid these long years. Sitting there before him in her mauve cardigan and cream blouse, in her low-heeled shoes and old-fashioned gloves.

He looks down at the tin of tacks in his hand and she tells him of the high esteem she holds him in. For doing what he did for the sake of the village, although not one of them knows to thank him for it. And now Mahony won't rest until he gets to the bottom of his mother's disappearance, and Mrs Cauley is snooping, and Bridget Doosey is in on the act too. Annie recounts Mahony's refusal of her bribe: a sum she had reserved to build and furnish a new conservatory, and she stops, just for a moment, to recall in her own mind the rattan furniture she has been willing to forgo.

When she has finished, Jack puts down the tin of tacks.

He stands with his back to her, taking off his uniform jacket. 'How did you know, Annie?'

'I saw you walking into the forest that day and I saw the look on your face. As soon as Bridget Doosey started putting it out that Orla had disappeared, I just knew.'

He hangs up his jacket. 'And you've never told anyone?'

'Not a soul.'

He takes off his tie and drapes it over his jacket and turns to face her. 'And what's the town's opinion of this great crime?'

'A few think it never happened, that Orla left town. A few think that Tadhg or Jimmy Nylon might know something about it, or Tom even, up in the forest. That one of them might be involved.'

Jack shakes his head.

Annie nods sagely. 'Well, I don't think anyone really believes that.'

'And what about me?' Jack rolls up his sleeves. 'Is Jack Brophy a suspect?'

'You'd be the last person—'

He sends her spinning then picks her up again and again. He pushes her up against the workbench, holding her face pinched in his fingers. 'Look at me,' he says.

Annie tries, really she tries. Whenever her eyes close or she looks away he bangs her head against the wall.

'Didn't I tell you to look at me?'

He tells her, over and over, that he didn't do it for the fucking village.

He did it for himself.

'Have you got that, Annie?'

She asks him if she can go home, please. Her lips don't seem belong to her any more, so she speaks slowly. 'Can I please go home?'

'You can't,' says Jack. 'You talk too much.'

This time she hardly sees his fist move.

She looks up at him. He is rifling through a drawer, whistling. She is curled in on herself, lying awkwardly on her shoulder. Pain rinses her mind of thought and keeps her breathing shallow.

He shuts the drawer and comes over to her with a sheet of plastic. He kneels next to her, looking down in dismay at his uniform trousers as the blood blotches and flowers on each dark-blue knee.

He wraps the plastic around her face, tucking it closely in at her throat and up under her chin, ignoring her body moving under him. He tightens the sheeting until her eyelids are splayed, then he secures it at the back of her head with nylon cord. Her breath starts to fog the plastic.

He leans over her, stroking her back with his face close to her. He's telling her something she can't hear.

Chapter 47

May 1976

In Mulderrig Village Hall the audience sits silent and blinking, their attention fixed on the stage curtains lit by a single solitary spotlight. The curtains undulate gently, although there's no breeze to speak of, for the windows are covered with black card and the doors are closed against the afternoon sun.

A figure steals into the hall, ticketless and uninvited. It pads into a far corner of the room and curls up in the deep shadows there.

Backstage the cast are waiting. They grin and point and stifle laughs to see themselves all together, ready in their costumes.

Soon the cast too quieten down.

And everyone begins to feel it.

Even the sharpest of them would struggle to describe what they are feeling.

It isn't love, or nostalgia, or peace, or even excitement – not really. It isn't the sense that something remarkable is about to happen, although that is there, in the feeling.

In the shadows at the back of the hall a figure unties her scarf, shakes out her hair and leans back against the wall.

Eddie Callaghan's nephew trains a light on the band at

the front of the stage. A slow ripple thrills through the audience as Pat Nolan takes up the uilleann pipes.

The first notes come sweet and harsh and a lament of riveting beauty spreads over the room. It's felt in the spine and in the soul, in the mind and in the gut. The pipes sing about a land lost, about forgotten honour and wasted bravery. They sing of sedge-edged water and wide skies, of the mountains and the sea, of those who are gone and those who never even were.

As the last strains of Pat Nolan's pipes echo, the curtains open.

The actors are amazed to find that the words fall naturally from their mouths, as if they have just thought them up themselves for the first time. So that Mrs Moran forgets to turn over the pages of her prompt book.

The audience watch bright-eyed and open-lipped, and everyone knows for sure that real lives are being lived on the stage today.

But it is Mahony that they are waiting for and when he walks onto the stage the room sighs.

At the back of the hall the figure in the shadows lifts up her head and smiles.

During the interval the lights go on and the doors are propped open. The daddies go out into the late afternoon sun for a smoke. The babies, who have stored up their crying, start wailing in chorus for rusks and dry nappies. Finding it impossible to settle, Teasie Lavelle rubs the hairs on her arms back down and looks over her shoulder.

Bridget Doosey is handing around lemonade and biscuits. 'Will you have a drink, Teasie?'

Teasie pushes her glasses up her nose and takes a paper cup. 'How's Mammy?'

'I've locked her in the house. I think I'll go back and check on her.'

'She'll be fine for a bit. Have a break for yourself, now.'

Teasie shakes her head, 'I don't know.'

'Are you managing, Teasie?'

Teasie shrugs, her eyes filling.

'Would it help if I came over to see her?'

Teasie nods. 'It might.'

'Then I'll be over later. Take a few biscuits for yourself there, Teasie.'

Teasie finishes the lemonade too quickly, so that it catches in her throat, but Bridget has turned away before she can give her the paper cup back.

Backstage the cast hug each other and mock-scream. They're holding up. They're loving it. Mrs Cauley's told them to stay out the back for the interval and Shauna brings them a tray of drinks, beer and lemonade if they want it. Mahony kisses Shauna through his stage make-up and she laughs to see him with more lipstick on than she has. As Mahony walks on to take his place she puts her hand on his arm and undoes another button on his shirt.

'For the mammies,' she grins.

The curtains open and the audience watch Mahony, as Christy, delight in the luck he has to be a hero remade, and when he throws out a wink the room hops. The audience watch with a shared smile, riveted by every glance from Christy and foot-stamp from Pegeen and waft of the Widow Quin's shawl.

A man comes quietly into the hall and takes a drink from the tray on the table. He picks his way along the aisle to a vacant seat.

A voice calls out loud from the back of the hall.

'He is washed in the blood of the lamb.'

A few members of the audience laugh, believing it to be part of the play.

The voice rings out again: the high, clear voice of a young girl.

'He is washed in the blood of the lamb.'

Eddie Callaghan's nephew gives a cry of alarm, as above him the stage lights flare and turn around all by themselves in their sockets, leaving the stage in darkness.

The actors too stop and turn.

The audience hold on to their seats as, inexplicably, the chairs pivot round on their back legs, scraping the floor in unison. The front doors slip down their latches and drive home their bolts. In the kitchen, the tea urn reaches a rolling boil and the crockery starts to shake. The spoons begin to bend and the sandwiches curl up and die.

At the back of the hall Mrs Lavelle stands barefoot in the spotlight with an expression of finely wrought hatred on her face.

She raises her arm and points.

And everyone looks.

It is Jack Brophy, taking his seat with a paper cup in his hand.

Jack puts his drink down and cautiously walks over to Mrs Lavelle, as if he's a shy man asking a timid woman to dance. The village holds its breath as he lays a hand gently on her arm.

She screams. It's threadbare and piercing, like a hurt child.

Pat Nolan strikes up the band.

After the play, the buffet table is set for the aftershow party and within minutes it is gnawed so clean it's a wonder it still has legs. Many move quickly past the tea and on to the hard stuff as they stand around dusting down crumbs and joining in with one of several acceptable topics of debate: the high calibre of the acting, not just of Mahony himself, of course, but of the supporting cast, particularly Tadhg Kerrigan as Old Mahon, the murdered father, tripping in and out over the doorframe.

No one mentions Mrs Lavelle.

Father Quinn skulks amongst them, as welcome as a wet shoe.

Across the room Mrs Cauley catches his eye and toasts him. He moves across to her.

'Mrs Cauley.'

'Father Quinn, did you enjoy the play?'

'It was a remarkable production, but I hope it was worth it.'

Mrs Cauley smiles sweetly. 'Oh it was, Father.'

The priest bends forwards. 'We had a deal, Mrs Cauley. Mahony should have left town this morning.'

'When it came down to it he just couldn't, Father.'

Father Quinn's smile is pestilential. 'No matter. I'll be going home to make that call directly. Your protégé will be swiftly taken into custody.'

Shauna brings over a tray with two glasses of whiskey on it. 'Will you have a little tipple for yourself, Father?'

Father Quinn smirks. 'Why not? It seems that I have reason to celebrate.'

'Grand, so, that's your one there, Father. Not that one, *the one on the left*, Father, *the left one*. Yes. That one.'

Father Quinn raises his glass. 'Ladies, I wish you a good evening.' He bows slightly and weaves off through the crowd, grinning malignantly.

'And I wish you a lifetime of hard shits,' says Mrs Cauley, downing her whiskey with a widening smile.

At the parochial house Bridget Doosey cuts the telephone cord, locks the back door and dangles the key into the cup of her brassiere. She goes up to the guest room, takes off her overalls and opens her crocodile handbag. She pulls on grey tights and a leotard and flexes gamely in front of the wardrobe mirror before settling down to wait.

At the village hall the crowd shows no sign of leaving, not while the cast move amongst them like higher beings. The actors grin at the requests to run another night, or two, or ten. All of them radiant with stage make-up and success. In the kitchen the helpers are wiping up the plates and cups with the radio on. Mrs Moran flicks her tea towel in time to the Brotherhood of Man and even Michael Hopper joins in, although quite who he's saving his kisses for is a mystery to everyone.

By the side of the stage Mrs Cauley watches and smiles. There is Mahony, riding high with Shauna by his side blushing scarlet at being near the centre of attention. God love her.

Mrs Cauley's smile fades as she spots Jack Brophy making his way through the crowd, stopping to lean down to talk here and there. Nodding with a serious expression on his face, listening intently. Tadhg presses a glass into his hand, they speak for a moment and then Tadhg pats him on the back. Jack downs his drink.

Mrs Cauley studies Jack closely and for long enough for him to look up at her. He smiles and makes his way over.

'Now then, Jack.'

'Are you behaving yourself, Merle?'

'I am of course.'

'And how did you get those two shiners?'

'I ran into a pillow.'

Jack pulls up a chair and sits down beside her. 'Congratulations on a fine play.'

'You missed the first act.'

Jack shrugs and smiles. 'Garda business.'

'Then you're excused. And how is Mary Lavelle?'

Jack nods. 'She's quiet now. Maurice has given her a sedative.'

There's a great commotion as a group of lads pick Mahony up and parade him around the hall; a few young ones follow laughing. The band re-forms again in the corner of the room and pockets of dancing start to break out.

Jack smiles. 'The town has taken to him.'

'Unlike his mother.'

Jack doesn't answer.

'What happened to Orla Sweeney?'

Jack smiles at her. 'It's too late in the day to ask me that, Merle. I'm off home to my slippers and RTÉ. I've not the time to talk crime tales.'

'I'll only ask you again,' smiles Mrs Cauley.

'The persistent detective.' His voice is low, mildly sardonic. 'Don't you need a body for a murder inquiry?'

'We will find her.'

Jack looks amused. 'Who will? Bridget Doosey with a shovel?'

'We know she was murdered, Jack. Evidence or no evidence.'

'I credited you with better sense.' He sounds genuinely disappointed. 'There was no murder. The girl left town and dumped her brat at the orphanage. This crime story you've invented is not going to change that.'

Mrs Cauley narrows her eyes.

Jack stands up. 'Forgive me; it's been a long day. Goodnight, Merle.'

By the door Jack stops and shakes Mahony's hand and kisses Shauna on the cheek. He's telling him he's done a grand job, no doubt. Mahony's face is blank, unreadable. As Jack turns to go he looks back at Mrs Cauley and smiles.

In the kitchen Mahony and Shauna are dancing to a slow song on the radio. Mrs Cauley can see them through the serving hatch. Shauna has her head against his neck and her hand furled against his chest. Mahony rests his cheek against her hair. God help them, thinks Mrs Cauley.

Alone in a pool of electric light Mrs Cauley raises her glass and toasts the stage. But the stage is empty; there are only a few fallen sequins that will take Michael Hopper a month to sweep up.

Johnnie isn't there.

She closes her eyes.

Johnnie smiles and kisses her face again and again and again.

Chapter 48

May 1976

Father Quinn wipes his forehead with the curtain. He can't for the life of him find his handkerchief. He sits back down at his desk and tries the phone again but hears nothing down the line.

He feels very wrong. He blames the library. He hasn't liked this room since the frogs took it over. They are very active tonight, arranging themselves in patterns on the hearthrug like synchronised swimmers, leering up at him, kicking out their webbed feet, turning and merging.

Father Quinn wipes his forehead with the receiver. Wait a minute! If he holds it up to his ear he can hear a voice through it.

Perhaps it's God's.

Or The God Of The Frogs.

The frogs nod and grin up at him, melting together into colourful clumps: a horrific kaleidoscope of soft under-bellies and reticulated limbs, green and orange, gold and brown.

There's another sound inside the receiver: it is hooves, galloping. Father Quinn picks up the phone, wraps it in his jacket for safekeeping and edges along the wall to try to find a door.

Bridget Doosey looks at the sugar lump on the saucer; she's tempted to have a go of it herself. She'll have to ask Shauna how many she put in the priest's whiskey. Judging by his reaction there's a rake of fun to be had on the old LSD, what with the babbling and the muttering, the licking of the wallpaper and the swinging from the curtains. But now it's time for Father Quinn's trip to take a more unsettling turn, with a little help from last year's nativity play and the priest's equinophobia. She's had a good clop on the coconuts, but now it's time for the priest to meet his new friend face to face. She picks up the donkey's head. It's a work of art, complete with grey fur, foot-high ears and bulbous eyes. The jaw can be animated by way of a string to show off the set of long white teeth to full effect. Bridget stifles a laugh and opens the guestroom door.

Father Quinn sees the creature even with his eyes closed. He hears it even with his ears closed, haw-hawing at him. It has chased him through walls and over bedposts, around tables and through letterboxes, with its eyes swirling and burning. He holds his head in his hands and his fingers go straight through into the mush of his brain. He cries like a baby and cradles his telephone against him. From time to time he kisses it and dribbles into the mouthpiece.

In the kitchen of the parochial house, in the first grey light of morning, Bridget Doosey takes off her mask and pours herself a piña colada. She wipes her eyes and drinks. This is the best fun she's had in a very long time.

She takes off her tail and puts on an apron. Later she'll

fix Father Quinn a coffee, carefully stirring in two more special lumps, then she'll phone the Bishop and tell him that Father Quinn is acting strangely. In the meantime she'll tie the priest to his bed frame. Just so that he doesn't damage himself by jumping out of the window or doing anything stupid.

Then she'll go over and visit Teasie to see if she can't get Mary Lavelle freshened up a bit.

Chapter 49

May 1976

A flannel would be wasted on Mary Lavelle. That much is obvious to Bridget Doosey.

Bridget sends Teasie out of the room for a clean pillow-case then she gets up on a stepladder to cover Mary's face. For she is certain that Mary wouldn't have wanted her daughter to see such an expression. Blue tongued and pop-eyed, like a mouse Bridget once found strangled in a hairnet. Luckily Teasie only caught the back view of her mother swinging gently from the light fitting.

By the time Dr McNulty and Jack Brophy arrive Teasie has stopped being sick in the sink for long enough to make tea for the gentlemen, although she forgets to boil the water. Jack Brophy cautions Bridget for disrupting the scene of death but the doctor pats him on the back.

'It's OK, Jack,' he says. 'Isn't it a straightforward case of suicide? The poor woman was unravelled.'

A meddlesome wind plays about the bay today. It came in on the back of the wild Atlantic. It's curious and coy, jaunty and teasing. It slinks through the town, licking at the walls and rooftops with its salty tongue. It hustles through doors and windows and capers uninvited into hallways. It dances the washing and bounces the spiders on their webs. It fidgets Mary Lavelle's bedroom curtains and caresses Teasie's hair as she rocks on the floor by the side of the bed.

It's a ghost-ridden wind today that opens and shuts Mary's bedroom door, whistles down the stairs and rattles right out of the letterbox. It rushes past Bridget Doosey and she holds on to the brim of her fedora as she hurries up the road to Rathmore House.

Chapter 50

May 1976

Mrs Cauley contemplates the button on the table. 'So Jack had a hand in this?'

Bridget shrugs. 'Well, I found that in Mary Lavelle's hand and it's from a guard's uniform, isn't it?'

Mahony nods. 'I'd say so.'

'And I'd say Mary had a bit of help,' says Bridget. 'Unless she flew up to the light fitting.'

'There was no chair or furniture nearby?'

'Exactly, Mahony. And she probably didn't bruise her own wrists or tear her own slip either.'

Mrs Cauley raises her eyebrows.

Bridget frowns. 'To say nothing of the teeth marks on her left breast and the broken clavicle.'

Shauna shudders by the sink as she washes the teacups and wonders why things have to get so grisly whenever Bridget Doosey is around.

Bridget picks up the button with the sugar tongs. 'He had to shut her up; she was trying to tell us something at the play.'

Mrs Cauley shakes her head. 'We should never have left

her alone. What were we thinking? She was identifying him as the killer.'

Bridget drops the button into a plastic bag. 'And so now we have a body, only not the right one.'

Shauna turns to them, drying her hands on a tea towel. 'This is terrible, but what can any of us do?'

'You're right, Shauna, what can we do?' agrees Bridget. 'There's Jack, a real lightning bastard who's been getting away with murder for years.' Bridget taps the side of her nose. 'But it's made him cocky and that might just be his downfall.'

Mahony looks at her. 'How do you mean?'

'I mean something important was missing from the body.' Bridget leans forward and whispers. 'Mary wasn't wearing any drawers.'

Shauna stares at her, horrified.

Mrs Cauley ponders this. 'How do you know that Jack took them? Maybe Mary hadn't put any on? Maybe she was having a bit of an airing?'

Shauna is without words.

Bridget turns to Mrs Cauley with a venomous expression. 'Are you trying to provoke me, old woman?'

Mrs Cauley hides a smile.

'Now, I'm no expert,' says Bridget. 'But sometimes they just can't help themselves, these murderers; they have to keep something.'

'A souvenir?' asks Mahony.

Bridget nods. 'And I'm betting that if he kept something of Mary's he'll have kept something of Orla's.'

Mahony thinks of the river, of Ida coming across Jack getting rid of evidence, something he'd kept, drowning it like a sack of kittens. But why there and why then, all those years later?

Bridget puts her hand on Mahony's arm. 'There's something we need to do, son.'

Shauna glances at Bridget with a look of growing panic. 'What?'

'Search Jack's house.'

Shauna waves the tea towel at her. 'Are you crazy? He's a killer, a cold-blooded upfront killer. We should leave him to the guards.'

'He is the guards,' says Bridget.

Shauna scowls. 'All right, I meant go above him.'

'And we will, Shauna,' reassures Mrs Cauley. 'But you have to remember that the moment he's threatened with an investigation Jack will be covering his tracks. We have to take him down, truss him up and hand him over to them. Case opened, case closed.'

'I'll go,' says Mahony. 'Cover me, and I'll go.'

Shauna glares at Bridget. 'Now look what you've done.'

Chapter 51

May 1976

In the parochial house Father Quinn is experiencing the mother of all comedowns. He has managed to chew through his restraints and is now stealing down the stairs. He stops every now and then to make sure that the hell-donkey isn't following him. With profound dismay he realises the keys to the front and back doors are missing and his trembling hands will not allow him to open the temperamental kitchen window catch. For a while all he can do is curl up, sobbing brokenly, under the table.

Then from some place, some inner resourceful place, a memory comes.

It is of Mahony. Striding the stage in his tight britches with his dark eyes smiling. He is laughing at him.

By degrees Father Quinn crawls out from under the table and, seeing Michael Hopper's bag of tools lying next to the back door, arms himself with a hammer. He edges over to the countertop, drags himself up and summons all his remaining strength.

By mid-morning Father Eugene Quinn slithers from a broken window into a rose bush. It's a difficult birth.

The priest lies blinking up at the clouds, froth collecting at the corners of his mouth. Then he turns himself over, drags himself up and limps off down the garden path. Drugged, trouserless and howling for revenge.

Chapter 52

May 1976

In the village hall Shauna switches on the tea urn and butters a few sconcs. Just because they're running a covert operation there's no reason not to be comfortable. The others pull chairs around the foot of the stage. No one smiles.

Mrs Cauley lends a funereal air to the proceedings, dressed in black bombazine like an elderly crow, her bandaged face pale and regal above a lace collar. She has taken one of her most dramatic wigs out of retirement; it is her judgement day wig, she says. Johnnie steps down off the stage and, with a look of concentration, tries to pet it. The wig, a formidable black beehive, edges away of its own accord until Mrs Cauley reaches a hand up to straighten it.

She peers out through her dressings. 'So, Doosey, can you confirm that our target is currently ensconced in the garda station?'

Bridget pats the binoculars on her lap. 'He is, the murdering bastard.'

'Then let's synchronise our watches.' Mrs Cauley draws an ancient pocket watch from the folds of her cape and passes it to Mahony.

Mahony turns it over in his hands. It's gold, remarkably fine and engraved with the initials *J. M. S.* When he flicks the catch with his thumbnail, the casement opens as smoothly as a beetle's wings.

He glances up at Mrs Cauley. 'It reads half past five.'

Behind her Johnnie withdraws his watch from his waist-coat pocket. He taps it and gives it a shake.

Shauna rolls her eyes. 'It's a quarter past eleven.'

Mrs Cauley nods. 'Mahony, are you ready?'

'I am.'

At twenty minutes past eleven, refusing a package of sand-wiches and a flask of tea from Shauna, Mahony exits the west-facing door of the village hall. He takes the back road to Kerrigan's Bar and sees no one. He enters the saloon door at twenty-four minutes past eleven. Tadhg is stacking bottles of lemonade behind the bar. Mahony asks the crack of Tadhg's arse if he can have a lend of the car. The crack says he can of course but it's full of chickens. Mahony thanks the crack and runs out of the back door.

At twenty-seven minutes past eleven, Jack Brophy receives a visit, in person, at the station, from Mrs Cauley and Bridget Doosey. Bridget Doosey, having manoeuvred Mrs Cauley's wheelchair in the door, takes a seat in the corner of the room and clamps a pair of interrogatory eyes on the guard. From time to time she whistles in an attempt to appear nonchalant.

At thirty-four minutes past eleven, Mahony is still attempting to start Tadhg's car. Chickens are falling out of the open door and skidding along the bonnet. There's a cockerel in the footwell shitting on the accelerator and two hens roosting on the dashboard. Mahony ignores them; he is listening to the engine in despair. This time it really is terminal.

At thirty-eight minutes past eleven, Mahony goes back inside Kerrigan's and grabs a set of keys from the hook behind the bar. He cuts out and around the back of the pub and runs to the garage, passing the doorway where Father Eugene Quinn sits sucking his fingers and rocking. Father Quinn opens his eyes and clocks Mahony. It is twenty to twelve.

Mahony has the garage door open in moment.
    And time stops.
    There, in front of him, is Tadhg Kerrigan's 1956 Cadillac Eldorado Seville: a two-door coupé the blue of a cloudless afternoon. Her headlamps widen in surprise as Mahony reaches out to touch her bright flank. She is polished to a mirror, all curves and dazzling chrome.
    She starts first time and turns over with the bass purr of a chain-smoking tiger. She is halfway out of the garage when Father Quinn jumps in front of her like a bollox.
    The car clips the priest and sends him spinning, so that when Mahony looks in his rear-view mirror he sees the priest flat on his arse with his fist up in the air, like a figure from a comic book.
    To his credit, Father Quinn picks himself up and gives chase as Mahony swings the Eldorado out onto the Castleross road wondering why the priest is wearing little more than his underpants.

Shauna is manning the headquarters at the village hall. She has drunk six cups of tea and broken a milk jug. She has swept and washed the floor and cleaned the windows. She has had a good go at the cobwebs with a tea towel tied to a broom and has restacked the chairs. She has cut a mountain of sandwiches and rinsed out the dishcloths.

She resumes her position behind the serving hatch, where she eats another biscuit, absentmindedly, with her eyes riveted to the door.

The statement is taking far longer than anyone would expect, given that Mrs Cauley didn't see the suspect properly, can't remember the precise look or contents of her purse and has no real idea regarding the time of the theft.

Nevertheless her recollection of theatrical anecdotes is second to none today.

It is well known that Mrs Cauley is an expert conversationalist with a multitude of subjects at her disposal, from politics to poker, billiards to tractor mechanics. And it's all entirely bespoke.

So Jack Brophy shows little surprise when Mrs Cauley launches into a detailed account of the time she hung a door with Noël Coward and his comprehensive set of chisels. Bridget sits quietly in the corner of the room, sucking her teeth and narrowing her eyes.

Not only does Jack seem oblivious of Bridget Doosey's stony glare but he also appears to be genuinely enjoying Mrs Cauley's exhaustive description of Ivor Novello's tool bag. He listens and nods with an attentive smile on his face, without even a hint of murderous intent.

Emboldened by the effortless success of their plan, Mrs Cauley embarks on a rambling anecdote involving Alfred Lunt and a rotary lathe. And Bridget Doosey starts to relax a little and finger the leaflets on wife beating and vehicular speeding.

Then Father Quinn bursts limping into the station,

unshaven, red-eyed and gibbering softly. The moment he lays eyes on Jack Brophy he starts to cry.

'Now are you sure about what you saw, Father?' Jack takes off his jacket and passes it to the priest to put around himself for decency.

Mrs Cauley talks low. 'He's not sure of anything. Can't you see he's cracked?'

Father Quinn fixes her with a wide-toothed sneer. 'Mahony took a car and tried to run me over, I'm sure of that.'

'Yes, Father,' says Mrs Cauley. 'And an ass with burning eyes was chasing you around your house all last night. Remember?'

'It was you.' Father Quinn points at her with a shaking finger. 'You and her are behind it. I knew it. You're despicable.'

Jack leans forward and pats the man on the arm. 'Settle down now, Father. I just need to know which direction Mahony was driving in.'

The priest nods. 'He drove out onto the Castleross road.'

'Did he now?' says Jack, looking dead at Mrs Cauley.

Jack leans forward and pats Father Quinn on the shoulder. 'Don't worry yourself now, Father,' he says. 'Just take yourself home and leave everything to me. I'll deal with Mahony.'

Chapter 53

May 1976

Mahony spins the Eldorado into Jack Brophy's drive and kills the engine. It's a good-sized modern bungalow set out of town on the road to Castleross. The place is well built and well maintained with well-locked doors. Which doesn't surprise Mahony at all, given Jack's line of business.

Mahony walks round the back of the house, where the land falls away into an established orchard. Painted beehives nestle amongst the trees; a couple of decent horses pull grass in the field beyond.

Mahony picks up a stone from a nearby rockery and, holding one arm over his face, puts a window in with it. He reaches his hand in and unlocks the back door.

The kitchen is neat. Immaculate. As is the hallway and the dining room. It is pale beige and carpeted thickly throughout. In the sitting room there's a wooden unit with a turntable and a selection of records, all opera, evidence right there of a diseased mind. A clock from the Deputy Commissioner sits up on the mantelpiece, brassy and smug in its polished glass dome. There are a couple of seascapes hanging on the wall – otherwise, nothing.

The place is anonymous.

The bedrooms are the same. No photos, nothing *personal*. Mahony opens the wardrobe in the master bedroom, there's one side for uniform, all pressed and ready, and the other side for off-duty, all pressed and ready. Jack's civilian clothes are arranged by colour from brown to fawn, with a black suit and a grey suit. The bedside table holds a torch and an alarm clock set for six o'clock.

Mahony takes the torch, looks for a way into the attic and finds it in the third bedroom. He stands on the bed and pulls down the hatch and the steel ladder that's attached to it. He sees the cord of a light switch hanging above him, so he throws the torch on the bed and swings himself up through the hole.

There's fuck all in the attic. Mahony goes back down the ladder. He'll take one last scan about the place then leave. On his way out he passes the pantry and thinks to try the door.

And there she is.

Mahony's heart turns over with horror.

Crouched naked in an old tin hip bath and swaddled in plastic sheeting, Annie Farelly grins back at him with her eyes wide and sightless and her knuckles resting in the quarter inch of blood congealing in the bottom of the bath.

Fuck no. Christ. Ah no.

On the shelf behind her, between tins of corned beef and string sacks of onions, are her shoes, paired and resting on newspaper, blood dulling the tan polish. Next to them are her clothes. Stained and folded. There's a cream blouse, a mauve cardigan, a grey pleated skirt, bunched underwear and a bloodied reel of stockings.

Mahony falls out of the back door running as a car pulls up on the drive at the front of the house.

· 333 ·

Chapter 54

May 1976

Back in the village hall Mrs Cauley frowns and scratches up under her wig. Her scalp is hopping, which is never a good sign.

She attempts a reassuring smile. 'Mahony is quick, Shauna. In the wits department there's none quicker.'

Bridget nods sagely. 'She's right. Listen to her now. Dry your arse and drink your tea. Mahony will slip in and out. He'll be off up the coast with the evidence by now.'

'He'll be long gone by the time Brophy gets up to the house,' Mrs Cauley agrees.

Shauna wipes her eyes. 'Mahony will have left the house already?'

Bridget laughs. 'He'll be in Westport by now!'

Shauna squints across at Mrs Cauley. 'And he'll return with the guards?'

'He will of course.'

'And Jack will be arrested?'

'He will, Shauna,' says Mrs Cauley.

'God willing.' Bridget pats her arm.

Shauna stops crying and looks at them. 'That's all bollocks, isn't it?'

Bridget shrugs. Mrs Cauley purses her lips.

Shauna puts down her teacup and grabs her cardigan.

'It will be tomorrow before we're underway, Michael.'

'We'll be away in just a minute now, Mrs Cauley.' Michael Hopper manoeuvres the wheelchair into the boot. He has no clear idea where they are going, only that the Bishop himself would murder him if he knew he was taking the priest's car. But as Bridget pointed out, with Quinn carted off to hospital with paranoia and thorn lacerations to the backside, who is to know?

'Take us straight up to Brophy's,' calls out Mrs Cauley. She turns to Bridget, sitting in the back seat behind her. 'If that fecker is up there in his slippers watching RTÉ then we'll know Mahony's got away unchecked.' She looks out of the window. 'Michael, will you put a bit of effort into it?'

'I nearly have it now, Mrs Cauley,' says Michael. He glances across the back of the car at Shauna.

Shauna scowls back at him. She has a firm grip on a hurling stick.

'What are you doing with the hurley there, Shauna?'

'Weapon,' she snarls. She also has a paring knife up the sleeve of her cardigan.

Michael closes the boot and gets into the driver's seat. 'And why does Shauna need a weapon?'

Mrs Cauley narrows her eyes at him. 'Self-defence. Jack Brophy killed Orla and Mary Lavelle and now he's after Mahony.'

Michael laughs until Mrs Cauley fixes him with the glare of a gorgon.

He looks at the grim-faced women with wonder in his rheumy blue eyes.

They have clearly departed ways with the sense that they were born with. But not liking the set of their jaws or the steely glint in their eyes Michael decides the best thing would be to humour them and let Jack sort the lot of them out.

In the back seat Bridget nudges Shauna and opens her bag to let her see what's inside: a handgun, black and gleaming.

Shauna would be no less surprised to see a cobra coiled in there. The gun has the same terrifying aspect, the same threat, not just to life but also to reality, like the arse has dropped out of normal.

'Tell me that's not real, Bridget.'

Bridget grins.

'Where did you get it?'

'Let's just say I'm moving in different kinds of circles now. What with the drugs and all.'

Shauna raises her eyebrows. 'Would you know how to use it?'

'I would.' Bridget looks up at her. 'I most certainly would.'

Chapter 55

May 1976

Mahony slows his stride. The fucker's here now. It won't do him any good to be scuttling away like a coward.

He has to keep the head.

He spits, finds a fag in his pocket and lights it. He looks up at the sky, willing himself to stop shaking and wondering if he can trust either God or his own legs in any of this.

He says a prayer anyway and saunters round to the front of the house as if he hasn't a care in the world.

Jack is leaning on the bonnet of the Eldorado in his uniform. He doesn't look like a murderer. He looks like a calm, reliable guard. He nods to Mahony, and the dead collie, nosing down the drive, snarls gently.

'You're in a fair bit of trouble, son. Theft of a motor vehicle, hit-and-run.' He smiles. 'On a priest no less.'

The dead collie weaves to Jack's side and glowers up at Mahony with its one dim eye.

Mahony takes a drag on his cigarette just while he works out where the fuck he should aim. He doesn't fancy his chances. The dead woman in the pantry is testimony to this man's temper. Plus, Jack has the height advantage, to say nothing of his weight there. For an older man he's in good shape. Under that uniform the fella is solid.

It will have to be a surprise attack. Mahony has a knife in his back pocket and a pair of fists. There's gravel at his feet and stone ornaments in the flowerbed. He can see them: there's a toad, a rabbit and a disrobing nymph.

'I came to turn meself in. Will you bring me down to the station?' Mahony nods over at the squad car.

Jack, still smiling, looks Mahony up and down, like he's measuring his arse for plastic sheeting.

'Come round the back now until I get the keys for the station,' says Jack.

So you can whack me on the patio and hose it down after, says the depth of Mahony's mind, the self-preservation division.

What is really starting to get to Mahony is the thought of ending up in a bucket next to the Widow Farelly. Open-eyed, bollock naked and violated in all sorts of ways, with his boots on newspaper and his knickers folded up.

No fucking way.

'Lead the way, Squire,' Mahony says.

Jack turns.

Mahony surprises himself.

Really and truly he does. He wouldn't have known he had it in him.

All right, so he'd always known he could be a handy little bastard with a few jars in him, but this is another horse entirely.

Here he is, palming the head of the nymph, pulling her up off the ground and raising her up to knock the murdering head off Sergeant Jack Brophy.

It's as if he'd rehearsed it all his life.

Jack falls down to his knees as if he's seen the light. And the dead dog leaps around him howling.

And Mahony is off, barrelling back to the Eldorado. He has the car swung round and out of the gate in seconds.

After a minute on the road Mahony casts his eye over the fuel gauge. He even taps it like they do in the films but the needle is still on the red. He has another quick pray. Please God let there be enough juice to get me the fuck out of here.

God answers with a pothole that has him bouncing off the ceiling and which focuses Mahony's mind back on avoiding the worst bits of the road. His arse slithers up and down the polished leather seat. There is no purchase to be had at all other than holding tight onto the wheel.

And he's doing a grand job with all of that when a movement in his rear-view mirror catches his eye.

Mahony knows that if he could let go of the wheel he'd be blessing himself right now.

A car chase is one thing.

A car chase on a road bolloxed by craters with a guard's car a foot off your bumper is another thing. The Eldorado has no chance. She is too long and low and heavy. Mahony takes the corners badly. Branches and brambles score. His only thought now is to get back down into town where there will be witnesses. Where he is less likely to be whacked and put in a hole. He congratulates himself for staying an optimist there.

It's as if Jack's read his mind.

The first bump is not even a warning. The second runs Mahony off the road and into a ditch. Jack rams the cop car hard into the side of the Eldorado, scraping all down the flank so that the passenger door bows in and the wing mirror smashes off.

Mahony is up, out and across the field to the cover of the forest beyond, running like bejaysus before Jack has even climbed across into the passenger seat to get out of his car.

Jack watches Mahony run into the trees before he moves around to the back of his car, opens the boot and slowly takes out a knife, a sack and a shovel.

Chapter 56

May 1976

Michael Hopper pulls the priest's car over when he sees the smash up ahead on the Castleross road.

Bridget has her hand on the door handle. 'Stay here, the lot of you. Keep your heads down.'

The others watch Bridget approach the cars with the gun trained along on her forearm.

'It's just like in the films,' murmurs Michael in astonishment.

Bridget keeps her body low, moving with surprising speed and grace.

Mrs Cauley smiles. 'She's the dark horse, isn't she?'

Bridget crosses over and scans the field beyond, then walks back to the car. 'They went into the forest; there's clear prints. Mahony must have run for cover.' She puts the safety catch on her gun. 'I'm going after them.'

Michael Hopper sinks down in his seat and offers up a prayer.

Shauna gets out of the car. 'I'm coming with you. You stay here with Michael, Mrs Cauley.'

Mrs Cauley rears up. 'I will not. I'll bring up the rear. Michael, unload me.'

Shauna looks as if she wants to say something. Instead she leans in through the window and kisses the old woman on the cheek.

Mrs Cauley smiles. 'Watch yourself, Shauna. And keep an eye on Annie Oakley there.'

Shauna nods and follows Bridget across the wall.

Chapter 57

May 1976

Mahony keeps running. He's covered some ground but has no idea where he's been or where he's heading. He's like a shagged-out horse in a western: lathered white and beaded with sweat, with a mad hunted look in his eyes. He slows himself, for the forest is thickening, drawing in, and it's getting harder to gallop. His fags have fallen out of his pocket but it's no matter, he hasn't the breath left to smoke one He'll think of packing them in now, in the time he has left to him.

He must have put some space between himself and Jack. He leans his palms up against the trunk of a tree and thinks.

All he has to do is to keep the head, find his way through the forest and get help. If he can avoid being found by Jack that'd be great.

And if he is found, he'll have to properly knock the man's head off this time.

In the meantime he'll need a bit of stealth. He looks down at himself; his trousers are OK but his white shirt, laundered by Shauna, has a gleam you could see from the moon. He strips off the shirt and bundles it into a bush.

Then he picks up handfuls of dirt from the ground and rubs it over his chest, arms and face and as much of his back as he can reach. Feeling half eejit and half wild man he looks around him for a weapon and takes up a stout stick with a splintered end.

'If he comes near me I'll be ramming you right up his hole,' he says to the stick.

The wheelchair is wedged between two saplings.

Michael shakes his head. 'I've misjudged the clearance there, Mrs Cauley.'

Mrs Cauley counts to ten.

'I'll have you free in a moment. I'll try it again in a minute now.'

Mrs Cauley looks at Michael in despair as he scratches the big red bulb of his nose and ponders.

'I think the best thing would be if I go back to the car and see if I can find a bit of rope,' he says. 'You stay there, Mrs Cauley. I'll be no sooner gone than I'll be back again.'

Michael turns and wanders through the trees.

Mrs Cauley wishes for a lend of Bridget's gun.

Mahony sees the dead girl up ahead of him through a thicket. She's sitting on the ground with her back to him.

He calls out to her in a whisper. 'Ida. Fuck. Ida.'

She doesn't move.

Mahony climbs around the thicket and, moving closer, sees that she's holding her yo-yo to the place where her heart would have been.

She stares straight past him with her eyes fixed on a distant point, as if she doesn't see him, as if he's the dead one.

'Ida?'

She speaks to him without moving her eyes. 'You shouldn't play in the forest today.' Her voice drifts up reedy, as if through layers of static.

'I need your help, Ida. I'm lost.'

She dims and flickers.

'Ida, please.'

Ida jumps up and runs through a tree. She stops and looks back at him over her shoulder without a smile.

Half a mile into the forest they are rushing through dead leaves and stumbling over tree roots. And there it is, the flash in the bracken and Shauna calling out.

'It's him, it's him.'

Bridget takes the shot.

At the sound of the gunshot Ida stops in her tracks.

She covers her ears, her eyes wide.

The echoes fade and Mahony stands and listens. The forest is still, with a breath-holding silence, a shocked speechlessness that pulses about the trees.

Without thinking, Mahony holds out his hand. 'Let's go, Ida.'

Chapter 58

May 1950

Orla waited in the clearing.

Francis had lost one of his booties, so she rubbed his little foot warm.

She put her hair down and made a tent of it for him, his face and her face together under it.

She swore that his eyes were turning brown now, just like hers, just like his daddy's.

She touched his tiny face. He was the whole of her world, right there.

She waited in the clearing, not knowing how late it was getting.

They were alone but for the flash of a long-limbed hare turning mid-flight, her eyes distended with ancient panic. They were alone but for the bees bumping over the wood sorrel. They were alone but for the shiny-backed beetles threading the moss that swaddled the tree roots. And the man who had stepped into the clearing with a sack and a shovel.

Chapter 59

May 1976

Under the tree canopy, in the early evening sunlight, Mahony follows a dead girl through the forest. Now and again he imagines he hears a footfall alongside them, tracking them. His neck hairs agree. They lift as if under some unholy gaze.

Maybe Ida feels it too. She keeps close to him, turning often to look back at him and sometimes stopping to listen with one faded little shoe lifted mid-step. She holds her yo-yo tightly in her hand; from time to time she kisses it.

Then the forest becomes familiar.

Mahony sees the river just the other side of the clearing. But this time it's different.

It is too still: the still of a lake, or a pond; a bright ribbon reflecting the sky.

Ida crouches on the riverbank, rubbing her yo-yo up and down her sleeve and humming a ferocious little song to herself.

Mahony knows his way now, but he hesitates. Ida is looking straight past him, smiling. And all at once she is up on her feet, laughing with delight and patting her dimpled dead knees as a dead collie comes running through the trees towards her.

The first blow catches Mahony on the back of his head and he's on the ground without a thought in his mind other than to turn over onto his knees and get straight back up again. Jack stands waiting.

And Mahony remembers.

To his credit Mahony lands a few punches on Jack, for he's lost the head and thinks of nothing.

He wants to kill his daddy properly now.

And God, Mahony's tough. He can take the full weight of a fist that could shatter jaws and roll eyes blind.

But Mahony will keep falling; they both know it, knocked over and stumbling backwards in a comic dance. Touching his face in confusion, as if it doesn't belong to him any more. He must've bit his own tongue, for when he opens his mouth he's swearing blood.

But he will keep getting up, with the help of a fallen tree this time, watching his bloody fingerprints smear up the trunk with mild surprise.

Then he's down, with a sharp white pain as Jack kicks him in his back, again and again and again.

A voice in Mahony's mind counts him down.

Then Jack stops and smiles and bends down with his palm out. As if he's remembered something, as if he wants to shake Mahony's hand. The fight is over, says Jack's smile, we can go home now, it was all a big mistake.

Mahony lifts his hand up to him. Jack walks away and picks up a shovel.

Time slows.

Mahony looks around him. There's more than enough

time to see a crow fly low over the water or a newt turn in the mud. Or to watch the light shimmer in the branches above. Or to see Ida flit across the river, running after the dead dog and howling with glee.

Something jumps out from the undergrowth and onto on Jack's back. He hardly falters; it's as if he's been expecting it. He drops the shovel.

Thomas Sweeney is far smaller in real life than a bogeyman ought to be. He is ancient and shoeless and bleeding heavily from a gunshot wound to his shoulder.

Jack shakes him off and punches him through a drift of leaves.

Now that Thomas is in touching distance he reaches out to Mahony. Strings of spittle fall from the old man's mouth and his words come without letters in them.

Mahony can see the stubble on his chin and the fine white hair on his head. His grandfather frowns and looks at him in desperation.

'I know,' Mahony says to him. 'I know.'

The old man's frown softens, as if he's just comprehended something. He reaches out to Mahony, his fingers bow-nailed and filthy, and his smile toothless and radiant.

Jack picks the old man up with one hand and leans him against a tree. He takes a knife from his pocket and thumbs out the blade.

Mahony lies at the edge of the world and looks up at the passing shadows of the birds and the clouds moving above. Jack is kneeling next to him, he has his hand on Mahony's wrist, as if he's feeling for a pulse, and his voice is low and calm. He sounds just as he did when they sat alongside each other in Kerrigan's Bar. It could be a joke he's telling him, or it could be something profound, about this being the end.

In the distance a woman shouts out, her cry strident in the peace of the forest.

Jack stops talking and looks up.

At the side of the clearing Bridget slows her pace and raises her gun for the second time.

Mahony closes his eyes.

He sees her walking towards him, through the clearing, in her too-big shoes, with a twist of a grin, with her dark eyes on his.

She is familiar and lovely, everyday and unforgotten. Mahony knows at once every detail of her: the sound of her voice, the timbre of her laugh and the smell of her hair. He knows her sudden temper and her slow soft tears and the way she moves, with a careless kind of grace.

Now, at the edge of the world, Mahony remembers everything. She holds out her hand in a gesture of suppli-cation, of apology. She smiles down at him, her face lit with love. A dim gleaming rose of the forest.

Jack takes Bridget's shot like a well-thrown punch. He stum-bles forward, his face confused, tears in his frank blue eyes. As if he's grappling with the agony of memory, like a guest drunk at a wake.

He makes it to the river's edge, where he rocks a moment, his face lifted to the sky, before he lets himself fall, before he hits the water.

Chapter 60

October 1977

In the forest, past the clearing, is an island longer than a fishing boat and as wide as a bus. It has been hiding under the water all along. And now it has a crow on it.

She picks her way over its gilded surface. As if on cue the sun comes out, burnishing the offerings embedded there. All the warm colours of metal are represented: gold, copper and bronze.

Like most crows she remains unimpressed, even by supernatural magnetism.

She hops over horse brasses and candlesticks; she pecks at christening cups and belt buckles.

In the middle of the island lies an unbroken circle of wedding bands.

It marks a spot.

The crow, with her head on one side, stares at it with her sharp black eye, as the tide changes, as the water rises.

Chapter 61

October 1977

Even in Mulderrig, time passes, although not as you'd notice. A year or so can steal by when the rhythm of your days and nights is quiet and unremarkable. So that now, when Mrs Cauley looks up from under her poker visor, she sees the land let loose its furious display of autumn colour.

She sits on the veranda of Rathmore House, watching for the day's end, waiting on a good sunset. For a while still the sun will pour warm honey on her wheelchair. It will pool on the table before her, glancing the rim of her whiskey glass and shining up the patterned back of the topmost card of the deck that waits near her hand. She looks out over the forest, where all the mad colours of the trees brawl: vivid drifts of rust and copper and rich bolts of burnt sienna and raw gold.

This is Mulderrig's last great show of the year.

Now the air tastes of bonfires and dark days, now the land is forgetting warm winds and soft days and remembering bitter skies and keen dawns.

This is a grand time for goodbyes. Mrs Cauley knows that better than anyone and better than the man standing before her searching for a few right words. So when she lifts her glass, she is toasting him. And when she smiles, it's a benediction.

'You'll be all right, so?' He shields his eyes, looking back at her and into the sun with the light flooding his face.

And there is his smile, the same and different and immeasurably dear to her. With a new scar that twists his top lip on the upward rise. It's ghosting to white now. A smile almost scoured out, but stitched well and well healed. Only now it is rarer and more cautious, as if it still hurts a little.

And there are his eyes, narrowed against the light, the same and different. With lines at the corners and a softness that wasn't always there before.

'You'll be all right?'

Mrs Cauley nods. 'Don't I have Doosey for my every need? She's in there now behind the door with her ears flapping, waiting on my call.'

Mahony glances in the kitchen door; there's the flash of a floral apron as Bridget ducks. He laughs.

She smiles. 'It was a gas, wasn't it?'

And he's there with her and for a moment he's holding her, nearly on his knees, with her desperately small in his arms.

But then he's standing and shouldering his rucksack.

Mrs Cauley looks up at him with a fierce love in her eyes. 'Fair play to you, Mahony, fair play to you.'

In the pantry Bridget needs a tablecloth to dry her tears.

Mahony throws his bag in the back of the car and starts the engine up. A vehicle that once had its own notions of when to stop and start now behaves like a perfect lady. But then with Mahony as her new owner there are no longer chickens on the dashboard or ferrets in the footwell.

As for the Eldorado? Tadhg has almost forgiven him.

Mahony joked that she had as many dents in her fender as he had. But as Mahony's body healed he had worked on her too, and he had worked a variety of magic, so that now you hardly notice the damage to her lovely lines. And no longer perfect, Tadhg drives her wherever the hell he wants.

Mahony turns out onto the road with the sun behind him.

On the veranda Bridget Doosey wipes her nose with the hem of the tablecloth and downs a dry sherry. 'Oh, my grief, I've lost him surely.'

'Pull your beak in, woman,' says Mrs Cauley. 'Can you blame him for becoming restless? You've said yourself that a fatherless man is always searching.'

Bridget takes up a pack of cards. 'He knows where his father is: he's at the bottom of the Shand.'

A smile haunts Mrs Cauley's face. 'And isn't it a wise man who knows his own father?'

Bridget shuffles, deals, puts down the deck and arranges her cards. Mrs Cauley waits.

Bridget looks up and stares at her. 'It wasn't Jack.'

Mrs Cauley laughs. 'So that's why all the wives of Mulderrig are still having unquiet dreams?' She takes up her cards. 'Well, I'd say that's grounds for another investigation, wouldn't you, Doosey? I'd say it's time to give this town another good shake.'

A slow grin spreads across Bridget Doosey's face. 'You really are a horrific, meddling old bitch.'

Mrs Cauley tips her visor and surveys her cards. She has a great hand.

★

Mahony switches the engine off and gets out of the car. He takes a can from the boot and makes his way to the clearing, sometimes climbing over fallen branches, sometimes wading through flurries of bright leaves. He walks slower now, there's a drag to his left leg, but he holds himself easy through it, so you could say it was almost deliberate, a bar-room saunter, a pirate's landlocked roll. Sometimes he stops and puts down the can and looks around himself. Above him leaves spiral down from breeze-caught branches and crows sweep the sky and blacken the treetops.

Now and then Mahony imagines he catches a glimpse of pale blue in the bracken or hears a faint line from an angry little song, although he knows he is alone now.

In the months that have passed the forest has grown in around Thomas Sweeney's place. Mahony can see traces of other visitors. Local kids no longer held at bay by Jack Brophy and the threat of Tom Bogey. The door of his grandfather's caravan is hanging off and his mattress has been dragged outside and disembowelled.

Mahony puts down the can and climbs up the steps.

Inside the caravan there's a powerful foxy smell. A dark musk reek, as if a wild animal has been kept inside against its will. Mahony's boot heels skitter on broken glass: all that's left of the shelves of jars.

Someone has pissed in one corner and someone has tried to light a fire in another. Mahony can see where the bottom of the curtain caught and smouldered and went out again, leaving a melted edge of blackened lacework.

The floor is rotten, the wood bloated with rain and the laminate sloughing off in strips. In a couple of places Mahony can see right through to the ground below. He kicks aside bottles and fag ends and sits down in the doorway.

For a moment he thinks of a yellow yo-yo and an upturned nose, scuffed shoes and a serious smile. Secrets and untold stories, lost toys and found treasure. Spittle and sounds without letters, and the animal panic in a dying man's eyes.

He looks out at the clearing; the bathtub Ida once danced in is still there.

When Mahony has emptied the can of petrol he throws a lit match. The flames catch and leap. They run up the side of the caravan and over the roof. They catch the timber floor and blacken the window. The curtain twists and is gone.

Mahony drives into town as the light fades. He drives at a fast walking pace with the window rolled down and his elbow out.

Down past Roadside Mary, her ruddy face benign in the setting sun, watching over Desmond Burke, who sits looking out over the rooftops. As the car passes, Desmond stands. Mahony doesn't stop and Desmond doesn't want him to. Mahony watches him grow smaller in the rear-view mirror, standing at the side of the road.

Mahony drives past whitewashed cottages, where washing jackknifes on clothes lines and dogs bark at nothing. The town is quiet at this time of day, with the mammies inside getting the dinner and the daddies inside waiting to go out for a jar. The dead too are nowhere to be seen. They have drifted up into dusty attics to creak and settle with the floor joists. Or retired to disused guest rooms or dark neglected corners.

There they lie, watchful and forgetting.

In the village hall Mrs Moran switches off the urn and hangs the tea towels out to dry. For a moment she fancies she hears a noise coming from the broom cupboard, a rhythm maybe, a pattern of words, like someone speaking poetry. But it's only the radio, left on low.

Mahony drives slowly through town.

At the Post Office and General Store, Marie Gaughan pulls down the shutters and walks rolls of chicken mesh inside. Later she'll balance the books and dust the onions, count the stamps and tidy the eggs. She'll hang her tabard on the hook behind the storeroom door, pull up her stockings and head off up the hill with her carpet slippers in her handbag.

Mahony drives slowly through town.

In the library of the parochial house, the new priest wonders at the fog rising from the fireplace, the dampness of the easy chair, and the newt scurrying in the fringes of the hearthrug. Fortunately, he doesn't believe in magic.

In the kitchen the cabbage waits in the sink for washing. In the oven the priest's chop lies forgotten. Róisín Munnelly stands by the back door, waiting.

Mahony drives slowly through town.

At the corner of the road a big girl wearing the last goodness out of an ugly dress grins and waves. And there's Tadhg standing outside Kerrigan's Bar with his arms folded having changed a difficult barrel and threatened a cellar rat with his deadly tongue. He has the lights on already in the saloon bar and the door propped open ready for a good night's drinking.

Tadhg raises a hand solemnly to the passing car. He has been setting his red face up to the dying light and thinking of Bridget Doosey, the tilt of her fedora and the savage glint in her eyes.

By the painted pump in the middle of the square the old ones look up and look down again. Maybe there's a hint of a wink there but really it's almost time to call it a day.

In a moment Mahony will be gone, leaving Mulderrig's living and dead to their reveries, and if they see him leave, well, they let him go with a nod or a wave, a blown kiss or a silent prayer.

When he's nearly out of town Mahony stops the car and turns to her, sitting silently beside him in the half-light with her windblown hair over her face and her hands held small and calm in her lap.

'Are you ready?' he says.

She remembers what Bridget said and smiles. 'Is it blast-off then?'

He smiles back at her and Shauna holds him with her eyes.

When they reach the open road he'll take her hand as she watches the town fall away behind them.

Acknowledgements

I am deeply grateful to Susan Armstrong and Louisa Joyner, and the teams at Conville & Walsh and Canongate for making this book possible – thank you for your support, encouragement and belief. Thank you also to Russell Schechter and St Mary's University for starting me off and continuing to cheer me on.

To my friends, family and all those who have contributed their time and advice (you know who you are) I owe a big debt of gratitude. You have helped me in a thousand different ways and although I have thanked each of you in person I thank you again here for being part of this story.